The Magic Girl

Book Two of The Lonely Raven Trilogy

ERIKA FAIR

CLAY BRIDGES
PRESS

To the ones who helped me find my magic,
and the ones who feed that fire.

"It is only the dead who do not return."
—Bertrand Barère de Vieuzac

"The unfathomable deep forest,
Where all must lose their way..."
—Edward Thomas

CHAPTER ONE

The unexpected scent of the early-1900s Ramleh cigarette sent Fallon Quinn into a frenetic spiral of panic and hope. She looked up and down the long, shadowy hallway of the Nashville hotel, trying to trace the familiar smell. Adrenaline flooded her veins—all of her senses heightened as she turned one way, then another. But she was alone.

Where was he?

She could hear the distant buzzing drone of voices from the hotel bar area, the clinking of glasses in the kitchen, the pounding of her own heart. Patsy Cline's "Crazy" now played—appropriately, she thought—on the vintage neon jukebox.

Fifteen years he'd been gone from her. Fifteen years since that strange, fragrant smoke had last curled around her. She placed a hand to her throat, overwhelmed by the emotions that faint scent had elicited. It was gone now, as if she'd imagined it. The thought that she'd possibly been wrong about sensing it tore at her heart.

A waitress passed by, and Fallon tried to look at ease, but the woman glanced at her more than once, so she knew her distress must be evident. Her breathing was shallow; her skin was tingling. Someone her heart cried out for was near—she was not imagining it. Or possibly she was finally losing her mind.

Fallon turned one more time, and Jacob was there, standing right beside her, his body only inches from hers. Looking up into his handsome face, her world exploded violently with emotion, and her brain abandoned all logic. She put a hand out into midair, as if seeking support from some invisible thing. Jacob reached without hesitation and took her hand in his, steadying her. His touch, warm and strong, sent her mind reeling further. She'd been so long without him; she struggled to process his return.

Not much about Jacob Roth seemed to have changed since she last saw him at the old house in Austin when she was fourteen years old. Since the night he'd kissed her lightly on top of the head and told her to "be well, my secret girl." A goodbye she had not recognized as such until he was already long gone.

Observing him now, she saw that his appearance was still deeply striking, his wavy brown hair just past his shoulders like always. She was distantly aware that he did not appear to have aged at all. After a decade and a half, she felt the years should be more evident upon him, but they were not.

A dark, long-sleeved shirt covered the tattoos on his arms, but she looked down briefly and glimpsed a familiar tattoo on his hand. She also spotted the double, dark silver chain on his left wrist, the tarnished, square locket still suspended—as if she needed every sign to assure her it was really him standing before her. Jeans and loosely-laced biker boots finished off his ensemble. The same as ever.

The only noticeable physical change she could detect was that the goatee she remembered had been replaced by a face of artfully-trimmed stubble which only added to his rough and dangerous countenance.

Jacob smirked as he noted her careful observation. "Do not let the change in my shaving routine throw you off, Fallon. It is truly me."

All of the nervous tension left her body as she returned his smile. It was him. They were reunited—two souls lost to each other, now found. The single thing she'd endlessly sought for the past decade was now standing before her. She was conscious of the sensation that a circle had been completed. That an unforeseen path had opened up before her, glowing with some kind of divine magic.

Everything she thought she knew melted away as Jacob Roth grinned at her, and she marveled at the energy that swirled around them. Smiles from Jacob had been rare years ago, much less this devilish smirk which seemed to wield its own magic. He was different now in his way with her. She felt herself being carried away by it.

So much more self-assured now as an adult than when she last saw him, she found that she could actually read him, which had proven impossible in the past, though it was sketchy and incomplete, like a radio with a poor signal. She was well aware that whatever she was picking up from him, he was likely allowing her to know. With Jacob, she had always been sure—there were no accidents, no mistakes, no unfortunate slips. He was confident and strong, in control of his emotions. She'd often admired him in that respect. Her own emotions seemed to spiral easily, even if she was able to keep them hidden from most people.

Jacob was overjoyed to see her, relieved to be reunited with her. For Fallon this was a surprise, and it lessened the sting of her continued anger at his abandonment. She wondered again if it had not been his choice to vanish so completely from her life.

Still firmly holding her hand, Jacob took a small step back so as to better see her. He looked her over slowly with piercing blue eyes, taking in her face, her long, dark, honey-blond hair, the curve of her neck, the fit of her vintage black and gray dress.

"Look at you, Fallon." His rich, rough voice rang pleasantly in her ears, and a smile played on his lips. "You are as lovely in person as you are through the eyes of a raven."

"You always spoke in riddles," she whispered, and he winked, squeezing her hand.

Fallon's mind sought out Bret and Tayce, her companions whom she had left drinking at the bar when she'd excused herself to go to the restroom. She could sense that, while they were still engaged in conversation, both men were beginning to think she'd been gone a little long.

"Jacob." She focused fully on him and tried to sound as if she were not falling completely apart inside. "Why are you here?" Her heart felt as if it were now residing permanently in her throat.

Instead of answering, he turned and led her by the hand into a nearby office area, shutting and locking the door behind them as he finally released her. He didn't turn on the light, but with her ability to see in the dark, that wasn't a problem.

"Did you come because I called to you?" she wondered. Had it already been more than two months since she'd tried contacting him with the raven tattoo on her left wrist? In a moment of desperation, she had spoken to it, begging Jacob to somehow hear her, to help her, all the while not knowing if what she was trying would work. The tattoo had glowed in response to her attention, which had filled her with hope, but then months had passed with nothing. Until tonight.

Resting on the edge of a metal desk, Jacob gently pulled her near and took her face in his hands. "It was partly that—because you called to me—though you don't need a tattoo for that, I assure you." He chuckled, then tilted his head. "Fallon, there is so much you need to know, so many secrets kept from you." His manner was earnest and tender. "I came to you tonight because I found the opportunity to do so, and because I knew that after so many years apart, we needed to see each other, face-to-face, but I cannot stay. I wanted to tell you that I will be with you again soon, I promise you."

Disappointment rained through her. She held back stinging tears as she realized she was going to lose him again. "No." She shook her head. "You promised me things before." The tremor in her voice would not be stilled. How could he leave—he'd only just returned.

There was a pained look in his eyes. "Fallon, I have my reasons for leaving you tonight, but I will come back. I did not break any promise I ever made to you," he insisted. "But because you don't know the truth of so many things, you cannot yet see. When we finally have the time to talk properly, you'll understand it all. But that time is not tonight, I am sorry."

The feeling of his hands on her face was unnerving, in part because it felt so natural, as if he had touched her this intimately a thousand times before, when she knew he never had. "There's always so much unknown, Jacob. For my whole life. I feel like I will forever be struggling to figure it out, but never any closer to the truth than I was before."

He nodded, looking intently into her eyes. "When I come back to you, I'll tell you everything. I promise there will be no more secrets." His face changed then, and when he spoke, the pitch of his voice had grown lower. "Truly, Fallon, I never imagined we'd be apart for so long. That was never my intent." He pulled her into an embrace, holding her tightly against himself. Closing his eyes, Jacob allowed himself to relax, to drown a moment in the glorious feeling of Fallon Quinn in his arms.

She wrapped her arms around him, never wanting to let him go. Her own heartbeat, her blood, rushed loudly in her ears as she struggled with the cascade of emotions that poured over her. She'd thought he was gone forever, that she would be endlessly navigating life without him. Tears streamed freely down her cheeks as she struggled to accept that the relief and joy which were filling her up would be short-lived.

"What if my father tries to steal me again before you return?" she asked.

His hold on her tightened, his face resting against her hair. She could feel his heart beating fast in his chest. "I don't believe he will try again for some time. When next we meet, I will help you guard against him."

Are you okay?

Bret James' voice in her head was jarring, and Fallon hesitated, feeling something like guilt winding through her heart before she answered back in the telepathic way that was unique to them. *I'm fine, Bret. I'll be back in a minute. Talking to a woman I met.*

The lie was easy, as they always were for her. But she was startled that she had become so lost, so unaware of reality. For a moment she had forgotten everything. For a moment she knew only him.

Still holding her close, Jacob spoke into her hair. "I will come back for you, Fallon. It may be a few months from now, I'm not yet sure, but please do not doubt it. I will take you away someplace safe where we can talk to your heart's content, I swear to you. Alright?"

"Alright."

He heard the disappointment in her voice. "Even if months go by without hearing from me, do not lose hope. It won't be like last time—I will come for you as soon as I can. No matter where you are, I will be there." He finally released her, looking at her as if he were trying to memorize every aspect of her. "My beautiful, beautiful Fallon," he murmured. "How I've missed you. But I must go. I cannot linger here with you," he brushed his thumb against her cheek, and everything in her tingled from head to toe, her breath catching in her throat, "much as I would like to." His gaze went briefly to her lips, but then he closed his eyes, trying to break the spell her presence was casting upon him.

With a renewed attempt at focus, Jacob held up Fallon's wrist and touched the raven tattoo, tracing it with deft fingers. "This is my sacred promise—I am with you always." He pushed up his left sleeve to expose the larger raven tattooed on his strong forearm. With its striking appearance and prism eye, the tattoo exactly matched the one on her left wrist. "I have been with you, even when you couldn't see me. You were not abandoned. Wait for me—I'll be back soon." He sighed reluctantly. "But for now, I must go."

Her gaze left his raven and returned to his face. Reaching out, she placed her hand tentatively against his cheek—a shiver ran visibly through him. "Where will you go?" She struggled to picture him strolling out casually through the bar. After being mysteriously gone from her for so long, he had achieved near-mythic status in her mind.

A smile lit his eyes as he placed a kiss lightly on her palm. "Away." He held a finger to his lips. And then, as she looked at him, he was suddenly gone into thin air.

Fallon flinched, her lips parting in surprise. She and her brother Luca had always jokingly speculated that Jacob could teleport himself here and there, with the mysterious ways that he'd shown up and then vanished at all hours from the Austin house they'd shared. Had they been right all along? It would explain a lot. It would explain this.

Jacob's departure created a gaping emptiness in the room, in Fallon's arms, in her heart. She wanted to weep, to curl up in a ball on the floor and sob with the weight of everything. Immediately she wanted him back; she bitterly contemplated the unfairness of his achingly brief return. Her premonition skill would tell her nothing regarding if or when he would come back to her—she'd tried it often in the past and failed. In all her life, she'd never had a premonition involving Jacob.

Leaning back against a wall, she closed her eyes and focused on breathing in slowly, exhaling at the same pace. She needed to compose herself, for there were people waiting on her, people to whom she could not yet reveal this stunning event. Not until she'd had time to accept it herself. But she could not change the fact that she was entirely transformed.

A few minutes later she pushed off the wall and left the office, returning to the restroom to make sure her hair was not in disarray and to wash the tears from her cheeks. An older woman who was washing her hands gave Fallon a sympathetic smile as she turned and left.

Fallon looked again into the mirror. Her honey-blonde hair was smoothed, and her cheeks were dry, but her eyes were definitely red. There was nothing she could do about that but hope that the bar lighting was whimsical enough to hide it.

Mentally she collected herself as best she could before going back out to join the singer and guitarist who waited for her at the hotel bar. Moving with her usual athletic confidence, she glanced casually at the jukebox as she passed by it and exchanged a smile with a waiter. But inside she was rattled and raw, shaken to her core.

Jacob Roth was back. What an unexpected turn of events.

Bret and Tayce were sitting in conversation just as she'd left them, with her empty seat in between. Both men had been rockstars several decades ago in separate hard rock bands, and though their days of blazing glory were past, they were still fairly popular. They continued to tour and put out albums now and then, satisfying die-hard fanbases who remained loyal.

In his early fifties, Bret was enjoying a healthy solo career. A gregarious and energetic singer, he'd left his hard-partying ways behind him when his daughter Bergen was born almost ten years before. Bret and Fallon had fallen for each other back in the late spring—she had now saved his life twice via premonition, most recently at the end of summer—and they'd discovered they could communicate telepathically, a skill she'd only previously shared with her brother.

Feeling as if she'd been gone from them for hours, Fallon slid back onto the barstool between the two men. She ordered whiskey on the rocks with a charming smile and continued to concentrate on her breath. Her heart was hammering in her chest, her eyes burned with restrained tears, and her emotions were flying out of control.

Nothing could have prepared her for this, for Jacob suddenly appearing after all these years, grinning at her as if all the world's secrets were hidden in his eyes and that unlocking them would be her undoing.

She wanted more than anything to go back to the hotel room and hide away there, but she and Bret still had to attend a concert that night. She was not going to have a chance to be alone with her thoughts for several more hours. Now more aware of the raven tattoo than she'd ever been, she ran her index finger surreptitiously over it. The raven fluttered in response, and her heart leapt.

"That's my girl!" Tayce acknowledged happily, encouraged by her drink order as her whiskey was set before her. He and Fallon enjoyed a close friendship and were known to spend much time together drinking and chatting in quiet bars. The long-haired guitarist was currently on tour with his old band, Dangerous Eye. He was spending his pre-show time with Bret and Fallon, who had flown out from California to catch his Nashville performance. An outstanding musician who was always in demand from other bands to go out on the road, Tayce Williams was easy-going and friendly. Fallon had saved his life two years earlier in Las Vegas on the same night she'd first saved Bret.

Despite Tayce's happy-go-lucky reaction to her beverage selection, Bret looked at Fallon in concern. He hadn't missed her reddened eyes or the subtle shift in her mood. And the fact that she had been gone for quite a long time.

Placing a comforting hand on her back, he leaned in close to her. Then he sniffed. "You smell like some form of tobacco I can't identify."

She tilted her head towards him with a shrug. "Women's restroom." She wrinkled her nose.

His hand dropped to her thigh and gave a gentle squeeze. "That doesn't explain the whiskey."

She took a sip of her drink. "I didn't want to leave Tayce with the impression that I'd gone soft. I have an image to maintain."

But despite her usual artistry with lying, tonight both men thought she looked almost as if she'd seen a ghost, and they felt that nothing coming from her lips sounded true.

"Did you have a premonition about the woman?" Bret asked.

She looked at him in confusion.

He licked his lips. "The one you were talking to just now."

Fallon cursed her choices, realizing that claiming a premonition would have been a far better cover-up than that she was simply engaged in conversation with a stranger, which seemed unlikely.

She shook her head. "No, this lady was really into the history of the hotel and went on and on about it." It sounded ridiculous, she knew. Fallon was an ace at extricating herself from unnecessary small talk.

Tayce listened to them, rubbing his goatee. Not knowing exactly why, he felt compelled to change the subject—he could tell Fallon was struggling. "Believe it or not," he leaned in, "Jack Lane texted while you were in the restroom. He has more potential world tour updates. He's been blowing up my phone all evening."

"He's definitely pursuing it with aggression," Fallon noted vaguely, shaken with being so nearly caught in a lie, grateful for Tayce's intervention. And why was she lying? Bret knew that Jacob existed, that he'd disappeared mysteriously from her life fifteen years ago. Why had she not run back to them to tell them the unbelievable news of his return? Why was she holding it so tightly to her chest?

She sighed. Maybe because she could still feel Jacob's hands on her face. His breath against her hair. And because the raven on her wrist now seemed alive.

She focused purposefully on the ice in her glass. The lights in the bar reflected on the frozen cubes with dazzling effect, and she imagined that if she looked at them hard enough, she'd be able to see the future. She remembered the hours she'd spent between the ages of eleven and fourteen, staring into a small mirror as Jacob tried teaching her to scry. The practice—gazing into a reflective object such as a mirror or crystal ball (though the latter had always sounded a bit theatrical to Fallon) with the intent of seeing into the future had been a challenge for her. She'd mastered all of the other magical abilities he'd tested her with, but scrying had left her frustrated, tearful, and rarely successful, though Jacob had always been patient. After he vanished from her life at fourteen, she'd never attempted scrying again, though she had eventually been able to refine her other abilities without his guidance.

Has anyone ever attempted to scry using ice? she wondered, and then nearly giggled, feeling the hysteria building within her. With effort she willed herself to calm down, taking another sip of her drink. This entire night was out of control.

Bret stretched his muscular arms above his head and readjusted his baseball cap over his shoulder-length dark blond hair. "I'll admit I'd love a big European tour. No question."

"Same," Tayce agreed. "I love touring Europe; haven't done that in a while with Dangerous Eye. I've gone with other bands, though. We usually end up drawing bigger crowds than in the states. It'll be interesting to see if Jack can pull this off."

Bret glanced again at Fallon, but he could see that she was closed off, gone deep inside herself. And so he let her be.

CHAPTER TWO

"**J**acob is back."

Selah Lowe, Fallon's ride-or-die best friend since second grade, stood alone in her artist studio in her lovely Queen Anne house in the tiny Texas town of Gray. She read and then re-read Fallon's startling late night text, and found herself looking for a place to sit down.

Selah's husband, tired after a long day at his medical practice in the nearby town of Dutton, was in their bedroom reading. Their six-year-old son Indio was fast asleep. The big house was quiet but for the much-needed rain that poured outside, roaring on the metal roof.

There was no one to see Selah's face, the array of emotions that passed over it. She was astonished. Overwhelmed. Relieved. But most of all, she was deeply troubled by Fallon's news. It wasn't that Jacob intended her friend any harm—she had seen, years ago, the fierce way the man cared for her friend, and she doubted that had changed. What troubled her was his sudden reappearance after so many silent years. It had to mean something. And it was that "something" that worried her. Not the least of which being how this incredible twist was going to turn Fallon's currently stable-ish world completely upside down.

Selah gazed blindly at the floor, her brain working quickly to create a sense of order out of this news and all that it entailed. Fallon was not a child anymore but a beautiful young woman. Jacob Roth had been an undeniably attractive man. A strong bond had existed between them, a bond Selah had never been able to fully interpret, though it had always been innocent enough, considering Fallon's age. There had been unquestionably no parent-child dynamic—they'd seemed more like friends or conspirators, honestly, despite their age difference. But if that connection was still there, fifteen years later, Selah wondered speculatively how this particular sub-plot was going to go.

With steady, paint-smeared fingers, she texted Fallon back: "Does Bret know?"

Sitting on the hotel bed in Nashville in near-complete darkness, Fallon twisted her lips and narrowed her eyes. Annoyed. Of all the responses. "Not yet."

Selah shook her head in disapproval, dangling beaded earrings swinging. "Tell him. At once."

Fallon threw her phone aside and hugged a pillow to her chest, staring at the lights of the city that played on the white wall. Selah's voice of reason was not what she had been seeking. She wasn't sure what she was looking for. Even after her long, hot shower she could not calm down. She'd tried various breathing exercises, as well as some yoga poses, but nothing had helped.

The pain she'd felt during Jacob's years-long absence was nothing compared to this new unhinged misery she was experiencing after being so briefly reunited with him and then having to say goodbye. She could still smell him—mountain air, river rocks, and rosemary. The scent was imprinted in her now—being separated from the person who that scent belonged to cracked her heart open, leaving it to ache and bleed.

Azul whined and nuzzled her hip, and Fallon scratched his ears affectionately. The long-haired, black dog had been waiting in the hotel room when she got back that night. Just before midnight, she had left Bret to party it up with the band and crew at the venue where Dangerous Eye had played an excellent show.

Tayce had been phenomenal on stage. Fallon remembered little else from the concert because every nerve ending in her body, frayed from the sudden reunion with Jacob, focused itself entirely on the magic way he played the guitar. The passion that poured forth from his fingers.

"You were right," Bret had whispered in her ear. "Soul. To Devil. Sold."

"There can be no other explanation," she'd agreed.

When the concert was over, Fallon had felt too disconnected and jumpy to enjoy the after-party, but she could see that Bret was having a grand time. And so, she convinced him that it would be fine if he stayed while she returned to the hotel alone. She had maybe, on a whim, had to apply a little pressure to his mind to sway him to this way of thinking, but no harm done.

And then she'd swung open the hotel room door, and there had been Azul, laying on the bed, panting happily, thrilled to see her. Despite that they had not brought the dog with them on their trip. Azul's ability to show up magically wherever Fallon happened to be had long been a purposefully ignored aspect of her life. She simply didn't think about it. He had been with her since she was seven years old—longer than anyone else—which also made him possibly…immortal? Regardless, he was her most treasured companion, and she could only hope that as long as she continued to feed him endless cubes of cheese, he would never leave her.

"Did you know he was coming back?" she asked the dog now, as they lay together on the bed, knowing there would be no answer. "Is that why you're here? Because I was shattered into a million pieces?"

Azul, her faithful friend for the past twenty-two years, rested his furry chin on her thigh and closed his eyes.

Fallon's thoughts drifted to her brother, because of anyone, he would have been the one to experience Jacob's return with. He would have better understood. Luca had been gone for nearly as long as Jacob, and she missed him every day. Their friendship had been unshakeable; they'd foolishly believed they would always be in each other's lives.

After they lost their adoptive parents when she was seven and Luca twelve, Jacob Roth had materialized into their lives as a previously unknown benevolent cousin. The court had awarded him guardianship without much hesitation.

Life with Jacob in a quaint, old Austin neighborhood had been surprisingly pleasant. He was decidedly not a father figure, and in all honesty, he was not actually their cousin. He had not been parental towards them in any recognizable way, tending to be gone from the house more than he was there. The siblings had no idea where he'd come from, or why, but as always with things regarding Jacob, they hadn't questioned it. Fallon and Luca had ended up raising each other, though Jacob had always been available when they required something, and he had provided financially for their every need.

Besides their shared telepathy, the siblings also both received premonitions about future trouble on a regular basis. Fallon had spent most of her adult life interpreting premonitions so as to rescue strangers from peril as varied as mild misfortune or inconvenience to death. It was this particular skill which had led her to rescue Bret, Tayce, and Jack two years ago in Las Vegas, thrusting her into their world, or more accurately, them into hers.

When she was eleven years old, Jacob had taken Fallon aside and revealed to her that she was far more powerful than her brother. He explained to her that Luca would be frightened to learn the truth of her extensive magical skills. With her agreement, Jacob began training her in secret, teaching her about various abilities she hadn't known she possessed and helping her to strengthen them. He always cautioned her to keep their training a secret from her brother. And while Fallon believed they were keeping the secret from Luca, she couldn't shake the feeling they were keeping it from someone else. But who?

Over the course of this secret training, a connection formed between Fallon and Jacob, which strengthened and grew as time passed. But when she was fourteen, Jacob disappeared with no warning and never returned. The loss of her friend and teacher tore Fallon's soul in two, but she and Luca carried on together. A few years later, Luca was murdered while out for a nighttime run in Austin. Fallon received a premonition, but too late to save him.

With Jacob and Luca both gone from her, Fallon had descended emotionally into a terrible place. She existed there for a while, living in the darkness of her heart, but eventually Selah had been able to pull her back to life. Over the years, Fallon had slowly come to terms with Luca's loss.

But Jacob's perceived abandonment she had never been able to understand, let alone accept, even fifteen years later. It made his return, his clear kindness and affection, and the undeniably strong feelings between them, all the more overwhelming.

Back in Texas, Selah was experiencing a rare moment of regretting her words. Because now Fallon had shut down and would likely remain unresponsive for the rest of the night. And Selah had failed—epically failed, she admitted—to elicit any satisfying information. Was Jacob still there? What had happened? What did he say? Where had he been? Why was he back?

She gazed around her studio with a sigh. Fallon was sometimes stubborn. Selah could do nothing now but wait.

In the hotel room, Fallon must have finally fallen asleep, because she found herself waking up well after one a.m. to Bret slipping under the covers with her. He smelled clean, so he had been back long enough to shower. Wrapping her up in his arms, he buried his face in her neck.

She soon realized he was troubled and pulled away to see him better in the faint light. "What's wrong?"

He lay back on his pillow, staring at her. "You bewitched me, to make me stay at the party."

She snorted. "There was no bewitching necessary to make you stay at that party. You were quite happy."

"To let you come back here alone, then. In my right mind, I never would have let that happen, because I knew, all evening, that something was wrong, that you were shaken up. Hiding something from me." He looked hurt. "You made me let you leave. I never would have stayed."

She was regretful that she had upset him. "I'm sorry. I thought I was doing what was best for everyone."

"Have you ever done that to me before?" He looked positively devastated, and she tried to quickly register everything that was now going wrong.

"No, Bret! Never. I didn't even know I could do it, really, but it worked."

He stared at her, waiting.

"I mean, you know I've calmed you, many times. But never have I gotten you to do something like go or stay somewhere, just by my willing it." She searched his face. He was irritated and mistrustful. And still waiting for an answer. She took the deepest breath she could manage. "I needed to be alone, to think. I knew you would have a good time if you stayed and that Tayce wouldn't want us both to leave early. I didn't want to try to explain it to you then. There was no reason why you should have had to miss hanging out with everyone. The truth is, I took so long getting back to you at the bar earlier this evening, not because I was chatting with a stranger, but because Jacob Roth showed up."

Fallon allowed some time for her words to sink in. When they did, Bret sat up in bed.

"What?!" He looked at the dog. "Is that why Azul is here?"

She frowned, puzzled. "Azul has nothing to do with Jacob." At least she had never believed he did. She sat up as well and took both his hands in hers.

He instantly felt calm and comfort washing over him, and tore his hands angrily away. "Stop it! Stop manipulating me every chance you get!"

She jerked back, and Azul looked up. *Was that what she was doing?* she wondered. *Manipulating him?*

"So, you lied to me? Jacob comes back after all these years, and the first thing you think to do is lie to me?"

Fallon could read that he was scared. Jealous. He thought Jacob was going to steal her away. "Bret, I wasn't ready to talk about it. I can scarcely understand it myself. But I am not going to suddenly stop loving you and Bergen. Jacob is a piece of me, of my past, my entire life. He trained me. Yes, there is a connection between us. But I love you. No one is taking me away. I need him back in my life. There are things going on that I have to address, that I have to know, and he has the answers. But the relationship he and I have has no bearing at all on the fact that you and I love each other." Her eyes burned bright. She knew her brain was being duplicitous; her heart felt full of lies. Every word she spoke was slicing her lips with tiny cuts of deceit.

Bret still would not touch her, looking wounded, and she didn't blame him. "Did you know he was coming back?" He knew so little about Jacob, only the scraps of information he'd been able to glean from Selah and Fallon. Though he couldn't admit it, he'd been jealous of Jacob from the moment he'd first

21

learned of him and discovered how deeply Jacob and Fallon had been connected. It was a jealousy he'd found himself unable to handle well.

Fallon shook her head. "I had no idea he was coming." She tapped the raven tattoo once. "I've been figuring out that this tattoo ties me to him, more so than that it matches his. The raven in my visions, the exact same raven tattooed on his arm—they are connected somehow."

Bret looked incredulous. "I never knew you and he had matching tattoos."

Fallon stared a moment, then exhaled through gritted teeth. "Months ago," she continued, "I tried to use this tattoo to contact him. I begged him, basically, to help me. The tattoo glowed in response. I didn't know if it meant anything; it had never happened before. It was an act of desperation on my part. Now months later, here he is."

"Where is he?" He glanced around, as if Jacob might be lurking there in their hotel room.

"Gone again, but he said he would be back and that then he would tell me everything."

"I'm sure he will." Bret's expression was not friendly. "What the hell happened in August while I was missing with Jack? When you vanished? You've been changed since then. You've told me nothing about it. And you didn't tell me you tried using the tattoo to communicate with him, why would you hide that from me?"

Back in August, the president of their record company had orchestrated a bizarre kidnapping of Bret James and Jack Lane in an attempt to increase record sales and tour revenue. They had been missing for eight days, and during that time Fallon's premonitions had grown increasingly intense and violent, the raven from her wrist always a living, flesh and blood presence. On the day before their rescue, Fallon had mysteriously vanished as well, though she had returned in less than twenty-four hours, just in time to figure out the riddle of their disappearance and save them. But Bret was right—she had not revealed much of anything to him about her vanishing. She kept secrets, though in her mind they were necessary secrets.

Now Fallon looked at her dog, trying to center her thoughts. Bret's accusations, his clear jealousy, felt heavy on her heart. "You tell me that you want this, this craziness," she reminded him. "I try to warn you against it, and you brush it off, you say it doesn't matter, that all that matters is you love me. But I don't know if that will always be enough. And I can't tell you everything. I don't even know half of it. I told you in the beginning that I lie and keep secrets. None of that is going to change just because I love you."

He stared at her. Everything was getting tangled, and he wasn't sure how to approach it. He decided to repeat one of his foremost concerns. "Again, I feel like a lot happened while Jack and I were gone. During that week and a half. A lot with you, internally, I don't know. And then I finally realized that you had been stolen away literally while my daughter was in the next room. Which you didn't even tell me! You didn't tell me about any of it till I found the tattoo on your neck over a week later."

"I wasn't ready to talk about it." She unconsciously rubbed the unwelcome star tattoo on the back of her neck, a souvenir from that vanishing. "And to be fair, there were a lot of other things going on at that time that took precedence."

"It was still important, Fallon. In a relationship, we have to be able to discuss the important things."

She pulled one knee to her chest. "In this relationship, you have to be able to accept that you won't know everything. And sometimes the figuring-out part needs to stay internal. Because, honestly, there are just too many important things."

It was an illuminating moment for her. She realized that she would never tell Bret all of her secrets, and she knew that highlighted some harsh truths about their relationship. Squinting, she looked away, not wanting to face it.

Bret was rubbing his hands over his face, exhausted. "I don't want this for Bergen."

Fallon was immediately alert. "This. What do you mean, this? You mean *me?*"

"No, I mean this chaos, this uncertainty, the mysteries, the unknown." Fallon had told him on the flight to Nashville that his only child was also receiving premonitions. He hadn't had a lot of time to process the news, but now it was hitting home in a big way.

"Your daughter's life will not mirror my chaos. I've told you this."

"Is it because, do you think, because she's around you..."

"Bret." She looked hard at him.

Azul glanced at her.

"I did not cause this. Her proximity to me did not infect her like a disease. That's not how it works. She has been having premonitions since she was at least seven years old. When she was nine, she tried to read me within minutes of first meeting me, something she had probably been doing unconsciously for years. These things have been active in her, long before I arrived on the scene. Do not try to blame me for this."

Bret stared quietly at Azul. At the seemingly immortal, teleporting, black dog. Months ago, he had absorbed this news without much care, the dog's unexplainably long lifespan and unusual ability.

Bret had also accepted that Fallon's friend Simon was now a literal ghost trapped in his Seattle apartment. *A ghost.* Bret had remained blithely unbothered by most everything strange and unexplainable about Fallon. Why was he so concerned about all of it now? He'd been careless, he knew, caught up in his intense love for her, the excitement of the mystical unknown. He had been willingly blind to everything she, in good faith, had tried to warn him about.

Jacob's return was shaking him. He admitted it reluctantly to himself, though of course Fallon knew. But did she know the reason? Beyond the obvious jealousy? It was because Jacob coming back into Fallon's life reminded Bret that she seemed like a magical spirit who would slip through his grasp the tighter he tried to hold her. That she was impermanent and fleeting. That she belonged to others.

They were both exhausted, and though nothing had been resolved, they decided, with unspoken agreement, to go to sleep. Bret fell asleep rather quickly, though he woke frequently through what remained of the night, restless.

Fallon did not sleep at all. Her emotions were shot after dealing first with Jacob's return and then Bret's ensuing loss of faith. Azul curled his warm, furry body up beside her, nuzzling her in an effort to bring her comfort. She pressed her cheek against his soft fur, holding one of his paws in her hand.

The next morning Bret and Fallon joined Tayce and his singer, Paul Crist, for breakfast at the hotel. Dangerous Eye was heading off to their next venue in a couple of hours. Due to a mechanical issue with one of the buses, the band had not left in the night as previously planned, and so breakfast with friends was an unexpected and welcome surprise.

As Bret and Fallon sat down at the table with them, Tayce could see immediately that something was off between his good friends, but he smiled and pretended all was well. He knew it must have everything to do with the strange state Fallon had been in when she returned to them at the bar the night before, and he wondered what could have happened in the brief time she was away. He was glad at least that they'd been able to attend last night's concert. Fallon had seemed so enthusiastic afterwards, hugging him tight and telling him over and over how incredible he was. But he'd known something was off when, a little bit later, Fallon slipped away back to the hotel alone without saying goodbye.

Tayce knew he would ask neither of them what was wrong. Bret would come to him in time. Fallon always held much back. The best thing he could do, he felt, was give them space.

Bret spent most of breakfast conversing with Paul. Dangerous Eye's blond lead singer lived on a farm with his wife Katrine only a few minutes from Fallon's north Texas home. Paul and Katrine had been acquaintances of Fallon for years but had known her only as the sweet, quirky waitress at their favorite restaurant, Solu. When Bret had re-entered their lives earlier in the year, Fallon soon became more of a friend to them as she spent time at their farm with Bret and Tayce. They were oblivious to her unusual abilities, however. Fallon never endeavored to advertise her oddness.

While the two singers chatted, Tayce concentrated on Fallon, trying to engage her in conversation. Her long blond hair was pulled up into a messy bun, and she looked pretty in a striped gray and black shirt and jeans. But she was quieter than usual, and her tired eyes looked almost sad. He updated her on the most recent news regarding the world tour possibilities, for there had been still more updates since the previous night. She asked him about his plans for the upcoming holidays.

"Filing for divorce," he reminded her. "Merry, merry holidays to Tayce."

She smiled ruefully at him. "All the glad tidings."

"You didn't know you were going to score some bonus Tayce time when you went to bed last night, did you?" he asked with a grin, selecting another piece of bacon.

"I had no idea I'd be this lucky, it's true," she confirmed.

Wiping his hands on a napkin, he reached into his backpack and pulled out a folded Dangerous Eye t-shirt, which he handed to her. "As requested."

Her face lit up as she accepted the shirt. "Nice. Thanks for hooking a girl up."

He shrugged. "That's how I roll. Girls, hook-ups…"

She patted his arm. "It's a busy life you lead, I know." She stashed the shirt into her ever-present messenger bag. "The tour is done in another week or so, yeah?"

"That's right." He nodded, finishing off his coffee. "Ten more days. Short but sweet. The guys and I always have a good time."

"The world tour, it would fit into your schedule?" She added pepper to her eggs.

"Let's just say I would absolutely make my schedule conform to it."

"Yeah, I think Bret would, too." She glanced at Bret briefly as he continued to chat enthusiastically with Paul. Fallon looked at her phone and then gazed into the distance without expression.

Tayce observed this quietly. How, he wondered, had things suddenly become so different for them? Or had it not been so sudden at all? He admitted to himself that he hadn't been around them at all since the dramatic events back in August, having left immediately to go out on tour. Maybe this had been brewing under the surface for a while.

"Hey, I'm playing a show in L.A. on Christmas Eve," Tayce mentioned to her. "You guys should come. You can meet my girls. That is, if you were planning on being around then."

Fallon's face lit up. She had long wanted to meet the two daughters Tayce shared with his soon-to-be-ex-wife. The oldest, Jane, was in her early twenties, and she thought that Annie, the youngest, was seventeen or eighteen. He spoke about them often, and she knew that he adored them.

"I actually will be in California then. I'm coming for the holidays and Bergen's birthday. At least, that was the plan." She threw another quick side-eye glance at Bret. "I'll definitely make sure to come. Not Dangerous Eye?"

"Nah, just me and some friends. I'll be playing guitar and singing lead." He stuck out his tongue at her. "We do it every year. Throw in some Christmas songs as well."

She looked genuinely happy. "That sounds fun, I can't wait."

"Can't wait for what?" Bret asked, finally joining their conversation as Paul excused himself and left the table.

"We're going to see Tayce play Christmas Eve."

"You can join me onstage," Tayce invited. "It's going to be super casual and fun." He mentioned the guys who would be playing with him, and Bret laughed.

"We won't miss it," Bret promised. "I'd heard about your Christmas Eve shows, but I've never been able to make it."

"All I ask is that you bring your own Santa hat. Otherwise, you're not allowed on stage."

Later that day, Bret caught a flight back to California and his daughter while Fallon and Azul headed back home to Gray. This taking of separate paths had already been planned when they flew to Nashville, for Fallon had things to take care of at home before she joined them in California for the holidays.

She had to fight with the airline about suddenly needing to check a pet.

"Can't I just tell you to go back home in the same manner in which you arrived?" she asked the dog, wrestling with the pet carrier she'd had to quickly purchase. Azul licked her hand and leaned into her. She hugged him, resigned to her fate.

That evening a car service ferried Fallon and Azul from the airport in Dallas to her small garage apartment in Gray. Her only mode of transportation was the classic Dodge Dart convertible she'd inherited from her brother, and she didn't like to leave it at the airport when she traveled.

Once home, Azul raced around the backyard enjoying the mild November weather while Fallon climbed the wooden steps to the apartment she rented from an elderly widow. Decorated simply in a neutral mix of whites and grays, the apartment had splashes of brighter colors here and there, mostly from pillows or the vintage travel posters Fallon had collected. The layout was open: the kitchen and living area were all one, and her bed was off in a corner, hidden behind a black curtain embroidered with beads and ribbon. Only the tiny bathroom had a door, and it was made of old, antique, heavy wood, with three small squares of wavy glass near the top of it.

She'd always felt secure here; it had been her home for the past eight years. But now things felt different. Temporary. As if she were existing in an in-between, not fully present.

And she was aware that somewhere, somehow, Jacob was possibly watching her. What had he meant, 'through the eyes of a raven?' She thought about the raven that had met her in so many of her more powerful visions months ago. The dark bird that had bruised her with a wing and sliced her with both beak and claw, drawing her blood. But had, in the end, done all of this to shield and protect her, as far as she could determine. She ran her thumb absent-mindedly over the raven on her wrist.

Thinking of Jacob brought an ache to her chest. She missed him beyond reason, but told herself she was foolish for doing so. She half-doubted that he would return to her, despite his fervent promise. Where there was hope, there existed the space for heartbreak. And she was weary of heartbreak.

CHAPTER THREE

FALLON & LUCA

When fifteen-year-old Fallon got home from school that day, she immediately sensed the emptiness. Despite Azul's warm, welcoming presence, the house in Austin often filled her with sadness when Luca was out, because it sharply reminded her that Jacob was gone from her.

She'd spent the past year wavering between grief and anger regarding Jacob and his unexplainable disappearance. On the darkest days, she sat in his bedroom and wished he'd left behind his wicked-looking, silver dagger. Without it, she was instead forced to use a basic kitchen knife to make cuts into the side of her hip, momentarily quelling the emotional pain that flooded her by eliciting physical pain. She made the cuts on her hip so that Luca and Selah wouldn't see, though this was unnecessary, because her body healed the cuts in minutes, leaving not even a scar.

This was something Selah had commented on more than once over the years—Fallon's lack of scars. She herself had scars from scraping her knee as a child, burning herself on a skillet while making pancakes with her sisters, and various other mishaps. But Fallon's skin was smooth and unmarked, without scars of any kind.

Fallon shrugged it off whenever Selah mentioned it, commenting that she was clearly more graceful than Selah, the ballerina. Her friend wasn't fooled by this evasion—Selah had long ago developed immense patience in regard to everything unusual regarding Fallon.

Now Fallon stood in the middle of the house and looked around while Azul solemnly licked her hand. The car was in the driveway. Twenty-year-old Luca had not been scheduled to work, because it was his birthday. They had discussed going to the lake with their friend, Simon.

But Luca was not in the house.

Hey. Luca?

She was met with silence. They'd been communicating telepathically since she was four years old, and her brother had never not answered her. This new quiet in her head felt wide and heavy. Closing her eyes, she searched for him with her mind.

Luca was not in Austin. She touched a hand to her temple. He wasn't dead; she could tell that much. But he was no longer in her world—that was her singular thought. And she wondered, with a sinking heart, if he would ever come back, or if he was gone from her forever like Jacob before him.

Falling down to her knees in the living room, a loneliness like nothing she'd ever known covered her in a crushing wave. They were both gone. The two men who had anchored her to life. Azul nuzzled her and lay against her lap, whining to acknowledge her distress. She buried her face in his fur and wept.

Selah, when she had gotten home from dance class and heard the news, wanted Fallon to come stay at her house, but Fallon refused.

"I want to be here when he gets back," Fallon said stubbornly.

In her bedroom, Selah wiped away a single tear. She was thinking about Jacob, who had never come back. Whose loss had so deeply wounded Fallon. What would they do, Selah pondered, if Luca failed to return as well? She wiped away two more tears. She loved Luca Quinn. He was like a brother to her, and possibly she'd always had a bit of a crush on him. He was such a happy, handsome, lively boy. Where could he have gone? He would never have left his little sister behind.

"Let me know right away," she ordered Fallon.

As Fallon hung up, she rubbed her thumb over the labradorite stone in the ring Jacob had given her for her twelfth birthday. Azul burrowed against her.

"What would I do without you?" she asked, laying her face against the dog's soft fur.

For the next several weeks that Luca was gone from her, Fallon was numb, moving mechanically through life. Tallie, one of Selah's older sisters, gave her a ride to school in the mornings and didn't ask questions. In the afternoon, Fallon took the city bus home. She lay on Luca's bed at night and stared at the walls, sleeping little.

Simon, who was their closest friend besides Selah, as well as being an on-and-off boyfriend of her brother's, was busy with college life, but he was distraught at Luca's disappearance as well. He texted her daily for updates and stopped by many weekday evenings with take-out food to share. On the weekends, Selah stayed with her and took her grocery shopping, doing her own part to ensure that Fallon was still eating.

One Saturday night, Selah woke to find Fallon gone from the bed they were sharing. She looked around the dark house for a while, coming last to Jacob's closed bedroom door. She hesitated, feeling the oddness of this moment. In the seven years that Jacob had lived with the siblings, Selah had never so much as laid a hand on the doorknob to this room. It had been off-limits, an unspoken sacred boundary.

Swinging the door open now, she found Fallon sitting in an ornate, cushioned chair, her feet on a leather ottoman, illuminated by the moonlight from a nearby window. Azul was asleep with his back pressed against the ottoman, snoring peacefully.

Selah flipped the closest light switch, but instead of a ceiling light it turned on a nearby lamp. She took a moment to look around the room. It was richly decorated but absent of any personal touch. From offhand comments Luca had made in her presence, she knew Fallon had spent much time in here. Looking back to her friend, she found Fallon watching her closely. Selah crossed her arms over her chest and leaned against the doorframe.

"What if he never comes back, either?" Fallon's voice was a ghostly whisper.

Selah had no answer for her, and she had never been one for false platitudes. "This room brings you comfort," she remarked. "It's familiar to you." Her tone was careful.

Fallon's gaze dropped to Azul. "Jacob read to me at night in here. You know, he would sit on my bed and read to me when I was a little girl. As I grew older, we switched to here. He would sit in this chair, and I would sit on the ottoman, and he would read."

Selah nodded.

Fallon was lying. Jacob had stopped reading to her after she turned eleven. His main goal had been to train her. He'd been hellbent on helping her understand everything her mind was capable of, unlocking abilities she hadn't known she possessed: psychometry, becoming a shadow, healing, and various others. Though this had all been done in secret, creating a sense of intimacy between them, there had never been even a hint of impropriety on Jacob's part. He had been an excellent teacher and she a devoted and hard-working student, both of them singularly focused on the task at hand. And then he'd left her.

Now Fallon's eyes looked almost silver in the moonlight from the window as she stared at her friend. "You know there was never anything inappropriate about our relationship. I loved him, but he took great pains to hold me at a distance, physically and emotionally."

Selah was shaking her head. "I never really thought there was anything inappropriate. I would have brought it up to you at the time if I had, trust me. Or at the least, alerted Luca. I wouldn't have let a suspicion like that slide. No, I could tell that with you, Jacob was pure of heart and intention. No matter what kind of man he might have been in his life outside of you and Luca." For she'd thought the weariness and lines in Jacob's handsome face had spoken of a life of trials, of exertion. Of darkness.

Tears were streaming down Fallon's cheeks. Selah wanted to hold her, but she stayed in the doorway. She still felt Jacob's presence in this space and knew that Fallon must, too.

"Luca's disappearance is different," Selah offered tentatively. "I think he will return." Unlike Jacob.

Fallon nodded. "I think so, too. That's why I haven't fallen completely apart."

Selah reflected that Fallon had no other family besides Luca and herself. She had never seen Fallon look so alone. "I will always be here," she promised.

Fallon looked up. "I know."

Seven weeks to the day after his vanishing, Fallon felt a tug at her heart and ran to look out into the backyard, Azul at her heels. Luca was sitting on the grass, looking around. With a scream she ran out to him, tackling him and sobbing as he hugged her.

He was tired, but unharmed, and he had no memory at all as to where he'd been or what had happened. But they immediately noticed his wrists. Whereas before the skin on the underside of his wrists had been unmarked, each wrist now bore a tattoo. On the right wrist was an eye and on the left wrist was a black bird, both fairly crudely done. The siblings stared at each other and tried to imagine what it meant.

"Jacob would know," said Fallon.

"Jacob is gone," her brother reminded her flatly, and she bowed her head.

"I thought you were gone like him," she whispered. "Forever."

He wrapped his arms around her. "Fallon, I won't ever leave you. I promise."

Years later, when Fallon turned twenty, she also vanished, despite Selah's best efforts to keep an eye on her that day. When she returned seven weeks later, with no memory of the event, she had blackline tattoos on her wrists as well, but hers were different. Artistic. Beautiful. Her bird was clearly a raven, and its eye was a prism. The eye on her right wrist was surrounded by flames.

At that point Luca had been dead for three years, so there was no comparing. But Fallon had been certain of one thing: the raven on her left wrist was identical to the raven she remembered being on Jacob Roth's left forearm.

CHAPTER FOUR

The day after she returned from Nashville, Fallon headed into Dutton, the slightly larger town to the north of Gray, for groceries and to run a few errands. She had not been home much since the rescue back in August. She'd been spending as much time as possible with Bret and Bergen, first at Paul and Katrine's farm and then later in California. But now she was back in Gray, and there were things that needed to be done.

She was looking forward to being alone for a while. Though she loved Bret and Bergen, they each, in varying ways, took a lot from her. She had not been alone much in the past few months, and it had begun to weigh on her.

As she arrived in Dutton, she spotted the iconic red and yellow building that housed Sunny Girl Bakery. She slowed and turned impulsively into the parking lot. Bringing Luca's black, 1963 Dodge Dart convertible to a stop near a tree, she realized she hadn't been to the bakery since August, when Tayce and Bergen had tagged along with her. When their lives had been paused because of Bret and Jack. The bakery's cheerful, enigmatic owner, Sunny Lewis, was a favorite of hers, and Fallon was surprised that she'd allowed three months to pass without seeing her.

The lively, twenty-something proprietress was alone behind the counter when Fallon entered. Sunny's pretty face lit up with mischief and joy as she greeted Fallon with a charming smile and sharp flick of her black ponytail.

"Felicitous Fallon! How I've missed you. What brings you in today?" In black jeans and a sleeveless black shirt, Sunny's toned arms were an artist's sketchbook of tattoos, and as usual, she gave off edgy girl-next-door vibes. No matter Fallon's mood, Sunny could usually bring a smile to her face.

Fallon leaned against the counter with a grin. "As fate would have it, I've been craving scones."

Sunny winked. "The gods are smiling on you. I've got apricot-pistachio, fresh this morning."

"That will be perfect. Six, please."

"Anything else?" Sunny asked, as she filled a small box with a half-dozen, lightly-iced scones.

Fallon held out her hand, and Sunny came near and took it, scrunching up the skin on the bridge of her nose as she appeared to concentrate. Then she brightened.

"One cappuccino with a shot of mocha, coming up."

Fallon laughed. "You've improved."

Sunny shrugged as she added a pump of mocha syrup to a paper cup. "Eh, I was sharper years ago. I'm like a dull blade these days. Also, it's your most typical order."

"True. How's business?"

"Brisk and breezy, mostly thanks to you."

Through her friendship with Selah and her family, Fallon had been instrumental in hooking entire local offices of people on Sunny's decadent baked goods.

As she accepted the cappuccino, her fingertips brushed Sunny's, and Fallon frowned at the fragment that entered her mind. "You had a coffee shop in Austin?"

"Sure, back in the day," said Sunny easily.

Since Sunny looked barely twenty-five years old, this thread of conversation always puzzled Fallon.

"Hey, how was the concert in Nashville?" Sunny inquired. "Such a fun city."

Fallon mentally flinched, since she had not told Sunny about a concert. "It was phenomenal. They've always been good live. Tayce Williams is an absolute wizard on guitar. Mesmerizing."

"Ah, like his father before him," Sunny noted sagely.

"No," Fallon shook her head as she handed Sunny cash, "his dad ran a dairy his whole life, he's…" She dropped off and met Sunny's steady gaze. "He's adopted. He knows nothing of his real parents."

Sunny's expression betrayed nothing. She grinned. "Was just a guess!"

But as another customer came in and drew Sunny away from her, Fallon was certain that it had not been a guess.

Within days, it was announced that the world tour, which singer Jack Lane had been pushing for ever since he and Bret were dramatically rescued by the FBI, was finally coming to official fruition. It had been a feat of endurance and dedication on the part of everyone's management teams that such a thing had been worked out so thoroughly and with a fair amount of speed. Everyone had recognized that the publicity garnered by their kidnapping was worth capitalizing on, which was ironic considering the reason behind the crime had been exactly that.

All scheduled dates were in Asia and Europe, and included Bret and Jack's solo bands along with Dangerous Eye. It was scheduled to kick off in early February in Tokyo, six weeks after the end of Dangerous Eye's brief North American tour, and would last around four months. Despite their initial reservations and off-handed comments, all the guys were undeniably excited to participate. Previously scheduled projects for all parties were being hastily rescheduled.

Even though things still felt unsettled between herself and Bret, it was understood that Fallon would come along on the entirety of the tour. With her lifelong love of music, she was thrilled to be accompanying the bands, but she was conflicted, considering the situation with Bret. The ghost of Jacob's promise to return to her—again—still loomed. When she and Jacob had been in that hotel office together, she'd gotten the brief but undeniable sensation that the most important person in her life was standing right in front of her.

She had two months to prepare for the tour, and so she began making a mental list. The first item could be taken care of immediately, and this was to give her notice at Solu. The enchanting restaurant had been a constant for her the past several years, and her boss, Diego Sanchez, could handle her occasional month-long sojourns. But now her heart was being pulled in too many different directions, and she could guarantee nothing. She needed to focus.

She had never needed the waitressing money; working at Solu had been a way to get her out amongst people. When Jacob had vanished from the siblings' lives fifteen years ago, he had placed Fallon's name on enough stocks, bonds, and bank accounts to assure her financial security forevermore.

At first, Diego and his wife Marianna begged Fallon to reconsider her decision to leave Solu. She was their most trusted employee, and they considered her family. Upon meeting them years before, she had saved the lives of them and their three children via premonition.

But Fallon was firm. "I can't say when I'll be in Gray for any certain length of time. Already this year I've been gone more than I've been here. It's time for us to part ways. I'll come in now and then to say 'hello,'" she promised, "but I can offer no more than that. It's time for me to go."

They both hugged her, and Marianna wiped away tears. "I knew we couldn't keep you forever. You have been a joy, Fallon."

* * * * * * *

Barefoot in ripped jeans and a black tank top, Fallon sat cross-legged on a wooden stool in Selah's artist studio one evening with a glass of sauvignon blanc, watching as the growing shadows crept across the walls. She loved the studio. The splatters of color staining the dark wood floor. The smell of paint and canvas. The old blues that played continuously on the speakers. When Fallon stepped into the studio and closed the door, she felt like she was stepping into an otherworld, secure with the often-silent company of her best friend and the reliable crooning of Billie Holiday and Ella Fitzgerald.

Painting had been suggested by the therapist Selah's parents consulted with when they saw their daughter struggling mentally and emotionally in the aftermath of her shattered dance career at eighteen. They had secretly gone to Fallon and asked her to attempt to sway Selah into trying art therapy, knowing their former ballerina was stubborn and touchy about who gave her advice. Accepting the mission, silver-tongued Fallon had seamlessly persuaded her friend to try painting. Selah had fallen in love with it in spite of all her well-placed misgivings. It had become an enormous part of her life.

As evening fell, Selah was cleaning her brushes in the small porcelain sink her husband had installed for this purpose. Dressed casually in her usual painting attire of leggings and a t-shirt, she touched a hand absently to her dark hair which was pulled back from her face. Now and then she glanced over at her friend, but Fallon was far away. A few times, Selah parted her lips to say something and then closed them, remaining silent.

Finally, she joined Fallon, perching on a stool near her. Perusing the mini-charcuterie board Fallon had briskly assembled downstairs, Selah selected a piece of cheese. The ensuing rapid-fire thumping on the hardwood floor brought a smile to her face, and she tossed the cheese to Azul before choosing another piece for herself. Azul happily devoured it, gazing up at her with adoring, dark doggy eyes.

Selah pointed a stern finger at him. "You've reached your limit, sir."

Azul slid down onto his belly and rested his chin between his paws.

With a faint smile at the exchange, Fallon poured herself more wine. Selah rarely drank alcohol but kept a bottle in the fridge for her friend.

"It seems to me you only come to say goodbye these days," Selah mentioned, for Fallon had told her about the upcoming tour and about her planned December trip to California. "You've barely been in Gray at all the past months."

Fallon gazed at her. "I feel like lately my life is only goodbyes. But this isn't goodbye, I'm not leaving for another two weeks."

"I was making a general observation."

Fallon thought Selah looked quietly tense. "What's wrong?" She never read Selah. When they were children, it had been established that Selah did not like or appreciate the invasion to her privacy. Fallon had never broken her promise that she would never read Selah again.

Now Selah stared out the window at the darkening sky. Fallon had filled her in on the basics of what had happened in Nashville concerning Jacob. The sudden appearance in the dark hallway. The intense conversation in the nearby office. The promise to come back for her. Selah felt like Fallon was definitely holding back on some details.

"Why has he returned? Why, Fallon? And why now? Where has he been? Fifteen years. It's a very long time. I know you know this. The time that passed was longer for you than for anyone—except possibly for him. But I need to know *why now*?"

Fallon turned the ring on her left ring finger round and round meditatively, then glanced down at it. Brass was woven artfully and delicately around the labradorite stone. In the light, the greenish-gray stone flashed with hints of bright blue, then gold, then a faint coppery red, before going back to green and gray. She tilted it back and forth in the light, watching the colors flash.

"I don't know. I don't know where he's been or why he stayed away so long. He didn't have time to tell me anything, except to say that he hadn't thought he'd be away from me as long as he has been. But his return, I think, might have everything to do with my father. With the way he can steal me at will." She looked at Selah. "I want to stop him from doing that. Obviously."

"Obviously." Selah broke her rule, getting up and retrieving a glass from a cupboard. She poured herself a small amount of wine. "All the more unsettling," she murmured. She took a sip. "Is he changed? Jacob?"

Fallon drew a knee to her chest. "He looks exactly the same. As if I had just seen him the night before in Austin. Unchanged."

"Unaged?"

"Unaged."

"If he was around fifty when we last saw him, which I know was our best estimate, then he should be nearing seventy by now," Selah observed.

Fallon shook her head. "But he is not. He looks about the same age as Bret. I tell you, there has been no change."

They exchanged a short glance, then Selah tapped her glass with a paint-stained finger. "So, fifteen years ago he kissed you on top of the head, in what was for him at the time a wild display of affection, and then he vanished with no explanation or warning, along with all of his personal effects. He did not die, clearly; he simply went away and has failed to communicate with you until fifteen years later in the hallway of a historic Nashville hotel. With apparent teleportation as his grand finale."

Fallon downed the remainder of her wine. "That sums it up. And things between him and I are," she licked her lips, "different, now." She met Selah's eyes.

Selah took this in and then nodded in careful understanding. "Not unexpected, if I'm being honest." Setting aside her glass, she massaged her temples. "How is Bret with this development?"

Fallon set aside her empty glass as well. "How do you think? Angry. Jealous. Threatened."

"I don't blame him."

"Neither do I, Selah. It's just that I was unprepared for this."

"Of course." Selah nodded sympathetically. She knew that things between Bret and Fallon must be damaged by Jacob's return. How could they remain whole under the circumstances? And if or when Jacob came again, if he took Fallon away somewhere as he'd promised, the damage would only increase. As far as she could see, the only tie left binding Bret and Fallon together now was Bergen. Even if they did not fully realize this yet.

Fallon's green-eyed gaze was on Selah's latest work in progress, a dark and dreamy landscape with threatening skies. A single tiny spark of gold was evident in the sky, one small glimmer of radiant hope. Selah's art was always a mix of despair and heaven.

Sliding off the stool, Fallon approached the piece, staring at it intently. Raising one hand, she extended her index finger towards the golden mark, stopping half an inch from the canvas. As Selah watched, the gold began to shimmer and move—she imagined wings. And then she held her breath as the brush stroke she'd applied hours before changed to resemble the small golden shadow of a raven.

Fallon's hand dropped, and she looked quickly over her shoulder. "I'm sorry."

Selah appeared unbothered. "It's more interesting this way. And I know he's been on your mind." But she admitted to herself that she was surprised. She'd never witnessed Fallon do such a thing before. She wondered what other mysteries her beautiful friend held close.

They both looked instinctively at the raven tattoo on Fallon's wrist.

Indio ran into the room then and threw his arms around Fallon, lightening the mood and distracting them from their discourse.

Michael came trailing after his son. He looked apologetic. "I told him he needed to let you two have some time alone. But he's been missing Fallon. I even promised him video games, and he still chose to invade your world instead."

Fallon was holding the six-year-old on her lap. "Of course. I've missed him, too. I'm better than any video game, right?"

"Right!" Indio crowed.

"How is first grade, my boy?"

He showed her the dinosaur figure he'd brought along. "It's fun. Look what I won for being the best student this week!"

CHAPTER FIVE

Since Nashville, Fallon's video calls with Bret were sometimes difficult and fraught with easy misunderstandings. He was touchy about everything. She swore that often she would catch him trying to peer over her shoulder into her apartment, as if he suspected Jacob might be there. Considering all the factors at play, she didn't necessarily blame him for his doubt, but she found herself tiptoeing around his heavy emotions with more and more regularity. She tried to be kind, understanding that Jacob's surprise return to her life was a lot to deal with, but his frequently snarky comments and general bad humor were testing her patience.

Conversely, her calls with Bergen were lively and full of love. The spunky nine-year-old girl missed her desperately and couldn't wait to see her again. She was counting down the days till Fallon was scheduled to join them for two weeks, for Christmas and New Years and to celebrate Bergen's tenth birthday.

Fallon wondered how that time with Bret would go. Not to mention the upcoming four-month tour. When she'd asked if she should come along on the tour, he had sounded surprised that she would consider not coming. But she suspected that his reasons for wanting her on tour were tangled. And she was concerned at her own willingness to go.

Despite being twenty-nine years old, Fallon had never been in a relationship before now. Her teenage years had been marked by hours spent training with Jacob, hanging out with her brother, and then learning to carry on after Jacob left. She'd had no friends in school besides Selah. Good-looking, friendly Luca had been popular at school and had easily made friends, but his pretty little sister had been distantly aloof.

Throughout her twenties Fallon had been uninterested in either dating or making new friends, preoccupied as she was searching for an unsearchable thing and dealing as gracefully as she could with the premonitions that came regularly and without warning. She'd had a few casual flings during her extensive travels, mainly with musicians she met at small concerts. She was always clear upfront that she would be moving on eventually and that there would be no on-going communication. While most of them were fine with this arrangement, a few had been certain they could change her mind, but none could. She traveled under assumed names, partly so that no one could track her down later.

The connection with Bret last April had been unexpected. She had fallen into a relationship with him fairly quickly and against her better judgement. He'd been sweet, and kind, and loving, all things she had previously refused to acknowledge to herself that she craved. She believed her close bond with his daughter, as well as the mental telepathy between herself and Bret, had influenced their strong feelings.

So, she didn't know if the currently shaky state of their relationship was her fault? Because she was simply unpracticed at relationships? Were her years of being strong and independent, even with her brother at her side, stopping her from being committed to someone in the right way? Was she being selfish by not letting him all the way in? Was she not being honest, both to herself and with Bret, about what existed between herself and Jacob?

She didn't know the answer to any of these questions. She'd always assumed that she would be alone in this life; she had accepted it long ago. Holding everyone at a careful distance, she didn't form close relationships. After suffering those two early, devastating losses of Jacob and Luca, she hadn't wanted to love anyone else. Selah, she had felt, would be her only attachment.

Her love for Bret and Bergen had shaken her, and even her affectionate friendship with Tayce was not anything she would have anticipated. Those three individuals had undeniably changed her heart, and she knew she would give her life for them. She worried that she'd see Bergen so much less if she and Bret were ever to end their relationship.

* * * * * * *

Every weekday, Fallon drove to Dutton to lift weights at the gym where she had been a member for the past eight years. Luca might have gotten her into running, but losing Jacob and Luca had changed her. After her year of intense mourning and self-destruction following Luca's murder, she had plunged herself into weight-lifting. She was determined to be strong—stronger than anyone expected. It was the combination of weights and running that helped heal her mentally enough that she was able to reclaim the abilities she had foolishly let go after losing Luca.

Upon returning from Nashville, Fallon went for long runs every few days, trying to clear her head. To shake things up, she started going more often to run at Star Fall Farm, the establishment Paul Crist and his wife Katrine had owned and operated for years. About five miles east of Gray, the farm consisted of 120 acres and could be reached by a dusty gravel road lined on either side by wooden fencing. The main house and its associated buildings were located in the general center of the property.

Paul and Katrine resided in a beautiful, quaint, old farmhouse with a wraparound porch. There was an ivy-covered cottage-style guesthouse out back, as well as a more modern-looking metal building that housed a recording studio and an upstairs apartment.

The property included an old wooden barn that was still in use and a greenhouse where Katrine grew herbs, strawberries, and flowers year-round. There were roads and trails leading to fields of vegetables, rows of berry bushes, fruit orchards, and a pasture full of angora goats, plus a couple of donkeys. Chickens, guineas, and geese wandered around freely with three dogs and a number of cats.

Katrine greeted her on the porch the first morning Fallon showed up. The older woman looked pure and earth-goddess-like in a colorful, long skirt and white tank top. Three crystals hung from black leather cords around her neck, and her wavy chestnut hair fell around her shoulders.

"So good to see you, Fallon! Paul said you might be stopping by."

Fallon accepted a lavender-scented hug.

"Paul will be home from the tour soon," Katrine told her. "He promised."

Tilting her head slightly at the wording Katrine used, Fallon smiled. "Running out here is far more enjoyable that running in town, for sure."

As she always did, Fallon tried to read Katrine and got nothing. It again gave her pause. She was usually able to get at least something from everyone she tried to read. Some were loud and clear, like Bret and Tayce, whose thoughts and feelings she could easily see. Bergen was glitter and rainbows and happiness. Others only gave her bits and pieces. But Katrine was the only person she'd ever hit a complete brick wall with.

Until last August, when the FBI agent assigned to Bret and Jack's case had shown up at Selah's door. Detective Ashton had proven impossible for Fallon to read, which had been disconcerting, especially at the end of the investigation when she had sensed something intense and sinister from him. She'd been shaken yet strangely relieved to read of his mysterious murder one month after Bret and Jack's rescue, a case that still remained unsolved. It was a puzzle that she continued to turn over in her mind.

"Come in after you're done with your run," Katrine invited. "I'll have fresh lemonade for you."

Fallon promised that she would. Then she set out, falling into a steady pace, Azul at her side. She usually wore headphones when she ran, but at the farm she liked to listen to everything around her.

She timed her run so that at the midway point she ended up at a pond, which was hidden away in a far corner of the property. There was a large sycamore tree near the bank, devoid of leaves now, but offering copious shade during the spring and summer months. Tayce loved to sit under the tree with his guitar, looking at the water as he played. Fallon had observed early on in their friendship that the farm appealed to him in a way Los Angeles did not.

Taking out her phone, she took a picture of her view and texted it to him.

"Unfair," he texted back. "I'm eating waffles in Charleston, and you're there soaking up all the goodness. You probably just got done with a run as well."

"My soul is purer, no doubt," she confirmed.

"Maybe after my divorce I'll go live at the farm full-time."

"Yes!" She grinned. "Then we'd see each other all the time, and you could start running with me."

"Don't get carried away," he warned, laughing at her prediction.

CHAPTER SIX

FALLON AND SELAH

Eleven-year-old Fallon waved as Tallie drove away, having just dropped her little sister off at Fallon's house for a sleepover. Selah ran to her friend and hugged her tightly. Her family had been away on vacation for most of June, and the girls had missed each other. Usually, Fallon spent the night at Selah's, but on rare occasion, Selah was allowed to stay the night with Fallon.

The lack of a maternal presence in the house had for a long time given Selah's parents pause. Recognizing this and also recognizing that Selah was Fallon's only friend—as well as a decent, loyal kid—Jacob had gone to visit Selah's parents and had set their minds at ease. They were still, admittedly, more comfortable having Fallon over, but they did relent now and then to allow Selah to stay. The girls had been best friends for four years; every year that passed saw Selah's family warming up to and accepting Fallon's living situation more and more.

Now Fallon grabbed Selah's hand and led her inside. Dropping her backpack in a chair in the main living area, Selah could smell something delicious in the air as she followed Fallon to the kitchen. Jacob was cooking dinner. He often wasn't home, but when he was, Selah was always interested in observing the dynamics between him and the siblings.

Jacob greeted Selah with the brief, polite half-nod, half-smile combination which he always employed with her, and she greeted him in the same reserved manner. The man was such a mystery to her—agreeable and not at all unpleasant, but entirely not a parent to Fallon and Luca. More of a roommate, really. This had been such a shock to her when she and Fallon had first become friends, when she realized Fallon and her brother were generally unparented. But as time passed, she took note of how happy Fallon seemed, how well-mannered and engaging the siblings were. Selah now accepted that possibly not all children needed parents, or perhaps Jacob's low-key presence was just what the siblings required.

"Tonight is Italian. I hope you are both hungry," Jacob mentioned, checking on the rolls in the oven as Fallon got two small bottles of lemonade from the fridge.

"I'm starving," Selah confirmed, watching as Fallon went near to Jacob to peer at the contents of the skillet on the stove.

He winked at her, and she smiled at him, before turning with a flick of her braids and calling Selah to follow her to her room.

"Where's Luca?" Selah asked, as they sat on Fallon's bed and sipped their lemonade.

"At work. He gets off at six, though, he should be home soon."

"He's driving Jacob's car?"

Fallon nodded. "Jacob for sure never uses it much."

"How does he get around?" Selah was curious. "Bus?"

Fallon shrugged, unconcerned. "We never know." She leaned down to pet Azul, who had come in from the backyard, his black fur warm from the summer sun.

Selah got up and wandered around the room, stopping at Fallon's bookshelf to see if there was anything new. Fallon had a lot books—Selah knew that several of them were gifts from Jacob while others had been purchased at used bookstores around Austin. There were some medals from participating in 5Ks; Selah was aware that Luca had recently gotten Fallon into running with him.

And there was an amber glass bottle that looked to be antique, holding a collection of black feathers. Selah had seen it on Fallon's shelf for as long as she'd known her, and every time she thought to look, the bottle seemed to have gained a feather or two. She reached out and touched a feather tentatively. Then, in what she felt to be a bold move on her part, she selected one of the feathers and took it out of the bottle, looking it over.

"Where do you find these?" she asked casually, but as she spoke there was suddenly an electricity in the air. When she looked over her shoulder, Fallon was staring at the bottle, almost as if in a trance. "Fallon."

Fallon looked to the doorway, and Selah turned and saw Jacob standing there, looking at the feather in her dark hands. There was a faint smile on his lips. "Dinner will be ready in ten minutes. I'm not sure if your brother will be joining you?" He directed the question at Fallon.

She reached for her phone. "I think so. But I'll ask."

"Come and set the table after you find out. I am leaving in a bit, but the food will be ready for you." Jacob disappeared as silently as he had come.

Fallon looked back at Selah. "I find them everywhere, the feathers. They remind me of that raven tattoo on Jacob's arm. So, I started collecting them. For fun."

Selah replaced the feather and sank to the floor to pet Azul, who nuzzled against her with affection. "From crows, I assume. Since ravens are rare in Austin. As far as I know."

Fallon was staring thoughtfully out the window. "I assume."

CHAPTER SEVEN

Fallon flew to California the week before Christmas, and Bret picked her up at the airport. Their most recent calls had been less fractious—he was in a good mood as he looked ahead to the world tour—and she was hopeful that the next two weeks would go smoothly.

As she climbed into his car, he pulled her close and kissed her passionately. "I've missed you," he confessed, and she grinned.

"Same, handsome."

When they got to the beachside town where he lived, Fallon observed that Daisy, the café which Bergen's mother and aunt owned, seemed busy.

"Café still doing well?" she asked. The building had bright blue clapboard walls, painted tastefully with a few white daisies, and there was an intricate mass of umbrella-covered outdoor tables and strings of lights through the trees.

"As far as I know. Since Lis doesn't live with me anymore, I don't hear much about it."

Not long after Fallon and Bret got together in the spring, Bergen's mother Lisbeth married her architect boyfriend. It had been an uneven time for Bergen and was made worse when Bret and Jack were kidnapped later in the summer. Fallon had felt herself becoming a safe place, an anchor, for Bergen—a role which she had not entirely been prepared to take on. But she was drawn to Bergen as a mother to a child, loving her with a blind fierceness that defied explanation.

At the house, Bret carried her bag inside and upstairs directly to his bedroom.

"Where's Bergen?" Fallon asked, following him and listening to the silence of the house.

"Spending the night with a friend." Dropping her bags, he turned to her and wrapped her up in his arms. "Tonight, it's just us." He kissed her deeply, pushing her back against the wall.

In that instance, she realized he was doing two things: he was setting the tone for how the next two weeks were going to go; and he was, in a sense, claiming her as his. The latter, to a lesser degree, but because she could read him so easily, it was undeniable. As their kisses became more intense, the raven tattoo on her wrist—which had only tingled uncomfortably in the past—began burning. Fallon hissed in pain, eyes watering, her mind drawn immediately to Jacob—and maybe that was the intention. But as Bret paused, his expression questioning if she was hurt, she frowned in annoyance at the clashing duality in her brain.

This is ridiculous and unfair, she thought.

Returning his kisses, she ignored the continuing ache in her left wrist.

Later that night while Bret slept soundly, Fallon lay awake, staring at the raven tattoo in the moonlight. It was no longer causing her pain. Sleep was beyond her, some barely-defined energy filling her body with tension. When she focused on it, the energy felt like grief.

Tears came to her eyes, though she tried to blink them away, not wanting Bret to wake up and find her crying. The tears blurred her vision, and the raven's wings moved, as if in flight. Then the bird turned its dark head and seemed to gaze at her with the sparkling prism eye.

"*Stop leaving me.*" Her whispered voice was barely a breath.

The entire raven glowed red, pulsing with color and heating her wrist in a way that sent electricity tingling pleasantly through her entire body. And then it was still. Only an unmoving line drawing on her wrist. Trembling, she rubbed roughly at the tears on her face, hugging a pillow tightly and willing herself to sleep.

The next day was Bergen's tenth birthday, and the girl arrived home early in the morning from her sleepover, excited to see Fallon. Bret, who was in a light-hearted mood, took them out for a day of brunch, shopping, and hanging out on the beach, which were some of Bergen's favorite things. The majority of their time was spent at the beach, which was her happy place.

"I can't believe you're ten," Fallon told her, as she and Bergen lay on their stomachs together on a beach towel in the sand towards the end of the day. The sea breeze felt cool against their salty skin. Bret, a couple of feet away, was on the phone with someone for work.

Pretty Bergen was simultaneously eating a cupcake and playing with the ring on Fallon's left ring finger. Her long, dark-blond hair clung damply to her tanned skin. A California girl through and through, she spent all of her time at the beach, swimming and surfing, her body lean and athletic. She'd played softball for a few years, but was about to give it up. Now that her mother had married Leo and moved out of Bret's house, everything was different. Having to schedule and split her time between the two houses was a complication she'd never had to deal with. More often, Bergen wanted to spend her free time either at the beach or riding her dirt bike with her dad when he was around.

Her step-dad, Leo, was fine, his twin sons moderately tolerable. Bergen understood that her parents living in the same house for all her life had been unusual and not sustainable—they weren't in a relationship, after all. They'd always seen other people. Her birth had been planned by two former lovers who had believed they could successfully parent as just friends, and possibly it hadn't been fully thought out, but it had worked for nine years. It had been familiar to her.

Having Fallon in her life changed everything and filled Bergen with joy. Fallon had only been around her since May, but it sometimes felt like she'd known Fallon forever. Being able to confide in her when her parents were driving her crazy was everything. She was like a fun aunt and favorite sister combined, and Bergen couldn't imagine life without her.

Bergen's gray eyes, another trait she shared with her father, stayed on the ring. She had never known Fallon to be without it. "Where did you get this?" she asked, licking icing off her thumb.

Fallon looked out at the ocean. "Mmm, someone gave it to me when I was twelve. For my birthday, actually."

"Your brother? Luca?"

Fallon shook her head. "A close friend." She rolled up to a sitting position. "Come on, let's get in the water one more time."

Bergen hopped up and raced her to the water's edge. Bret put away his phone and joined them.

* * * * * * *

The Christmas Eve concert put on by Tayce and friends at a small venue turned out to be a fun night. Fallon did not get to meet his daughters, who were both home sick with the flu, but she had a good time. Bret joined Tayce onstage for several songs, and Fallon could only whole-heartedly agree that the entire band wearing Santa hats was a nice touch. She was impressed that Tayce could sing almost as well as he played guitar.

"You've never heard him sing?" Bret asked as they drove home. "He's put out some solo albums."

Fallon was mystified as she looked at her phone. "I somehow missed them over the years. I'm adding them all to my playlist right now."

All in all, Fallon's visit to California was going well until New Year's Eve. In the days before, Bergen decided that she wanted her father to invite people over.

"This is Fallon's first New Year's with us," she argued. "We have to do something."

Fallon might have assured them that they did not, in fact, need to do anything. She preferred quiet nights at home over large groups. But no one asked her.

She'd noticed that, though they were getting along fine, she and Bret went through frequent stretches where they didn't say much to each other. Which struck her. Earlier on in their relationship, they'd talked for hours. Had they simply run out of things to say? Truly, ever since the rescue in August, things had been different between them, even before Jacob's shock reappearance. Her focus had shifted. She'd developed a new awareness that there were shadow elements in her world. Dangerous ones.

Finally agreeing to his daughter's request for a party, Bret easily found some friends who were willing to forgo whatever previous New Year's plans they'd had in order to hang out with Bret James. He allowed Bergen to invite one friend of her own. And he called in a favor to Lisbeth, managing to have Daisy cater some food. Fallon resigned herself to her fate.

Bret's backyard was picturesque, landscaped with various plants and flowers. The high, stone wall all around gave it a secluded feel. The pool had a rough, asymmetrical shape and included a waterfall; the surrounding patio area was done in reddish brown stones with a Mediterranean look. For the party, the entire area was adorned with strings of tiny, white lights and music played through various speakers.

That evening, Bergen and her friend Gracie were usually swimming, getting out now and then to have a snack. The evening air was chilly, but the pool was heated.

Fallon, barefoot in a casual black slip of a dress, hair loose, was either walking around looking beautiful and unapproachable or sitting on the edge of the pool with her legs in the warm water in order to keep an eye on the girls. She'd had a premonition about one of the first of Bret's friends to show up that evening—something straightforward involving the man's car and his ex-wife. This had been handled successfully but with a fair amount of awkwardness—now more than a few people were looking at her speculatively from a distance.

Fallon ignored them, as she had always disregarded the backwards glances she'd gotten throughout her life. Most of the handful of people Bret had invited over were fairly decent, good people, as far as she could read, including his guitarist, Travis, and his wife Josie, both of whom she knew from the previous year's tour. But she was currently not in the mood to appear sociable.

She was aware that her role as Bret James' girlfriend was to smile and be friendly and hospitable, but tonight she couldn't bring herself to do it, and she could tell Bret was slightly disappointed. Usually, she was able to position herself as a ray of sunshine at his side, charming everyone they came in contact with. But tonight, she was simply tired after spending nearly two weeks in California with a child who loved her immensely and a man who was now unsure of her yet still intent on enjoying the physical side of their relationship.

Her primary goal that she'd set for herself this evening was to keep an eye on the two girls, who she knew could be easily overlooked by the adults who were drinking and socializing. Lisbeth had texted her more than once to see how things were going. This loss of control was something Lisbeth had rarely experienced—her daughter living with her father only—and Fallon saw that it was not easy for her. When Lisbeth finally realized that Fallon had established herself as the girls' guardian for the evening, she stopped texting.

At around eleven-thirty, Bret came and sat down next to Fallon at the edge of the pool, kissing her and slipping an arm around her. He'd started off the evening in black swim trunks and a white t-shirt, but he had stripped off the t-shirt hours ago. His body was fit and toned, his reward for a decade of intentional clean living and dedicated weight-lifting that had all been sparked by Bergen's birth.

"I'm so glad you're here," he told her, running a hand through her hair and kissing her again.

Fallon leaned against him. She thought he'd had far more to drink than his usual. Truth be told, she and Tayce out-drank Bret the majority of the time. But because she wanted to monitor the girls, she was drinking only sparkling water tonight.

"You're not going to go with him, are you?"

She blinked at Bret, trying to interpret his question. The sounds of the waterfall and the distant chatter became secondary. "What?"

He was staring at her intently. "Jacob. If he ever comes back, to take you away, you won't go, right?"

Adrenaline spiked in her chest, her heart beginning to beat rapidly. "Let's talk about this tomorrow." *Or never*, she thought. She glanced over to the girls, who were sitting under the waterfall, laughing.

"Fallon, promise me you won't go." He was grabbing onto her hand.

Her eyes flashed at him. "Bret, this conversation is not happening right now."

He looked angry. "You're going to go with him."

The adrenaline exploded. "Of course, I'm going to go with him! He holds the answers that I've been needing for the past fifteen years! There is a lot going on that I need an explanation for, that I need protection against. Absolutely, I will go with him. How can you ask that I not? How can you ask that I remain ignorant of everything that I need to know?"

Various emotions were at war across his face. He leaned in to kiss her, but she pulled back, glaring. He was stricken and uncertain; Fallon had never been angry with him before.

Her head was spinning. Had they ever even argued? Besides the fraught night in Nashville? She couldn't remember. This was certainly uncharted territory. She noticed that Bergen was staring at them with concern from across the pool, and she gave the girl a bright smile.

Bret saw the smile, saw where she was directing it, and pulled himself together. Diving into the water, he swam out to his daughter.

Fallon got up and disappeared into the house. She needed space to breathe.

Upstairs in the sanctuary of Bret's dark bedroom, Fallon's phone began vibrating, and she saw that it was Tayce calling.

"Hey, trouble," she greeted him, sitting on the bed and wiping a stray tear from her cheek. "Ready for the new year?"

"I love a new year! Full of possibilities. Clean slate."

She smiled. "Typical Tayce."

"What about you, beautiful? You still in California?"

"I am." She looked around the room, listening to the sounds of the party-goers that continued down by the pool. "I have a strong feeling that this new year will be epic."

"Your tone of voice doesn't match your words, but okay."

"Where are you?" she asked.

"Party at my cousin's. My girls are here, too; I'm kind of hanging with them. Fairly low-key. Just soaking up being with them. They've both recovered from the flu but still not feeling very lively."

Fallon smiled, glad that he was getting to spend time with them. "Happy New Year, T. I'm excited to be out on tour with you in a month."

"Yes!" He was grinning. "All the shenanigans! Happy New Year, sorceress. Take care."

She was still smiling as she went back down to the pool, the shouts and yells announcing that she was missing the countdown. Bergen ran to her side when she appeared, wrapping her arms tightly around her waist. Bret and Gracie soon joined them.

Bret leaned in and kissed Fallon lightly on the lips as everyone around them yelled and cheered. "Happy New Year," he whispered.

She took his hand and stood there with him while Bergen still held her close, and they all watched as fireworks filled the sky. Where had she been last New Year's? She reflected—likely helping out at Madrigal, the Mexican restaurant in Gray that was owned by Diego's uncle. They were always open on New Year's Eve. She and Tayce had spent many hours sitting together at Madrigal's bar last summer.

Where would she be next New Year's? As she pondered this, a combined feeling of sweet warmth and ice-cold dread filled her from head to toe. She flinched in alarm and tried to shake the feelings away, for the dread was chilling her to the bone. Bret noticed her momentary distress and pulled her closer.

Fallon took a deep breath, coughing, as if she couldn't get enough air. On her wrist the raven tattoo fluttered in a soothing way, and strange tendrils of comfort began wrapping up her arm—it felt almost as if someone was holding her forearm, comforting and strong. The gripping panic dissipated, and she stole a glance at her wrist. But the tattoo was still.

The next day, Bret was apologetic. "I don't know what came over me."

Fallon had just finished swimming early morning laps in the pool and was sitting on a lounge chair, a sweatshirt pulled on over her bikini and a towel wrapped around her. The party had broken up shortly after midnight, and Bret had more or less passed out in his bed not much later. Fallon had overseen the girls going to bed at a semi-reasonable time.

That morning Bret had slept late. After taking a quick shower to wake himself up, he'd come looking for Fallon. Now he was holding a cup of coffee and had brought one for her as well.

Fallon accepted the coffee. "You had too much to drink last night, for one."

He nodded, accepting the charge as he sat down next to her. "I know you want answers to all the questions that you have. I understand there's no one but him who can possibly give you information."

"There is not," she confirmed, sipping the coffee.

He put a hand on her bare thigh, where the towel had fallen away. "I'm sorry I acted like that. I love you."

She squeezed his hand, staring at the pool water glistening in the sun. "I love you, too."

"Just…where…where would he take you?"

She sighed. "Bret. I have no idea. I know no more than I ever did." The raven tattoo was pulsing gently on her wrist like a soothing lullaby, and she resisted the need to lay her fingers against it.

Bret was quiet for a minute. "Does Bergen know anything about Jacob?"

Fallon looked into his troubled face. "She knows very little of my past. Only that my parents died when I was young, and I lived with Luca in Austin in that house. Possibly we mentioned, last summer when we stayed there, that I'd had a legal guardian while I lived there? But I don't remember. She was not interested in my history last year. She is very much an in-the-moment girl."

He nodded in agreement. "She is."

Fallon glanced at the ring on her finger. "I feel that is changing, though. She is starting to ask questions. She's curious about things." She pulled her hand from his and lay back in the chair, taking another sip of coffee. "Her curiosity will continue to grow. Of course, I'll be careful with what I share. There's no need for her to know about anyone in my life being murdered, for example."

He pinched the bridge of his nose.

"I'll have to tell her about Jacob at some point, especially if he comes back. But for now, I'm only addressing what she asks me about directly."

CHAPTER EIGHT

FALLON & JACOB

The day after Fallon's twelfth birthday, Luca had gone hiking with Simon. Fallon was laying on her stomach on the floor in her room, Azul sleeping nearby. She was going through the box of records Selah had given her the night before. It was a wide variety of music from many decades ago, and Fallon was interested in all of them. She was playing select albums on her portable turntable.

"Always the music, with you," said a rich, rough voice from her bedroom doorway, and Fallon smiled to see Jacob standing there. He came in and looked down at the box of records. *Houses of the Holy* was currently playing.

"Selah gave them to me as a birthday gift."

He nodded. "I saw you looking through them last night."

Fallon sat up. "Her grandfather saved them from an Austin store that was closed or something, a long time ago. He never did anything with them, and her dad had them in storage. Selah found them and asked if she could give them to me because I love music."

A strange look had passed over Jacob's face. He crouched down and sniffed the box. "It still smells faintly of smoke," he observed. Fallon gave him a questioning look as he rose back up. "Interesting," he mused, "that it would find its way to you after all this time." Turning abruptly, he left the room without another word.

Fallon crawled closer to the box and sniffed. It smelled old. Musty. And yes, there at the end, the slightest hint of smoke. Sitting back on her heels, she stared curiously at the empty doorway through which Jacob had so quickly departed.

CHAPTER NINE

Packing for the upcoming tour made Fallon happy, for she was especially looking forward to returning to Europe. She'd spent a large amount of time there over the years and sometimes felt more at home across the Atlantic than she did in the States. The age, the history, the hidden pasts that went back centuries—she felt it all deep in her bones. If not for the ties that seemed to bind her to Selah, she thought she might have moved overseas long ago.

Bret spent much of January rehearsing for the tour with his band. He was also spending extra time with Bergen, who was beyond disappointed that she would be left in California for the majority of the tour.

In truth, Bergen was frustrated and sad that Fallon and her father were not going to be around. She was currently back in school after the holidays, splitting her time between her father and the chaotic homelife she'd inherited when her mother married Leo. She didn't relish the idea that she would spend the next several months with her twin step-brothers, unable to escape to her dad's for a break.

Bret relayed to Fallon the frequently tense conversations in which he tried to soothe his daughter regarding his upcoming absence. Fallon, in turn, fielded many calls and texts from Bergen on the subject as well. Bergen's vibrant mother, usually quite communicative, had gone oddly silent through all of it, an observation Fallon made but kept to herself. Nonetheless it troubled her.

As she always did before a long trip, Fallon headed to Sunny Girl Bakery to stock up on kolaches. She usually purchased several dozen for Ms. Landrum, the eighty-something widow she rented her apartment from, as the woman was no longer able to drive the distance to Dutton to fetch the favored treats herself. Fallon kept her well-supplied and made sure to buy extras when she knew she would be away for a time. Ms. Landrum happily stored them in her freezer.

Fallon was still feeling unbalanced regarding the things Sunny had said and revealed during her visit back in late November. She'd been into the bakery a few times since then, especially during the festive pre-Christmas season, but Indio and Selah had been with her. When Fallon came in with guests, Sunny was reliably on her best behavior. Today, Fallon felt almost nervous about seeing her alone.

Sunny emerged from the back when the bells over the door announced Fallon's arrival. No one else was there. "My fearless Fallon friend!" She was smiling her usual self-assured smile. "What can I do for you today?"

Fallon smiled back as she approached the counter. "I need to order extra kolaches."

Sunny's long black hair was loose around her shoulders, shiny and flashing almost purple in the light. "Ah, you're leaving again. Peach and lemon as usual?"

"As always. And no rush, later this week is fine. Let's make it three dozen, since I'm going to be gone a while."

Sunny scribbled a note on a piece of paper on the counter between them. After a moment, Fallon realized Sunny had stopped writing and was studying her wrists. Specifically, the tattoos. The raven in flight with the prism eye and the lone eye surrounded by flames.

Sunny reached out and touched the raven tattoo with the end of her pen. "Exquisite detail. An artist's touch, for sure."

Fallon wanted to tell her that she didn't know who had done the tattoos. That it was one of her life's many unsolved mysteries.

For years she had not thought anything of them. Until the eye-with-flames tattoo unexpectedly burned Jack Lane's arm nearly a year ago. And then months later, the raven tattoo had glowed with a phosphorescent light as she'd tried calling to Jacob to help her. Since Nashville, the raven tattoo seemed almost sentient, able to respond to her and affect her physically. She now regarded the tattoos with far more curiosity and wariness than before, giving them the respect they seemed to warrant. Surely Jacob would be able to tell her who had done them. And why the raven mirrored his.

Sunny was staring at her strangely. "These," she tapped each tattoo with her pen in turn, "these were done with love."

Fallon's face darkened. "No. They weren't." She left the bakery without another word.

Back in her car, she tried to steady her uneven breathing. When Jack and Bret had been missing in August, she had vanished again, just like on her twentieth birthday, mysteriously stolen against her will. It was the same event Bret remained frustrated about, unable to understand her continued secrecy.

This time when she disappeared, she'd ended up with a tattoo of a star on the back of her neck, though as with the wrist tattoos, she'd apparently been unconscious during the application. During that disappearance, she'd learned the man responsible for her vanishings was her biological father, which had been a startling revelation. Up until that point she'd been unaware that the Quinns had not been her real parents, though it did explain why she'd never felt a connection to either of them, only to Luca. She definitely did not trust the man who called himself her father. He'd hidden his appearance from her during the brief visit and had threatened her at the end. He'd laughed at her seeming weakness in the face of his power. And she'd been tied to a chair the entire time. The whole episode had been jarring and had filled her with anger.

Upon her return, she'd been able to think of nothing else but how to stop him from ever stealing her against her will again. It was what had prompted her to finally try to contact Jacob.

She had felt no love, nothing good in the place where she'd been taken, and certainly no love from her nameless father, despite his poisonous words to the contrary. Therefore, the tattoos on her wrists and neck could not have been done with good intent if they had originated in that dark place. Even if the raven did seem to link her to Jacob.

* * * * * * *

On the February day she was to depart for the tour, Fallon implored Azul to remain in Gray with the Sanchez family at Solu. She was flying from Dallas to L.A. to meet Bret, and they were then flying together to Asia.

"You know there are rules about pets in Europe," she reminded the dog. "I cannot bring you, and you cannot just show up. You have to stay here. I'll come back to you; I promise. You need to stay put."

Tongue lolling, Azul panted happily and nuzzled her.

Fallon exchanged a glance with Selah, who had come to see her off. "I'm sure it got through." She stood and looked around the apartment, contemplating if she had forgotten anything. A car was coming soon to take her to the airport.

Selah was going to deliver Azul to Solu. Fallon had also gotten her to agree to pick up the kolaches and deliver them to Ms. Landrum. Unwilling to face Sunny again so soon after the tattoo incident, she told Selah it was simply because she had run out of time.

Now Selah hugged her tightly. "Be safe, love. Let me know when you hear from Mr. Roth again."

Fallon hugged her back. "Of course. Who knows when that will be," she added dismissively. More than two months had passed with no word from him. As if she had simply imagined his appearance in Nashville.

She couldn't fool Selah, who heard a world of emotion in her voice. *Even I have been waiting all these years for Jacob to return to you*, Selah thought to herself with an inward sigh. *I, the only living soul to remain who remembers the two of you together.*

CHAPTER TEN

The tour kicked off with high energy, delivering two spectacular sold-out shows in Tokyo, where historically their fan bases had always been strong. Fallon was only able to catch the performances of Dangerous Eye and Bret's band, but she felt they'd put on excellent shows. Immediately afterwards, the three bands were enroute to Europe.

On the plane, Fallon was seated between Bret and Tayce, and the latter was grinning even wider than usual as he put away his phone just before take-off. She looked at him questioningly, sliding her headphones down to hang around her neck.

"My girls are joining us in Italy," he informed her happily.

Despite that Fallon had still never met Tayce's two daughters, she knew he loved them tremendously, and she smiled at his obvious joy. "I can't wait to finally meet them! That's wonderful news. Are they going to stay with the tour for a while?"

"A week for sure, maybe longer." He stowed his backpack under the seat in front of him. "Ah, I miss them all the time. They surprised me—I had no idea they were going to try to come! They've been planning it since the tour was announced."

Fallon consulted the tour schedule on her phone. "They'll be with us in a few days, then." Bret and Tayce both looked at the screen as well. They were currently flying into Amsterdam, but then immediately taking a bus to Belgium. The Amsterdam show would come later. After Belgium they were headed to Berlin for a show and then on to Italy.

Tayce leaned back, closing his eyes. "I can't wait for you to meet them. Of course, they're going to love you."

* * * * * * * *

A man with long, black hair leered at Fallon from the shadows, and a bemused smile touched her lips as she paused before him.

"Jack Lane," she murmured. "How I've missed you." They were in Belgium at the first venue for the European leg of the tour. She and Jack had not crossed paths until now, which Fallon felt had been a fortunate thing.

"Likewise, darlin'." He leaned in and kissed her cheek. Smelling of cigarettes and leather, his fingers, wrists, and ears were adorned with silver jewelry. At nearly sixty, Jack was the quintessential aging rockstar. "How have you been, wicked one?" he inquired, unconsciously rubbing the faint scar on his left arm, an eye with flames. The scar matched the tattoo on her right wrist.

She lifted a shoulder. "Mostly the same. I see your world tour dreams came true."

"The other guys wanted it as badly as me, they just didn't admit it."

"You're right about that," she agreed. She glanced curiously at his left arm, which hung loosely by his side. The previous year, when he and Bret had been kidnapped and held underground, Jack's left arm had been badly damaged. She wondered how far physical therapy had brought him back.

"Yeah, it's still pretty fucked up," he confirmed, seeing her stare. "Day by day."

They fell into step together, wandering back into the main auditorium in companionable silence, which was odd in itself, Fallon mused with half a laugh. Bret's band was in the middle of soundcheck, and they both stopped and watched.

"You and James having troubles?" Jack inquired.

She cut her eyes at him. "Are we really having this conversation?" she asked. But she was curious that he would have noticed anything amiss, enough to comment on it. "I'm here on the tour, aren't I?"

"I don't know." He stuck his lighter and a pack of cigarettes in his back pocket. "You seem a million miles away. Every time I see you."

She smiled her crooked smile. "And you were, of course, deeply concerned about my relationship status."

"I'm all about being the first to know the good gossip." He grinned unabashedly, and she chuckled.

"I've got a lot going on," she allowed. "But no need to interpret things that aren't there."

"Hmm. Maybe."

An hour later, Fallon sat in the auditorium with Bret watching Jack's band's soundcheck. She observed immediately that Jack was only holding the microphone with his right hand. Having not seen either of his Tokyo performances, she hadn't realized the gravity of the handicap.

"Can he not hold the mic with his left hand?" she asked.

Bret shook his head. "Not with any degree of success. His guitarist, Kris, said he kept dropping it during rehearsals when he used his left hand, which you know embarrasses the hell out of him. So now he's not even trying. From what I've heard, he's been going to physical therapy, but I imagine it's difficult to regain strength in his arm when he can't hold weight in that hand. Nerve damage or something."

Fallon frowned, deep in thought.

That night Bret and his band performed first—it was a schedule that rotated every night, all three bands being treated equally—and shortly after he went on stage, Fallon sought out Tayce.

"Do you have a few minutes?" she asked. "I need to talk to Jack alone, but I don't want to be all alone with him, if you get what I'm saying."

Tayce got to his feet. "Sure, hon, what's up?"

"Come and you'll see."

They found Jack in his dressing room, and he let them in, amused when Fallon turned and locked the door. "I mean, sure, I've got time," Jack quipped, looking her over. "Don't know why you brought him along, though," he added, gesturing at Tayce, who rolled his eyes.

"Calm down. This is just a quick visit." She indicated the couch. "Sit with me a minute."

Jack obliged, and Tayce sat across from them, curious. Fallon, on Jack's left, took his arm in both hands and looked it over.

Immediately Jack sobered up. "What's going on?"

She put her right hand in his left. "Squeeze my hand."

He scowled at her.

"Jack, please. As hard as you can."

With a sigh he gripped her hand; she felt the weakness in it. She ran her other hand up and down his arm, concentrating. Tayce recognized that Jack was too strangely vulnerable to make a sly comment about her hands being on him.

Fallon was now looking hard at Jack. "Remember the night at the pool at Bret's? Remember how I made the burn on your arm stop hurting?"

He stared at her a moment and then nodded cautiously. Left unsaid, but known by the three in the room, was the fact that Jack had the burn on his arm because he'd been making an ass of himself that night at the pool by forcibly kissing her.

"Close your eyes," she told him. At first, Jack looked like he wanted to resist, but then she repeated, "Close them," in a soft, song-like way, and he felt his eyes shut tight. She held his hand firmly and wrapped her other hand around his forearm, closing her eyes as well.

Tayce watched the scene, frozen. He had no idea what Fallon was up to. He saw her tremble once, as if with effort, and then suddenly her face cleared. She released Jack and sat back.

Jack immediately looked at her, opening and closing his left fist. "What did you do?" he asked, his voice low.

"You already know." Getting to her feet, she wavered a little, and Tayce leapt up, putting an arm around her. She looked exhausted. "It was pretty messed up, still," she addressed Jack. "You weren't lying. I think it will be better now." She looked up at Tayce. "I need to go lay down."

He guided her swiftly from the room, alarmed at how heavily she leaned on him.

Jack did not move or say a word.

Tayce saw that she was nearly falling asleep in his arms, and he thought hard about where to put her. Even though everyone involved with the tour had been vetted and gone through security checks, he had never been one to completely trust everyone on the road; he couldn't imagine leaving her alone backstage in such a vulnerable state. When his girls had traveled with him, when they were small, he had never left them with anyone but a handful of fully-trusted friends.

In the end, he enlisted the help of Seth, Bret's long-time bodyguard. Tayce knew that Fallon liked Seth, who had been Bret's guard back in the heady BlueStar days decades ago. Seth always worked Bret's solo tours and could be trusted, especially with Bergen. And so, Tayce knew he could be trusted with Fallon.

Seth didn't ask any questions as the two men took her out to the buses. He spoke to the driver while Tayce guided her back to her bunk. Sitting her on the edge of the bed, Fallon lay back heavily, mumbling at him.

"Are you actually okay?" he asked doubtfully. "Can I leave you here?" He glanced at his watch. He needed to get ready.

She half-opened her eyes. "I'm completely fine; I need to sleep. I promise. I'm good. Go." Her eyes closed again, and he could tell she was immediately unconscious. Accompanying her to see Jack had turned into far more than Tayce had expected, but he knew there was no discussing it with her now.

After removing her shoes, he lifted her further into the bunk, just getting her head onto the pillows. He set her phone next to her, drew the curtain closed, and left with Seth, who was confident that the driver would not let anyone onto the bus without contacting him first.

On the bus later that night, enroute to their next destination, Bret was concerned by Fallon's continued exhaustion. "Are you getting sick?" he asked, touching her cheek as he sat beside her on the bunk. He'd been told by Seth and a few others that she'd been asleep on the bus since the beginning of the night. "Did you have one of those headaches where you had to give yourself a shot?"

Fallon occasionally suffered debilitating headaches, which were seemingly tied to her premonitions. Selah's husband kept her supplied with custom injections that knocked her out, dulling the pain and quieting her mind. Bret had experienced one of these rare episodes, and he knew she was often unconscious for hours.

But Fallon shook her head, yawning. "No shot. Just tired."

"Guess what? Remember we were talking about Jack earlier? Tonight, he held the mic with his left and right hands, interchangeably, no problem. He looked unstoppable. I wonder what happened? The change is night and day. Almost like..." A thought struck him, and he narrowed his eyes at her. "Like magic."

Fallon smiled her crooked little smile. "Talk to Tayce," she instructed, yawning again and turning away from him. She was back asleep in seconds. Bret sighed.

She slept for the next eight hours. The buses stopped mid-morning for everyone to grab brunch. It took some maneuvering, but Bret finally got Tayce alone at a table while most everyone was still getting their food. Knowing they didn't have much time, Tayce rapidly relayed everything to him that had happened in Jack's dressing room the previous night.

Bret was surprised to have his suspicion confirmed. "She did heal him." He shook his head. "I can't believe it. I knew she'd healed the burn on his arm enough to make it stop hurting—though she made sure to leave the scar. Almost like a little reminder."

Tayce smiled ruefully, nodding. "Agreed."

"And I knew that her own body heals itself unnaturally quickly," Bret continued. "But I guess I had no idea that she could do something like this. I mean, his arm was pretty wrecked. No wonder she was exhausted." He looked across the restaurant at where Fallon was enthusiastically filling her plate at the buffet. She looked like a stranger to him, mysterious and beautiful but unknown.

"Man, I was kind of blown away," Tayce admitted. "I didn't know any of that, going in. About the healing. I feel like I'm always the last to know everything. I mean, what else can she do that I don't know about?" He looked thoughtful as he drank his coffee. "I'm surprised Jack's not talking this up. And you know he's never said a word to me about the burn, even though there's a literal scar on his arm that matches her tattoo. It was you that told me about that."

Bret crossed his arms over his chest. "It's entirely out of character for him, but he's been completely loyal when it comes to keeping her secrets. I can't explain it."

The conversation ended as a crew member joined them at the table.

CHAPTER TEN

It took even longer for Bret to be able to speak privately with Fallon that day. Not until they were alone in his dressing room at the Berlin venue late in the afternoon.

"Since when do you have a soft spot for Jack?" he asked.

Clad in Doc Martens and a casual, above-the-knee, black skirt and black tank top, Fallon slid on a leather jacket as she perched on the arm of a couch, considering him. He was very nearly jealous, which she hadn't expected. Though maybe she should have.

"Let's just say, that I know what it's like to seem a certain way and to play into that role for everyone's amusement or expectation." She rubbed a bruise on her knee, a sign of her body's continued recovery from the day before. Rarely did a bruise last more than a few hours on her. "You know that half of the jewelry Jack wears these days belonged to Peter, right?"

Bret looked down, chastened by the reminder. Three years ago in Las Vegas, Fallon's premonition had saved Bret's life—she had impulsively saved Tayce and Jack's lives as well. Peter Stillson, Jack's bassist at the time, and a woman named Cynthia had remained outside the club when the other three went in. Peter and Cyn had disappeared without a trace and were later found murdered. The three men who lived eventually all came to understand that, but for Fallon's careful intervention, they would have died that night as well. Bret knew the senseless death of the young guitarist had hit Jack hard. He looked back at Fallon.

"And do you know that the woman who died, Cyn, had a son?" she continued. "Jack anonymously funded the kid's college tuition. Because the sad truth is, Cyn and Jack had been

85

flirting all night, and she went out on that sidewalk because of him. Deep inside, Jack believes those two died because of him. Because otherwise they would have been inside the club. In his mind, their deaths are his fault. Even though that's an illogical line of thought to follow."

Bret frowned. "Cyn stayed out there when we all went back in because she wanted to finish her cigarette," he remembered, the memories of that night still feeling surreal, "and because she thought Jack would be right back. Peter stayed to keep her company." He shifted his weight from one foot to the other. "So how do you know all of this?"

"I listen. And I read people." She ran the tip of her tongue over her lip. "Peter's death is still tearing Jack up inside, knowing that if only he'd ordered the kid to follow him back into the club that night, he'd have lived. He'd probably be on this tour with Jack right now. Jack wears that jewelry both to honor him and as a kind of penance, because it constantly reminds him of what could have been." She stretched her arms over her head. "Jack needed help with that arm. He didn't deserve the injury he got. He'd seen me heal him before, so it wasn't going to be too bonkers. He wasn't going to cause a scene."

"And so, you healed him."

She nodded.

"I feel petty."

"No." She shook her head. "It was a legitimate question. Jack's kind of an ass, in general. Borderline disrespectful most of the time. Why would I put myself out for him? Exhaust myself to that degree? It was an understandable question that you had. I hope my answer was enough."

He leaned down and kissed her. "It was." He tilted his head. "Did he thank you?"

She grinned. "Nope. Too much pride, that boy."

"Did it make you that tired because…"

"Because of the complexity of the injury, yes. I was glad I was able to do it. Some things are beyond me. Or maybe they wouldn't be if I were stronger? I don't know. Selah's dance career ended at eighteen because I'd let my abilities go after Luca died, and so when she was terribly injured during a performance, I was unable to heal her knee. It was ruined. By the time I regained my ability to heal, the damage was too ingrained—I wasn't as strong as I am now. I was able to make the swelling go away so that she could start physical therapy, at least, but I could not fix her."

CHAPTER ELEVEN

Jane and Annie Williams, twenty-two and eighteen, were tremendously full of life and overflowing with love for their guitarist father. Sparkling, witty, and engaging, they crashed onto the tour in Milan with laughter and stories and jokes. They were endlessly teasing and hugging their dad and taking selfies with him. Now you could always tell where Tayce was by the sound of his daughters' voices.

Fallon was happily intrigued. "I can't believe you are the father of these two fully-grown humans," she commented. "They're so grounded and joyful."

"They're away from their mother," he pointed out.

"They love you immensely. You are such a great dad."

He smiled, his whole face lighting up. "I did something right in my life, didn't I? Maybe not in the right way, but I did it."

She hugged him. "I really think you did."

As predicted, both girls were obsessed with Fallon, and when their father was busy, they were at her side. They spent as much time with her as they could, though often their conversations with her were completely one-sided.

"You're so gorgeous!" exclaimed Annie, who was petite, blond, and animated.

"We knew you would be," Jane added. Taller and striking, with darker hair, she had her father's brown eyes and lithe figure, as well as a manner quieter than her feisty younger sister. She was a singer in a small band, Sweet Jane, which played clubs around L.A and occasionally festivals in various U.S. locations. Her boyfriend, Sam, played drums in the same band. "Dad has a thing about beauty," Jane explained. "He can always find it."

"And he told us how amazing you were," said Annie.

"Sometimes we doubt his opinion."

"But he was right about you!"

"He adores you," Jane told her sincerely.

"We love Dad's real friends. He chooses good ones."

"Weren't you the one who asked him if he'd sold his soul to the devil?"

"We know for a fact, he totally did." Annie's eyes were shining. "No one plays like Dad does."

"It's so cool you're on tour, and we can hang with you a while!"

"We've been wanting to meet you forever!"

On their second night in Milan, there was no concert, and Bret and Tayce took Fallon and the sisters out for drinks. Jane ordered ginger ale, and after the drinks had been delivered, Tayce raised an eyebrow at his oldest daughter. She sipped her drink shyly while on the other side of him, Annie giggled.

Fallon read her loud and clear, and winked at Tayce. "Jane, don't make him wait."

Jane grinned at her father. "Yes, I'm pregnant." She kissed his cheek. "You're going to be a grandfather."

Tayce's expression changed from surprise to joy as he hugged her. "Janie, that's amazing. I'm so happy for you and Sam!"

Annie threw her arms around both of them to join the hug. "Mom doesn't know yet. We wanted you to know first because you usually find things out after everyone else."

He sat back with an arm around each of them, beaming, and as they each leaned close against him, Fallon took a picture.

"Do you know boy or girl?" Bret asked.

Jane shook her head. "Not yet." She looked around at the table. "Guesses?"

"Girl!" cried Annie.

As Tayce and Bret looked to Fallon, her gaze seemed to go temporarily out of focus. Then she smiled. "It's a boy," she declared softly, not meeting anyone's eye, and at this Tayce high-fived Bret.

"We shall see," said Jane, sipping her drink.

Tayce was smiling across the table at Fallon. "*You* shall see. *We* already know."

* * * * * * *

Stuck on tour with the same large number of people—bands, crews, and guests—proved to be a minor nightmare for Fallon, as she proceeded to get premonitions about everyone, including Annie. She handled the majority of them fairly well, but the constant proximity was making her tense. Usually when she saved someone with a premonition, she was able to steer clear of them for the rest of her life. On the few occasions when she did have to continue seeing the person, she had often been so smooth with her orchestration of their premonition-based salvation, they were unaware anything at all had happened. Not so this time.

The last tour had not gone like this. There were so many more people attached to this tour and her premonitions seemed to currently be in overdrive. Rumors swirled about her as people were able to compare notes and speculate. Fallon wished, not for the first time, that the premonitions would somehow go away.

"It's difficult to stay below radar," she told Bret one afternoon as they watched Dangerous Eye's soundcheck, "when you've saved the lighting guy from a serious burn and Jack's drummer from financial ruin all in one day. People begin to look at me funny. Like I'm either a witch or a talisman."

"You're tired of the premonitions," he realized.

"Of course, I am. It's stressful, constantly having to seek people out and low-key steer them from error or pain. Being responsible for their well-being in that moment. And then, as in the current situation, having to still be around them every day for months. Usually, I can slip off into the sunset, never to be seen again."

"I never thought of it that way, that it was a burden," he admitted. "I guess I just thought it was cool."

She turned her head so he couldn't see her rolling her eyes. "Maybe it would be cool," she countered, "if I hadn't had them my entire life. Or if they only came once or twice a year."

"You'll have them for the rest of your life."

A look of weariness flashed across her face. "I guess so," she said quietly. The raven tattoo quivered in a comforting rhythm on her wrist, and she rubbed her thumb across it like an answer.

Beside her, Bret sank deep into troubled thoughts as he considered that his precious daughter might one day view her own premonitions as a burden. Another one of those items that didn't show up in the parenting handbook, he thought with a sigh.

From across the room, Tayce was watching Bret interact with Fallon. Every time he saw them together on this tour, he was reminded of that breakfast in Nashville back in November. The distance between them remained.

Not physically, though. There was no distance there. Bret seemed to spare no opportunity to touch Fallon, to grab her, to kiss her. Of course, they'd been pretty touchy-feely with each other early on in their brief romance, but something about this struck Tayce as different. And because he was fairly in-tune to her these days, Tayce could see that in all of this public display, Fallon was slightly displeased, though she went along with it. To Tayce, it looked like Bret was losing her. And doing nothing at all to stop it.

What, he wondered, had happened in that Nashville hotel?

CHAPTER TWELVE

Bret's expression was dark several days later when Fallon, overstimulated after a rainy afternoon of shopping with Tayce and his girls in Zurich, entered their hotel room. The lights were all out, and Bret was sitting in a chair near the window, the glow from outside illuminating him, casting everything else into shadow. He was holding his cellphone, and Fallon got the idea that he had just ended a conversation. She read him less and less these days, unaware if it was from avoidance or simply disinterest, and so she didn't always know what was going on with him.

"What's wrong?" she asked, setting down her bag and slipping out of her damp clothes.

He sat back in the chair and stared out the window at the falling rain. "It's Leo. He's taking a job in London. Some big architecture firm. A huge opportunity."

Fallon's heart dropped as she pulled on a pair of leggings. "What?"

He met her gaze. "Exactly."

Putting on a black hoodie, she sat cross-legged in a chair near him. "What's Lisbeth saying?"

"That it will all work out." He looked back at the window. "That we will figure it out somehow."

Fallon twisted the ring on her finger, her mind whirling with thoughts, rolling everything she knew about Leo and Lisbeth around in her head. "They're going to move Bergen to London with them."

"No." He shook his head, sitting up straighter. "They wouldn't do that. Uproot her from all she knows. Lis and I have always worked things out regarding Bee. Always. This will be no different, it will just be complicated."

She knew his judgement was clouded, his reasoning false. "Well, just in case, I think you should have your attorney look into things." Uncrossing her legs, she bent down and began tying her black Converse shoes. "To know what your rights are in a situation like this."

"You don't know Lisbeth like I do," he snapped, getting to his feet abruptly. "Attorneys are the last thing that would need to be brought into this situation. We can handle it."

Bret was nearly to the door when Fallon said softly, "She waited till you were overseas on tour to tell you this news. That was not by accident."

He paused, his back to her. And then he was gone. The door closed behind him with a slam.

Fallon looked at the window, watching the raindrops chase each other down the glass. There was a deep sadness forming in her chest. The raven tattoo pulsed gently, and a soothing sensation wrapped around her wrist. She held her wrist to her face a moment and felt sweet comfort washing over her. *Madness,* she mused, pulling out her phone.

She sent a quick text to Bergen: "I love you, honeybee. Forever. Never forget that. You are always in my heart, sweet girl."

Bergen, sleepy in her California bedroom, read the text several times, smiling faintly. "I love you, too, Fallon. Forever plus forever."

* * * * * * *

Only a few days later, Bret learned that Lisbeth was on her way to London to look at housing options. At his request, she flew into Germany to meet up with the tour on their next stop in Hamburg so they could discuss the future, face-to-face.

On the day that she was to arrive, Bret was tense and short-tempered with everyone. He snapped at Fallon whenever she tried to speak to him, and so she spent most of the day hanging out with Jane and Annie.

It was late in the afternoon when Fallon saw Lisbeth arrive. She glimpsed her entering the hotel lobby as she herself disappeared into an elevator with Tayce's girls. Dangerous Eye was at soundcheck, and Fallon had gone out briefly with Annie and Jane to grab cappuccinos. They would be heading over to the venue in about an hour, but right now they were sitting cozily in Tayce's room, the girls chattering away to each other while on their phones, momentarily ignoring Fallon.

Sitting purposefully apart from them, Fallon tuned her mind in to Bret so as to follow the conversation with Lisbeth.

She was unsure if he would share anything with her later. And she was not optimistic about how it was going to go.

In Bret's hotel room, Lisbeth looked beautiful, if a bit tired. Her long golden-brown hair was glossy, her clothing stylish. She stared at Bret with large, dark eyes that brimmed with near-puppy affection, a look he remembered from long past that she had always employed when trying to get her way. She had just informed him that she intended to obtain full physical custody of Bergen. That she would move Bergen permanently to London and allow her to see her father during school breaks or else when he was touring in Europe. That she and Leo had already chosen the children's school and informed their California schools of the impending change.

Bret was caught entirely off guard by her intentions. Her words were a sucker punch to his heart. He had not listened to Fallon's warning, and he had not, he now realized, truly listened to what Lisbeth had been saying regarding the London move.

"I thought Bergen would stay with me," he said, the disbelief that he would lose his child to a home overseas beginning to grow painfully within him.

"Bret." Lisbeth shook her head at him, as if at a troublesome child. "We cannot separate that girl from me, her mother."

The pain in his chest glowed fiery with anger. "But from her father, no problem," he snapped.

"I have always been the most constant person in her life! I never leave her."

His face burned at her words. "I love her no less than you do, Lis! I am as much her parent as you are! You don't have the right to take her away from me! You knew what my job was when we had her. You knew I would travel. She understands. I spend as much time as I possibly can with her."

There were now tears in Lisbeth's eyes. Bret recognized the tactic. "You would have her on long holidays," she tried to soothe him. "For much of the summer. But even then, I have to know that Fallon will be around. I won't agree to anything, unless I know that when Bergen is with you, Fallon will be, too."

"Fallon is not her family," Bret reminded her acidly. "You don't get to dictate who I keep company with. I love that you've mapped out my future with my daughter without consulting me. You must think I'm an incompetent parent. I'm surprised you allow her to stay at my house at all."

"You are a wonderful father, Bret, of course you are. But I cannot be across the ocean, in London, knowing you and Bergen are alone. The two of you need Fallon to be there."

"Again, this is between you and me, this doesn't involve Fallon," he growled.

"It does involve her!" Lisbeth argued. "She is currently Bergen's biggest female influence besides me. Bergen is obsessed with her, in love with her. While she is so far away from me, she needs to have Fallon with her."

He was fully glaring. "Well, I'm not in charge of Fallon. You'll have to ask her yourself. Will you be formally naming her in the custody proceedings? Seems a little unorthodox, considering Fallon has no legal authority in this situation whatsoever."

Lisbeth hesitated, confused by the quiet anger in his voice. "But do you think, I mean, if ever you were going to marry a girl..."

"He will not be marrying me." Fallon's words cut like ice as she came into the room, and Lisbeth jumped, which Bret appreciated with the briefest smile. Fallon looked cold and beautiful as she stood there, arms folded across her chest, blond hair falling around her shoulders. She had hurried to join them when she heard the turn of the conversation. She was furious that Bergen was about to be dragged into a full-blown custody dispute. And she was annoyed that Lisbeth was throwing her name around like a bargaining chip.

"I will always be around when Bergen needs me. I will protect your daughter to the end of time."

Lisbeth didn't know why, instead of relief, she felt somewhat alarmed. Fallon looked so strange and powerful.

"But I cannot guarantee that I will physically be with her," Fallon added. "And how dare you use me against him. Bret and Bergen don't need anyone to babysit them when they're together."

"I won't agree to you having full physical custody of her, Lis. I will never agree to that." Bret was furious.

Lisbeth was now nodding. "Then we have a problem."

Not much later, Lisbeth left, for there was nothing else to say. Bret's mood was bleak. He was immediately on the phone with his attorney.

Fallon was torn between wanting to comfort him and knowing that any attempt she made to do so would only anger him further. She wished she could calm him without physical touch, but that was the only way she knew her power to calm worked. Since Nashville he had not wanted her to manipulate his emotions in any way. It starkly showed her how much she had used her calming power on him in the past year.

That night at the concert, Tayce and Fallon sat alone together in a dressing room, and she filled him in on the gist of Lisbeth's visit.

Tayce was incredulous. "I didn't think one parent could move far away with a kid, much less out of the country. I mean, I didn't think that was even legal."

"I didn't think so, either, but Lisbeth and Leo seem to have better attorneys, for one. Courts like to side with the mother, as well. And Bret's erratic schedule hurts him tremendously. He's not home consistently. At all. So, I can see a court siding with her on that. The question is, would he give it all up— touring, traveling around for recording sessions, all of it—for Bergen?"

They considered.

"It's not fair," said Tayce. "He'd have to give up everything he loves, his entire career, just to have the right to have his own daughter live with him?"

"Even Bergen wouldn't agree to that. She would never accept him having to give that up."

He took a long sip of water. "The alternative is her in London, though. Full-time."

"Bret and Bergen are amazing together. There's no reason to demand that I or any other female be around. It was ludicrous for Lisbeth to say that."

"She won't win that one, for sure. And doesn't her sister live in town? Bergen literally has an aunt right there." He screwed the lid back on the water bottle.

"Such a mess."

"What about Leo's ex?" he asked. "He has the two boys, right?"

She shook her head. "He does, but he's a widower."

"Ah. So, no issue there."

She bit her bottom lip. "I get the feeling this is going to go on forever."

* * * * * * *

The day his girls departed the tour, Tayce came to Bret and Fallon's room. Fallon was alone doing a series of body weight exercises on a black yoga mat. This hotel had no gym, and she accepted the irony that the one time she had space in her schedule, there was no gym to be found.

Tayce sat on the end of the bed, resting his arms on his thighs and clasping his hands.

"Hey, grandpa," she greeted him.

He smiled, overwhelmed with happiness. She could swear his face was glowing; her heart swelled with love for her friend.

"It's crazy, isn't it?" he asked. "So, I think you already know, but my girls loved you more than they can even express. They wish I would marry you and grow old with you and all the things."

Fallon laughed.

"They asked why I didn't meet you sooner." He chuckled. "I didn't tell them that you saved my life three years ago, though of course we didn't meet that night. That would only further endear you to them."

"They were a lot of fun. Kind of high-energy for me, though, especially Annie. Kind of like you when you've had multiple cups of coffee."

Tayce smiled. But then he sighed, and she could tell he had something else to say. She sat back on her heels and waited.

"So, Paul's got something going on," he began, glancing to make sure the hotel room door was closed. "Katrine is missing. I mean, not in a tragic way, but in a this-has-happened-before way. But still. Missing. Like for days. Then she's back at the farm. Then gone again, I don't know." He shrugged. "He doesn't tell me everything, but I know enough. It's becoming a huge distraction for him. A weight. So yesterday I told him you could possibly help. That you have some unique sources, and you sometimes help people in trouble."

"*Tayce.*" She practically growled his name. "I've gotten no premonitions about Katrine!"

He winced. "I know, I know. But he's been so upset. I thought, maybe…"

She was glaring, and it unnerved him.

"You're not going to kiss me, are you?" he asked nervously.

She glared and made some noise for which he could find no translation. "Bring him to me. I'll listen to what he says. Give me fifteen minutes to change clothes."

Paul looked preoccupied when Tayce brought him to her room, and she didn't know why she hadn't noticed before.

"She gets nervy when I go on tour," Paul explained. "Agitated. I don't know why, she can't really say. I try to talk about it with her, but it's almost like it's a conversation she can't have. Every time I leave, it's gotten progressively worse. She's never disappeared like this before. Well, once, but that was for less than twenty-four hours." Paul ran his fingers through his short blond hair and wavered between being worried and simply tired. "I mean, she's always been very flighty, free-spirited. She comes and goes; it's never been a big deal. I usually know where she is, for the most part. It would be normal that I couldn't reach her for a while. But this thing with touring, like I said, it gets worse each time, and now she'll be gone for days, with maybe only one text to let me know she's fine. No explanation of where she's been, and when I ask, she doesn't say. As if she didn't hear me. I think, if the tour is truly what's caused this, that this will have to be the last time I tour."

No expression touched Tayce's face as he listened, but he looked quickly to Fallon to see what she would say.

Fallon, in cut-off denim shorts and a black t-shirt, sat cross-legged in a chair, facing them. "Make me a list, contact information of everyone she's close to, including family," she directed Paul. "I'll work on it, you concentrate on the tour, okay? I'll work on it. See if I can determine what's going on."

Tayce smiled and flashed a peace sign at her. She rolled her eyes. Paul distractedly thanked her and went away.

"What the hell," murmured Tayce. "I wonder what this is all about?"

Fallon shook her head. "I have no idea. I could never read Katrine, so I couldn't ever get a feel for her. Kind, loving, generous, of course, but that's just how she acts. Anyone can recognize that in her. But a real sense of who she is, I could never see. And I can usually see into everyone." She thought briefly again about Detective Ashton.

"What do you see in me?" Tayce challenged, raising an eyebrow.

She smiled easily. "A big goofball with a pretty face and mad guitar skills."

"I don't think you need special powers to interpret that," commented Bret, as he entered their hotel room. "Except for the pretty face part—I don't get that at all from him."

"That hurts!" Tayce exclaimed. "I happen to find you extremely attractive, James."

Bret pointed at the door. "Out."

Laughing, Tayce departed.

Bret lay down on the bed, propped up by pillows. He looked tired, which was the only excuse Fallon could see for his somewhat gruff dismissal of their friend. "I saw Paul leaving," he mentioned. "What's up?"

She relayed the situation to him, and he frowned in concern. "That's odd. And sad. I had no idea that was going on." He drank some water and tried to hold back a yawn. "Why did he come to you, though?"

Fallon looked out the window. "Tayce was trying to help. He offered me up like a sacrifice."

He gave a short laugh. "Can you, though? Help?"

Her forehead creased in thought. "I guess I have to try."

* * * * * * *

Fallon sat cross-legged on the hotel bed early that evening, eyes closed, hands resting lightly on her knees. Everyone was at the venue for pre-show VIP activities, but she had stayed behind ostensibly to take care of a few things, promising to show up later.

The truth was she needed some alone time. The tour was a lot. She loved the excitement of traveling from city to city and watching all the guys pouring their hearts out night after night.

But the constant togetherness with Bret had worn her to the bone. She felt herself withdrawing from everyone but Tayce, who remained a warm, joyful touchstone for her.

She knew Bret was deeply unhappy. Stressed out because of Lisbeth and Leo's machinations as well as the distance that continued to grow between himself and Fallon. He spoke to her at times as if she were a stranger. Though she was still in his bed at night, they were beginning to avoid each other more and more during the day. The raven on her wrist was now more of a constant companion than anyone, though she didn't understand it, and wondered if it was some kind of mental instability on her part.

Fallon wanted to leave the tour. She and Bret needed to end things. But Bergen was coming soon for spring break, and Fallon had to be there for that. It was non-negotiable.

Tears streamed down her cheeks as she opened her eyes. She missed Jacob. She wanted him back. She wasn't used to feeling completely powerless, but currently that was her state. Over three months had passed since Nashville, and despite her offhand remarks to Selah, she'd secretly been certain that he'd have returned by now. He'd promised, but what if something had happened to him? What if she never saw him again? It would break her.

Fallon buried her face in her hands. Her life had been an endless uncertainty, save her bond with her brother and her connection with Jacob. She'd felt unwanted and alone since she was born—those two men had been her sentinels, the fuel to her fire. Over the past three months, she'd shown herself a brave face in the mirror, but behind the scenes, she was shattering, the brief reunion with Jacob having ignited more emotions—and more realizations—than she could handle.

She pressed her face harder into her hands, sobbing silently, her body shuddering. Being alone was what she'd always accepted as her destiny. But she no longer wanted that to be her fate. Despite her close friendships, there was an inviolate chasm within her which friends like Tayce and even Selah couldn't fully breach. In those few moments alone with Jacob three months ago, he had easily crossed that chasm—nothing within her was hidden or unreachable for him. She'd felt everything, including her magic, coming alive in his presence.

Through her tears, she wondered if she would ever feel that way again. She screamed in painful frustration, muffling the sound with her hands.

Suddenly her left wrist tingled sharply. A strange comfort began winding around her forearm, traveling upwards to her shoulders, and then flooding her, until her whole body felt as if she were being carried, rocked gently, soothed. Closing her eyes, she willingly gave in to the sensation. As blackness sweetly overtook her, she knew that somehow, she was in Jacob's arms.

When Fallon woke up, she felt lucid and refreshed, and her phone was ringing. It was Tayce, but she couldn't yet move to answer it, still somewhat existing in the odd dream state the raven tattoo had sent her into.

Looking at the time, she understood why there were so many missed texts and calls. Four hours had passed. She sat up with a yawn and texted Tayce and Bret that she had accidentally fallen asleep and was fine. Then she retrieved a bottle of water, drinking it down. She felt revived from her emotional sinking spell. And somewhere, buried deep in her heart, she now knew without question that Jacob would come back to her.

CHAPTER THIRTEEN

FALLON

Fallon glanced over at Selah's homework. She squinted. Then she looked back at her own calculus textbook with a glare. She sighed dramatically.

Selah bit back a laugh and didn't look up.

Closing the book, Fallon stood and began gathering up her papers. "I'll do it later."

"Your favorite little phrase."

Fallon gave her friend a dark look. "I'll get it done. I need to schedule time with my math tutor."

Selah sat back and stretched. "Speaking of, where is Luca?"

"He and Simon were meeting up. But he'll be here soon. We're going running tonight."

Sipping her unsweetened iced tea, Selah glanced at the time. "I'm going to do the last five problems. Then I'll head home for dinner." Since Jacob had been gone from them the past three years, meals at the Quinn house were no longer as reliably delectable as they had been. Selah did miss that man's cooking. But more than that, she missed the lighter spirit Fallon had been when he was around.

Fallon disappeared moodily down the hallway with her school backpack. Their senior year had just started, and she was already ready for it to be over—for school in general to become a distant memory. Selah had been accepted to The University of Texas there in Austin. Fallon had no such plans.

In her bedroom, she dropped the backpack on the floor near her desk, then dug around in a drawer for her favorite running shorts. Locating them, she switched her leggings for the shorts and replaced her t-shirt with a tank top, grabbing a pair of socks from the top drawer. As she turned to leave the room, however, she froze.

There was a book lying on her bed. A worn, well-loved paperback. She knew immediately which one it was; she knew the cover by heart. *To Kill a Mockingbird* had been the first book Jacob had ever read to her, when she was seven years old. They'd probably read it at least three or four times over the years. Jacob had been well-aware that it was special—it was the only book they'd read more than once.

And now there it was at the center of her neatly-made bed, as if on display. It had not been there two hours ago when she and Selah had arrived at the house. And Selah had not left the dining table at any point that afternoon. Luca was not home. There was no one else there.

Fallon's gaze traveled slowly over the room, but everything else was in place, undisturbed. The bookshelves were across the room; the book had not simply fallen onto her bed. It had been placed there.

She trembled. Only Jacob knew what this book meant to her. Only Jacob, who had been gone now for years. Her face felt hot with tears that wanted to fall. She blinked them back and sat on the bed, picking up the book—her heart skipped as a folded piece of white paper fell out from within the pages and onto the quilt. With shaking hands, she picked up the paper and unfolded it. Written in sweeping script, was a quote:

"One weakness is enough, and love is the deadliest."[1]
—Bertolt Brecht

The tears coursed freely down her cheeks, and she dropped both book and paper. She looked around the room again, getting up and running to the window—locked—but there was no one outside. She went to the fireplace and shone a light up inside. Ridiculous. There was nothing there. No one. Who could have done this? It was cruel. The book they'd read and re-read, and the quote he had often told her. His mantra, truly.

No one else could have known this. It was impossible. But Jacob would not have shown up after three years just to do this thing which he'd have known would cause her pain. Would he? She couldn't make sense of it.

Carefully she tucked the paper back inside the book and then she went to the bathroom and washed her face, letting the cold water run over her wrists.

When Fallon reappeared in the dining room, Selah was on the last math problem, and Luca was pulling into the driveway. Selah saw the book in her hand and the redness in her eyes, and surmised that Fallon was missing Jacob. Her grief for the man still came and went, Selah had observed. She felt that possibly Fallon would miss him for the rest of her life. Even she missed seeing them in this house, existing carefully together.

Luca called out a greeting to them on his way to his room. Fallon sank quietly into a chair at the table, staring into space.

When her brother emerged half an hour later, dressed to run, Fallon looked at him sadly and shook her head.

"Not feeling it tonight?" he asked. "Scared that with my new shoes, I'll leave you in the dust?" But his teasing voice was gentle, as it always was with her. He pulled his shaggy blond hair back into a ponytail as Fallon got up and wrapped her arms around him.

Still holding the book, Selah noted privately.

Luca hugged her back tightly and kissed her forehead. He gave Selah a look, and she nodded. A promise that she would stay with his sister till he got back. Then he waved and was gone.

Never to return.

When they got to the park later, red and blue lights were flashing harshly in the darkness. Fallon had to be restrained from running to his body, screaming into the night as they awaited the forensics unit. Selah sat in the grass for an hour and held onto her as she cried and cried. At some point Simon joined them, grief stricken and bereft.

And Selah knew, then, that she had lost both the Quinns that night. The brother and the sister. For how could one exist without the other?

CHAPTER FOURTEEN

The bands were in London for five days, doing press as well as playing two large shows, but they had some free days to relax. Bret was unable to find any peace as he corresponded with his attorney daily regarding the custody situation. There was now even more creeping tension between himself and Fallon because he knew that he should have listened to her. Should have immediately contacted his attorney and begun the process of protecting his rights regarding his daughter, instead of allowing time to go by and then being blind-sided by his former lover.

Fallon's announcement to Lisbeth that she would not be marrying him had stung, even though he knew things were incredibly fragmented between them. Despite being together less than a year, he had, at one point, assumed he'd marry her. Had expected that this magical woman whom his daughter loved passionately would be with them forever. Fate, destiny, and all the rest.

But he knew that he'd been purposefully blind to all of the aspects of her life that were otherworldly and troublesome. He'd been especially blind to the specter of Jacob Roth.

Fallon was slowly working her way through the list Paul had provided her with, posing as Paul's assistant and attempting to elicit information from friends and relations without raising alarms. So far no one had any knowledge of the situation regarding Katrine. Fallon thought briefly of enlisting Simon, her ghost friend who resided in Seattle. He had been so useful with his research skills the previous year during her search for Bret and Jack, but she wasn't sure exactly what she could ask him to do in this situation. Katrine was back at the farm now, and all was seemingly well.

On their third night, Seth, a native Londoner, organized an outing to a few of his favorite pubs. Eventually a group of eighteen various band and crew members convened in the hotel lobby and then made their way down the sidewalk towards the first pub on Seth's list.

Fallon was shivering in a thin black sweater, her wool coat and black knit cap doing little to cut out the brisk London air. Bret and Tayce were with her, though Bret had come only to please Seth. His mood was low after a long afternoon of speaking with his attorney. Bret and Lisbeth were now communicating solely through their lawyers; he was amazed at how quickly they had gone from best friends to this current nightmare state.

After everyone had downed a pint and soaked up the atmosphere at the first pub, they moved on loudly to the next establishment on Seth's itinerary. Four members of the party chose to remain behind.

When Fallon showed reluctance towards going back out into the cold, Bret and Tayce readily agreed to separate from the group. Unexpectedly, Jack hung back with them. With their numbers greatly depleted, the quartet established themselves in a private back room that held an old, round wooden table and a stone fireplace where a fire crackled and blazed. It was growing darker outside and shadows were closing in, making the room even cozier. Other than the fire, the only light in the room came from some strategically-placed tin lanterns spread around.

The group sat around the table, drinking whiskey and beer, relaxing, and telling stories—except for Fallon, who told no stories, only drank and listened.

"Have you ever knowingly refused to save someone?"

At Jack's question, all eyes fell upon Fallon, who was curled up in her chair, staring at the fire. An hour had passed, and they were all warm from the alcohol. Even Bret was looking at ease. Fallon had shed her coat; she looked small and vulnerable in the chair, her eyes far away. Bret and Tayce, on either side of her, waited curiously for her answer.

For a moment she continued to watch the flames, as if possibly she hadn't heard the question, but then finally she turned her head slightly, glancing at Jack. "Yes."

Jack smiled as if he'd just won a game. "Isn't that a little like playing God?"

"Is God sending me the visions?" she wondered. "Maybe they come from something darker, elemental, and following them at all is a sin in itself."

"That doesn't matter," he countered. "You're making a conscious decision with each one. You're essentially deciding who lives or dies. If it's a life-or-death situation."

Tayce looked thoughtful. "I can see that, though. Surely, you've gotten some visions about people who are truly horrible souls."

"That I have," she confirmed.

"Is it up to her to judge, though?" Jack asked. "Whether or not their souls are too horrible to save?"

"Well," she slid her now-empty glass across the table, a warning tone of finality in her voice, "no one has yet died simply because I thought they weren't worth saving. And we know I've saved your ass twice, Lane, so my scale must be pretty low, don't you think?"

Bret and Tayce laughed. Jack's self-satisfied smile didn't waver, but he said no more about it, rising and going out to get everyone some more to drink.

After he returned, the guys were all drawn enthusiastically into a conversation about something that had happened in Los Angeles long ago during their years of raging glory. Knowing that these particular paths of story-telling could sometimes take ages, Fallon tuned out and resumed her quiet study of the flames that flickered in the fireplace. Tonight, for some reason, she felt strangely on edge. The fire kept drawing her in. There was an odd anticipation fluttering in the periphery of her mind. The raven tattoo had been very quiet, and she pressed her thumb against it, hoping that it might react, but all she could feel was her own pulse.

It was several minutes later that she sensed a tingling deep in her chest, even before she felt the draft of cool air from an outside door being opened. And so, she was already staring at the doorway when he walked through it.

Jacob Roth filled the entire room with his presence as he came to stand beside their table, confidently at ease as he intruded upon their intimate gathering. The three guys looked up at him with curiosity, but Fallon simply smiled at him, relief and joy flooding her body. Jacob returned her smile with a tender familiarity that everyone noticed.

Getting to her feet, Fallon went around Tayce to get to Jacob, and he wrapped her up in a tight hug. "You did return," she whispered. She could feel the cold from outside on his arms as he held her close.

"I don't break my promises to you," he murmured, so that only she could hear. "I never will."

She introduced him to her friends, and he shook hands with them all—Bret was tense even as he tried not to be, while Tayce and Jack were entirely clueless as to Jacob's identity.

"He was mine and my brother's guardian when we were growing up, after our parents died," Fallon explained. "A friend of the family, so to speak." She and Jacob exchanged a glance.

Tayce liked Jacob immediately, feeling drawn to him as if to an old friend, and invited him to join them for a drink. Jacob agreed to this, taking off his long dark coat and pulling up a chair between Tayce and the fire. Fallon returned to her seat between Tayce and Bret, wondering how this would go. She hadn't expected that Jacob would show up amongst her companions. Bret was not meeting her eye.

"So, where are you from?" Jack asked the newcomer, leaning forward with his elbows on the table, intrigued by the situation as he noticed the quiet tension in Bret's face and the radiance in Fallon's. He could see that Tayce was likely as clueless as he was, and he had a feeling that the details of this scenario were extremely important.

"I'm a bit of a gypsy, Mr. Lane. Not unlike the rest of you." Jacob accepted the whiskey a waitress had brought for him, leaning back in his chair. With the fire reflecting on his handsome face, illuminating bits of gold in his wavy brown hair, he looked relaxed, as if he had nowhere else to be but there in the pub drinking with them.

Tayce lifted his glass. "Cheers to that. My home is the road."

"What brings you to London?" Bret asked pointedly.

Jacob observed Bret with a cool gaze, before smiling slightly at Fallon. "This lovely one. She is the sun I revolve around, at least that's how it feels at times. She's told you there is much she and I need to discuss."

Bret also rested his elbows on the table, thrown off by Jacob's honesty but rallying at the last second. "She did tell me that." With great effort he sounded steady and controlled. Jacob was nothing that he had expected and everything he feared.

Shifting his gaze away from Fallon, Jacob glanced at the fire. "I must take her away for a short while, but I will take good care of her. I will bring her back. I know it may trouble those that care about her, but it is important."

Even Jack was too stunned by the conversation to say anything, watching the interaction quietly.

Despite his initial good feelings about Jacob, Tayce was growing nervous, reacting unconsciously to the different energies in the room and realizing that once again there were things going on which he knew nothing about. And then, as Jacob pushed up the sleeves of his dark shirt, Tayce noticed the raven tattoo on Jacob's strong left forearm.

"Hey! That looks exactly like Fallon's raven! I mean *exactly*, all the way down to the prism eye!"

Jacob looked warmly at Tayce. "Well, Mr. Williams, about that, let me tell you a story. There exists a raven that sees all that can be seen about Fallon—and about her brother, when he was living. He has always been their guardian, this dark bird, forever watching them, unseen, since they were small children and even to this day."

Fallon took in this revelation without expression, though internally she was spinning.

The raven was real.

"And Fallon here," Jacob continued, "with her magical self, could right now place a hand on the raven on my arm, close her eyes, and see anything she wished that the raven had ever seen."

She looked at Jacob alertly, while beside her Bret frowned, and Tayce's eyes widened.

"No way!" Jack was grinning. "You got your tattoos done at Satan's workshop, too? Come on, Fallon! Show us how it works."

Tayce looked at her in concern, trying to see—but unable to tell—what she was thinking. He was wishing very hard that he had not made any mention of the raven. There was, he thought, a wild, reckless look in her eyes.

Fallon was staring at Jacob with laser focus. "Really?" she asked softly, and he nodded. Her heart thrummed wildly. She was aware that she'd had too much to drink to think clearly, but she knew she was going to try it. And she knew exactly what she wanted to see.

Without a second of hesitation, she leaned across the table and lay her hand on his forearm, her palm on the raven tattoo, eyes closing tight. She was seeking Luca's murderer. She wanted to see it unfold.

Jacob realized immediately what she intended, and the smile went away from his face.

It was twilight in the park in Austin, no one else on the running path. Luca was sitting beside a tree, staring in the direction of the creek that ran below. Fallon remembered running the same path with him a thousand times, but why had he stopped to sit down? They had never paused there in that spot before.

She heard someone approaching at the same moment Luca did. She watched as he looked over his shoulder and smiled in surprise, his face lighting up. When she looked, she saw Jacob heading towards her brother with a smile on his face. And then as he reached Luca, Jacob drew out a gun and shot her brother in the head.

In the pub Fallon cried out in terrible pain, a scream from deep in her soul. She tore her hand away from Jacob's arm and stared at him in confused anguish, tears in her eyes.

"You?" she whimpered.

Jacob's features grew dark, his stare intense. He was shaking his head. "Fallon, no."

Everyone else was watching in rapt attention, but no one dared to move or speak.

Swiftly Jacob reached out, seizing Fallon's wrist. "We need to talk."

And then he and Fallon were gone, vanishing into thin air.

Jack stood up so fast his chair fell over. "What the hell? Where are they?" He was looking around with wild eyes.

Tayce, who had also gotten to his feet, was silent as he waited for an explanation. He could see that even Jacob and Fallon's coats were gone. The messenger bag that had been hanging on her chair—gone. As if the two of them had never been there at all. His heart was racing as he felt panic rising up in his chest. His friend was gone. Fallon was gone.

Still seated, Bret was momentarily frozen in place, but he finally looked up. There was an acute mix of disbelief and annoyance in his face. "Jacob can teleport. From one location to another, boom, like magic. That's what she told me once, though I don't think I believed it till now. And I had never even considered that he could take her with him."

Jack picked up his chair, breathing unsteadily. He was still looking around the room. "What did she see when she put her hand on his fucking arm?"

But that was not Tayce's foremost concern. "Is she going to be alright?" He was worried. Jacob had looked intriguing, he thought, but also dangerous. Fallon had looked so upset. That scream.

Clasping his hands behind his head, Bret shrugged, giving in to anger and jealousy. "Regardless, if she is or isn't, there's nothing we can do about it. I've known for a while that he was going to take her away so they could talk. Now it's here. She's gone."

Still more shaken than he would have admitted, Jack drained his glass, drank Fallon's as well, and then looked at Bret. "I know one thing, James. When or if she comes back from wherever she's gone to, that girl won't be yours anymore." He slipped his jacket on as he swiftly left the room.

Scraping his chair back, Bret got to his feet without a word, and Tayce followed him silently back out into the cold London night.

CHAPTER FIFTEEN

A brisk, sobering wind hit Fallon in the face, and as she looked around, she saw that the London pub had disappeared. She and Jacob were standing alone together on a lush green mountaintop. The sky above was growing dark, the setting silver-gold sun all but gone.

She felt a wave of mingling dizziness and euphoria. Jacob's hands went to her waist to steady her as she took in the reality of the teleportation that had just occurred. To their right was a pretty stone cottage surrounded by a short fence—they were standing outside the little worn wooden gate. Much further past the cottage on the left was what looked to be an old barn with an enclosed area for animals—she could see a few chickens wandering around, and the *baaing* of sheep reached her on the wind.

She took one small step away from his hands, hugging herself against the cold as she noticed her messenger bag and coat at her feet.

"Come inside, Fallon." His voice was gentle as he bent to retrieve her coat, placing it carefully around her shoulders to protect her from the chill air.

But she remained rigidly still, staring up at him with darkened eyes. Her cheeks were damp with tears.

He touched her chin to tilt her head slightly. "Fallon. I did not kill your brother. It was not me. You know that in your heart. Come inside, and we will talk."

She had trusted him for her entire life. And she was freezing. Wiping away the tears, she grabbed her bag and allowed him to guide her through the gate, up to the front door and inside where it was warm and comfortable. Jacob closed the door firmly against the cold wind.

Fallon was still trembling, both from the sight of Luca's murder and at the reality of having been somehow transported to another place magically—though regarding the latter she tried to play it cool and seem entirely unalarmed. This was different than when she'd been stolen by her father. For this, she had been fully awake and aware.

Inside, a fire was burning brightly in a primitive-looking, stone fireplace. The cottage smelled faintly of herbs and flowers: rosemary, sage, lavender, and roses. There was a minimal amount of furniture and decoration, but it was cozy in its simplicity. It felt safe. It felt like home.

In spite of herself, Fallon's body began to relax. She set her bag on a chair by a window, hanging her coat next to his on a metal hook.

Knowing she needed space, Jacob turned to the right and went into the kitchen, which looked as if it had been added on to the cottage. The kitchen walls were red brick, and there were a few shelves holding dishes and glassware. Herbs hung drying over the large stove, and pots and pans hung from a metal rectangle suspended over the small, butcher block-topped island.

Clad in black dress pants and a black, button-up shirt which was now untucked, Jacob pushed up his sleeves and tied his hair back as he moved around the kitchen with ease. Fallon recalled the wonderful meals he had prepared for them in Austin, and her stomach growled in response. She had not had anything to eat since lunch.

"I know that you're hungry," he said. "Let me fix us something, and then we can talk." When she didn't respond, he threw her a look over his shoulder. "Fallon." His voice was hard.

"Why did I see you, at his death?" Her voice shook more than she would have wanted it to. Her throat felt raw from holding back tears. "Why did he see you? Were you there? I saw you shoot him in the head!"

Iron skillet in hand, Jacob was getting out a basket of eggs and some green onions from the moderately-sized silver fridge. "I was actually at the house that night, watching over you. I was nowhere near Luca. A shape-shifter was sent, with my visage."

"A shape-shifter?" She sounded surprised, and he met her stare.

"Yes, they exist. Anyway, it fooled your brother easily. That is the point of your tattoo, the eye with flames—why it is different than his was. Yours holds magic that ensures you cannot be tricked by false guises. That you will be able to always see through such things. It was not me who took his life. Even the raven was fooled, which is why you see my image in the memory. You are seeing the raven's memory."

The last bit of tension left her body. He was telling the truth.

Jacob came over to her, handing her a glass of ruby red wine as he looked at her intently. "And deep in your heart, Fallon, you know that a gun is not my weapon of choice."

She thought of the wicked dagger from her first psychometry lesson so long ago, and nodded. "I know."

He returned to continue his task in the kitchen while she stared at the firelight glinting in her glass, then took a long sip of the wine.

"This is very good," she observed, as she went over to the window and looked out at the sweeping, rugged landscape, trying to fill her mind's eye with something other than Luca's death. Darkness had fallen quickly, but with her ability to see in the dark, she could still observe the general idea of her surroundings.

"The wine is local. Ahh, Spanish grapes. Why else should I choose to live here?"

She was surprised that they were in Spain. She had never been able to pinpoint, in her mind, where she thought Jacob might reside. "In Austin you never drank wine," she pointed out. "Only whiskey."

"Because no other wine compares, yet it was too much trouble to get this there. You cannot buy this at a store in America, and I stopped myself from hauling in cases." He smiled, amused with himself. "Many of my neighbors on this mountain, they are somewhat unsure if I am a treacherous villain or not—I am perhaps a bit intimidating at times, though friendly—and so they are constantly plying me with gifts of wine in order that they might remain in my good graces."

"You do nothing to dispel the myth, otherwise your supply of wine would fade away," she guessed. She squinted at something out the window in the distance, and he noticed.

"What do you see?" he asked.

"A light at the barn. A flash of white and blue. It reminded me of someone I saw a long time ago."

"Colette."

Fallon turned sharply towards him. "The white-haired woman." The one who had appeared at her door when Fallon was fourteen to deliver the shattering news that Jacob was gone from her. "What is she doing here?"

"She is almost always here. She takes care of me. You see the kitchen fully stocked with fresh produce and other things? That is her doing."

"You mean she actually knows your schedule?" Fallon came closer.

"My schedule is erratic, at best," he admitted. "She keeps the kitchen fully stocked, no matter my situation."

"Doesn't that waste a lot of food?"

He shrugged. "She feeds her pigs. It all works out."

"But who is she?" Fallon pressed. "Why does she do things for you?"

His eyes sparkled a little as he looked across the kitchen at her, taking a sip of wine. "She is known as The Heart of the Ravener. She is always at my call."

Fallon took another step forward. "The Ravener?"

He emptied the contents of the skillet onto two plates. "That would be me."

Her eyes widened. "You have a title? Are you immortal?" She sat down on a tall wooden stool, weak under the weight of everything coming together. "The raven. My visions. Your raven tattoo. My raven tattoo. Are *you* the raven?"

"I am not. And yet I am. I am him and he is me, but we are never in the same place at the same time. He is under my control. Maybe I am under his." He laughed as he set their plates on a small dining table by a window, turning out the lights and lighting a few candles. "Come, Fallon. You have much to discover, but we can delve into it all after we dine. Come. Sit. It has been a long evening for you."

She sat down across from him, watching as he refilled her wine glass. "Why was it Colette who told me you were gone, when I was fourteen?" Her tone was slightly accusatory.

He did not meet her stare. "I was not allowed to be near you anymore. I was ordered away. She was able to go in my stead."

"By my father. He ordered you away from me."

"Yes."

"And now?" she asked. "Has the ban been lifted? On staying away from me?"

He shook his head. "On the contrary, it remains firmly in place, such as it is. But you needed me. I felt it was time for you to know things. And to be honest," he looked up, "I needed you."

His gaze ignited a flame deep within her—it began to burn and illuminate areas that had long been darkened. The world around them shrank, and she was conscious of only the two of them existing. The candlelight created a golden sphere about them from which she never wanted to depart.

He gestured at her with his fork, smiling. "Please. Eat."

As she had anticipated, the meal was delicious, and she realized how much she'd missed his cooking. Dining with Jacob felt as natural as anything ever had, and they spoke casually of unimportant things. At one point, there was a familiar bark at the door, and he got up to let in a dog.

Fallon's face lit up as Azul raced to her side—he nuzzled against her as she leaned down to hug and kiss him.

Jacob chuckled as he watched their reunion. "He was always your dog," he observed softly, and she grinned at him.

"What animals are up here?" she asked. "In the barn, I mean."

"Ah, Colette is quite the homesteader. She has chickens, a few pigs, and a flock of sheep. The sheep, I feel, are preference only, for her—she likes to watch them. They amuse her, bring her a sense of peace. She has the pigs slaughtered now and then, and cures the meat. There's a large vegetable garden which she tends to, and she collects fruit from all over. In the winter it is sometimes difficult to get supplies here. She always seems to have enough of everything, as well as plenty to share with various neighbors around the mountains. She's invaluable, really."

Moving about in the kitchen, he set down a water bowl for Azul and fed him some cheese and a piece of meat. The dog wagged his tail fiercely in a show of pure joy.

"You know he showed up tonight mainly for the cheese," Jacob told her. "Your friend Marianna is stingy with cheese offerings."

Fallon laughed as she carried their dishes to the sink. "How do you know that?"

He shrugged with a grin. "The raven keeps me informed of the important things."

"And Azul's cheese consumption is most definitely on the list of important things," Fallon agreed, kneeling down to give the dog a bigger hug.

Together, she and Jacob cleaned up the dishes and put things away. When they were done in the kitchen, Jacob blew out the candles and brought two glasses of wine to the dark leather sofa, where they sat together before the fire. His feet rested on a large ottoman while she tucked her legs up beside herself.

It had grown completely dark both outside and within the cottage. The fire glowed and crackled, the light reflecting on their faces. Azul was sound asleep on a rug in front of it, sprawled on his side with his furry belly aimed towards the heat.

Fallon's gaze followed the shadows that played on the walls. She was still acclimating to the reality of being reunited with the one she had sought for so long, now sitting beside him in his home, far away from everyone she knew. Her weary body was content, like one who had completed a long, difficult race and emerged the victor.

"Are you always alone here?" she wondered, sipping her wine. "Aside from Colette. Am I not allowed to ask that question?"

"Fallon, you can ask me whatever you like." He sighed. "I was in love once. A lifetime ago. She had many of the same powers that you do, which is the reason I knew enough to begin teaching you when you were younger. She had a premonition one night, she wouldn't tell me what it was really about, but she said I must learn all of her abilities. And so, she began teaching me. I have an irrevocable memory—once something is in my mind, it never leaves, so I was able to recall it all for you as needed. I don't know if the vision she had was of you? That she knew one day I'd be in charge of a girl who desperately needed to be trained? I can only guess. I believe so, though. I believe her vision was of you. She was extraordinary. And very kind."

She read sadness off of him, and faint longing. "I'm so sorry."

"Yes," he seemed to snap out of a reverie, "yes, it is sad, she died, too young. As I said, it was long ago." He clinked his wine glass against hers. "You and I, we are the King and Queen of Loss." He laughed lightly, running a hand through his hair and pushing back some tendrils that had escaped his ponytail. "It is better to be alone, though. Sad but true."

"I've always felt that I should be alone," she agreed. "That it would make more sense."

"Ahh, but you loved that music man."

She stared hard at the fire, hearing something in his tone. "I do love Bret and Bergen—they've become like family to me. I've had no family but Selah for so long. But I always somewhat feared that it was not the best idea for him, being involved with me."

Turning fully towards him, Fallon allowed those thoughts to blow away like petals on a breeze. The complete darkness of the room, the golden light from the fire illuminating each of them, made everything feel intimate and sacred. The cares and concerns which she usually carried now seemed distantly unreal. The only true thing was the man sitting quietly beside her.

Jacob's gaze stayed mainly on the fire, though occasionally he glanced at her, as if assuring himself that she was truly there with him. There was a contentment in his face which was new to her.

Swallowing the last of her wine, Fallon allowed him to take her glass, feeling his fingers lightly brush hers, her heartrate soaring in response. She watched as he set both glasses on a small table.

"Do you know my future, Ravener?"

He graced her with a devilish side-eye. "I do not, lovely Fallon. How could I?"

She raised an eyebrow. "You seem to know a lot," she countered, running her thumb slowly over his wrist and feeling his pulse quicken. Her own breath felt ragged in her chest. "You keep reminding me of how much I don't know."

"I have access to things which you don't, that is true. But your future?" He lifted a shoulder. "Your future is yours." He paused, a sly smile on his lips. "You will win all the wars. How does that sound?"

"Like a lie."

Reaching out, Jacob held her face tenderly in his hand, his gaze delving into hers. "You're so beautiful," he whispered, brushing her lips with his thumb as her breath caught in her throat. His eyes were gleaming. "Fallon, you are tired. Believe me, I would love for this evening to go on forever, but more than anything, you need sleep. Much has happened that your mind needs to work through. You're exhausted, and you've had a lot to drink," he chuckled, "even for you. I very much need you to be the clear-headed woman I know you to be. And that will require rest."

As she stared into his eyes, she felt incredible exhaustion winding through her body and became aware of the chaos of emotions in her head and heart. Overwhelmed with the events of the day. With the reality of him.

"I am so tired," she murmured in agreement, allowing him to lay her back on the couch, where she curled up on her side. She was unable to keep her eyes open any longer. The alcohol she'd been drinking all night long had caught up to her.

Jacob lifted a wool blanket from the back of the couch and wrapped it securely around her as Fallon watched the flames in the fireplace dance and flicker. He carefully covered her bare feet against the cool night air, tucking the blanket around them.

Fallon thought about the flames in the old stone fireplace back at the pub in London. How many hours had she been gone from there? Time seemed different here. What had Bret, Tayce, and Jack thought? What did they do when she vanished before their eyes?

"We'll still be here when I wake up?" she asked, looking back at him, his face illuminated by the flames. Her heart was flying as she gazed at him. She never wanted to look away, but she could feel her eyes closing.

He gave a low laugh, his hand a comforting weight on her hip. "You are not dreaming. We'll still be here. Tomorrow we will talk. I know it seems that I keep delaying, but I have been rather enjoying our evening together. We have much to discuss, however. There is knowledge that has been withheld from you. But it will wait till tomorrow."

"Alright," she whispered, drifting off.

* * * * * * *

In the morning when Fallon awoke, she was still on the couch under the blanket, but the fire had died out. She had been so tired that she'd slept through what remained of the night without waking. Turning over and stretching, she felt her skin flush with the memory of the night before.

Raising up a little, she saw that outside the sun was shining, warming the cottage. Some of the windows had been cranked open to let in the fresh air. No one was around, not even her faithful Azul.

On her way to the bathroom, she was startled to see her suitcase and backpack sitting against the wall. How had he managed that? Regardless, she was relieved, and knelt to rifle through them.

The cottage's single bathroom proved to be a spectacle of uniqueness. There was no mirror over the old-fashioned white porcelain sink—instead, there was a tall window of square panes of colored glass. A small, round mirror was attached with an accordion-style mount to the side of the window—for shaving, she assumed, spying a man's razor on a nearby metal shelf. The shower was a large, walk-in affair, tucked around a corner and out of sight. It was done entirely in rough, dark gray stone, with an array of metal fixtures cleverly directing sprays of water.

After taking a quick shower, she dressed in leggings and a black, long-sleeved shirt. In the kitchen, she drank a glass of water and slid on her running shoes before heading outside.

It was warmer than when she had arrived the evening before, though the wind still blew steadily. The sun felt glorious, and her surroundings were breathtaking in their loveliness and scope. Not seeing anyone around, she followed a well-worn path from the cottage up to a grassy spot on a wide precipice, which overlooked a greater expanse of the mountain range they seemed to be in. Her gaze took in the gray rock, the emerald green pastures, full, leafy trees, dramatic cliffs, and flower-filled meadows where sheep were grazing—all of it was bathed in majestic beauty.

Sinking down to the ground, she looked around and drank it all in. Her body felt alive with magic; every cell in her seemed to sing, and the air fairly crackled with energy. She had never before been in a place that spoke to her as powerfully as this, and she soaked it all in like new life.

"This is my favorite place to sit," Jacob commented when he appeared beside her about twenty minutes later. His smile could not hide that he was overjoyed to see her there. When he'd woken up that morning and found her laying curled up under the blanket where he'd left her, his heart had wanted to beat out of his chest. "You're still near the cottage, but you can see it all, the wonder of this area."

She got to her feet with a smile, stepping closer to him. "This is an amazing place to live."

He put an arm around her shoulders to steer her back towards the cottage. "I'm happy that I was finally able to bring you here. It's something I've wanted to do for a very long time. Would you like to see the river?" His smile turned sly as he squeezed her close. "I happen to know how you feel about water."

She laughed. "Yes, I want to see it, very much."

"It is much further down the mountain into the first valley. Let's grab a picnic, and we can make the trek. And I promise, we will talk about things."

* * * * * * *

The river was cold and beautiful and everything she could have hoped for, roaring wildly over rocks, then spreading out into little areas where one could safely wade around.

131

"Sometimes, at this time of year, there is still snow on the ground," he explained, "but not this year. This year spring has asserted itself rather early. Perhaps the mountains knew you were coming."

It had taken them an hour to hike from the cottage. Fallon sat on the edge of a large rock and stared at the water while Jacob spread out a blanket on a wider rock in the sun.

"Do you come here a lot?" she asked.

Jacob began pulling food from a backpack—bread, salami, cheese, and fruit—and setting it out on the blanket. "I wouldn't say a lot, but it is a ritual I enjoy now and then—spending a day down by the river."

She joined him on the blanket, accepting some grapes that he held out to her. He poured them each a half glass of wine. For a while they ate and drank in silence, listening to the music of nearby birds and the water rushing over the rocks. The wind did not blow here as it did further up the mountain, and the air was warmer. Azul had launched an in-depth exploration all along the riverbank.

As they ate, Fallon found herself staring reflectively at Jacob. "Tell me something."

"Anything, Fallon."

"Why do you still look exactly the same? Why haven't you aged?"

His gaze drifted to the river. "Beginning with the hard questions," he murmured.

"I'll throw some easy ones in, too," Fallon promised, with an impish head tilt. She marveled at his distinctive profile, his strong jaw, the lines at his eyes. The sun glinted gold flecks in his wavy brown hair, and all his movements, even a simple turn of his head, were marked with grace and strength.

We are here together, she thought. *I am at peace—there is no more searching. And he is achingly beautiful.*

As if sensing her thoughts, he looked at her, lips curving into a grin.

"How old are you really?" she pressed, trying to hide the slight blush that bloomed on her cheeks. "Because I don't think the answer is fifties."

He sighed, his grin fading. "I don't know, Fallon. I don't know how old I truly am. I was a young man when I became the Ravener. Younger than you are now. My becoming, my transition, immediately aged me to this that you see before you and kept me here. And so, I was twenty-seven when I became this, yet I am not the man I was then. For I have seen too much of the darknesses of this world and beyond, decade upon decade, than any twenty-seven-year-old should. For over a century, I have been this. I've lost track of how old I would truly be, because it hasn't mattered in a long, long time. It would serve no purpose to know how many years. It would make me tired. More tired than I already am."

Fallon had gone still. *A century.* Her heart shattered for the twenty-seven-year-old she glimpsed in the sparkle in his eyes, and for the lines of suffering and hardship on his handsome face.

Seeing her sadness, Jacob reached out and touched her cheek. "It is not for you to fret about," he told her, his voice husky. She placed her hand over his, and for a moment they stayed there, adrift in each other's eyes.

"Are you immortal?" she asked softly.

"I can be destroyed. But until then, I go on." He sat back and picked up his wine. "Ask me another question."

Fallon gazed out at the water, blinking away tears, not trusting herself to look at him. "It's surreal to me that we're here together after all these years. Two people sitting by a river having a picnic. As if it were the most natural thing in the world."

He nodded, breaking off a piece of bread. "I agree. It is a bit like a dream."

"I feel like I don't know you, and yet at the same time I feel as if we are beloved, old friends who have known each other for centuries. My head doesn't know you well, but my heart does. As if that makes any sense. It's a strange, strange thing."

He smiled as he took a sip of wine. "Life is a strange thing, I have found. I long ago stopped trying to make sense of it."

"You were such a stranger to me, for all of my life. You were rarely around when I was growing up and yet you became so important to me. When you disappeared from our lives, I missed your companionship—you were the strongest, most intelligent person I knew. I felt lost, even though I still had my brother. As the years went on, as I grew into my late teens and early twenties, my thoughts about you changed. Not only did I miss the knowledge you possessed and our rapport, but I missed your devilishly beautiful face." She raised an eyebrow. "My feelings for you became something different entirely."

Jacob was grinning. "Since we're confessing. The way I regarded you changed drastically when you turned twenty. After I left you years before, at fourteen, the raven kept me up to date—I was not watching you all the time, busy with other things. In truth, I rarely saw you, and your teenage years came and went, for the most part, without my notice. But on the day that you turned twenty—when I saw you, my whole universe shifted. You had grown into a beautiful woman, and I was stunned, caught off guard, by my reaction."

Fallon looked suspicious. "You saw me the day I turned twenty? That's the day my father stole me the first time, for seven weeks."

Jacob stared off into the distance. "Yes. We will get to that part eventually."

Sensing a darker turn to the conversation, Fallon scrambled to pose what she hoped would be a lighter path. "What do you see when you close your eyes at night?"

Jacob hesitated for several seconds, then leaned in towards her, fully amused. "Fallon, is that supposed to be an easy question?"

She ducked her head with a sheepish grin. "Sorry."

He studied her a moment before sitting back. "What do you see?"

Tracing a pattern on the blanket with her finger, she glanced up at him. "For the past decade? Honestly? You."

A genuine smile lit his face, but as he saw she was still waiting on his answer, he looked down at his hands. "It depends on what kind of day I've had. Sometimes, when I close my eyes, I see only death."

Digging her nails into her palm, Fallon silently cursed her conversation skills.

Then Jacob leveled his gaze with hers. "But often, I am able to block those images, and instead I see colors."

"Colors?"

"Yes. Almost like a filter sliding over my conscious mind, in a soothing way. One color in particular comforts me the most." Reaching out, he touched a finger to her right temple. "The particular shade of green which your eyes turn when you are in sunlight. That is my favorite." His hand dropped, and he hooked his index finger around hers, giving it a gentle squeeze. "What would be your favorite?"

Fallon tried to think around the fluttering nonsense of her heart in her chest. "Well, don't be offended—your eyes are spectacular—but I think my favorite would be the color of this river."

He was smiling. "Somehow, I knew."

When they were done with lunch, Fallon knelt on the blanket and began putting things away. "I needed your help when Bret and Jack were missing," she mentioned, her tone mildly critical. "I needed you. So much was at stake, and I was next to useless."

"You were nothing of the kind." He was lighting a cigarette, the same fragrant ones she remembered. "And I couldn't have helped you. I didn't know where they were, honestly. I would not have withheld that information from you, I assure you."

"You could have helped me figure it all out, then," she pressed, setting the picnic things aside.

"No one else would have interpreted Bergen's dream as quickly as you did or known enough to think to question her about her dreams. You had already secured the necessary information from Simon. That was your doing. All of it was your doing. In the end, it all came together because of you."

"I wasted precious time going inside my mind like I did. I think that made everything worse for me. But I was desperate, because day after day there was nothing, and I knew they were both dying somewhere."

He nodded, hearing the slight catch in her voice. "I knew the pain you were in, the frustration at your seeming helplessness. I followed every moment that I could; I realize you would have rather I'd been there physically beside you. But I was there, in my own way. The raven and I did have to save you several times during that period, though, didn't we? From your own charming recklessness." He smiled, but she did not share in his amusement.

"Is that what the raven was doing? Saving me?"

"Believe it or not, yes."

She looked skeptical. "Now Katrine is off and on missing," she continued, "and certain people think I might have the answers, but I'm as useless as I was looking for Bret and Jack."

He gazed at her. "I taught you how to scry. That would help in this situation."

She lowered her eyes. "That's the one thing I didn't practice." Learning how to clear her head enough to stare into a mirror and see hidden things had never come easily to her.

"That's not my fault. I remember you struggled with it. Sometimes the abilities that challenge you the most require your deepest attention."

She bit her lip. "The universe really messed up when it chose me to have all this potential," she remarked lightly.

He leveled a sober gaze at her. "It did no such thing. You are endlessly incredible. You just don't see it."

She rubbed her thumb repetitively over the smooth surface of one of the black river stones. "During that time, when I was in the backyard at Selah's, going so far into my mind—at times it felt like I was becoming the raven." She cast a look at him.

He nodded. "I felt it, too. It was unnerving."

"So, it wasn't normal?"

"Not at all. It was nothing I had ever experienced before. You are very powerful, Fallon. Dangerously so. But there is always so little anger in you. Where is your fury?" He grinned, rubbing his jaw. "With true madness in your heart, you would be deadly."

She hurled the stone into the rushing water. "I guess no one's found my breaking point yet."

He sighed, smile fading away. "They will." He crushed out the cigarette and shoved their basket of picnic things further out of the way, moving closer to her. "One thing I want you to know, is that I did care for you while we were living there together in Austin, but I could not show affection for you or Luca. The house was monitored, and officially I was not there to form relationships—I was there to guard. Early on in your lives, your father was jealous of any love his children showed to anyone. Selah's survival during that time period surprised me, but possibly he was not so threatened by your love for another girl."

Fallon pushed back the alarm that welled up within her. "But they saw you training me? How was that allowed?"

He shook his head. "But they didn't. Remember I told you we must keep it a secret? My bedroom was the only area in the house that was cloaked from their view—that is why we always trained there. They thought, as Luca did, that I was only reading to you in my room. Little attention was paid to us over the years, but inevitably they noticed that your powers were growing. They investigated. They found out what I was doing and saw that we had grown close to one another."

"When I was fourteen."

"Yes. And I was threatened and ordered away."

She had a difficult time imagining anyone being able to threaten Jacob. "What did they threaten you with?" She smiled in anticipation of his answer.

His jaw tightened. "Your death."

She was surprised and briefly felt a chill, as if the sun had gone behind a cloud. "So, despite that he had tried for years to keep me alive and make sure I was safe, my father would have rather seen me die than endure defiance from you and a bond between us?"

"Correct. Kian's views have always been slightly senseless. He has been wasteful of others' lives for as long as I've known him."

"Kian? That's his name?"

He picked up a rock and held it in his hand. "That is one of his names; he has many. That is the name I use for him, yes."

She looked thoughtful. "Did you even have any fondness for Luca?" she wondered. "It never seemed that way."

"Of course I did. He was my nephew. I was honored that I was able to watch him grow from an uncertain boy into a confident young man. It grieves me that he was taken from you so young."

Her eyes had widened. "Your nephew?"

"Yes, his mother was my young great-niece Lea. Your father killed her four weeks after Luca's birth, because he decided she was too in love with her son. With *his* son." His tone was bitter. "Lea was a sweet girl who loved Luca dearly. She would have been an incredible mother to him. She did not deserve the fate that was dealt to her. Life would have turned out quite differently if, when I placed you with Luca, she had been there to be a mother to you as well."

Fallon's lips parted as sorrow touched her heart. "That's horrible." She blinked back a tear. "Did he also kill my mother?"

Jacob looked uncomfortable, shifting around. "No. Your mother continues on, in her way."

"Really?" Fallon was startled. "Where is she? When and why was I separated from her?"

He threw the rock into the water. "Your mother's name is Carolina. When she was eighteen, your father came across her and was completely enchanted with her beauty and her spirit." He smiled at her. "I am maybe a bit biased, but I feel that you are far more beautiful."

Fallon touched his hand, ducking her head to hide her own smile.

"She was mortal, simply a human girl. He pursued her, charmed her, seduced her, and she became pregnant with you. When it came time for you to be born, she was taken to your father's world. Being half his, you needed to be born there. Your first breath needed to be of that air, don't ask me to explain why. A normal human can only survive in that world a few hours before their mind begins to fracture—they cannot stay there for long. It is a different place."

"How long can I survive there?" she asked.

"No one's certain. The longest you've been there were those seven weeks when you were twenty. By the end, your mind was beginning to show early signs of stress and fatigue." He picked up another rock. "So that she would not be in that world for too long, Carolina was not brought there until she was fully in labor with you. But there were complications with the delivery, and she ended up being there for several hours. Her brain was stressed, torn, and changed. Kian was either unable or unwilling to repair the damage, depending on who you ask.

"It made Carolina unstable, broken, and what was worse is that she knew she was damaged, what had been lost, and it drove her mad. You were given to her, but a nanny went along to help. After a couple of years, when you began showing an attachment to the nanny, Carolina sent her away. Another nanny was employed, one of many. None lasted long. I was directed to make frequent surprise appearances to check on your well-being."

"You've known me always." She was staring at him, partly surprised, but somewhat aware that she'd known.

Jacob nodded. "Since the moment of your birth, yes. I was never fond of children, as you recognized early on. Though I was not around you often, we had somehow developed something of a kinship by the time you were two. You looked forward to my visits. We were comrades, in our own way. Two old souls. You trusted me whole-heartedly. You were a very different child, old before your time due in part to the chaos you existed in with her. I felt something of a responsibility towards you. That was a shattering realization for me—it was not in my nature to form attachments."

"My mother allowed you to pop in like that?"

"She could fire nannies to her heart's content, but my welfare checks were non-negotiable under Kian's order. When you were nearly four years old, things had grown dire. Carolina's physical and mental abuse of you had become more violent. Your bruises healed too quickly for her liking, which only angered her further. I could no longer stand by and allow it to happen—I was nearer and nearer to the point of killing her every time she harmed you, which would not have turned out well for you and me.

"There was finally a day when I told Kian that I believed your survival was in jeopardy. He knew I would not come to him unless the situation demanded attention. Fortunately, he agreed with my assessment and approved your removal from your mother's possession. And so, one night I tricked her and stole you away."

Fallon sat back on her heels. "You placed me with Luca."

"It was out of the question that you would stay with me— my life was no place for a child, though Colette would have aced the assignment, I'm certain. I knew you needed Luca, who I had determined to be a good, kind-hearted boy. The last six months with your mother were an assault on your mind and spirit, not to mention your body, but your brother put himself in charge of healing you, and I believe he succeeded."

There was a warmth in her heart as she thought wistfully of Luca. "He was the best brother." She studied the water, the shades of blue and the foamy white, the dark rocks that broke through the rough surface. "Luca was my father, mother, and brother all in one." She sighed. "Where is my mother now?"

"I'm not sure. She frequently moves about. Still mentally damaged. Out of pure jealousy, she orchestrated the murders of the Quinns. She tried to steal you several times while I was living with you, but was, of course, unsuccessful. She has been quiet for many years now. Maybe she realizes the power you have and is afraid to confront you. I don't know."

"What could she possibly want from me now? I'm no longer a child she can possess."

He looked at her. "Justice. She is bitter. You are alive, free, beautiful. Life as she knew it ceased at nineteen. She's jealous. Angry. I don't know what her intentions would be, but I would not trust her."

"My father is an extraordinarily evil man."

He cast his gaze aside. "It gets worse."

She tensed up. "Tell me."

He tucked his hair behind his ears. "When your father ordered me away, he believed you would suffer emotionally with the separation from me. That with no one actively training you, your powers would dim. But you were my warrior, you continued on—in my room where no one could see you, which was clever, though at the time you didn't know the training was supposed to be a secret from anyone other than Luca."

"I did it there to feel close to you," she explained. "It was very difficult for me to continue on without you. I was so destroyed, emotionally, by what I viewed as you abandoning me when I needed you the most."

He reached out and caressed her cheek, a look of true tenderness in his eyes. "Fallon, I am sorry that you were left so much in the dark. But navigating the treacherous waters with someone as cruel and unstable as Kian is never easy, and it was made more tenuous by your youth and inability to protect yourself." He dropped his hand down to take one of hers. "Your father eventually noticed your powers did not fade, but instead grew stronger. He watched nervously for a few years as this went on. And then he panicked and decided to play the one card he knew would shatter you."

She waited.

"He hired the shape-shifter that murdered your brother."

Jacob grabbed her as he saw her about to lose control, her eyes filling with tears, her face wrecked with sorrow. "I killed him. I killed him because I kept training. He didn't have to die." A sob tore from her throat.

"No." He held her close against himself. "Your cruel, controlling father killed him. Killed his own son in order to weaken his daughter. I have always said, about you, that they will not know what to battle you with, and so they will try to destroy you with loss."

She buried her face against his chest. "You knew they were going to kill him that night."

"No, I had no idea."

"Don't lie to me." She lifted her head. "Isn't that why you left me the quote in the mockingbird book on my bed? Knowing that finding it would shake me up and probably cause me to stay home that evening?"

He held her face tenderly in his hands. "I am not lying, Fallon. I did leave you the note for the reason you say, to unnerve you and keep you at home, but I did so because I thought they were going to try to kill *you* that night. They floated that line of false information for weeks ahead of time, so that I would focus my protection on you and look away from everything else. There was enough truth in it, enough menace, that I couldn't easily dismiss it as false.

"I was at your house that evening, as I said, watching you, so fearful they would kill you before I could stop them. But it was a trick. The raven was watching Luca—by the time he saw what was happening, it was too late, it all happened too quickly. I saw you collapse on the floor with the vision at the same time the raven saw the shape-shifter approaching your brother. It was then that I realized my mistake."

Fallon could do nothing but shove the feelings of guilt deep down inside, knowing they would do no one any good. She could not change what had happened, could not go back in time and alter her choices. Save her brother's life. Luca was gone, never to return.

But Jacob was here. The sounds of the wild river filled her head as he continued to hold her close, and she felt some kind of energy passing back and forth between them, settling in her bones, healing her.

After a minute or two, she got to her feet and faced the water. She watched it for a while, before she finally spoke. "I don't understand why my father doesn't want me to be trained. For my powers—whatever they might be—not to fully develop."

Getting to his feet, Jacob stood beside her. "The reason he wanted you to be kept untrained is that your father is afraid of you." His fingers brushed her cheek. "You are more powerful than he is."

His words were startling. She stared out at the vastness of the mountainsides, the fierce river that roared before her, the wide blue sky overhead. She felt hollow inside, till she felt Jacob's hand close around hers. Taking a deep, shuddering breath, she looked at him. "How was that determined? My power?"

"There is a test. There are crystals known as the Ruen Crystals—when someone holds one in the palm of their hand, the amount of light that emanates from the crystal gives an idea as to the level of power that person is imbued with."

Her gaze was wary, a memory flickering faintly in her brain.

"When you were three years old, your father instructed me to test you out of curiosity. The gem had burned moderately for Luca, and not much more was expected of you."

Fallon was aware she was holding her breath.

"I waited till your mother was out. I placed the gem in your little hand, and it glowed immediately. It grew brighter and brighter, and then it did something I'd never seen before." He turned to her and ran a comforting hand up and down her arm. "It exploded in a fiery storm, sending tiny crystal shards flying."

Tears were in her eyes. Jacob folded her up protectively in his arms as she trembled.

"I remember the explosion," she whispered, her head against his chest. "I didn't know what it was. But you told me not to be afraid." She closed her eyes. "I am afraid."

He stepped back and tilted her head so she was looking at him. "You have nothing to fear, my lovely Fallon." There was a glint in his eye, a faint smile hinting at the corner of his mouth. "You will win all the wars."

"So you say."

Closing the distance between them, she kissed him tenderly on the lips. Her face was immediately cradled in his hands as he returned the kiss with an intensity that shook her soul. Her arms wrapped around his neck, the noisy chaos of the river filling their heads. There was nothing Fallon could imagine wanting more than this. She'd been swimming lost and alone in a darkened sea the past ten years, and now the water around her lit up with sizzling sparks of fire, illuminating orange and yellow as it heated her skin. She still didn't fully understand why he was back in her life, but if he wanted to break her and destroy her, she would let him. Because as the glittering waves crashed around her, she recognized that it was the most alive she'd ever felt. A phoenix soaring up from the ashes of her old life. She would never be the same Fallon again.

Jacob pulled her body against his, losing himself in the kiss, everything in him in danger of coming undone. His long-time spirit of careful self-control disintegrated with every touch, every taste of Fallon.

She is unraveling me from the inside out, he acknowledged. *Once I embark down this path with her, there will be no turning back.*

Azul brought them back down to earth, barking and running around happily. Pulling reluctantly apart, they connected each other's gaze, their breathing jagged and quick. Fallon trembled as he ran his hands delicately up and down her arms.

Then Jacob glanced at the time. "We should head back. The sun will be setting soon, and the cold will come in."

Gathering up their things into two backpacks and putting their shoes back on, they began the long hike back to the cottage. Fallon watched curiously as Azul trotted confidently ahead of them.

"It's like he already knows the path," she commented with a little laugh as they walked.

Jacob was nodding. "Yes. He has been to this river many, many times before."

Fallon stopped abruptly on the path and looked at him. Jacob also stopped, breaking into a smile.

"What do you mean?" she demanded.

Jacob cocked his head slightly. "How do you suppose, Fallon, that Azul made it here to us, to the cottage?"

She shrugged. "He usually turns up wherever I am. I never know how or why. I assumed this was the same."

"No." Jacob shook his head. "No one can show up here without my bidding. This entire land around us is heavily protected, even against teleporting dogs. He would not have been able to 'just show up.' Unless he was already an established resident, like Colette."

"What?"

He rubbed his chin thoughtfully. "Do you still truly believe, after all these years, that an immortal black dog appeared to you as a stray when you were seven—by pure happenstance—and decided to remain with you forever?"

Fallon blinked and said nothing.

"Who else showed up when you were seven?" he prompted.

She bit her bottom lip, reflecting. "You did."

He nodded encouragingly.

Lines formed between her eyes. "Azul came with you?"

Jacob wrapped a lock of her long hair around his finger and then watched as it slowly unwound itself and fell away. "Yes, lovely. He was my dog. I brought him along because I knew that for several years I would rarely be here, since I was assigned to be in Austin with you and Luca. I did not want him to grow lonely."

She shifted the weight of her backpack.

"He fell in love with you," Jacob continued, "not wholly unexpectedly, and completely switched his allegiance from me to you."

She touched a hand to her face. "I can't believe I never realized. That he was yours. And you never corrected me."

"I was amused. And your assumption was sweet. I knew that, with you, he would be in the best hands." They turned and began walking again, side-by-side. "You were only seven. A lot had been going on in your life. It was an understandable misunderstanding."

She moved closer to him and slipped her arm through his, deep in thought.

A few minutes later she stopped him again, and he looked at her with a soft smile of anticipation.

"Yes?" he inquired.

She appeared to be minorly struggling. "I named him 'Azul,' though, right? That was me?"

He laughed a deep, rich laugh. "I named him 'Azul' decades ago, my sweet girl. Long before you entered my life. I am sorry to shatter some of your core memories, but it is true. When he showed up with me in Austin, and you were deciding what to name this brand-new dog, I told you a story about a dog named Blue. You were cautiously interested. I knew you had been taking Spanish at school. I suggested 'Azul' as an interesting twist on the name, and you latched onto it immediately and informed the dog that his new name was Azul." He wrapped an arm around her shoulders as they continued walking. "It was completely self-serving on my part. I didn't want to change his name, both for his own comfort and because I didn't want to have to learn a different name for him."

She looked up at him. "And you said you were no good with children."

He kissed the side of her head. "I am not. But somehow, I was always good with you."

* * * * * * *

It was early evening and inside the cottage the colder air was settling in. Fallon, just out of a shower, was barefoot and cozy, curled up with the blanket on the couch before the blazing fire. She was staring at the raven tattoo on her wrist while Jacob rearranged something on a bookshelf behind her. They had eaten a marvelous dinner, and now she was slowly drinking a glass of wine as she examined the intricacy of the raven with its prism eye.

She looked over her shoulder at him. "Who did my tattoos?"

His eyes met hers. "I did."

She was surprised, sitting up. "You can tattoo magic?"

He smirked. "It is one of my talents, yes."

"But you were supposed to have no contact with me."

"You were unconscious," he told her dryly. "I suppose, to them, that didn't count. But I had long known that Kian planned to take you away at the age of twenty like he had taken Luca. And, of course, nothing in hell could have stopped me from being there with you when he did. Seven weeks was a long time to keep you there, unconscious and vulnerable—it made me uneasy. I trust no one in that place. I stayed beside you throughout."

Somewhat astonished, she watched him as he joined her on the couch. "You didn't do Luca's tattoos," she noted.

"I did not," he confirmed. "His were done poorly. An experiment. After that, I campaigned for years to be the one to do yours, because I had confidence in no one but myself to take the care that was needed. Yours needed to be perfect."

"You changed the raven's eye to a prism. You made it the identical twin of yours."

He nodded. "I did that without their knowledge and later claimed it was aesthetic only, though they were initially suspicious. That tiny detail very much deepened the link between you and me, allowing me to know where and how you were, even without the raven's watch. Kept at a distance as I had been, I wanted every avenue open to me to be able to protect you. It strengthened your link to the raven as well."

"And you added the flames to the eye." She glanced at her right wrist.

"Again. I knew what I was doing. I knew what I needed to protect you against. Your brother's tattoos, as I say, were an experiment to see if they could harness his powers through the tattoos. I saw the ways they failed him, and I knew exactly what I wanted on your wrists. Most everyone thought I was simply being dramatically artistic with your tattoos—that it was ego-driven on my part. It was well-known that I was fond of you, as evidenced by my constant presence at your side throughout your time there. But no one realized how much my heart was now beating with every beat of yours."

Fallon felt her own heart react to his words, leaping in her chest.

"Kian, if he had been paying closer attention, would have suspected that I was being disingenuous. But he was distracted. And so, I was able to accomplish everything I intended on your wrists."

She was surprised at the emotion she felt when she finally understood that for those mysterious seven weeks, so long a dark unknown in her life, Jacob had been with her. He had not left her side. *Of course you were with me,* she thought, following the dancing flames of the fire. *You have always been with me.*

He ran his fingers over her arm. "I believe I began falling in love with you, during that time. As I said earlier, I had not paid much attention to you during your teenage years, except for the months surrounding Luca's death. When I saw you on your twentieth birthday, it was as if I was seeing you for the first time. I was utterly destroyed and changed. I memorized every aspect of your beauty. I imagined conversations we'd have if you'd been awake—I wished again and again that I could wake you. I went positively feral on the few occasions when they attempted to separate us." He made a face. "It was an odd seven weeks, to be sure. When you were finally sent back, I felt your loss deeply. I was forever altered. There was an empty space in my chest that hadn't been there before. I began watching you through the raven's eye every chance I got. I could no longer look away from you."

She laced her fingers through his, cupping his jaw with her other hand as she stared into his eyes. There was so much she wanted to say, but her throat was tight. "How," she swallowed, "how were you able to stay with me? He ordered you away from me when I was young—how were you able to manage that?"

"Like I said, it was apparently not as much of an issue since you were unconscious. Kian was also not around much during that time, and when he was, he was not interested in a fight. Everyone else there is slightly afraid of me, so no one challenged me. Honestly, I think he was a bit intrigued at my interest in you."

A new thought occurred, and she pointed accusingly to the back of her neck, but he shook his head.

"That was not me, that star." Jacob made a derisive noise. "You were to be there for less than twenty-four hours, and I was not to accompany you—that was the agreement. I couldn't believe it when I noticed what they'd done. Things have been breaking down further between me and your father for some time now for various reasons. When he took you this most recent time, I should have known they would try to put their mark on you in some way. They've been aware now for years that your wrist tattoos are not what they seem."

She held her wrists close, against her stomach.

"The timing was terrible, but I knew that if I attempted to stand in the way of him taking you, he would initiate other means of getting to you. And I did not want that to happen. At least not while you were so mentally weakened trying to locate Bret and Jack."

"Kian told me he knew what I was doing when I was at Selah's. In my mind. Going too deep and such."

Jacob shook his head. "He was lying. He was guessing based on what others relayed to him. He cannot see into your head like he suggests he can. You are too powerful for that. Your power now is so far beyond any that you had as a child."

She pulled her knees up, watching him curiously. "Who is The Ravener?"

Jacob leaned back, relaxed, his arms on the back of the sofa. "A protector. A deal-maker. A guardian. A seeker of vengeance." He tilted his head at her. "It's a full-time job, believe me."

She laughed out loud. Then she sobered quickly. "So, one of your jobs was to protect me?"

"Since your birth, until you were fourteen, yes, it was one of my primary duties. I can cast shades of protection that keep something or someone hidden. That is why I called you my 'secret girl'—for many years your very existence was a closely-guarded secret. Your father does have a number of enemies and because of that, you and Luca had always been vulnerable. I kept you both a secret for as long as I could. Have you ever wondered why no harm has ever come to Selah and her family? Why the troubles you and they have seen have only occurred outside of Gray?"

Fallon nodded. "It's been a puzzle."

"I cast protection over the entire town. No one can find you or harm you there, for the most part. It's not foolproof. But it keeps your friends there fairly safe as well. I included the farm the first time I saw you go running out there. That was my own doing, by the way, not any order from Kian."

"So, when I leave Gray..."

"You are exposed. But you are a strong, clever woman. And you are always in my raven's eye."

She pursed her lips. "Have I ever truly had a moment's privacy in my entire life?"

Jacob laughed. "Never, my girl."

"And how does one become The Ravener?"

His blue eyes went almost black. "Those are long stories. Not to be recounted." Rising abruptly, he left the cottage, disappearing into the night.

For a long time after he left, Fallon sat alone on the couch, quiet and still, regretting her question. Jacob did not come back. She listened to the fire crackling in the fireplace, to Azul's faint snoring sounds from the rug, and the wind against the roof.

Her hand was over her mouth. As if she could reverse time and call the words back. She should have known not to ask. Not to probe too deeply. Despite his willingness to be open with her, to shine a light on all of the secrets that had followed her throughout her life, she knew, in her heart, that there were some tales too dark to tell.

Getting to her feet, she went to the door and opened it, hoping he was just outside, that she could call him in from the cold. But there was nothing before her but the night and the wind, and after a moment, she closed the door and turned away, shivering.

Her gaze went to the doorway to his bedroom, into which she had not yet gone. It was the cottage's lone bedroom, from what she could tell, and there was a faint golden glow emanating from it.

Pausing now just inside the doorway, she looked around with interest, her bare feet chilled on the wooden floor. The bed was in the near-center of the room. Large and cushioned, it was low to the ground and covered in pillows and down-filled comforters. It looked heavenly. The warm, golden glow she'd noticed was coming from a fire blazing in a small, silver, wood-burning stove in the center of the room. A floor-to-ceiling, arched, multi-pane window showed her a sky full of stars.

She wanted desperately to curl up on that bed. It had been a long day wildly filled with emotion and information, and Jacob's current absence was weighing on her soul. Yawning, Fallon gave in without a fight and went to the bed, crawling in amidst the pillows and the comforters, curling up and closing her eyes. She was asleep in seconds.

Jacob stood in the bedroom doorway at 3 a.m. and watched her fondly for a moment as she slept. The fire had died down, and it was only the faintest light that still lit the bed. The joy her presence brought him filled his entire being with warmth and a lightness he'd long forgotten. Drawing closer, he smiled to see her buried under the comforters, a look of pure serenity on her face.

He removed his shirt and then carefully sat on the bed, stretching out beside her on top of the covers. He looped one arm around her, and Fallon opened her eyes. She smiled softly when she saw him, practically purring with contentment as she turned into him, falling back asleep against his chest. Jacob rested his cheek against her head, closing his eyes and falling into a dreamless sleep.

When Fallon awoke the next morning, she was alone in the bed, though she was aware she'd spent half the night sleeping in Jacob's arms.

After getting dressed, she found him in the kitchen with freshly brewed coffee, and he handed her a cup.

"Sleep well?" he inquired, eyeing her over the rim of his mug.

"I did," she confirmed, feeling slightly guilty for taking over his bed, uninvited, but also somewhat not.

He was distractingly shirtless, and she wondered how he could appear even more beautiful. There were tattoos on his muscular chest that she'd never seen before, but also a wide array of cruel scars all over his torso. Startled, her fingers immediately went to the scars, tracing the history of pain she knew nothing about. "Jacob…"

He shuddered at her touch, and closed his hand over hers. "Fallon, I must leave you for a few hours this morning. Will you be alright? Is there anything at all I can do for you?"

She bit her lip as she looked into his eyes. For a moment she was sure she had forgotten how to speak. "Just…come back to me."

A smile spread slowly across his face. "Believe me," he placed a kiss on her forehead, "I will never leave you again for long." He kissed her softly on the lips, lingering there, before she saw him grab his shirt off the counter and then he vanished.

Fallon exhaled slowly. "I miss you already," she told the empty room.

Beside her, Azul whined, snuffling against her hand.

She smiled down at him. "Yes, we will go out and enjoy this beautiful morning. Let me get my shoes."

Fallon and Azul explored for several hours. They didn't go far because she wasn't sure of the boundaries of Jacob's property, though she could tell it was extensive. She did not fully trust the dog to know where they should and should not go.

Colette was nowhere to be found, but Fallon did come across the smaller cottage tucked away from view where she assumed the woman lived. She also found the vegetable gardens, newly-tilled in preparation for planting.

They went to say hello to the sheep—though Fallon quickly realized that Azul had a penchant for chasing the sheep with riotous glee. The sheep were displeased, but no harm done.

"All this time." She looked at the dog with narrowed eyes. "You've been living a double-life. Secretly a sheep-chaser."

Azul panted happily.

Jacob returned in the early afternoon, and found Fallon in his bed again, taking a nap. "Sleeping beauty. You and that bed have developed a bit of a relationship."

She propped herself up on her elbows, gazing at him with a small yawn. "It's a dreamy bed."

He cocked his head to the side as he looked at her. "Even more so with you in it." He tossed a black t-shirt at her face, and Fallon gave a laughing yelp as she sat up, holding the shirt up to look at it. The white design on the front advertised Cosmic Records in Austin, Texas, and she appreciated the soft, vintage-y feel of it.

"Cool. Where's this from? I never knew a Cosmic Records. Was it a real place?"

He sat beside her. "It was. From before your time there. I knew the owner, a really nice guy. One day, the store burned to the ground and took him with it." His stare went far away, his jaw clenching. "It was an unfortunate thing."

Hearing something dark in his voice, she lay a hand on his arm.

He looked at her and smiled, his face brightening. "Anyway. I've had it so long, and you can definitely be a t-shirt and jeans girl at times, so I thought you'd like it."

"I love it. Thanks." She got up and went to place the shirt with her suitcase. As she knelt, she looked over at him. "That record store. The one that burned."

He gazed at her and nodded.

"Was that where … you remember the records Selah gave me for my birthday once, was…"

"Yes." His expression was momentarily strange. "Your records came from there. I believe her grandfather must have salvaged them during or after the fire. It always struck me as odd that they came to you. It's not anything I want to think much about, honestly."

In the early evening, Fallon explored more of the cottage—she was beginning to suspect that it was magically larger inside than out—and was excited to discover that a room behind the kitchen housed a full gym. She had been off-handedly wondering how it was that Jacob was in such incredible physical condition, and this explained it. Though she frequented the gym in Dutton five days a week, she dreamed of having something of her own.

Wandering around the various machines, weights, boxes, bands, and benches, her body tingled in anticipation. She wanted to try it all. Being on tour was rough on everyone's schedule, and though various hotels had gyms, there was usually little time to utilize them. Her workout routine had been absolutely ruined by the tour.

"Shall we work out before dinner?" Jacob asked with a grin, coming in and straddling a bench as he sat down to watch her.

Fallon drifted over to him and knelt on the bench between his legs. "As long as I won't be a distraction."

He moved a lock of hair away from her eyes. "Oh, you'll be a distraction." His gaze dropped to her lips. "But I will fight the good fight." He slid back away from her and hopped up, pulling his hair back and removing his shirt. "I've seen how much you can bench. Let's see how badly the tour has affected you."

"Or how badly you've affected me," she murmured, looking away from his bare torso and taking a sip of water.

He chuckled softly.

That night after their workout, Fallon cooked dinner while he went to shower, telling him he'd been spoiling her. In return, he volunteered to clean up the kitchen while she showered.

When she finally emerged from the bathroom much later, the cottage was quiet. Azul slept soundly before the fire, and no other lights were on. Fallon headed to the bedroom.

In the shadows on the edge of the room, Jacob was sitting on a cushioned chair, leaning forward with his elbows on his thighs. He was staring into nothingness, the firelight reflecting on his face. As Fallon drew near to him, she saw notes of sadness in his features, an unspoken weariness. Gently she placed a hand on his head, and he rested it against her hip, closing his eyes.

"Remember what you always told me?" she asked softly, running her fingers through his hair, feeling him tremble beneath her touch. "About love being a great weakness?"

"'One weakness is enough...'" he quoted, looking up at her. "And you are most definitely mine."

He reached for her as she sank down into his embrace, his lips finding hers. Their arms wrapped around each other, and he pulled her tightly against himself as the kiss deepened.

He breathed her name, and Fallon's body was electrified in a freefall, Jacob's kisses a wicked combination of gentle sweetness and fiery passion.

Sliding her hands under his shirt, Fallon leaned back long enough to pull the shirt up and over his head. As she tossed it aside, she took her time looking him over; a sly smile curved her lips as he watched her with fire in his eyes.

Rising from the chair, he carried her over to the bed and lay her gently down. He started to take a step back, but she grabbed his hands and pulled him down on top of her. Kissing her deeply as she clung to him, he pulled back a little.

"My beautiful one," he murmured, lost in her eyes and her touch, her every breath, "do you know that you are mine?"

"Yes," she kissed him, running her fingers through his hair. "Jacob, I am yours."

At some point much later in the night, Jacob awoke and unconsciously reached for her. He found her awake, watching him in the moonlight. Tears were streaming down her face. He raised up on one arm, concerned.

"What is it?" he asked softly, worry creasing his brow. His fingers trailed tenderly up her bare skin, from her hip to her collar bone, and she shivered pleasantly at his touch, catching her breath. He kissed her forehead. "Tell me, my love."

"I looked for you everywhere." Her voice shook as she ran her hand slowly over his bare chest, over the scars. Some of them appeared to be old, but many were recent, and it was on these which her fingers lingered. "All over the United States. Europe. Even South America a couple of times. I told myself I was taking necessary breaks from Gray, from my predictable existence there. But subconsciously, I was forever searching for your face in a crowd."

He covered her hand with his, then he brought it to his lips and kissed her knuckles, one by one.

"I imagined every scenario: running into you at an Italian restaurant; spotting you on a balcony in Greece; finding you on a beach in Belize, a bar in Lima." More tears fell on her cheeks, and he leaned in to kiss them all away. "Since Luca died, I have searched for you. I knew that he was gone, that I couldn't seek him out. But I thought that maybe I could find you."

There were tears glistening in his eyes. "I will never leave you again. I promise, Fallon, I will be with you always. There is none in all my life I love as I love you. Even in death, I will be with you. Nothing will tear us apart." He pulled her to him in an impassioned embrace, kissing her intensely as he moved his body to cover hers.

* * * * * * *

When she awoke in the morning in Jacob's strong arms, Fallon felt, for the first time in her life, that she was where she belonged. She was home. She wanted, truly, nothing more than to stay there forever and gaze into his eyes when he smiled at her. It was a selfish thought, she knew. But she was currently reveling in a bout of much-deserved selfishness.

She stared at him in the morning light—the peace on his face as he slept, the beautiful line of his jaw. Her fingers softly touched his hair, moving it away from his ear as she studied his features, absorbing them into memory.

Jacob stirred, opening his eyes, a smile touching his lips when he saw her close attention. He rested his forehead against hers. "Good morning, my lovely one," he murmured. "I will admit that I have long-dreamed of waking up to this. To you."

She caressed his face, wriggling closer to his warmth. "Can we stay here all day?" she asked.

He grinned. "In the cottage or in this bed?"

"In this bed," she whispered, and he dragged her on top of him.

"Absolutely."

* * * * * * *

That evening they dined by candlelight on vegetable soup and fresh bread. After they were finished, Fallon sat on Jacob's lap, staring languidly at the flames of the candles on the table. His arms were wrapped around her tightly, possessively, as if he never planned on letting her go.

"How was my mother able to 'orchestrate' the murders of the Quinns?" she wondered, taking a sip of wine. "You told me she's a mere human, correct? No powers, nothing?"

"That's right." He ran a hand down her arm, resting his chin on her shoulder. "There are a few individuals in your father's circle who are sympathetic to her, after what happened with your birth and then later with me stealing you away—though, me stealing you is mostly viewed as a necessary act, since I was taking you essentially to save you. Still, there has been some debate. Anyway, those in her corner have helped her get by over the years, and I feel they have lent their power now and then, especially in an attempt to right the wrongs they feel were levied against her by Kian." He kissed her bare shoulder, brushing his thumb along her collar bone and sliding the strap of her tank top aside. "I am not concerned that they would do anything against you, however. The general consensus is that you personally have wronged no one. And besides, there is a limit to their sympathy for her, and everyone knows you are under my protection."

She set aside her wine and held onto his arm, leaning back comfortably against his chest. "Will my father be aware that you and I have spent time together?"

"Yes. He has spies around this world. None here—this place and the land around it are my sanctuary, and no one can find me here. But all the same, he will know that we have been in contact. He's already sent me a message asking if I know where you might be, testing me. It will take him a while to figure out how much we've communicated, but eventually he'll know that our alliance means you are aware of the truth, and that he has lost you."

He sighed. "Fallon, my guess is that he will want to destroy you out of fear. Your existence will suddenly be a threat to him, and he does not do well with threats. He will wage a war against you." Jacob's voice was grave and troubled. He closed his eyes, pressing his face against her hair, breathing her in. "I am so sorry. I feared that when I returned to you, it would spark a chain of events. But I could no longer stay away."

She reached up to place a gentle hand against his face. "Never apologize for returning to me. Ever." She looked back at him. "You are the greatest gift, Jacob. No matter what fires it sparks."

His eyes shone as he gazed at her. "I have never been seen as a gift before," he murmured, voice husky. "A weapon, a threat, a monster—yes. But never a gift."

She caught a thread that passed through her mind, a stray thought, a realization, and she sat up with a frown. "You have viewed yourself as a monster." His gaze dropped, and she shook her head. "No, Jacob. You are not."

"Fallon, you don't know what I do. What I've done."

She leaned her forehead against his. "But I can see who you are." Her voice dropped to barely a breath. "And you are not a monster."

Closing his eyes as he leaned into her, he wished he could say she was right.

She held him close for a long while, till the candles on the table burned down into pools of wax, and the only light in the cottage came from the fireplace. When she finally spoke, her voice cracked.

"You said a war. I'm not powerful enough to face someone like Kian."

He sat up straighter. "Powerful enough? Yes, you are, Fallon. But you are not yet confident enough, as you have no idea of your true capabilities. I will get you there. He won't act yet; he will take his time as he always does, and so we have time of our own." He pushed her hair back, kissing her throat. "It is time for you to realize the power that has been simmering beneath the surface for all your life. He will be the biggest danger you have ever faced. And I will do everything possible to ensure you are prepared for it."

Fallon took a deep breath, turning everything over in her head and her heart. "I have to go back to them for a while.

Katrine is still an issue; I promised Paul I would help figure out what's going on. And Bergen is about to be dragged into utter hell."

"I know." He hugged her against himself. "Go back, and do what you can. Then I will come for you again, and you must stay with me a few weeks. You will be invincible when I am done with you."

She narrowed her eyes at him. "Your expectations concern me."

He gave her a heartbreaking smile. "I aim high because I do not want him to kill you. It would destroy me."

She twisted towards him, touching her thumb to his lower lip. "So, it's all about you, is it?"

His eyes turned molten at her touch, and he kissed her till they were both breathless. "Of course, it is all about me, Fallon," he remarked with a smirk. "As it always is." He moved his chair back, letting her feet touch the floor. "Come. Focus. I must fix the tattoo on your neck before you go back."

"Fix?" She got up and followed him doubtfully into a back room she hadn't noticed before. Fallon was now certain that the cottage was much bigger inside that the outside led one to believe.

As Jacob turned on a lamp, Fallon was delighted to find that the room was a cozy study. Two walls were entirely filled with floor-to-ceiling bookshelves, overflowing with books. The wood floor was covered in elaborately-patterned rugs in rich jewel tones. Lamps with amber shades lit each corner, and a dark, wooden rolltop desk sat against the farthest wall. There were two comfortable-looking, deeply-cushioned, velvet chairs positioned near each bookshelf. A small wood-burning stove warmed the space.

Fallon's knees were literally weak with joy, and she realized Jacob had paused to observe her with a soft smile.

"You knew this would be my favorite room."

He nodded. "I knew."

"How have I not seen it yet? Has it been…hiding?"

Holding back a grin, he indicated a small table in the corner. "Perhaps. Sit there, rest your forehead on the table."

"What does it do? The star tattoo?" Sitting down in a chair, she accepted the small towel he handed her for cushioning her head.

He was digging around in a metal case he'd retrieved from a drawer of the rolltop. "They attempted to mark you with a tracking tattoo, not unlike a GPS tracker. But as I have always said, their tattoo artist does shabby work. The protective ring on your finger has dulled their new tattoo to the point of uselessness, but I would still like to rid you of it."

"My ring from you?"

"Protects you. Obviously. What have I ever done that was not about protecting you?" he asked lightly, turning on two more bright lamps and aiming them at her.

She cast her gaze up at him. "I can think of a few things you've done recently that had nothing at all to do with protecting me."

His entire face lit up with a smile, and she laughed, resting her head back on the table.

"You're not supposed to get labradorite wet," she mentioned, "but I've been showering and swimming with this ring since I was twelve. Because I didn't know. But it doesn't seem to have suffered any ill effects from my misuse."

"Ah, it wouldn't. It is special, as I told you. Nothing can damage it."

She rolled her eyes. "Of course nothing can."

"Nor can it be removed by anyone against your will, or your father would have taken it from you long ago."

When his task was completed, the star on the back of her neck was gone, only a red mark remaining.

"How did you manage that?" she asked, looking in the mirrors he held up.

"I have the necessary tools. To undo poorly-wrought magic."

She looked like she was thinking of something, an idea, but when he cocked his head at her in question, she shook her head.

That night was to be their last together before she returned to the tour, and neither of them slept. By mutual agreement, they had decided she must go back the following day. If she stayed with him any longer, they were both aware she might never return to her old life at all.

They lay on his bed facing each other in the lights of the fire and the moon. Over the past days, Fallon had gained no more knowledge about what being the Ravener actually entailed. But she had seen all of the scars on his chest and discovered more on his back. She had caught the haunted look in his eyes when he wasn't looking at her. When he was deep in thought, when he wasn't smiling at her, he looked tired. Whatever it was that had come to him and made him the Ravener, she felt it was something no one would ask for. She could sense that much, as he continued to let down his guard around her. He might speak lightly of it to her, but she knew it was actually a heavy thing. A torment. And the truth of that broke her heart.

Fallon sighed deeply now. "Part of me wants to stay here, in this bed with you, for the rest of my life."

He squeezed her ankle. "Most of me agrees that would be a stellar idea."

Her gaze fell upon the tarnished locket at his wrist. He never took it off. In her entire life, she had never seen him without the double chain. She reached for it now, fingertips hovering just before touching it, engaging her psychometry skills to read its intentions and history. Her mind came up against a wall of cold, dark metal, and she flinched.

She looked at Jacob, but he was quietly watching her, his head resting on a pillow, unconcerned by her interest. Sitting cross-legged next to him and inhaling deeply, she clasped the locket with her thumb and index finger. It was smooth and cool to her touch, and tiny sparks of energy pricked at her thumb, but she could see nothing about it.

"Jacob, what is this?"

His gaze flicked down to the locket and then back to her face. "Something of mine that I've always had. Something from before."

"Before you became the Ravener."

He closed his eyes briefly. "Yes."

She tried to open it, but it remained firmly closed no matter what she tried. "It won't open."

He glanced at it again. "Not today, no."

"Is there a photo in it?"

Staring deeply into her eyes, he nodded. "There are two."

And she saw so much sadness there in his blue eyes that she let go of the locket and again took his face in her hands, leaning down and kissing him deeply. "You've carried so much weight for so long," she whispered. "Your soul has been in chains, in shackles. I can see it. I want to free you from it all."

He slid his arms around her and pulled her down against himself. "Little by little, you chip away at all the darkness that has been around me. When I hold you, when I kiss you, I'm so free, my heavy heart feels light. It's a sensation that has been gone from me for so long, I can scarcely remember it. But I would never give any of this burden to you."

She kissed him again, nipping at his bottom lip and eliciting a groan from him. "You know I'm stronger than I look. I will help you carry it."

He rolled over on top of her. "Fallon," he kissed her, "I don't deserve you."

She snaked her fingers into his hair. "Maybe you do."

After a moment he paused, looking her over with a smile. "You, my love, are a journey I never want to return from."

CHAPTER SIXTEEN

As expected, her return to Bret was awkward and not without pain. She had been gone nearly five days, unreachable, her fate unknown, and his imagination had been hard on him.

Jacob determined what hotel the bands were staying at in Munich, Germany. He took Fallon there in the night while everyone was away at the concert, kissing her a long goodbye in an empty hallway and then leaving her abruptly—she didn't think she would ever get used to the teleportation.

When Jacob was gone, she immediately reached out to find Bret with her mind. She located him at the local music hall, hanging out backstage with several people, his band having already performed for the evening. She closed her eyes and breathed in and out a few times to steady herself.

Hello, you. I'm at the hotel; I'll see you when you get back here.

She sensed his immediate joy at hearing her voice, followed quickly by the pain of his helplessness in the situation, his doubt and soaring jealousy.

Are you back for good? he asked.

No. For a while. I'll be going back soon, for longer. I'll explain as much as I can tonight. If you want. Is Bergen alright?

Seems to be. No change. Let me grab a taxi and go back to the hotel.

I'll be here.

Fallon sat nervously in the small hotel lobby, suitcase, backpack, and messenger bag at her feet, contemplating the current state of her life, the new and perilous twists: Kian, Luca, Bret, and overwhelmingly Jacob—everything connected and changed with every new revelation.

Sighing at the degree of melodrama, she rested her forehead in her hands, blinking back tears. Life was such an unpredictable trickster. She didn't want to cause pain to anyone—she had always endeavored to do no harm as she navigated through her strange existence. But she knew that she was about to hurt Bret terribly. Had already hurt him. Their relationship had been hanging on by the tiniest of threads even before Jacob's return, and she recognized with clearer eyes that she'd truly been sticking around because of Bergen. She had never allowed herself the luxury of imagining that Jacob would ever truly come back to her, or that when he did, he would consume her, body and soul.

"Fallon!"

She looked up as Seth and Bret entered the lobby, forcing a smile and going into the latter's open arms when he held them out to her. He hugged her close for a while, and she rested her head on his shoulder. She was filled with absolute dread at the night that lay before them.

"Tayce didn't join you?" she teased, trying to lighten the mood, knowing their happy friend would be overjoyed at her return.

He made a face as they headed towards the elevators together with her bags, leaving Seth behind in the lobby. "He would have, of course, but I neglected to tell him you were back."

"That's almost mean. I'm sure he's been nervous without me around to read his fortune and such."

"A complete wreck, yes. But his relief will have to wait till morning."

"Actually, I texted him once I knew you were already safely in a cab. I convinced him to stay and perform with his band, though."

In Bret's room they encountered an immediate obstacle. "Come on," he was sliding his shirt over his head, "let's go shower and then we can talk."

But she hesitated, before sinking down into a chair. She understood he was testing her. And she had failed the test. Her eyes were seas of misery.

As he stood and stared at her, Bret knew Jack had been right. It was brutally obvious. She was no longer his. The pain sliced through him unmercifully as hot tears blurred his vision, but he blinked them back. Even though he'd more or less expected this, it still stung.

"I'd like to tell you everything I learned," she offered, her voice barely above a whisper. "If you want to hear it. If you don't, though, I understand."

Tossing his shirt aside, he helped himself to a beer from the mini fridge, steeling himself. "Sure." He sat down on the bed, kicking off his boots and leaning back against the headboard. "Go ahead."

She began speaking in the guarded privacy of their minds, but he stopped her, shaking his head.

"No. Don't. Tell me out loud."

Understandable. Speaking in their minds was too intimate. She told him everything she'd learned about her father, including the deaths and the reason he'd ordered Jacob away from her. Kian's fear of her powers and what would happen once he found out she would never align herself with him. She told him about the tattoo on her neck, why Jacob had removed it, and what the tattoos on her wrists meant. And who had done them.

When Bret heard her speaking about how Jacob had fought to be the one to tattoo her wrists, how he had carefully added all the elements he felt necessary to protect her and stayed at her side for the entire time she was stolen at twenty, Bret knew that Fallon had never truly been his. She had been Jacob's all along. Even if she hadn't realized it at the time. This knowledge did nothing, however, to lessen the pain in his heart.

Despite her betrayal and the reality that he had lost her, he did still love her, and he recognized with wisdom that his daughter loved her even more. He was, frankly, horrified by the dark turn of her tale, which was nothing he had expected.

"So now this ultra-powerful madman is going to try to hunt you down and kill you?" he summarized in slight disbelief.

"Yes, apparently. Eventually. Not quite yet." She hugged a knee to her chest.

"For many reasons, I wish Jacob had never come back into your life."

"It's not his fault," she protested.

"Tell me how it isn't!" he growled, finishing his beer and fetching another.

She sat back in the chair with a sigh. "I'd already more or less declared war on my father while you were missing with Jack. When I was taken by him, while you were gone, I realized how much of a power play was going on, how much this man thought he was in complete control of me. Not only did this affect me, but my loved ones as well—he could have kept me away long enough to let you die in the storm cellar; he had the power to do so. Your death would have affected many more people than just me.

"I came back furious. I didn't want anyone to have that kind of power over me and the people I love. But I had no idea what to do. I wanted information on how to block my father from stealing me again, and there was no one in my life to ask. The only person I imagined who could help me was Jacob, so that's when, out of pure desperation, I tried calling to him with the raven tattoo. I'd never tried such a thing before. I didn't know if it would even work or if he, wherever he was, would help me. He'd been gone for fifteen years. I didn't know what to expect." She plucked at a loose thread in the chair cushion. "Obviously, there was much more going on than I could have realized, and when Jacob saw that I was showing signs of being defensive towards my father, he knew he had to act, that I needed information and training. If I faced my father tonight, he would likely win. We want *me* to win, right?" She looked at him from across the room.

He nodded. "Of course. I would never wish for you to lose a battle like that. It all seems so unbelievable."

"As usual."

A ghost of a smile touched his lips, but only briefly. "Yes, as usual." He looked away. "It was hard for me to watch him take you away, that night in the pub. And then to hear nothing from you for days. Not knowing if you were alive or dead. And now, I realize, that everything has changed, and I never saw that coming. Or maybe I always did, and I was just fooling myself. Afraid of the truth." His face showed his anger and hurt; he was unable to look in her direction. "I know things have been difficult with us for months now. But I still never imagined this. Though in some ways I feel like I lost you last summer. Like I lost you the first time I heard you say Jacob's name."

Fallon looked down at her hands, tears sliding down her cheeks. "I'm so sorry. A part of me will always consider you family. But the simplicity of that is gone now."

There was nothing left to say. Fallon knew that they could obviously no longer share a hotel room, but she hadn't been think-ing that far ahead. And so, at two o'clock in the morning, she was knocking on Tayce's door, crossing her fingers that he was alone.

The guitarist swung the door open, shirtless in dark shorts, long hair loose. He observed her—backpack and messenger bag slung over one shoulder, suitcase at her feet. Eyes red. "Hey, sorceress." He gave her a gentle smile.

"Hey, trouble," she greeted him, her voice hoarse with weariness and restrained tears. "Does your room have two beds?"

He stepped back and held out his arm, welcoming her in. "Yes, but even if it didn't, I'd scoot over for you," he vowed, and she smiled as she went by.

"Always so selfless," she murmured. "Hey, can we talk in the morning?"

"Sure, hon." He locked the door, returning to his own bed while she set her things down and opened her suitcase.

Half an hour later, the room was dark, and they lay in separate beds, both unable to sleep. Yellow light from the street filtered in through rough, green curtains.

Tayce was relieved she was back—felt selfishly happy even, that she was here in his room after her mysterious adventure. When she'd needed a place to go, she had turned to him. He had a mountain of questions regarding everything that was going on, but he knew she and Bret must have just ended things and that she needed, more than anything, some peace.

"Can I ask you one thing?" he ventured.

She glanced at him in the dimness and nodded.

"Are you going to be alright?"

She smiled, and he saw true happiness in her face. It brought a smile to his own.

"Yes," she said simply.

Still smiling, he turned over and went to sleep.

The next morning Fallon was showered and dressed before Tayce was even awake. She sat on her bed texting back and forth with Bergen and Selah while he jumped in the shower.

Bergen had been hurt that Fallon had seemingly ghosted her for five days; her father had not been forthcoming with an explanation. Fallon told her there were things going on that she would explain when they were face-to-face, not before, but that she loved her always.

Selah had also not known that Fallon had been whisked away by Jacob, and she very nearly pressed the icon on her phone for a video call, but stopped herself. Processing everything in her brain as rapidly as she could, Selah knew that Fallon was likely still reeling from everything that had transpired, from what she'd learned and—Selah assumed—from the inevitable showdown with Bret. It was difficult, but she would allow Fallon space before she demanded too many details.

But she would ask for a few.

"How is Bret?" she texted.

"Wounded and angry," Fallon answered back.

Selah nodded to herself. "How is Jacob?"

Fallon smiled at her phone. "He is heaven."

Selah pinched the bridge of her nose and again willed herself to not force the video call. "How are you?"

Fallon hesitated. "I don't know how to answer that. See previous response?"

Selah smiled. "Take care, love. We must talk soon. Oh," her fingers kept typing, "Marianna said Azul is missing." The black dog often went missing when Fallon was out of town; it had never been a problem. Somehow the dog always found his way to his mistress. No one questioned it. Not officially, at least.

"He's safe. He's with Jacob, they don't need to worry. Get some sleep, I know it's late for you."

By the time Fallon finished with Bergen and Selah, Tayce was out of the shower and dressed, and they were soon walking arm-in-arm down a sidewalk to a small café, which Fallon had located in a quick online search. The weather was delightful, the morning sun shining in a clear blue sky. The buses were leaving at noon for Austria, and so they had a few hours available for breakfast. They had not seen Bret anywhere at the hotel, and Tayce had wisely not mentioned him.

"You're lucky I wasn't entertaining groupies last night," he told her with a raised eyebrow.

Fallon laughed. "The thought did occur to me. My next option was knocking on Jack's door."

He looked at her in horror.

"Just kidding. I'd have slept in the lobby."

He chuckled. "Clearly safer in the lobby."

In the crowded café, they managed to find a small table where they sat together and ordered coffee and croissants. Tayce was wide-eyed as he folded his arms on the table.

"I'm so glad you're back, Fallon. Truly. I can't believe teleportation is real and that you apparently survived it. I wish you could have seen Jack's face when you guys vanished. It was classic! His chair went flying! I doubt he's ever been so shocked in his life."

"You, on the other hand, were all cool and calm about it, huh?" she teased.

He hung his head guiltily. "I was a mess. I didn't know what to think. And I did feel that Jacob looked dangerous there at the end and that he had possibly taken you somewhere to kill you. I mean, you were obviously really happy to see him when he showed up. Suspiciously happy, if I'm being honest. But by the time you guys left, you were so upset by whatever happened when you touched his tattoo. And he grabbed you with this seriously intense look on his face, and then you were both gone—I guess I thought I'd never see you again. For all I knew, you'd been stolen away by the devil himself."

She smiled, touched by his honesty and by the obvious emotion in his voice. She watched as the waitress set their orders in front of them. "He is not the devil, I'm back, and all is well."

Tayce stirred his coffee thoughtfully. "You know, you don't lie as well as you used to."

Smile fading, she looked away. "Lies are easier when the heart is not involved."

"Speaking of that, Bret was a hellish mess while you were gone," he commented, taking a sip. "Everyone learned to stay out of his way. And no one knew where you'd gone to, which was mysterious and didn't help the overall situation."

"Ah, you're right. Me vanishing for several days with no explanation, I'm sure only fueled the gossip fires, which probably didn't help his overall mood. I wasn't even thinking—you guys left London without me. And my luggage was also gone. Brilliant." She shook her head. "Bret had every right to be a hellish mess. Everything has changed. Everything."

He took this in, nodding. "Mmm. You're still my homegirl, though, right?"

She smiled into her coffee. "Till the end, my friend. Ride or die." She felt a brief chill creep across her heart, similar to the sensation she'd experienced at Bret's on New Year's Eve. But Tayce's laughter, his hand patting her thigh, brought her out of it.

"So, what are you going to do?" he asked. "What happens next? I don't want you to leave the tour, but Bret is going to have a hard time if you stick around. He was pretty distressed while you were gone, as I said. Jack kept saying helpful stuff to him like, 'time to move on, bro' and 'not your girl anymore.' Turns out Jack knew what he was talking about, I guess."

She sighed and tore off a piece of croissant. "Clearly the end is near, when Jack Lane starts prophesying." She added milk to her coffee, chewing thoughtfully. "I think I would leave immediately, but Bergen is coming in a few days for spring break. She's staying with the tour for ten days. Part of the reason she's coming is to see me. If I'm gone, Lisbeth will hold things up trying to secure a nanny last minute, wrecking Bret's whole week."

"Ah, I see. Yeah, you need to stick around for the girl. Roomies!"

She smiled slightly. "Yes, if you're okay with that. Not every hotel is going to have two beds."

He placed a hand solemnly over his heart. "It's a sacrifice I'm willing to make, Fallon." She laughed, and he grinned. "I can't wait to stay up late with the flashlight telling ghost stories," he enthused.

"I've got some ghost stories," Fallon murmured, sipping her coffee. She smelled cigarettes and leather just before Jack Lane dropped into the seat beside her.

The accommodations in the café were so tight that his thigh was pressed completely against hers. "This is cozy! Have you already moved on from Bret to this guy?"

Fallon and Tayce both stared at him with no reaction.

Jack held up his hands in surrender. "Too soon?"

Focusing on her coffee, Fallon shifted her chair closer to Tayce.

"Glad to see you made it back, wicked one," Jack acknowledged. "It was wild seeing you and that cat disappear from the pub." He accepted a cup of coffee from the waitress, thanking her and saying a few phrases to her in German.

Fallon was eyeing him. "His name is Jacob."

"Jacob, that's right." Jack drank some of his coffee and then set it carefully on the table. "Where did you guys go?"

Tayce glanced at Fallon, wondering what she would say.

"To where he lives," she answered. "Far and away."

Jack grinned. "Always the secrets, this girl." He looked between her and Tayce. "Five days is a long time, when you think about it. What did you and this Jacob guy do?"

Fallon rested her elbows on the table. "Jack. You're pushing the limits of my niceness."

He smiled like a satisfied cat as he drank his coffee. "Just checking in with you, darling. You know how much I care."

No one made a big deal about Tayce and Fallon's new roommate situation, though Jack did continue to make comments here and there, for the sport of it. It was clear to most of their comrades that there was nothing going on between them beyond platonic friendship. In private, a few people teased Tayce, but he shrugged them off.

Several people were shocked at the seemingly abrupt end to what they had viewed as a solid relationship between Bret and Fallon, though others pointed out that they'd been sensing tension between them for the entire tour, and soon the general consensus was that the relationship had been in trouble for a while.

No one said a word about any of it to Bret, whose mood was fairly cold when he wasn't on stage. Having Fallon still around on the tour was more difficult than he'd anticipated, but he needed her there for Bergen. She did her best to stay out of his way, which he recognized and appreciated. And as they traveled from city to city, Fallon noticed that he was never lacking for female companionship, as he was no longer constrained by the need to remain faithful to anyone.

Not only were she and Tayce sharing a hotel room, but Fallon was also now riding on Dangerous Eye's bus. Everything had shifted, and she often found herself at Tayce's side throughout the day at venues and such, when she normally might have been hanging out with Bret.

During the times when they were all alone, Tayce began asking questions, mostly about her childhood. He wanted to know details about Luca, Selah, and Jacob. He wanted her history. All the things he hadn't really focused on or thought much about until Jacob Roth materialized in a London pub and quite literally spirited her away. He was curious about what else she could do besides heal. And how and why she had these gifts.

Fallon knew she could trust Tayce. She regaled him with stories about her brother. She told him all about Jacob, including the secret training and the eventual abandonment. About Selah's constant presence throughout her life. She shared with him what she'd learned about Jacob being in her life since she was born, in one way or another. And about Kian—what he had done and what he could do. She described the cottage to him, Colette, the mountains, and the river, and to Tayce it sounded like she was weaving a fairytale, especially when she added in details about Jacob and his love for her, his tenderness.

By the time the day arrived when Bergen was to join the tour, Tayce felt he had received quite the education regarding Fallon's life, though it only left him more troubled. He loved Fallon and felt a deep connection with her, more so than with most, and therefore he wanted her world to be secure and filled with joy. While the things she shared helped him know her better and deepened his affection for her, they also frightened him. Whenever his daughters brought their troubles to him, he always wanted to help. Fallon's troubles, however, he felt entirely unequipped to assist with.

"Did you know there are two songs I wrote about my daughters?" he asked her one day. They were sitting in their hotel room, waiting to be called to head to the next venue. He was on the bed with an acoustic guitar.

Fallon shook her head, watching him from where she sat curled up in an upholstered red chair. "I didn't even know you sang lead or that you'd released solo albums till last December. I feel like I failed as a best friend."

He smiled, strumming the guitar. "Not a big deal. They weren't exactly commercial successes."

"Not that you intended them to be."

He raised an eyebrow. "You're right. I put them out because I could. Because I had a good time writing and recording them."

"Anyway." She sat up straighter. "Your daughters."

His left hand moved with skill as he elicited the most beautiful tune from the instrument. "Yes. For Jane, I wrote a song called 'My Sweet Jane.' And for Annie, I wrote 'Electric Annie.' Which is a play on another song title."

"'Dreamboat Annie.'"

"Yes," he confirmed. "But 'electric' because she's…"

"Lively."

He chuckled. "Exactly. Since birth." His expression became unreadable. "I tell you this because over the last few weeks, I wrote a song about you."

Her eyes widened. "You did? What's it called?"

"'Fleeting.'" His fingers continued to work their magic as the song he was playing wove its way through her soul.

Fallon met his gaze when he glanced back up. "Is this it?" Tears pricked at her eyes, as she already knew the answer. He was nodding, closing his eyes as he continued to play. "My sweet boy," she whispered, knowing he probably didn't hear her. She tilted her head. "One day, will you sing it for me?" Both of their phones were flashing, indicating that their ride was there.

He winked at her. "One day."

CHAPTER SEVENTEEN

S eth accompanied Fallon to the airport in Poland to pick up Bergen. After some identity confirmation with a member of the flight crew, the girl ran happily into Fallon's arms while Seth took charge of her carry-on luggage.

"Hi, Seth! Oh, I've missed you so much, Fallon!"

"Same, my beautiful Bee. How was the flight?"

"So long, but the lady watching me was really nice. Where's Dad?"

"Soundcheck. When we get out of here, we'll go straight there. Let me text your mom that you made it."

At the music hall, Bergen left Fallon's side to race across the auditorium and leap into Bret's arms. He crushed her tightly against himself, a wide smile lighting up his face.

Fallon hung back, looking around for Tayce. She could sense that he was nearby, but there were so many people running around, she couldn't quite place him. She was positive Bret had, as yet, said nothing to Bergen about their changed relationship, and she was tense in anticipation of how that would go. The girl was going to be less than forgiving. Slinking back into the shadows, she waited till Bret and Bergen had gone back towards the stage, and then she left the auditorium.

Back at the hotel in their room, Bergen took a quick shower and changed into the clothes she would wear to the concert.

"Make sure your bags are packed up," Bret directed. "Tonight, right after the show we're getting directly on the buses and driving all night to Hungary. So all of our things will already be on the buses after the concert."

"Okay." She looked around as she bent down to tie her red sneakers. "Where's Fallon? And where's all her stuff?" She'd been so rushed to get in the shower, she hadn't noticed the lack of luggage in the room.

Bret shifted uncomfortably and looked at his phone. "Umm, we're not in the same room anymore."

She straightened up and turned to him, momentarily speechless. "Well, what room is she in?" She felt breathless, her chest heavy and tight.

"She's been staying with Tayce." He wouldn't meet her eyes.

Bergen was frowning. "But why is she with Tayce? You guys always share a room."

Getting to his feet, Bret grabbed a water bottle. "Not anymore," he said briskly. "Come on, we'll go find her. I have to leave to get back to the venue; you can stay with her."

Suspicious, she shoved her phone in her back pocket and followed him out the door and into the hall. She noticed he was texting and walking slowly; she stole a quick glance at the screen. "You don't even know what room she's in?" Bergen felt her heart flutter in panic. "Dad, what's going on? You have to tell me!"

"We're just, we're taking a break, it's fine."

"Fallon!" Bergen ran to her as Fallon stuck her head out a door.

Bret looked at Fallon. "I can make sure her luggage gets on the bus with mine. Can you keep her from now till the show?"

Fallon nodded. "Of course."

He kissed Bergen's cheek. "I'll see you later tonight."

As Bret walked away with Seth, Fallon looked at the time. "Your dad's band plays first tonight. Dangerous Eye is last, so Tayce is taking a quick nap. Let's go down to the lobby for a bit. Are you hungry?"

"Starving." Bergen yawned as Fallon put an arm around her shoulders, and they headed for the elevator.

"Let's see what we can find for you downstairs."

Bergen didn't mention the separate rooms or the clear lack of affection between Fallon and Bret. She kept it to herself. She hoped she was wrong. Coming in the midst of the turmoil she was already facing with her parents, her first instinct was to panic.

Fallon easily noticed. "My sweet honeybee. What troubles you?" Though, of course, she already knew.

"You and Dad, are you not together anymore? You don't stay in his room? Why are you with Tayce? What's going on? He said you guys were taking a break."

Fallon squeezed her close, silently cursing Bret. "We are not taking a break. We're no longer together." She saw tears forming immediately in the girl's gray eyes, and so she stopped, putting her hands on Bergen's shoulders. "Relationships change all the time, Bergen, that's the way the world works sometimes. But my love for you does not change. My promise to be there for you when you need me, that does not change. Okay? It doesn't matter what's going on between me and your dad. I won't stop loving you. I will always be somewhere in your life."

"I thought you would be with him from now on." Bergen's lower lip was trembling; she was biting it to try and make it stop. "I thought, I don't know, that maybe one day you'd marry him and be my second mom." Her eyes were more and more watery with tears. "What happened? Are you with Tayce now?"

Fallon looked away, annoyed with Bret for not handling this ahead of time. As the parent in the situation.

"I am not with Tayce, sweetheart. He's one of my best friends. There is nothing going on between us. The thing with me and your dad, it's difficult to explain." She glanced at the raven tattoo and wondered how to say the truth without Bergen hating her.

They were soon seated in the hotel restaurant, and Fallon ordered the girl a sandwich and some soup.

Bergen had noticed her attention to the raven tattoo. "It's something with that. Isn't it?"

Fallon looked up in surprise. "Yes."

"Is it also something to do with the five days you didn't have your phone?"

Taking a sip of water, Fallon nodded.

The girl stared at her. "Tell me. The truth. You told me you'd tell me when we were together in person. What is going on?"

Thinking for a minute, Fallon finally told Bergen an abbreviated tale about Jacob. Bergen listened intently. When Fallon was done, Bergen was stirring her spoon slowly in her soup.

"So, the truth is, you fell in love with someone else."

189

Fallon rested her chin against her clasped hands, her jaw tight. On her wrist the raven fluttered soothingly. "It has more layers than that. Many more. But, yes, I guess, that's the basic idea. I am wildly in love with Jacob. There is no one I love like I love him." The raven tattoo grew briefly warm at her words, and she almost smiled, but the stoic expression on Bergen's face stopped her.

The girl lay down her spoon. "I'm not hungry after all, I guess."

Fallon sighed.

Bergen's sadness at the ending of her father's relationship with Fallon was stark and palpable. When Bergen fell for Fallon the previous May, she'd fallen hard and completely, beyond reason. Never before had she become so attached to someone her father was dating, and because Bret had initially been so blinded by Fallon, he had not been at all alarmed by how intensely his daughter loved his girlfriend.

Fallon guessed that the only reason Bergen had been so graceful regarding her mother's marriage to Leo last June, was because she'd been holding onto an idealized dream in her heart of a future where her dad married Fallon. Even though at the time of that wedding, Bret and Fallon had barely been together two months. Bergen's imagination had taken some enormous leaps, and no one had bothered to temper her expectations.

Seeing that brilliantly-imagined future so totally erased and understanding that there would be no reconciliation was difficult for the girl to make peace with. All of the adults in her life, as far as she was concerned, had gravely failed her. She put on a smiling face, but Fallon and Bret could sense her deep disappointment.

"What did you tell her?" Bret asked.

Fallon rubbed her forehead. "The truth."

He stared at her. Waiting.

She shrugged. "What do you want me to say? I told her the truth. That you and I are no longer together and will not be reconciling. Since you obviously didn't have the courage to tell her yourself, I did, and you don't get to control the narrative. I don't lie to that girl."

He briefly narrowed his eyes at her sass. "Did you tell her about Jacob?"

"Yes, of course, I did, and fear not, she hates him with every ounce of her being. Only because she can't bring herself to hate me."

He crossed his arms over his chest. "She's not being super nice to me, either. She told me that Lisbeth and I are screwing up her life, and I'm pretty sure she blames me for losing you. That's why I wanted to know what you told her."

"What I told her regarding us put the blame fully on me, but her ten-year-old mind is going to shift it how she sees it." Fallon sighed. "A lot of things are being thrown her way. She was having a hard enough time adjusting to living five minutes away from your house. London is pretty shattering."

"London is not really my fault." He kicked at a spot on the ground. "I think you're the only person she semi-likes, currently. Her mom is definitely at the top of her hit list. Top of mine as well. Though you're a close second, if I'm being honest."

Fallon glanced away, brushing off the jab. "Bergen needs time to process everything. All that she knew and was comforted by has been flipped and changed. It's a lot, but eventually it will work itself out."

"I guess." But he sounded doubtful. If he lost custody of his daughter, he didn't know how he would survive.

She looked him fully in the eyes. "Bret." She did not try to touch him, but her voice somehow reached into him, and he felt the ensuing sense of calm filling him. "I think eventually it will be okay. I'm not certain, but I feel like it will be. In time. Do not lose hope." Then she turned and was gone.

Down the hall, away from him, she performed a low-key mini celebration dance. She had calmed him without physical touch. Finally. It was possible. She had watched as the lines of worry eased in his face. Because she wasn't touching him, he hadn't thought to blame her. She would continue to work at refining it, for that particular ability was invaluable.

* * * * * * *

Bergen sat cross-legged on an amp case during soundcheck that afternoon, chin in her hands. Fallon, several feet behind her in the shadows, watched her. Despite the impossible disruptions going on in her life, Bergen was a patient, well-mannered child on tour. She was cognizant of being in her father's place of work and recognized that being a brat would endear her to no one, nor help him. She did not complain about logistics, didn't blink an eye when plans abruptly changed, when her father had to hand her off to Fallon's care because he was suddenly demanded elsewhere. She paid especially close attention to Bret and his band, studying the movements of everyone involved in their performance. She was monitoring. Reading everyone. She wanted everything in her father's world to be well.

Fallon recognized that Bergen had long ago put herself in charge of taking care of Bret. She loved her mother. But her father needed her. That was Bergen's view, and Fallon thought she was probably right. It was part of what was making the potential move to London so horrifying for the girl. Bergen honestly thought that Bret would not survive without her. Fallon felt she was mostly correct in her assumption.

Fallon's gaze traced Bergen's slim bare shoulders, her perennial summer tan, her shoulder blades like bony wings trapped beneath her golden skin. Sometimes she seemed so fragile, it made Fallon's heart ache.

CHAPTER EIGHTEEN

One afternoon in Amsterdam, while Bret's band was performing on a local radio program, Fallon and Tayce took Bergen out for a sunny afternoon of walking along the waterways and enjoying some touristy moments. Away from the chaos of the tour and her stressed-out father, Bergen felt relaxed and at ease in the company of two people she was enormously fond of—who kept her laughing with their back-and-forth banter.

The trio discussed the pros and cons of living on a houseboat full-time. They contemplated renting bicycles; Bergen expressed serious doubt at Tayce's ability to ride a bike. Which he claimed hurt his feelings. Which in turn made Bergen giggle. And which Fallon was relieved to see.

Bergen made them pose for numerous selfies all afternoon, most of which she sent on to her dad, though Fallon privately doubted that Bret wanted his phone so deluged with her own image. Still, she was sure he was at least pleased that Bergen was smiling and enjoying herself.

Several times Tayce was stopped by fans wanting selfies and autographs, and he was friendly and kind to all of them.

"I forgot he used to be super famous or something," Bergen mentioned to Fallon as they stood to the side.

"Like your dad," Fallon reminded her. "And it's not used-to-be. He still is. Everyone who ever knew of him, still knows of him."

"True." Bergen looked thoughtful. "So weird when people know Dad. They're always nice. He doesn't let them take pictures with me, though, when they ask."

"He does try to protect you. There are plenty of photos of you online already. From when you were really little up to recently. It's difficult to avoid."

As the three of them were crossing over a pedestrian bridge, Jacob Roth suddenly appeared before them from out of nowhere, like a specter, grabbing Fallon up in his arms for a long, passionate kiss. Startled, Bergen and Tayce stared openly at the pure joy on both their faces as the kiss ended and they simply smiled at each other, faces alight.

Letting Fallon's feet again touch the ground, Jacob turned to shake hands with Tayce, greeting him like an old friend. Then he knelt down to be properly introduced to Bergen, who, despite her best defenses, her determination to hold him up as the enemy, couldn't help liking him. She was charmed by his smile, his kind eyes, and his earnest, attentive manner towards her. He did not seem at all like the villain she had created in her head.

"It's such a lovely day," Jacob explained, rising back up and addressing them all, but looking only at Fallon, "and I couldn't bear to let the opportunity to enjoy it with Fallon and two of her favorites pass me by."

"And so here you are," Fallon murmured, with crooked smile.

He smiled back at her, clasping both her hands. "Here I am," he echoed. For a moment, they were the only two people in the world.

Bergen and Tayce exchanged a look.

The foursome strolled on for a while, chatting and buying food. Fallon felt the entire situation to be somewhat surreal, and no one questioned where Jacob had materialized from, or how. He had an easy rapport with Tayce and Bergen, who were both pleased by his company. Though Fallon stopped Bergen from adding Jacob to her series of selfies.

"You being with us is the best surprise," Fallon told Jacob quietly at one point.

Jacob held her face in his hand, smiling. "They're your two favorites. I am enjoying myself." He kissed her cheek.

There was something electrically beautiful about Jacob and Fallon, walking hand-in-hand and smiling at each other; Tayce couldn't take his eyes off of them. Jacob was handsome in black pants and a dark, button-up shirt, all of his movements marked with poise and a rough grace. He truly seemed as if he had stepped out of another place and time. At his side, Fallon looked ethereally pretty in a swirly, daringly-see-through long black skirt and black tank top, her blond hair loose. Tayce had never seen two people look so much like they belonged together.

They'd stopped to get tea and coffee nearly an hour later when Jacob looked up alertly. Fallon paused in her conversation with Bergen, sensing the change in him. The blue, cloudless sky above darkened strangely with fast-moving clouds. The wind was changing, and shadows grew around them as if a storm approached—everyone on the street was looking around, puzzled by the abrupt change in the weather.

Jacob seized Bergen's hand, motioning to Fallon and Tayce. "Come. Now." His tone did not allow for argument or hesitation, and they followed him quickly into an alley, stepping into a shadowy doorway. "Take hold of Fallon's hand," he instructed Tayce. "We leave immediately."

Tayce and Bergen were mystified, but Fallon grabbed Tayce's hand and looked at him soberly. "Don't let go." Then she held out her other hand to Jacob, who gripped it tightly.

Immediately they were gone.

And standing on the same beautiful, cold mountaintop that Jacob had brought Fallon to a month ago.

Tayce looked around in wonder, stumbling a little and pulling his hair back into a low ponytail as the wind whipped it around. "No way." He knelt down and touched the grass and rocks around him, as if to check that they were real. "What world are we in?"

Jacob mildly rolled his eyes at him. "Spain."

"Oh." Tayce looked slightly disappointed as he stood back up.

"First teleportation experience: not as cool as previously hoped," Fallon teased, hugging herself against the cold, her attire proving no match for the chill mountain air.

But Tayce grinned at her. "Are you kidding? That was wild. *This* is wild." He gestured at everything, shrugging off his leather jacket and handing it to her.

Jacob had released Bergen immediately upon arrival, and she was spinning slowly in a circle, her gray eyes drinking in the beauty of the landscape around them. She seemed to have taken her first teleportation in stride.

"This is amazing," she whispered, continuing to turn, taking it all in.

"Did we really just teleport?" Tayce was pinching himself and looking at Fallon, who nodded as she gratefully slipped on his jacket.

"We did," she confirmed. "I told you he could. You saw it happen in London."

"I know, I know. I seem to have a hard time accepting some of the crazy magic stuff. And why are the four of us here, exactly?" He fell in step with her as she began walking along a path, upwards towards where he could see a small stone cottage behind a short fence. Bergen trailed close behind them, still gazing about curiously.

"Fallon and I needed to be quickly gone," Jacob answered him. "If I'd left the two of you behind," he shot a glance at Bergen, who was listening to him too intently, "I couldn't leave the two of you there. So here you are."

"Is he always this cryptic?" Tayce asked.

"He's usually pretty over the top, yes," Fallon confirmed, and Jacob smirked at her as he passed them on his way to the cottage. Bergen caught up to Fallon and took her hand.

A dog's excited barking made them all look up, and they watched as Azul came racing towards them from the area of the barn.

"Azul!" Bergen was thrilled. Letting go of Fallon, she ran to greet the dog, falling to her knees and accepting all the doggy kisses and wriggling.

"How is he here?" Tayce asked, confused.

Fallon was smiling at the girl and dog. "Little did I know, this was always his other home."

He glanced at her in question, but she shook her head and said no more, and he followed her into the comfort of the cottage.

* * * * * * *

Without elaborating, Jacob told Fallon and Tayce that in order to ensure their safety, he wanted to wait at least twenty-four hours before returning them to Amsterdam. The three of them were standing before the fireplace while Bergen explored the rest of the cottage. In the kitchen Azul was noisily drinking water.

Tayce looked at his phone. "I just have a show tomorrow night. Gotta be back for that. Otherwise, I definitely don't mind this unexpected stopover." He was grinning. Fallon thought he had possibly not stopped grinning since they'd arrived.

Jacob gave him a half smile. "I did not anticipate you being a problem."

"But Bret…"

Jacob looked to Fallon as she left her sentiment unfinished. "Yes, of course he is displeased by Bergen's disappearance, but I have sent Colette to speak with him. Her calm manner will soothe him. It will be alright."

She shook her head sadly. "It will never be alright with him anymore."

* * * * * * *

Alone in his hotel room, Bret stared at his phone, at the lack of a text from either Fallon or Bergen. The two girls and Tayce were an hour late in returning from their afternoon excursion. His daughter's constant stream of selfies had stopped two hours ago. The tracking app on Bergen's phone showed him nothing, as if his child had vanished into thin air.

Only he was aware of the trio's failure to appear. He kept his concerns to himself for now. Despite his anger and sadness regarding Fallon, he still trusted her completely with Bergen and knew that she would give her life before letting his daughter come to harm. Whenever Fallon was out somewhere with Bergen, she was always incredibly responsive to his texts. The lack of communication from her was worrying, as well as the complete absence of his daughter's phone on the tracking app—"Bergen cannot be located at this time," it reported to him helpfully. *That isn't alarming at all*, he thought.

He wanted to throw his phone at the wall. Instead, he texted all three of them again and then sat heavily on the edge of his hotel bed, telling himself not to panic. But deep down he knew that the only thing that would keep Fallon from responding to him was if something had happened. Something not necessarily good. He'd tried speaking to her through their shared telepathy, but had been met with silence.

Bret's attention was drawn to a tapping at his closed window. A pure white dove was resting on the sill, seemingly staring in at him. After a moment, it tapped its beak against the pane again, then looked at him expectantly, blinking.

He was reminded of Fallon's raven. *What is it with birds?* he thought with a sigh.

Clutching his phone in his left hand, he rose slowly, not looking away from the bird. He approached the window, unhooking the latch with care, marveling at the way the dove moved to the side to allow the window to swing open.

With a flutter of white, the dove entered his room, and then there was a flash of bright light, and a woman stood before him. Her face was kind, her hair in a long white braid. A necklace of smooth blue stones hung around her neck, the color matching the cerulean of her eyes. Her dress was modest and mostly white, her age indeterminate. He thought he caught the scent of cinnamon and sugar. He also had a flash of an idea that Bergen would love her.

"Bret, dear boy." Her warm tone filled him with comfort. "Bergen is safe. I have been sent to assure you she is secure and unharmed. There was a threat this afternoon while they were out walking. Jacob and Fallon could not guarantee Bergen and Tayce's safety, and so Jacob immediately swept them all away to his cottage in the mountains. All is well there."

"Swept them away..." Despite the calm she was filling him with, his heart was beating hard.

Colette nodded. "Teleported them away, to be accurate. Bergen was, as you might imagine, thrilled."

Bret had expected as much. Then he narrowed his eyes. "Who are you?"

Her smile deepened. "My apologies. My name is Colette. I am Jacob Roth's housekeeper-assistant. I take care of certain things for him. As the host, he did not want to abandon Bergen and Tayce so soon after arriving, but he and Fallon knew that you needed to quickly be informed. They sent me to speak with you, to assure you that your child is well. There is no way to communicate with them via technology where they are."

He clenched and unclenched a fist. Of course there wasn't. "Why didn't he bring Bergen back to me?"

Colette clasped her left wrist with her right hand. "The danger from this afternoon lingers for them, over this entire city; Jacob feared bringing them back too soon. Even bringing her to you would not be safe. Twenty-four hours must pass before he is comfortable returning them, and by then the danger will have subsided."

Bret inhaled and exhaled as deeply and slowly as he could. "And my daughter was in danger because…"

Colette looked away from him for the first time. "Because someone was attempting to destroy Fallon and Jacob. I can tell you no more than that."

The realness of her words momentarily pushed away the calm. He rubbed his hand over his face and felt himself panicking. "Bergen is alright?"

Sweet happiness shone again on Colette's face, and in turn warmth filled his chest and steadied his heart. "As I said, Bergen is thrilled with the teleportation experience and with her current location, I assure you. There are farm animals galore. The setting is lovely and wild. She is in her element. She remains very much under Fallon's care."

He slid his phone into his back pocket and crossed his arms over his chest. "Okay. I mean, I don't have much choice, right? Thank you for coming to tell me. She'll be back tomorrow?"

"Yes, Mr. Williams will need to be back in time for tomorrow night's show, so Bergen will be brought back with him."

"If her mother contacts me—she's unaware of Jacob's existence, let alone the whole teleportation thing."

"Lisbeth will not try to contact you or Bergen for the next forty-eight hours." She sounded serene and certain. "No worries there."

Bret nodded his understanding and sank into a chair, gazing out the window. A minute later the white dove soared out and disappeared into the evening sky.

He closed his eyes. His body ached with missing Fallon, and his anger was sparking because of the easy way Jacob had now taken away both of his girls. He knew he was being irrational; he understood that everything was being done to keep his child safe. But he was angry, all the same, that she had been in danger in the first place.

Getting his phone back out, he scrolled to Selah's number and pressed 'call.'

That evening in the cottage, Jacob cooked for them while Fallon entertained Tayce and Bergen with tales of her life in Austin. Bergen loved hearing about Luca and about Selah as a young girl.

Tayce was enthusiastic about the meal, and Fallon remarked that Selah had all but stopped eating at their house after Jacob left.

Jacob chuckled when he heard that. "I spoiled her, apparently," he observed.

"You spoiled us all," Fallon told him. "Luca and I suddenly had to learn to cook. It was a harsh awakening." She pursed her lips thoughtfully. "I excelled at it far more than he did. But we ate out a lot. It was Austin, after all."

After dinner, Jacob mysteriously located an acoustic guitar. They pushed the ottoman closer to the fire, where Tayce sat as he played and sang for them. He invited Fallon to sing along when Jacob reminisced about the songs she used to sing with her brother.

"You didn't tell me you could sing," Tayce accused her, after she aced the first song.

"You never asked," she countered.

Azul snoozed on the floor beside them as Fallon sat on the ottoman with Tayce, performing song after song. No matter what song he threw at her, she met the challenge. She hadn't sung since Luca was alive, but her face was flushed with happiness as she sang with Tayce. Jacob, sitting on the couch with Bergen, looked pleased with himself.

The musical duo finally ended their performance with a haunting version of "Moon River," at Fallon's request. As she sang the song directly to her guitar-playing friend, in an achingly pretty voice, her cheeks were streaked with tears. Soon everyone else, including Tayce, was in tears as well. Even Jacob was blinking rapidly.

When the song ended, Tayce reached across his guitar and gave her a long hug. Then he set the guitar aside, and they continued to sit together before the fire, talking quietly.

On the couch, Bergen and Jacob sat in silent companionship. Throughout the course of the evening, Jacob had utterly won her over. Bergen felt as if the entire day had been some sort of fever dream. Would unicorns suddenly appear out of the mist? Were dragons lurking outside the window? She wouldn't be surprised.

Jacob's shirt was completely unbuttoned and hanging open, revealing his toned chest and torso, and his sleeves were pushed up. Bergen was studying the various, unusual tattoos on his hands and forearms, as well as those on his chest, squinting at them in the firelight. She was caught off-guard when she saw the scars.

"What happened?" she asked, and he could tell from her tone what she meant.

"Life."

She accepted this, nodding sagely, though she was troubled. Her father didn't have many scars, just a few on his leg and arm from a long-ago dirt bike accident. Nothing like what she could see on Jacob's body.

"You must work out as much as my dad," she commented, acknowledging his physique as she changed the subject.

Jacob gazed at her. "Being strong is an asset."

"Fallon feels the same. About being strong." Bergen tilted her head. "You have more tattoos than my dad, though. Way more."

He looked back at the fire. "I have seen far more of life than he has."

Fallon glanced briefly back at them over her shoulder, then turned her attention back to Tayce.

"Do you know my dad?" Bergen asked.

Jacob draped his arms across the back of the couch and considered her question. "Not well."

She played with the bracelets on her wrists. "You look like you could be a rockstar."

He broke into laughter. "I can assure you, little one, that the only similarities between me and a rockstar would be the amount of traveling that I do."

Bergen looked over at Fallon and Tayce as they chatted before the fire. "Have you seen Fallon's tattoos?" she asked.

Jacob's stare was also drawn to the pair on the ottoman. "The ones on her wrists?" he asked casually.

Bergen nodded. "Yes, those."

There was a ghost of a smile on his face. "Yes. I have seen them. I'm the one who did them."

She looked at him with sharp surprise. "Does she know?" she demanded, in a hushed conspiratorial tone. She had always heard Fallon disavow knowledge of who had done her tattoos.

He was smiling fully now. "Yes, she knows. For a long time, she did not, but she does now."

Lines appeared on Bergen's forehead. "Last year, I dreamed she had a scorpion tattoo on her arm."

Jacob's face darkened. "We will avoid that. That particular vision of yours will not be coming true."

She pushed the blanket away and hugged her knees to her chest. "You know about all that?"

"About your premonitions? Of course. I know everything about Fallon, and therefore I know everything that she knows about you."

Bergen looked down at her toes, which were painted with a purple glitter polish. "I didn't tell Fallon, but it scares me. Being able to have visions."

He reached out and lightly touched her shoulder. "You are a brave little thing. And strong. Do not let it frighten you. Fallon will help you to understand it all." He took back his hand and stretched his arms over his head, stifling a yawn. "It is late," he announced. "I'm going out for a walk, and this girl needs to be in bed, I think."

Bergen wanted to protest, but she was undeniably tired, and so she allowed Fallon to lead her to the bathroom and show her the workings of the large, impressive shower. Fallon brought her fresh towels as well as a t-shirt, which she held up.

"You can sleep in this. The fire keeps the bedroom warm enough. Since you'll have to wear your same clothes tomorrow."

Yawning, Bergen agreed.

Thirty minutes later, Fallon tucked Bergen snugly into Jacob's bed. The girl, who was elated by everything about this unforeseen side trip, couldn't recall ever seeing such a cozy bedroom.

"I love this cottage," she sighed, as Fallon ran her fingers lightly down her arm. "It's like something from a dream. It's not even real."

"I love it, too," Fallon agreed.

"You'll be sleeping in here with me, right?"

Fallon kissed her forehead. "Of course. Jacob and I will be back in a little while. We're going for a walk. Tayce will be here while we're gone."

Bergen's eyes shone in the firelight. "You love him. And he loves you. He loves you so much. He can't take his eyes off of you."

Brushing a lock of hair off Bergen's cheek, Fallon smiled.

Tayce was sprawled on the couch staring at the fire when Fallon and Jacob escaped outside for a moment alone, and he smiled to himself.

They walked in the cold night with their arms around each other till they came to the precipice and sat down, a thick wool blanket wrapped around them as he held her close. He kissed her cheek, and she leaned back against him, looking out as the starry night spread out in front of them like a sparkling canvas.

"I used to wonder if you were looking at the stars at the same time I was," she admitted. "Especially when I was traveling. I thought, maybe the stars will tell him that I'm thinking of him. That I need him to come back to me."

He held her closer. "I thought of you when I looked at the stars, too, Fallon. Every night. Seeing them made me feel alone, yet reassured me that you were—usually—under the same sky."

"What was coming, earlier?" she asked. "And why?"

He buried his face against her neck, breathing her in, taking his time in answering. "Kian, while aware of our reunion and our renewed contact, was seemingly unaware of the exact nature of our current relationship." Jacob gazed up at the dark, gray clouds that sailed past the bright moon. "Remember I said that he has spies everywhere? They are not always watching you—for sure, at times they rarely do—but they did take notice of me kissing you passionately on a public street in Amsterdam. It was not something they could ignore.

"Judging by what Kian sent, I'd say he was furious and reacted with emotion, wanting to kill us both. The entity that he employed, I've seen in use before. You and I could have defeated it, but I couldn't guarantee Tayce and Bergen's safety, and I didn't have much time to prepare you. It was easier to just jump away with you all, safe and sound. Sometimes the entity hangs around, invisible but very present, in the area into which it was dispatched. That is why we are not yet returning. It angers me that Bergen was in danger, as she is only a child, but I should never be surprised at Kian's callousness. I've observed it for countless lifetimes."

"Will he try again?"

"Not in that way. It was an extremely reckless move on his part. A knee-jerk reaction if you will. Kian usually takes his time. Because he does not know you well, our feelings for each other will have caught him off guard. Despite our known bond, he'll have been blindsided by this turn of events. Regardless of his anger, however, he gets easily distracted by other things. We have time. He may now and then try to lash out at someone you love, out of spite. I have cast my net of protection over everyone I can think of. Years ago, this was an easier task, but lately your heart has spread itself around quite freely."

She bent her head. "I was meant to be alone."

"No, never." He turned her head, kissing her. "You were meant to be with me."

Her heart and soul swelled with love for him as she looked into his eyes. "What about you?"

He squinted questioningly.

"I mean, Kian—can he truly harm you?"

Jacob gazed up at the moon, set like a white jewel in the wide, starlit sky. He felt the cold wind against his cheek and felt also the unusual sensation of time moving forwards and backwards on some odd, chaotic track. Ever since Fallon had come back into his life, he had felt unbalanced and wonderfully strange.

"Do you know the song, 'Clair de Lune'?" he asked. "Or the poem that inspired it?"

She shook her head, puzzled. "I mean, I'm sure I've heard it. I know of it. Debussy, right? I doubt I'd recognize it, though. And as for the poem, I don't know. Why?"

"Sometimes it comes to me in memories. Sometimes it haunts my heart, and sometimes it brings me you." He returned his gaze to her. "He will not destroy me directly. He will try to destroy me by harming or killing you. It has been my fear for all your life, though it is a fear which has gripped me even more powerfully in the past nine years. It's a wonder I've gotten anything else at all accomplished in the past three decades, honestly."

He held her closer to him, his lips against her hair, and whispered in her ear, "*Votre ame est un paysage choisi, Que vont charmant masques et bergamasques…tristes sous leurs deguisements fantasques… Ils n'ont pas l'air de croire a leur Bonheur Et leur chanson se mele au clair de lune…*"[2]

> Your soul is a chosen landscape
> Where charming masquerades and dancers are promenading…
> Sad beneath their fantastic disguises…
> They seem not to believe in their own happiness
> And their song blends with the moonlight…

Listening to him recite fragments of the Verlaine poem to her in French brought tears to her eyes and fire to her skin. She kissed him fiercely, twisting around and pulling herself against him. They fell back in each other's arms, the warmth of the blanket surrounding them as they lost themselves in the night.

* * * * * * *

It was easy to wake up early in the cottage with the sun shining in the bedroom's large arched window. Bergen sat up in bed, feeling overwhelming happiness and peace of mind. She wished she could stay here forever with Fallon and Jacob, her memories of her parents blurring as the environment filled her blood and bones with the magic of the little Spanish refuge.

Beside her, Fallon was beginning to stir. Bergen thought that Jacob had slept in the study. Not a lot of room for guests, she'd noted.

She felt a deep pang of sadness for her father, whom she knew still missed Fallon, but without question she was aware that Fallon and Jacob belonged together. Seeing them in love made her heart sing. She understood now. She understood what Fallon had tried to explain to her—it was only ever Jacob.

There was the sound of knocking and a door opening, and then Fallon and Bergen heard a woman's voice from the front of the cottage.

"Good morning to you all! Bergen James, may I see you?"

"That's Colette," Fallon explained. "Go get dressed."

The child scurried away to the bathroom. When she re-emerged, Fallon and Jacob were both dressed and in the kitchen with Tayce, speaking to a woman whose long white hair hung in a thick braid down her back. The woman looked at Bergen with kind blue eyes, and as she came near and rested a hand on Bergen's shoulder, Bergen smelled cinnamon and sugar.

"Sweet child, I am Colette. It is my sincere pleasure to finally meet you. I've been told you are good with animals; is this true?"

Bergen lit up. "I love animals."

"Do you think you'd like to help me out this morning?"

Bergen, completely at ease in the mountain retreat, went out the door with barely a backwards glance at Fallon. Tayce trailed behind them, holding a cup of coffee.

When everyone was gone, Jacob pulled Fallon close and kissed her as she wrapped her arms around him. If he kissed her till the end of time, he thought, it would still never be enough.

"I'll need to return Tayce to Amsterdam in time for soundcheck," he told her. "But you and Bergen can stay another day if you want. Being here seems to agree with her. Though I realize that will complicate things with her father."

"It does agree with her. She's so relaxed. She's been tense and upset about everything that's going on. But, yes, Bret is going to hate me, more than he already does. Yet another thing he won't be able to forgive me for."

He ran a thumb gently over her cheek bone. "He's struggling to gain control of his emotions regarding you and me, which of course is understandable. And additionally, he's facing a nightmare he never envisioned: a custody battle with Lisbeth. He'll make peace with you sooner than he's going to make peace with her for forcing this on them. Losing you to me is painful. Losing Bergen would be…" he trailed off, unable to find adequate words.

Fallon looked sad. "I wish I could fix this for them. But I know I can't."

Jacob kissed her again—long, lingering kisses that made her feel as if she were flying. Kissing him was an intoxication she had never known. Everything about him was an exhilarating euphoria she never wanted to live without.

He told her he needed go away to deal with some Ravener things but would be back in time for lunch. After he vanished from the kitchen, Fallon ate a slice of toast spread with homemade jam while she sipped her coffee. Then she headed out to the precipice alone, glad that she'd left a pair of jeans behind the last time she'd been at the cottage. The long, see-through skirt was not practical for the mountains.

A few minutes later, Azul joined her, stretching out on his stomach in the grass nearby.

She was still on the precipice thirty minutes later, sitting cross-legged with her eyes closed, when Tayce came up the path. He had left Bergen happily eating breakfast in Colette's smaller cottage. Tayce looked out over the majestic beauty that surrounded them as he sat down beside her. Azul opened an eye to regard him, thumped his tail twice, then went back to sleep.

"You love it here," Tayce noted, seeing peace in Fallon's face.

"I have no worries here." Even her voice sounded calm and clear. "No concerns. Everything from the real-world fades away. It is intoxicating and dangerous."

"Everything fades, but him."

She lowered her eyes with a smile. "Yes, that's true." She looked back out at the view. "The wind never stops here. The river I told you about is much further down—the one Jacob took me to when I was here last time."

"Have you ever thought that, when we die, what if we could become some element of nature?"

"I would be water," she told him immediately.

"I figured as much." He looked around. "I think I would be the wind. It goes on forever. Powerful and gentle all at once." He looked at his phone. "I have no service here, you know."

She laughed. "No. Not here."

"I'm assuming Bret has somehow explained my absence to my band?"

"It's been taken care of," she assured him. "I don't think Bret was involved. But Jacob made sure that your guys know that you and I took a little side trip."

"Nothing strange about that at all," he quipped. "No awkward questions will arise, I'm sure."

"It's simpler than that. When you show up later today, they won't even remember that you were gone."

He stared at her silently for a minute. Then he looked back out at the view. "Explain why we have no service. Surely there are satellites, something? Doesn't Jacob ever need, you know, wi-fi?"

Fallon was pulling her hair back into a messy bun, tired of having the wind whip it in her face. "Jacob has so many means of communication that require no electricity or technology," she explained. "We're lucky he has solar up here for the hot water and other things. As for the lack of internet, I can't fully explain it to you. Let me just say that the security he has around this whole place is intense. It must block out and protect against a multitude of threats, magical and otherwise. No one can see us here, no one can find us, even with magic. That's huge. The entire area is cloaked—it took him decades to secure it. Therefore, something as simple as wi-fi doesn't stand a chance."

Tayce managed an impressed look. "I mean, when you put it that way." He looked at her soberly. "Why did we have to leave

Amsterdam so suddenly? Tell me the truth, since Bergen's ears are not here right now."

She fiddled with a blade of grass. "My father realizes now that Jacob and I have an alliance. He cannot accept it; the bond between us had been a thorn in his side for years and years. To see that it continues on and has actually turned into something even more powerful—he can't abide it. He wants to destroy us. Something under his power was coming to get us yesterday. Clearly, we couldn't leave the two of you behind."

Tayce's eyes widened. "Clearly."

She tore the piece of grass in two. "Everyone I care about is in jeopardy. Jacob protects you all, but the wider a net he has to cast, the thinner the protection."

Tayce placed his palms on his thighs, thinking of his daughters.

"Even them," she confirmed. "See the danger of Social Fallon? It was better when I was more of a loner."

But he couldn't joke, concern on his face. "What's going to happen? How will this end?"

She smiled her crooked smile. "Apparently I have to destroy him before he destroys me."

He leaned over and wrapped his arms around her. "Things seemed so much more innocent that first night I met you at Solu. Everything has gotten complicated."

She sighed, hugging him back. "It was always complicated. You've just been pulled deeper into it."

He released her and sat back, his fingers absently playing with the two long chains around his neck, one suspending a cross, the other the silver crescent moon.

215

Fallon's gaze was drawn as usual to the crescent moon pendant, something about it calling out to her. She reached to touch it, hesitating when she felt love and pain coming off of it, but there was no threat, so she took it and held it on her palm. Then she closed it up in her fist and shut her eyes, while Tayce watched her curiously.

Light flashed in her mind, she felt overwhelming maternal love, then great sadness, fear, terrible loss, and finally an image of a baby shone long and hard in her inner vision. Then everything abruptly went black, startling her, and she was aware of the coppery scent of blood.

She opened her eyes and released the pendant, taking a moment to collect herself before looking at him with kindness. "She loved you so very much. Your mother. This was hers."

He was shaking his head as he pointed to the crescent moon. "No way was this my mom's. Not her style."

"Where did you get it?" she asked.

"It was always with my things. As far back as I can remember. I thought it was cool. I started wearing it when I was a teenager because finally the long chain worked, you know?"

She played with the fraying hem of her jeans. "It belonged to your birth mother, not your adoptive mother. Your birth mother's name was Isla. She was beautiful and loved you passionately. She's the one who named you Tayce Elliot. She never wanted to lose you, but she died," she frowned, "and not easily." Fallon indicated the necklace. "Someone very close to her placed this with you, as a memento. You were taken far away to keep you safe."

And strangely, though she left this part unspoken, she now knew that Jacob had once held this necklace, which left her feeling more than a little unsettled.

Tayce was shaken to his core. He had never questioned his origins because his adoptive parents had been so loving, had so completed him. He had grown up in a situation of such pleasant normalcy, the only thing lacking had been his need to leave and play his guitar around the world. His parents had both been older than most of his friends' parents. They had adopted him later in life, but they had nurtured and cared for him so much better than many he knew. He'd never asked where he came from; it had never been important. They'd both been dead for years now—he'd never contemplated the existence of anyone else.

But Fallon's declaration of his birth mother's love and death, the revelation of her actual name, that was all searingly real to him. He held the crescent moon in his hand and looked out at the gray skies. *Isla.* He wanted to tell Jane and Annie about their grandmother's real name.

He looked at Fallon. "What about my father? My real one?"

Her thoughts went immediately to Sunny, but she shook her head. "The necklace has no attachment to him that I could see." She placed a hand on his forearm. "If I had to guess, though, I'd say he probably played guitar in a band."

He smiled, nodding. "Probably so. It's interesting to wonder who he might have been." He rubbed a worn spot on his shoe. "Where was my mother from? Could you tell?"

Fallon was quiet, her eyes going distant. "I couldn't tell."

But she knew one thing for certain: Isla had not been of this world. She glanced at him and thought about Las Vegas.

"When I saw her face," Fallon admitted, "I was immediately reminded of Annie."

Tayce grinned happily, looking up at the sky.

* * * * * * *

Several hours later, Tayce and Fallon stood together watching the sheep, which were grazing peacefully against the backdrop of the glorious mountains and cloudy blue-gray skies. The wind was blowing more gently now, cool against their faces.

"I'm going to miss this place," he declared. "After a little while it kind of sinks its teeth into you and doesn't let go." He looked at Fallon. "In a good way, I mean."

"I understand what you're saying."

"Bergen doesn't want to leave, either, I can tell. And you were right, everything starts to fade, everyone you once knew, all of it. If I never went home again, I don't think I'd mind."

She squeezed his arm as she leaned against him. "I'm glad you got to come along, even if the reasons were poor. I'm so happy that you got to experience this place. But you have to get back to the tour and to preparing for an illustrious stint as best-grandpa-ever."

He grinned from ear to ear. "Ah, there is that."

Bergen was coming towards them from Colette's small cottage. She looked light-hearted and at ease.

"So, you are going to stay another night here with me?" Fallon asked, and Bergen nodded happily. "Your father will not be pleased," she warned. "He won't understand."

"Isn't it better to ask forgiveness than permission?" the girl wondered.

Fallon exchanged a look with Tayce. "So they say. I don't know if that's always the best path. I think it's something people say when they don't want to be told 'no.'"

"I will be asking your father if you can stay. I'll give him the option to demand your return." Jacob had joined them. "Of course, that puts him in a position of being unpopular, which will displease him even further, and he will then reluctantly allow you to stay. But he'll be bitter about it. Understandably so."

Bergen looked troubled only briefly and then beamed at them. "I cannot leave this place any sooner than I have to. Do what you have to do."

"Alright, then." Jacob turned to Fallon, kissing her. "Tayce and I will be on our way."

Fallon hugged Tayce. "We'll see you tomorrow, trouble."

Jacob took his arm, and the men were gone.

Bergen tugged on Fallon's hand. "Colette has a pony behind her cottage, the cutest pony I've ever seen. Come and meet him!"

Jacob held back as Tayce entered Bret's Amsterdam hotel room, sinking into the shadows down the hallway so as not to be seen. He heard Bret asking immediately for Bergen, followed by Tayce's quick reassurances. Jacob sighed and wished to return to Fallon, but he waited to see what Bret's decision would be. Fallon had insisted they give him a choice. Tayce had undertaken the task alone, for Jacob knew that seeing him would do Bret's mood no good.

After nearly fifteen minutes, Tayce reappeared in the hallway, looking around. Jacob stepped into his view.

"He's angry," Tayce reported, "I can tell. But yeah, of course, he relented. I showed him the video."

Bergen had filmed herself with Tayce's phone, telling her father how much she loved him but also how much she was enjoying being with Fallon in the mountains and to please let her stay one more night.

"The video is what sealed it," Tayce added.

Jacob nodded. "I assumed it would."

Tayce was gazing at Jacob with an odd look on his face. "It's so weird. It's almost like you're familiar to me."

Jacob smiled mildly. "That would be due to how much Fallon speaks of me, I'm sure."

Tayce laughed. "That's true, we have had some talks."

"Take care, Tayce. I will return them tomorrow."

* * * * * * *

Jacob was back at the cottage in time to prepare dinner. Afterwards, Bergen went with Colette to feed and secure the animals for the evening, as well as to play a card game at her house.

When he had finally finished cleaning up the kitchen for the night, Jacob came into the bedroom and found Fallon sitting cross-legged on the bed. She was rubbing her temples as if she were in pain.

"What is it?" he asked, sitting beside her.

"My head. It's been hurting on and off all day. Not like my normal headaches, this feels deeper. Odd." She looked into his face and was surprised at the alarm she saw there, though he hid it away quickly. "What?" she asked.

But he kissed her hard, dragging her down into the pillows. "Let me make it go away," he whispered roughly, and she faintly wondered what was wrong.

Bergen slept on the couch that night under blankets, Azul curled up beside her. Jacob and Fallon lay in his bed and stared at each other in the firelight. Neither wanted to fall asleep, because in the morning he was returning her to the tour.

Fallon wanted to ask what had disturbed him earlier, about her headache, but she didn't want to tarnish this perfect moment. Jacob seemed happy and at peace now. She would fight wars, she thought, to bring him peace.

Early the next morning, because she had requested it, Jacob and Fallon took Bergen down to the river for a quick visit. Fallon waded in the cold water with her, and Bergen filled her pockets with smooth black river rocks. Jacob sat on their favorite wide rock in the sun and watched them.

At one point, Bergen stopped and looked over at him curiously. "How many worlds are there?"

He leaned back on his elbows, somewhat surprised at her question. "Ah, little one, they are without number."

"Which one are you from?" she asked.

He smiled. "Fortunately, this one."

Bergen tilted her head. "Why 'fortunately'?"

"Because in this world, I found Fallon."

A smiled spread slowly across the girl's face. "And then you both found me."

When they got back to the cottage, Fallon disappeared into the bedroom, and Bergen set about stacking all her rocks artistically in the front windowsills.

"I'll be coming back here, won't I?" she wanted to know, wrestling with a variety of emotions at the thought of saying goodbye to this place.

Jacob gazed at her from the kitchen where he was preparing brunch. "I am not the future-seer in this arrangement."

She continued with her placement of the rocks. "I hope I come back here."

After they ate, Bergen looked around, soaking it all in, no one having been able to promise her definitively that she would ever return to the cottage. Finally, she looked at Fallon. "Okay. I'm ready to face Dad."

Jacob took both their hands, and they were gone.

And then they were standing in the hallway outside Bret's hotel room in Gothenburg, Sweden. The door was slightly ajar. Bergen entered first, Fallon behind her with anxiety, Jacob trailing last, radiating confidence and strength.

Bret cried out in relief when he saw his daughter, grabbing her up tightly in his arms.

Fallon felt a jolt of surprise as she saw Selah sitting on the edge of the bed, looking simultaneously serene and troubled. Jacob came to stand close behind Fallon, placing a hand on her waist.

When Selah saw Jacob, her face only barely masked her astonishment at seeing him again after so long. Hearing that he was back in Fallon's life and actually seeing him were two entirely different things. As she took notice of the tender way he held onto Fallon, Selah's heart wanted to burst.

Overcome with emotion and not wanting to deal with the other adults in the room, Bret was not letting Bergen go. She was indifferent, however, still feeling the loss of the Spanish mountains in her bones like a deep sadness. Finally, she began to squirm and complain in his arms.

"Are you alright?" he asked, letting her feet touch the floor, looking her over as if to check for injury.

She gave him the type of incredulous look that only a ten-year-old can.

"Bergen was taken in order to keep her safe. Not to bring about harm," said Fallon, unable to hold her tongue any longer. She briefly met Selah's gaze. Selah gave her a difficult smile. The room was full of tension.

Bret was now staring steadily at Fallon. "My girl has never been teleported away from me before. Since her mother knows nothing of Jacob and his abilities, I was tense as I waited to see if she would question Bergen's whereabouts before you could get her back to me. Despite Colette's assurances that I should not worry about it. Don't ever take her again without asking."

Fallon's eyes gleamed with anger. "If we hadn't taken her, she might have died. There was no time to ask your permission. You know this. Don't pretend I did it merely on a whim." Jacob's hand on her waist tightened its grip, though his face remained impassive.

Bret held Fallon's gaze, resolutely avoiding looking at the man at her back. Bergen's voice pulled him back to her. "Dad, I'm safe with Fallon and Jacob," she said. "They'd never let anything happen to me."

Selah stared hard and purposefully at the floor.

Fallon leaned back a little against Jacob.

An array of complex emotions passed over Bret's face as he turned over the phrase she had used with such familiarity—"Fallon and Jacob"—as if they were one person. As if they were special to her.

There was an ensuing heavy stretch of silence; the room was unbearably stuffy from the indoor heating even with the window cracked open. An insect buzzing in the windowsill was the only sound.

Fallon kept stealing looks at Selah, who had never been to Sweden, to Europe, not even once out of the United States, and yet there she sat with her quiet strength, absorbing the proceedings.

"We're trying to keep everyone I love safe until I can finish this," Fallon tried to explain, breaking the silence. "I hate that everyone is in danger, of course I feel responsible, because it's my father at the heart of all this. Jacob protects you all, but it's not foolproof."

"At times like this," said Bret coldly, "I truly wish neither of you had ever entered my life."

Fallon turned without a word and left the room. Bergen followed after her, glowering at her father over her shoulder.

"Do not be too hard on her." Jacob's rich voice filled the room with a strange mix of intensity and calm. Selah was nearly overwhelmed to hear it again, so much a ghost from her past. "For one thing," Jacob continued, "if Fallon had never entered your life, Bergen would, by now, have already sung a sweet, sad song at your funeral."

Bret turned away from him in anger, fists clenched, despising Jacob for being right.

"Much of what is going on now," Jacob went on, "Fallon has had no control over. Even the timing of my return has been fully affected by her father. My own desire was to return to her long before she met you, which would have saved you the pain of this separation from her. But instead, life has taken this path, and so we must make our way. There is a war coming. And she must be strong enough to face it. Alone."

Bret looked back at Jacob. "She shouldn't have to face it alone."

"Haven't you heard her favorite quote?" Jacob asked.

"'One weakness is enough'," Selah's words drifted to them from the doorway, "'and love is the deadliest'." She was staring at Jacob with hard eyes. He looked back at her thoughtfully. "She said that you always told her that," Selah remembered, "but she never believed you."

"She believes me now."

"She does." Her forehead was creased with concern. "You will guard her. You will keep her close."

Jacob gave a nod. "As I always have. As I always will. While I live, Fallon is never alone."

Leaving Bret to sulk and simmer, Jacob helped Selah locate Fallon in Tayce's hotel room. Tayce and Bergen were both gone, the former having recognized that Fallon needed some time alone. Tayce was currently leading a reluctant Bergen back to her father, telling her that no matter her feelings on what was going on between Bret and Fallon, her father needed to spend time with her. That she more or less owed him as much after staying longer than necessary—and without his permission— on a magical mystery tour with Fallon and Jacob.

When Jacob and Selah appeared, Fallon jumped up and went to Selah, wrapping her arms around her. "You flew halfway around the world." She still could not believe it.

Selah held her at arm's length, studying her. "You are even more different than when I last saw you, Fallon." Solemn in her assessment, Selah had one eye on Jacob as he wandered over to a window and stared out at the city. She was still a little dazed by his presence. "You have been transformed by him."

"I'm still me."

"You are wiser than before." Selah sighed. "And yet you have always been wiser than most."

Jacob moved into Fallon's view, his face alight as he met her eyes. "I must say goodbye, my love."

Releasing Selah, Fallon went into his arms.

"Selah," he gave her a warm smile, "I am glad to see you again after all these years. You have been a loyal friend."

Selah bowed her head to acknowledge Jacob's sentiment. "I am even more glad to see you again," she muttered to herself. "For her sake."

But Jacob heard her and gave her a smirk, before he kissed Fallon sweetly and held her close, bending to rest his head on hers. "I will see you again soon."

After a moment she looked up, cradling his face with her hand. Then with one last kiss, he vanished, startling Selah.

Fallon motioned to her, and they sat together on one of the beds.

"You are in love," Selah declared. "I can see it without question now—you are both deeply in love." She was smiling, her face bright with joy. "This is not as it ever was before. This is new. New and, dare I say, wonderful. There is a light in both your faces. A light I never dreamed I'd see in Jacob's face, for sure. I have never seen him so joyful as when he smiles at you." She looked momentarily troubled. "Though now there is darkness in the face of someone else."

Fallon looked away. "I didn't intend for Bret to be hurt. I never would have wanted that."

"No, of course not. It was a dangerous thing, him falling for you. Like a sailor loving a mermaid." Selah made herself more comfortable. "Now, love. Tell me everything that is going on. Including all the things you held back from me before."

"Where's Indio?"

"Tallie came to stay while I'm away." Selah raised an eyebrow. "Global travel was an unprecedented request on my part. She was eager to assist. And she always did have a soft spot for you, the little blond orphan girl." She grinned at the memory, and Fallon laughed.

"She used to sing 'It's a Hard Knock Life' whenever I was at your house," Fallon recalled.

Selah was nodding. "It made me angry at the time—I was protective of you—but I see the humor in it now."

"Bret convinced you to come here?" Fallon was still in disbelief.

"He has often relied on me when he is unable to handle, or seeking answers for, your… unexplainableness. Yes, Bret called me, since Jacob is a bit of a specific subject. He was angry, I could tell, because suddenly Jacob had you both—you and Bergen. It was more than he could deal with. Which I get, though I also fully understand why Bergen was taken. But Bret was all alone, without anyone to share his concerns and frustrations with, as Tayce was also gone."

"Still. Having you come all the way here was a big endeavor. A big ask on his part. Though I am so happy to see you!"

Selah nodded. "I agree; it was a big ask. I will admit a large part of me leapt at the chance to experience this all firsthand." She smiled. "Seeing Jacob again, it's surreal. Seeing how much he loves you—that makes the whole trip worthwhile."

Fallon squeezed her hand. "What about a passport? How was that managed?"

"Ah, that. I never told you, but Michael and I had planned an anniversary trip a couple of years ago to Paris. It fell through for various reasons, but it meant I had a valid passport available for just such an event as this. And Bret's assistant somehow obtained the most expedient flights and transportation to get me here. It was a feat. I had little to no time to pack. Michael's head was spinning as I departed, as you can imagine."

"So, when you got here, though…did it ease Bret's mind?" Fallon asked doubtfully.

Selah made a dismissive noise. "You know it didn't. What do I know about Jacob these days? Where he lives or what he's up to? What did I ever know? Nothing. I haven't seen him in fifteen years; nor have you and I been able to discuss any real details since he took you away from them in London. All I could do was reassure him that Jacob, as I have mentioned before, is pure of heart and intention when it comes to you, and therefore the same applies to Bergen." She looked annoyed. "He knew all of this. I don't understand what he thought getting me here would accomplish. But here I am, and I'm going to enjoy every second of you telling me absolutely everything that is going on." She leveled her gaze at Fallon. "Everything."

* * * * * * *

That evening as Bergen sat on the hotel bed staring at her phone, she was thoughtful. "So, Tayce is really excited about Jane having a baby."

Selah, who was getting dressed while Fallon took a quick shower, glanced at her. "People do tend to get excited about babies," she agreed.

Tayce had managed to coordinate rooming temporarily with one of his bandmates so that Fallon and Selah would have a room of their own for a few days.

Bergen looked up from her phone. "What about Fallon? Doesn't she want babies? She would have such beautiful ones. Especially if Jacob was the father!"

Selah looked solemn before answering. "Never." She shook her head. "The idea distresses her greatly. Her life has always been so full of chaos and the unknown, one of her deepest fears has been that she might unintentionally bring a child into this world. As soon as she turned twenty-one, she had surgery to prevent any pregnancies. She's not naturally drawn to children anyway, though she very much loves Indio. It was surprising, the way she bonded with you, to be honest. But she loves you beyond all reason, as if you were hers."

Bergen beamed. "I am hers."

At the concert that evening, Bret was hanging out in his dressing room with Selah and his daughter. It was as awkward, yet easy, as anyone might expect. Not ideal, but having the three bands and their crews on tour meant things backstage were often cramped and busy. Fallon had just left them to go help out briefly at one of the merchandise booths. Selah, knowing no one, had nowhere else to go. Considering he was the reason she was there on the tour, Bret had, of course, accepted her company without hesitation.

It was a surprise to all three of them when Jacob appeared in the room. Since he allegedly always knew where Fallon was, Selah was struck by the thought that he had waited purposefully for a time when Fallon would not be around. But why would that be?

Jacob looked directly at Bret. "I was wanting a moment alone with Bergen, if that was alright with you."

Bret was so surprised by the request, he at first didn't know how to respond. When he glanced at Selah, she nodded that he should say 'yes.' Bret looked at his daughter, who was watching him as she waited to see what he would do. She was trying to be on her best behavior, even though everything in her had wanted to immediately run to Jacob's side.

Every bitter comment that Bret wanted to say fell away, and he found himself agreeing. "Sure, I guess. Now?"

"Now would be best," Jacob confirmed.

"Why do you want to be alone with her?"

Jacob's face revealed nothing. "I wish only to briefly converse with her. Less than five minutes."

Selah drew nearer, giving Bret a reassuring look. She wondered what Jacob was playing at. What he intended with this odd request.

In the end, Selah and Bret stepped outside the dressing room door, closing it behind them and waiting together in silence. Jacob was alone with Bergen for less than five minutes, as promised. As Bergen opened the door for them, Selah looked past her and glimpsed Jacob before he vanished. His face was stone. Selah was riddled with worry as she and Bret re-entered the dressing room.

Bret bent down to look at his daughter. "Are you okay?"

She looked at him quizzically. "Of course, I'm okay. Why would I not be okay?"

He let that question go. "What did he want?"

Bergen shrugged. "Nothing really. He had me hold a small crystal in the palm of my hand."

Bret frowned as Selah came near. "A crystal?"

"Yeah, a clear, yellowish crystal, I don't know. But Dad," her eyes were wide, "all of a sudden it started to glow, and then it exploded into tiny pieces. What does that mean?"

Bret exchanged a look with Selah. "I don't know, Bee. What did Jacob say?"

Bergen shook her head. "He stared, like, into space, not at anything, he just stared. He didn't say a word." She looked troubled. "I think we won't tell Fallon."

Selah touched her shoulder. "Why? What do you mean?"

"I don't know." Bergen shifted uneasily. "I think, for now, we won't tell her. I can't explain it. He came when she was gone. He knows where she is every second of every day. He knew she wouldn't be here."

Bret and Selah glanced at each other again, this time with some concern. But they both knew, without saying anything out loud, that they would not tell Fallon, despite that they didn't know why.

The next day Bergen tearfully returned to California. She'd begged to stay with them on the tour, sobbing hysterically in Bret's arms, pleading with him to keep her. She cried so hard she was nearly sick. Bret had looked to Fallon with such naked desperation that she'd immediately taken Bergen aside for a talk.

Fallon told Bergen that, for now, Bret had to follow all the rules, and that meant sending her back to her mother. "It's not that he doesn't want you on tour with him. Never think that,

Bee. Your dad would want you with him all the time. Don't ever convince yourself otherwise. But because of the things the lawyers are discussing, it's important that he follows the rules right now." Laying her hands on the girl's arms, she radiated calm to her.

Bergen, sobs finally abated, went back to her father and hugged him tightly goodbye. Over the top of her head, he gave Fallon a look that could possibly be described as grateful, and she nodded.

Selah stayed with the tour for a few more days, and Fallon attempted to give her a bit of a pleasant European vacation. Despite the bands' uneven traveling schedule and a mishap with one of the buses, Fallon was able to take Selah to museums, cathedrals, and cafés. Though she seemed to enjoy herself, Selah's rare, dazzling smile remained mostly hidden.

"You're troubled," Fallon acknowledged, as they sat on the edge of a fountain with cups of gelato.

Selah looked at her. "Of course I'm troubled." She had gotten her wish, and Fallon had revealed everything to her the first evening. "A powerful, magical, devil-man who can steal you away at will is likely going to want you dead shortly. How can I not be troubled? He stole you away from Gray last year, the one place you and Jacob say is protected. I don't understand," she pushed on, before Fallon could speak, "what that man, your father, ever intended for you? Once he realized he had a child imbued with the level of power you allegedly possess, what was his end goal? Why keep you untrained? Why not just destroy you at age three, if your power was his fear? Why allow you to grow up at all?"

Fallon shook her head, her face shadowed by her long hair. Around them was a bustle of activity, people laughing and talking, kids shrieking. The fountain was splashing loudly at their backs. "I don't think he ever truly understood how much I was in Jacob's heart, the loyalty Jacob felt towards me. And therefore, my father maybe thought that he and Jacob together would always be able to overpower me, control me. Maybe he thought one day he would use me for his own devices. But then, I think his concept of time is nothing like ours. And he never anticipated that Jacob and I would fall in love."

Selah finally smiled. Like the sun coming out from behind clouds. Jacob had been showing up now and then while she and Fallon were out being touristy, and so Selah had been able to witness again and again the sweet, powerful connection between them. The love Jacob had for Fallon made Selah want to sing to the highest heavens. It brought her immense joy amidst the fear.

Jacob's past was another matter, and of course, it troubled Selah, though she tried to put it out of her mind. Who was he really? Who was the Ravener? How had he come to be this? What did his future hold, and what did that mean for Fallon? The questions kept her awake at night, though she knew there would apparently be no answers anytime soon. But Fallon and Jacob's love for each other, their life together, was near the forefront of her prayers.

CHAPTER NINETEEN

JACOB

Tension bloomed in Jacob as he watched the young woman approach him. Her long brown hair fell in waves around her shoulders, the light sprinkling of freckles on her cheeks were endearing, and she had a baby in her arms, but all of this he noticed only peripherally. Because what his gaze was drawn to was the blood on the woman's hands and pretty face.

"Violet." He took a step towards her, then stopped when he saw her eyes. Her beautiful eyes were full of torment—he watched as she struggled against it. Glancing at the baby, he was reassured that the child was alive. "Is Isla," he began, but Violet shook her head.

"She's gone." Her voice was strange. Unnatural. "She had to die, Jacob. You knew it would come to that. But look, I saved him. Do you see? I saved him." She showed him the baby, as if he needed further proof.

Upon closer examination, Jacob could tell that the child was seemingly unharmed. Was the boy six or seven months old?

He couldn't recall. Admittedly he hadn't been paying much attention to Isla's life.

Looking back into Violet's eyes, he finally saw her, the sweet girl he knew and loved. There she was. He held out his arms and she melted against his chest, trembling.

"Isla," she sobbed, shuddering in pain as he held her close. "Oh, Jacob, she's gone, that beautiful girl. I can't even understand it." She choked on a sob. "You have to take him. This child, he has to go somewhere safe. Somewhere lovely and safe and far, far away. Promise me."

Somewhere you will never find him, Jacob thought with a sigh. He accepted the baby from her. Violet tried to wipe her hands clean on her jeans before she tucked the blanket more snugly around the child. Then she pulled the long silver chain from around her neck.

"This must go with him. A memento. A memory from his mother—she loved him so much." She stared transfixed at the shining crescent moon. Then in a voice that was oddly cold she sang, *"I wished for you, I wished for you, and for all I know, you came from the moon, Clair de Lune, my Clair de Lune."*

Jacob felt his chest tighten. He had heard that made-up rhyme from Isla more than once over the years, but never from Violet.

She was staring hard at the baby now; he was reminded of a predator observing its prey. "I could keep him. Couldn't I? Tayce Elliot. What a sweet boy. What do you think?" She held out the silver necklace to Jacob, giving him a knowing smile.

In her eyes, he could see his girl slipping away again, and he shuttered his heart against the pain.

"I will take him somewhere safe," he promised, accepting the necklace from her and closing it in his fist. His mind was already brainstorming locations, even as Violet hummed a wicked little tune and rubbed her body against his.

"Come back soon," she instructed him with a purr, "you know where I'll be."

Jacob nodded once. And then he was gone.

Standing at the end of a long, dirt driveway, fields surrounded him, golden with wheat and green with soybeans. The wide sky was blue and cloudless, the sun bright overhead. He looked down at the baby in his arms. The child was watching him intently with brown eyes. Jacob tucked the crescent moon into the folds of the blanket as he walked down the driveway.

"Come, little one. Let us set you on a new adventure." He looked around with interest. "This looks to be a good place. I know, at least, that you will be safe from all that I am taking you away from." He sighed. "I cannot say if we will ever meet again. Life does take its strange turns, though. So perhaps. Perhaps one day I will know you. I've learned not to imagine how I think life will go. Inevitably, it surprises me."

The baby smiled at him and made some soft sound. Jacob grinned in spite of himself.

"I will tell them your real name, Tayce Elliot. It is a good name and suits you. I apologize that I cannot take you to your real father. He would love you, I feel; it is unfortunate that he can't have you and raise you. But if I left you with him, she would find you." He looked at the simple house he was approaching. A dog gave a friendly bark from the yard. "Yes, you will be safe here. I will not leave you with them unless I am certain that you will be loved."

CHAPTER TWENTY

Upon Selah's departure, the tour moved on to France. On the day they arrived in Paris, Tayce and Fallon went for a long walk, knowing that their time together on the tour was drawing to a close. Fallon was stylish and sweet in a black dress; Tayce was rockstar casual in jeans, t-shirt, and leather jacket. Eventually they stopped at a café for coffee, sitting at a small table and watching the sparrows that gathered on the ground nearby.

Tayce admitted to Fallon that he was nervous about her father and the impending unknown. He talked excitedly about Jane's pregnancy, and he updated her about Kat, informing her that Katrine had been unreachable for three days.

"Paul is on the phone constantly with their main worker at the farm, trying to decide what to do. Call the police? She always comes back. Always. There's no obvious sign of anything being wrong. But it's a huge drain on him, a major distraction, obviously."

Fallon bit her lower lip. "I've been avoiding dealing with this. I've been letting myself be preoccupied with everything

else. When we get back to the hotel, I'll see what I can do."
Jacob had run her through a crash course in scrying while she
was at the cottage with Tayce and Bergen. She was still dragging
her feet about it, but hearing the latest about Katrine was the
impetus she needed to at least try.

Tayce sat back and studied her. "A year ago, I honestly
thought that by now you might have moved in with Bret."

She narrowed her eyes at him briefly.

He shrugged. "It was interesting. I'd never seen him with
anyone like you. Then again, I've never met anyone quite like
you." He winked. "And I've met a lot of people."

She clasped her hands together and rested her chin against
them. "Things started changing last August when Bret and Jack
were gone. You probably noticed, since you were around me
constantly at that time. When I was going so far into my mind
at Selah's, I interacted, I guess you could say, with the raven,
more and more. And there was a change in me. When Bret
was rescued, he didn't come back to the same girl. My father
stealing me against my will while Bret and Jack's lives hung in
the balance was eye-opening. And then when Jacob returned to
me, I learned things that have altered everything."

"And you fell madly in love with Jacob, and your life was
transformed. Eternally."

She stared at him steadily, while on her wrist the raven
pulsed with her every heartbeat.

Tayce held her gaze and spoke carefully. "You were very
obviously changed from the moment he came back to you that
night in the hotel bar in Tennessee. Your face was flushed, and
I thought that if I touched you, I'd get an electric shock; you

were that tense. You may not want to admit it, but Bret lost you that night. Which makes sense, now that I know so much more of the story. Then when Jacob stole you away from the pub in England—when you returned to us, you were even more different."

"I learned some painful truths."

"Beyond that. It was your heart that was changed."

She stared at the ring on her finger, twisting it back and forth.

"When we were at his cottage together…" He shook his head. "What's the phrase I'm looking for? 'A blind man could see how much he loves you.' That's how it is with the two of you. It's like you and Jacob are two otherworldly parts of a beautiful whole—it's impossible for me to adequately explain. I've never experienced anything like it. You seem like a normal young woman when it's just you and me together. But when you're with him, I can see the magic shining off of you.

"Bergen came to me that night in the cottage, when you and Jacob were outside looking at the stars or whatever lie you gave, and she said to me, 'I don't want my dad to be sad. But I want Fallon to be where she should be. And she belongs with Jacob. Tayce, aren't they just like a love song?'"

Tears pricked at Fallon's eyes. "My whole life I've been waiting for him to come back to me."

Tayce nodded. "I know that now. And I think Bret knew it and feared it."

She tried to blink the tears away, failing. "I feel like I've loved Jacob for thousands of years. Like I've known him and loved him through countless other lifetimes. Maybe I should have done things differently, with Bret. But I didn't know if Jacob would ever come back or if I'd simply long for him forever." She ran a finger along the edge of her cup. "When we were reunited… it was like an ignition, and it feels at times like we've both been waiting a lifetime for this."

There were still tears on her cheeks, and Tayce touched her wrist. "Why are you still crying?"

She wiped the tears away with the back of her hand. "Because I love him so much. And I'm scared. And I'm not sure why."

CHAPTER TWENTY-ONE

B ack at the hotel, Fallon was heavy with the pressure of too many things in disarray, knowing she was about to be unreachable for possibly weeks. The situation with Bergen, she knew, was mostly out of her control. The girl was being plunged into a full-blown nightmare: her parents fighting over custody of her, with lawyers. There was not a lot that Fallon felt she could do besides continuing to be a loving figure in Bergen's life.

Getting out an old silver pocket mirror Jacob had given her, she sat cross-legged on the bed and lay the mirror on a pillow in front of her. Closing her eyes, she stilled her mind, letting all her senses settle. She felt she was still fairly awful at scrying, and so she didn't expect much from this session, but she was desperate for information about Katrine.

She wondered if the woman Jacob had loved had been excellent at scrying. She wondered why she'd died young. She knew she would never ask. There was a lot of painful darkness looming in Jacob's past, and she didn't want to ask him to relive any of it just to satisfy her curiosity. Who had he been before he became the Ravener, and how long ago did it happen? Had he had a family before? What became of them?

None of this would she seek answers for. She understood that she needed to be comfortable never knowing his full story, despite that he knew hers, apparently better than she did.

Taking a slow, deep, belly breath, she pictured Katrine in her mind's eye and concentrated on her for a moment, before gazing down at the mirror. For a while, there was nothing, then a blur that came and went as if with a breeze.

After several minutes, her mind was tired as she continued to search the mirror, which had unfortunately grown cloudy with a fog. She was lamenting her poor scrying skills when suddenly she saw red and yellow, then Katrine's face, followed again by red and yellow. Then the mirror cleared completely, as if announcing to her that the session was over.

Fallon sat back, blinking rapidly. There was one thing in her world that was undeniably red and yellow: Sunny Girl Bakery. What did that have to do with Katrine? She lay on her stomach and scrolled through her phone. She didn't have a personal phone number for Sunny Lewis, but she did have the number for the bakery. Checking the time zones, she placed the call.

Sunny answered on the third ring. "My fearless Fallon friend, how's the tour going?"

"It's been interesting. I have a question for you."

Sunny paused. "I have Katrine."

Fallon rested her forehead on her hand.

"She's staying at my townhouse. I found her wandering in the park one night. She needs someone to keep an eye on her till Paul can come home. She's in an odd state."

"I'll come as soon as I can. I don't want to tell Paul yet, till I've seen her. Thank you, Sunny."

Claiming to be tired, Fallon stayed behind at the hotel when everyone left for the concert venue late that afternoon. As soon as they were all gone, she kissed the raven tattoo, and Jacob was immediately with her, wrapping her hair through his fingers and kissing her hard on the lips.

"The effect that has on me..." His breathing was jagged.

She grinned as she slid her arms around his neck. "New super-power, unlocked. Hey, I found out where Katrine is; she's with Sunny, my friend who owns the bakery. I don't know how long Sunny's had her, but I need to go right away." She looked coyly up at him, and he laughed out loud.

"Don't want to bother with that transatlantic flight?" he asked huskily.

"Only if you have the time."

He kissed her forehead. "For you, there is always time."

"Let me pack up my things. I don't want to leave anything on the tour. I doubt I'll be returning to it."

She texted Paul to let him know Katrine was safe and that she would find out more information. Then she alerted Tayce and Bret to her departure, but gave no reason—Tayce was sad, Bret ambivalent—and then Jacob spirited her away.

They ended up in her apartment in Gray.

"That's the only way to travel internationally," she declared. "You've spoiled me forever."

He kissed her softly, his lips lingering on hers. "You're going to have to wait till morning to go see Sunny."

"Am I?" She returned his kiss, feeling the intensity building as he traced her collar bone with his thumb, running his other hand over her hip.

"Yes. You're going to be occupied for the rest of the day. Sunny would understand."

CHAPTER TWENTY-TWO

When Fallon arrived at Sunny's townhouse early the next morning, Sunny was outside waiting for her. "Yesterday when we spoke, you were in Europe," her friend remarked, leading Fallon inside.

Fallon licked her lips. "Yes."

They went inside and headed up some stairs. Sunny stopped at the top. "Here we are." She motioned to Fallon to enter a closed door.

Fallon could hear someone inside humming a tune. Turning the knob, she stepped into what looked like a sunshine-filled office/guest room.

Katrine turned and smiled at her. "Just tidying up. How are you today, Fallon?" She was wearing one of her usual long skirts with a tank top and she looked healthy and serene as usual.

Fallon pushed aside her alarm and smiled back. "I'm good, Kat."

"Haven't seen you around lately, did you leave again on one of your trips?" Katrine returned to fluffing pillows and straightening a stack of books.

"Ummm, yes. I've been on tour with Bret and Tayce. And Paul."

"Oh, how nice!" She shuffled a stack of magazines, fanning it out on a coffee table. "How's that going?"

"Paul is worried about you. He couldn't, couldn't find you."

Katrine began to hum again, moving away to dust a bookshelf.

Sunny stood at Fallon's side, threw her a sideways glance, and then smiled brightly at Katrine. "Kat, you've got your necklaces on! Remember I told you not to wear them when Fallon visits?"

Fallon frowned.

Katrine touched her throat. "Oh! Goodness, you're right. Sunny, you did say that. Just a minute." She unclasped the three necklaces that suspended different crystals and set them on a nearby table.

Immediately Katrine was loud and clear—Fallon took a sudden step back as she read the terror and chaos inside her friend. She pressed her fingers to her temples, tearing her mind away.

Sunny was watching her closely. "It's bad, isn't it?"

"Can you read her?" Fallon asked. They both kept their voices low.

With a brief, impish smile, Sunny shook her head. "No, I'm not magic like you. I have some enhanced senses, but I am nowhere near your league. I observe people. Katrine has interested me for years, because I suspected some sort of disquiet in her mind, despite her 'peace, love, happiness' outward appearance. Over the past few months, she kept mentioning that Paul was leaving on tour again, and that's when the humming started. I asked why she didn't go with him, and she said she couldn't. But with a smile, you know? Like it was all okay."

"How did you know about the crystals?"

"She told me about them once, when I asked." Sunny pulled her black hair back into a ponytail. "I don't remember what the other two are for, but the dark one I remember, she told me it blocks negativity. I laughed and said I could use something like that. I researched it and realized it wasn't quite what she thought. It doesn't block negativity. It blocks people from seeing into her. People like you."

Fallon stole a glance at Katrine. "This is full-blown mental illness."

Sunny nodded sadly. "Exacerbated by her husband's perceived abandonment when he goes on tour. He's the glue that holds her mind together, though he may not even know it. I'm thinking it's not been terribly bad till recently. I don't think he's toured globally in a long time, right?"

"You're correct." Fallon again looked over at Katrine, who continued not to notice them. "She needs a doctor. I can't heal mental, only physical. Thank you for keeping her safe, Sunny."

"I adore Kat and Paul. They're so creative and interesting, and that's hard to come by around here, present company notwithstanding."

After ensuring that Katrine was happy to remain in the spare room arranging furniture, Fallon went out to the privacy of her car and called Paul in Paris. They talked for a long time, and at one point he wept. When she finally hung up with him, she knew he was first calling a doctor, and second informing his bandmates that he would have to leave the tour immediately. She admired his decision to place Katrine's well-being over all else, but she felt bad for his bandmates—especially Tayce—who were so enjoying the tour.

She texted Bret a brief summary of what was going on. She had a feeling she knew what he would do with the information.

Jacob was suddenly watching her fondly from the passenger seat, and she flinched slightly.

"How is it that you're so accurate when you teleport?" she asked.

"Decades of practice and mild misfortune. I can see where I'm going, though, so it's not total guesswork."

"Ever teleported into a moving vehicle?" she quizzed.

He smirked. "Easy."

"What about a deep underwater submersible?"

"Oh, that's a good one. A pro-level move, for sure. I assume I could manage it, though."

He leaned over and kissed her temple, seeing that she was still troubled by the storm she had seen in Katrine's head. She held tightly to his arm, eyes going glassy as she leaned into him. Wrapping his arms around her in a comforting embrace, he rested his head against hers.

"Does the raven still watch me when I'm away from you?" she wondered.

Jacob smiled faintly. "He watches little else, Fallon, but you."

Later that day, Paul texted Fallon the pertinent information about where Katrine would be going and who would be coming to collect her. He explained that he had attained permission for Fallon to accompany his wife to the hospital, and she promised to do so. Katrine's sister would meet them. Paul's return flight from Europe was to arrive the following day.

As Fallon had privately anticipated, Bret and Jack were going to share filling in for Paul during the few remaining shows on the tour.

* * * * * * * *

After Katrine was gone, Fallon seemed to hang in the balance. "I feel like I should return to the tour, because that's where I was, but I also know that I definitely don't belong there anymore. Bergen is back with Lisbeth. Katrine is being taken care of."

Jacob kissed her wrist. "I think it's time for you to come with me."

She met his eyes. "Let me talk to Selah, since I'm here. And I want to thank Sunny again for keeping Katrine safe. And then I will go with you."

In jeans and the Cosmic Records t-shirt, which was now her favorite, Fallon entered Sunny Girl Bakery that afternoon and found it empty. Sunny was alone behind the counter, drinking iced coffee and sketching something on a piece of paper. She smiled when she saw Fallon coming towards her. "Hey!" She squinted at Fallon's attire. "Cool shirt."

"Thanks. It was a record store in Austin about fifty years ago. It burned down, something tragic, killed the owner, too. My friend gave it to me. He used to go to that store a lot; he knew the owner."

"Sure, he did," Sunny murmured, nodding. "You know, I lived in Austin once."

"That's right, you had a coffee shop there." Fallon tilted her head. "I lived there till I was nineteen, where was your shop?"

"Just off Guadalupe. It was a long time ago, though. Before your time." Sunny's gaze hadn't left the shirt. "The owner of that record store, Ben, he was young and sweet. Obsessed with music. Always wore the coolest hats. Looks like a comfy shirt."

Fallon was holding her breath, trying to do the math in her head. Again, she swore that Sunny could not be more than twenty-five years old. And why did she sound like she'd known Ben? He'd been dead for over fifty years.

"It's one of my favorites, for sure," she said with some uncertainty. Why was every visit with Sunny now throwing her violently off balance?

Sunny smiled as she turned away. "Eventually, everything connects."

Leaning on the counter, Fallon eyed a tray of donuts and decided to let the Austin thing go for now. It was too much to tangle with. "I wanted to thank you again for looking out for Katrine."

"Like I said before, I could have done no less. Kat's a cool lady. This is so tragic for them. I wish I was as in tune to things as you are."

Fallon pulled her stare from the donuts. "It's not all it's cracked up to be." She straightened up. "I'll be gone for a while. Take care. Keep Michael's office supplied with sugary treats."

Sunny grinned. "I will do my best. Good luck in your endeavors. And do enjoy your time with your old friend." She had a sly, knowing look on her face.

Fallon locked onto Sunny's dark-eyed gaze for a long moment. There was something there, some emotion in Sunny's expression that she couldn't interpret. And something familiar in her eyes.

Fallon found Selah upstairs in her studio, painting. When she saw her, Selah hesitated, brush in hand. "Are you coming to say goodbye, love?"

"For a while. I'll be back."

Selah set aside her brush and wiped her hands on her black leggings. "How will I know that you're alright?"

"I'll be fine, you know. And if anything ever happened to me, Jacob would come and tell you."

Coming over to her, Selah hugged her tightly. "Sometimes I dream of a quiet life," she sighed.

"One day, you will have it," Fallon told her sagely.

Selah looked at her. "I would choose you over a quiet life any day."

Fallon smiled. "I do love you, my friend."

Despite the look of confidence and calm in Fallon's face, Selah felt a sense of dread, and she wasn't sure if it was her own dread or something she was picking up from Fallon, who was so like a sister to her. "I love you with all my being," she said softly.

When she returned to her apartment, Fallon started some laundry in the garage and began packing a couple of bags for Spain. The whole place felt empty without Jacob and Azul.

Coming up the outside stairs a few hours later with her last basket of clean, dry clothes, she shut the apartment door behind her and dumped the clothes out on the couch to fold.

"My love in her most domestic habitat."

She looked sharply into the kitchen, where Jacob was suddenly going through her fridge. "Do you just hang out waiting for cool moments to pop in on me?"

He glanced at her over his shoulder. "I do have other things to do, you know. I am a busy, busy man. It's just that you're lucky. That I appear when I do." He got out a bottle of sparkling water.

"Ahhh. Lucky. I see."

Coming over to her, he kissed her. "Yes. Lucky." He sank down onto the couch amid the laundry, opening the water. Fallon sat comfortably on his lap and composed a long text to Bergen, explaining where she would be. Leaning back against Jacob's chest, she sent shorter, similar texts to Bret and Tayce. Only Bergen and Tayce responded, both clearly anxious about her open-ended departure.

"We can't leave until I fold this laundry," she told him.

Jacob set aside his drink. "Then by all means, let us commence with the folding."

"When's the last time you folded laundry?"

He looked offended. "You think I don't fold my own laundry?"

She raised an eyebrow.

His look turned to sheepish. "Possibly Colette handles my laundry for me," he admitted.

"I suspected as much. After all, as you say, you are a busy, busy man."

"Busy loving you." He wrapped his arms around her and pulled her down into the laundry, kissing her as she giggled.

"This gets us nowhere near our eventual goal," she pointed out.

"Depends on what you think our eventual goal is," he murmured, deepening the kiss, and she grinned as she wrapped her legs around his waist.

CHAPTER TWENTY-THREE

Fallon's return to the cottage filled her with joy. Jacob stood and watched as she and Azul rolled around together in the cottage's yard, both so happy to see each other.

"I think he is pleased to have you here, in the place that is his true home," he commented.

On her back, with the dog's front legs across her chest, Fallon smiled up at him. "I can tell he belongs here." She held out a hand to him. "When's the last time you frolicked in the grass with your dog? Get down here."

He grinned, dropping lightly to his knees beside her. Azul glanced at him and then moved aside as Jacob lowered himself down onto Fallon. He kissed her as she ran her fingers through his hair. "He's cute," he murmured, "but I'd rather frolic in the grass with you."

She tenderly caressed his jaw. "I say we take the frolicking inside—I'm cold."

He chuckled as he gathered her up in his arms and rose to his feet. "Absolutely, my girl."

* * * * * * *

The next afternoon Fallon stood at the cottage's small dining table peeling a satsuma. She didn't know where it had come from, but there was now a large bowl of bright orange satsumas in the kitchen—she assumed it was the work of Colette, who often seemed to move about like a ghost, unseen. Jacob was sitting at the table drinking hot tea as he gazed out the window.

"I didn't mention this before," Fallon began, "but last year I saw that FBI guy who helped me find Bret and Jack, Detective Ashton was found murdered, clutching a large amount of cash. Stabbed in the heart." She was eyeing Jacob closely. "Stabbed with precision."

He did not move his gaze from the window. "Ashton was a dirty cop and an evil-minded man."

"Odd," Fallon mused, still watching him, "that whoever killed him was apparently uninterested in the money. No weapon was found at the scene." She chewed on a sweet wedge of orange. "I could never read him; it was extremely frustrating. He was good to have around. He followed through with things I told him. Obviously, he followed my instructions to the letter when I realized they were being held in Kansas, and it saved their lives. But there at the very end, he was making me uneasy due to his, intense interest, let's say, in me. I could read that much. And that he was hiding something from me."

Jacob finally looked at her, setting down his cup. His face was grave. "Fallon, the degree of harm that man intended for you still makes me ill to think about. He had grievously injured other women in the past. He was not a good human."

She stared back at him thoughtfully. "Jacob Roth, you are my prophet and my executioner, my lover and my soul."

A genuine smile spread slowly across his features. "And you are my poet." He pulled her down onto his lap and kissed her. "My magician."

She smiled as she ate another wedge of orange, offering him one, which he accepted. "How did you know about Ashton anyway?" she asked. "That he was bad, or that he intended me harm?"

He swept her hair aside and ran his index finger down her neck. "Because I'm the one who hired him. I bribed him. I paid him rather a lot of money to work with you and do what you wanted. When Bret and Jack were taken, you weren't having visions that helped; you were struggling, exhausting yourself. Making yourself vulnerable in a way I did not like. Once the FBI was brought into it, I needed someone to immediately go to you and make a connection you could use. I had him carry a crystal in his pocket that blurs and hides feelings and intentions, so you wouldn't realize he was being paid off and get unnecessarily distracted by that detail. Likely the same type of stone Katrine wore around her neck. I didn't realize till the end that he might be a danger to you. And it turned out he intended to be quite a serious danger."

Fallon was surprised. "It was you. You did all of that to help me find Bret and Jack, because..."

Tenderly he tucked her hair behind her ears, cradling her face in his hands. "Because you loved him. Because he had your heart."

She nodded, lost in his eyes. "He did. But you have my heart and my soul." She frowned. "But again, how did you know what he intended? You don't read people."

"The raven had noticed your interaction with Ashton, there at the end, and he became suspicious. Uneasy."

"The raven was uneasy." She narrowed her eyes.

"Yes. The raven can read intentions, but the crystal was blocking him from seeing clearly, so he couldn't be sure. I had the raven come with me when I met Ashton that final time. As soon as the detective handed the dark crystal back to me, the raven could immediately see every horrible intent the man had for you, all the things he'd done to many other women before you. He cast this to me, and I took the necessary action that would keep you from harm."

She wrapped her arms around his neck, laying her head against his.

"Honestly, with what he intended for you, Fallon," Jacob's voice had an edge to it, "I wish I could kill him again."

It was a gloriously sunny day. After lunch, they hiked down to the river with Azul, spreading a blanket out on their favorite smooth rock. They took off their shoes, Jacob shed his shirt, and they lay down in the sun.

"While we were living with you in Austin, were we being constantly watched?" she asked, wriggling her bare toes and listening to the sounds of the water. Small birds darted in and out of the tall grass closer to the river's edge, making musical, staccato noises as they tweeted at each other.

"No. Not at all. Especially early on. They trusted me to keep them informed. Most everything they knew about you when you were younger was what I chose to tell them. For a long time, they had no reason to believe I would ever hold anything back. Not till you were fourteen, and they realized your powers were increasing."

"And how did they know that? If they couldn't see us in your room? I wasn't exactly walking around showing off my abilities. Obviously even Luca didn't know."

"Your father had a woman who can look at people and see how powerful they are, she sees a glow about them. She was familiar with your look, which was one of immense power but undeveloped. One day, maybe a couple of years after she'd last seen you, she looked and saw that your glow was far more brilliant than it had been—it indicated a change in your power. A refining.

"At that point, an investigation was launched, spies that were unknown to me were sent. They saw you leaving my room in secret one too many times. Either I was training you or something inappropriate was going on. They quickly determined it to be the former."

Fallon stretched her body like a cat, soaking up the warmth of the sun. "I'm surprised after all that, which I assume was taken to be quite the betrayal on your part, that they allowed you to be the one to tattoo me."

"Well, like I said, I had campaigned for years to be the one. And there aren't that many people who can tattoo magic well. Let's just say that when the time came to do yours, their usual tattoo artist could not be found." He gave her a sideways glance.

She raised up on an elbow. "And now? Do they continue to watch me?"

"Your father, despite what he may tell you, and while he is kept informed, knows little about you, Fallon—who you are, what your life is like. In spite of everything that has transpired, it is still held that I am most knowledgeable regarding you. Regardless, he is too busy to pay much attention."

She narrowed her eyes. "What exactly is he busy doing?"

He wouldn't look directly at her. "All the things he does."

She let that go. "And you. You seem pretty powerful in your own right. *Ravener.* Why do you do anything at all that he wishes?"

He gave a rough little laugh. "Ah, because of you. Always because of you."

She sat up all the way. "Explain."

He rose up to a seated position as well, pulling his hair back from his face. "One night, around thirty years ago, I had a dream. Now, I do not dream often. Since I became who I am, it simply doesn't happen. And so, it was significant. I dreamed about a girl, maybe ten years old, wearing a black dress, sitting on a rock out in this river.

"On her lap was the raven. Comfortably the raven sat, as if he belonged there on her lap, and she had a gentle hand on him. She was watching me, as I stood on the shore, with unwavering green eyes. And I knew that I loved her more than anything in the world." He sat up straighter. "That was the extent of the dream. I had no idea who the girl was or what it might mean, if anything. The next morning, a message was sent to me that Carolina was pregnant, it requested that I guard her for the duration of the pregnancy. I had the option to decline the job. But coming so soon after the dream as it did, I felt the two things were connected, and I accepted immediately." He looked into her green eyes. "Of course, as it turned out, the girl on the rock was you."

Fallon was in tears. She placed her hands in his, feeling the strength with which his hands closed around hers. Shutting her eyes, she listened to the river pouring over the rocks, unendingly beautiful. Jacob leaned forward and rested his forehead against hers.

CHAPTER TWENTY-THREE

"I love you, Jacob. Forever, I will love you."

He kissed her, gently squeezing her hands. "And you know, my love, how I love you."

She looked at him. "But why did you wait fifteen years to return to me? How could you wait that long?"

He smiled a sad sort of smile. "Ah, yes. Those fifteen years." He sighed. "When Selah graduated from college," he began, "and was getting married and moving away, I wanted to go to you then. You were lost, as you so often were, not knowing where to go or what to do. Not knowing your purpose. And, I know, missing your brother and me." He watched as tears came again to her eyes. "I knew," he said gently. "I always knew how you missed me. And your pain wrapped around my heart, entwining itself with my own pain. As you grew into the beautiful woman that you are, I longed to be with you, that feeling consumed me. It took much self-control on my part to stay away from you."

He gazed at the river. "I knew that when I finally returned to you, I would never again want to be apart from you. As I mentioned before, I understood that it would set into motion your father's vengeance. Fallon, I didn't want to endanger you any sooner than I had to. I thought that by staying away, I was keeping you safe from him." He looked into her eyes. "I was doing what I thought was right, even though it was killing me."

She drew closer and knelt beside him, leaning against him. "I understand. You've been protecting me since before I was born. It's the first thing you think to do." She kissed him. "But you should have come back to me sooner."

He grinned, sliding his arms around her. "It has become abundantly clear that, yes, I should have."

CHAPTER TWENTY-FOUR

For the next several days, the weather was pleasant, and they spent that time exploring the mountains together, discovering beautiful spots which thrilled Fallon and which Jacob had long been absent from. On one of the days, he borrowed a pair of horses from a neighbor, and they spent the entire day riding. Fallon had never been on a horse before, but Jacob was at ease.

"You were never on a horse, even when you were young?" he asked, puzzled as he saw her anxiety.

"You were there." There was a challenge in her eyes as she stared at him. "You know there were no horses."

His forehead creased in thought. "At least just sat on a pony?"

"Never. No one sat me on a pony for a birthday pic or even ever took me to a petting zoo. Never." She threw him a wicked side eye.

"Someone failed you," he declared.

"Apparently."

He shrugged. "I'm not good with kids."

"You keep rolling out that excuse, but it's starting to show signs of being untrue." She sniffed. "Except for the lack of ponies."

He chuckled. "I will try to make it up to you. You see, I am making it up to you now! I borrow this one frequently," he admitted, stroking his horse's dark neck. "I enjoy riding around, spending time with such a magnificent animal."

"You got a calm one for me, right?" she asked nervously as her horse moved around. She was glad that her legs were strong, feeling that she might need all the help she could get to not be thrown off.

Jacob was smiling as he brought his horse up beside hers. "You know how to radiate calm. It works on animals the same as humans. Keep your horse calm or she'll take advantage—she can be a bit tricky."

Fallon growled at him, her brow creased with worry.

He laughed. "She is tricky but gentle, Fallon. Not unlike yourself."

She swatted him away ineffectively.

Despite her initial reservations, Fallon thoroughly enjoyed their horseback outing. They rode for several hours and then had lunch by a small stream they came upon, letting the horses graze nearby. After lunch, Jacob lay on the blanket in the shade, and Fallon lay comfortably on top of him, her head on his chest. She closed her eyes as the breeze gently blew her hair, listening to the steady beat of his heart beneath her cheek and the stream running a few yards away. They both dozed off lightly for a bit, waking each time the horses snorted and snuffled.

"Remember when I was nine, when I fell out of that tree in the backyard and broke my arm?" she asked sleepily.

"I could never forget. Luca's face was absolutely white with fear. You cried and cried. But I knew you would heal."

"You gave me whiskey."

"Yes, I did." He chuckled. "Just enough to calm you."

"Thus began my path to near-alcoholism."

He laughed out loud. "You've traced it all back to me, then?"

"I have, actually. Though I know you'd like to blame Tayce." She turned her head to lay on her other cheek. "How did you know I would heal?"

Jacob gave a little sigh. "I had already known for years. Since you were very young. Because your mother broke two of your ribs when you were three years old. And that night I held you in my arms until you healed."

She raised up on her arms. "What?"

He looked at her. "I wasn't certain that the ribs would heal, but I had observed early on that cuts and bruises did not last on you. And so, I suspected that your body possessed accelerated self-healing. But I didn't know if it could handle broken bones."

She dragged herself up his body so that they were face-to-face.

He grinned slyly. "Do that again, and I won't be able to finish my story."

She smirked. "Continue."

"It just so happened that I had arrived that night for one of my surprise checks, though she was unaware. I heard you screaming in pain, and I knew something was very wrong." His eyes looked briefly dark, and she remembered that he kept every memory. She thought this one must be unpleasant to relive. "I immediately took you to a different part of the house and locked us away and held you—I didn't know what else to do. I was explicitly not allowed to teleport with you without permission. No one from your father's circle was appearing to offer assistance, though that did not surprise me. They had turned a blind eye to your abuse for years. As long as I held you against me, you calmed down somewhat, whimpering in pain, but no longer screaming. So, I sat down and held you and waited. Eventually you fell asleep. I held you for hours, not wanting to wake you because I knew then you'd hurt again. After a few hours, I also fell asleep.

"When I woke up, you woke up as well. And you were fine. The ribs I'd determined to be broken seemed whole. You could take deep breaths without pain. But that event was the catalyst, the beginning of the end of your time with your mother. I went immediately to Kian and insisted that you be removed from Carolina. If it had been anyone else, he might have ignored the request. But you, filled with the potential for great power, appealed to the greed in his heart. He wanted you to live. And so, he let me save you."

There was an ache in Fallon's heart as she watched him. "Jacob." She shook her head. "The Ravener and The Child. What a strange twist from what I can only imagine your story had been up till then."

"Yes." He laughed. "It was definitely the plot twist no one saw coming."

She leaned down and kissed him. "I like this twist as well."

He grinned as he slid his hands up her body, rolling over so that she ended up beneath him. "It's my favorite," he agreed, kissing her back.

That evening in the cottage, Jacob found Fallon sitting cross-legged in front of the fire, staring at the flames. He watched with interest as, under her intense gaze, the tips of the flames changed to purple, then blue, then green, then back to yellow. Then her shoulders relaxed, and her breath returned to normal.

Crouching down beside her, he touched her jaw. "You are drunk on your own power," he observed with a laugh.

She looked at him, blushing. "I feel like lately every time I try something new, it just happens. I don't know, it's some kind of strange confidence I've not had before." She swept her arm around. "It's this place. And it's you. Awakening everything in me. I'll be teleporting next."

"Ah." He sat on the floor beside her. "Maybe not that."

"No?"

"Teleporting is a natural skill," he explained. "It is not easily taught—I'm not certain if it even can be taught. There is danger in the potential error. You can imagine."

"Hmm." Staring into the flames, Fallon sank deep into her thoughts while he rubbed her back, massaging her shoulders with his strong, tender hands.

After a while he nudged her. "What is on your mind, my love? You've been contemplating something for a while. Not just this evening, but over the past few days."

"I wanted to ask something." She glanced at him. "But I wasn't sure until now."

He waited patiently, the fingers of his left hand soothingly tapping out an entire piano concerto on her back.

She took a deep breath. "I don't want the premonitions anymore." Blinking rapidly, as if to push back tears, she looked at him again. "Is there some way, something we can do, to block them?" She sounded emotional. The premonitions had been with her for so long, she could barely remember a time when she had not had to deal with them. She felt guilty and hopeful all at once.

Jacob looked thoughtful, his fingers stilled on her back. "I've wondered before about that, if you would ever ask. I know that they've troubled you for some time now."

"It's incredible to look into the future," she admitted, "but it's also a burden. And I don't want that burden anymore. I'm so overwhelmed with everything else."

His hand slid up behind her neck, and he softly kissed her temple. "I can make them go away. Of course, I will do that for you, Fallon. There is a tattoo that will accomplish just this." He stood up, pulling her to her feet. "Come."

Her heart was thrumming anxiously as she followed him to the study, to the table where he'd removed the star tattoo during her first visit.

"Pull your hair all the way back," he instructed. "I need to get to your ears."

"My ears?"

He ran a finger over the bone of her skull just behind her left ear. "Here. On both sides."

She pulled her hair up in a bun and sat with her forehead on the table. He began rattling around in his metal box.

"I'm nervous," she confessed.

"There's no need. A bit more pressure than usual, because of the proximity to bone, but nothing you cannot handle."

"What will they look like? The tattoos?"

"A short, silver line behind each ear."

"Silver?" She glanced back at him.

"Yes. It's unusual-looking on skin, that's true. But it's a special ink, powerful enough to break the premonition line in your mind." He sat on a stool and scooted close to her. "You know I won't hurt you. It will be, for you, a mild discomfort."

"I know you won't hurt me, that's not why I'm nervous. I'm anxious. About the premonitions stopping."

"Ah." She felt his gloved hands on her skin, cleaning the area behind her ears with alcohol. "You've never not known them. I understand." He squeezed her shoulder. "You know this already, but I must remind you—be very still. I am breaking a line, not simply tattooing you. It is a delicate process."

She nodded and closed her eyes.

He started behind her right ear, taking his time. The pressure to her skull caused her to catch her breath a few times, but there was little pain. Moving to her other side, he carefully added the second mark behind her left ear.

As he finally finished and his needle left her skin for the last time, she whimpered at a sharp pain that zinged through her head, from ear to ear. It was gone in seconds. Jacob placed a comforting hand on her shoulder, setting aside his tools and removing his gloves. She felt his lips brush against each tattoo tenderly, in turn, and then she leaned back against his chest as a new feeling settled over her. He wrapped his arms around her and held her close while she looked around, wide-eyed. Different.

"They're gone," she murmured. "I can tell that they're gone." She was shaken, despite the relief. The premonitions had defined her for all her life. It was startling that they were no more.

He kissed her cheek. "Let's go to the kitchen, you need to drink water."

She sat up shakily, and as he held up two mirrors for her, she saw the faint slashes of silver behind each ear. And she felt the freedom they provided her. Turning and kissing him, she allowed him to help her to her feet. He guided her to the kitchen, where she sat on a tall stool and held a glass of cool water to her lips. Her hands were shaking too badly to hold the glass herself.

"They have been a distraction for you, the premonitions," he observed, releasing her hair from the bands that held it back and watching as the golden locks fell around her face. "They needed to be put to rest. It was time."

CHAPTER TWENTY-FIVE

In the morning when Fallon opened her eyes, she could smell food cooking. She had a vague, sweet memory of Jacob waking her in the night and kissing her goodbye, whispering that he would be back in a day or two, then kissing her again passionately. The sense of his reluctance to leave her had been pouring off of him in waves, but eventually he'd vanished, his gaze never leaving hers.

Getting out of bed and remembering the look in his eyes, she felt mild unease as she dressed—where had he gone that he'd looked so troubled at leaving her? She headed out to the kitchen where she found the source of the enticing aromas. Colette was making breakfast.

The woman smiled at her when Fallon appeared, blue eyes twinkling. "It will be ready in a moment."

Fallon was surprised. "You don't need to go to this trouble." She looked around, hoping that Jacob had been wrong about being gone from her. But she and Colette were alone in the cottage except for Azul, who was in the kitchen eating kibble.

Still smiling as she slid some eggs onto a plate, Colette set some warm tortillas on the table. "Ah, but I don't mind at all, Fallon Rose, and besides, Jacob requested it. He felt badly that he had to leave you so suddenly. He hasn't had to leave you like this before, not for this long and not for this particular type of assignment." She paused. "He never wants to be apart from you, I can see it in his face, and regardless, I know his heart."

Fallon sat down at the table and tore a piece off of a tortilla. "Can you explain that to me? Why are you 'the heart of the Ravener'?"

Colette set a glass of water and a plate of food before Fallon. Then she poured her a cup of hot tea and one for herself as well. "It's a long story and not easily explained. He and I are linked, due to things that occurred on that terrible day when he became the Ravener, and I take care of him as best I can. I am not truly his heart, of course, but I know his heart. I know what he needs." She sat down across from Fallon. "Eat, child."

Fallon sipped the tea. "Can I not ask how you became this? It was a mistake when I asked him how he became the Ravener."

Colette's face was grave. "Jacob has been through hell. He goes through it still, time and again. His is not an easy job, not an easy life. It is a curse upon him—it destroyed everything. He took it on in an act of selfless compassion. It was a cruelty of the universe that such an act would be met with such darkness." She was frowning into her tea, seemingly lost in thought, and Fallon listened without breathing.

"But then," Colette's face lightened, "there is you." She looked up and gazed at Fallon. Then she gave a small sigh. "No, I cannot share my details without telling you his story. That remains his to tell. Though I feel he will tell it to you, one day. When he is ready."

"Did you two know each other? Before?" Fallon wondered.

Colette shook her head. "We were strangers."

"And are you immortal?" She added salsa to her eggs.

"I am ageless while I am in the Ravener's service. If he were to die, my body would begin aging again as before. At least that is what I've always known in my heart. I don't like to speak of death with you. Let me speak of love, since you have reintroduced that particular joy into our world. Jacob has several places of residence around this globe which he uses when necessary. But this Spanish cottage, this is his sanctuary, the place he feels most at home. It is sacred to him. Do you know you are the first person in all his history to be brought here?"

Fallon took another sip of tea, her hand trembling slightly. "That can't be. That woman…"

"Whom he loved? Her name was Violet. Yes, he loved her very much. And yet contrary to what you may think, he did not ever bring her here, not once. You, on the other hand, he brought here immediately, without hesitation."

Fallon's breathing had quickened. Adrenaline was surging through her. "He brought Tayce and Bergen here as well," she argued.

Colette was looking at her intently. "Fallon, he hears your name on the wind, in the rush of the water—this whole place now literally sings your name in his soul. For over a century he has been broken, a dark shadow, even while he loved and lost Violet. But you heal him. You make him whole, fill him with wonder and joy. You are unlike any other. You, Fallon, are his salvation." Colette lightly touched the rim of her teacup in a meditative fashion. "That is my belief."

Tears slid down Fallon's face. *A century.* She dug her nails into her palm. *His salvation.*

"He brought Tayce and Bergen here because they are two people who are very much in your heart, whom you love and trust," Colette explained. "And I think he was showing off. Showing two people who adore you, where it is you go with the one who adores you most."

Fallon placed her hands against her temples, closing her eyes. She had never felt anything like the emotions that were pummeling her heart, bruising it with their power. She wished that Jacob was there with her. She was overwhelmed with her need to see him, to hold him close.

Eventually she wiped away her tears and resumed eating, composed. "Again, I ask: not how, but who are you? Who were you?"

Colette gazed out the window. "I no longer wonder who I was. Before. Jacob remembers himself, but I do not. Whoever I was, I became bound to him at the moment he became the Ravener, and now I remember little else." She smiled slightly. "I would like to say perhaps I'd been the white dove in some magician's act. But then, how do you explain the cooking skills?"

Fallon allowed a slight smile. Finished with the meal, she sat back from the table. "Do you think I'll be able to defeat my father?"

Colette's warm face changed. "Don't call him that." She spat out the words. "Kian was never a father to you. That murderer. Luca was more a father to you than Kian."

"Yes, Luca definitely was more a parent than anyone," Fallon agreed. "He started parenting me as soon as I entered his life. Jacob was certainly not paternal."

"No, that he was not," Colette laughed. "He was not paternal to the two of you at any point. But then, he was never a father, before. A son, a brother, yes, but not a father. He was an uncle as well, but he was not much interested in his nieces and nephews."

"He had a family." Fallon spoke the thought aloud. "They…what…"

Her face full of sorrow, Colette shook her head. "You must never ask. I said too much. I know he will likely tell you one day, in his time. But do not ask him. I can say no more."

Fallon fell silent, folding her hands together.

Colette smiled gently and changed the subject. "It was amusing to me when he was first placed with you and Luca in the Austin house; I was not sure how it would go. There was a contingency plan where I would come and stay as well, to take care of the two of you. But that ended up being unnecessary— you and your brother rarely asked anything of him, having already been fairly self-sufficient on your own with the Quinns."

"Did you know that he was training me?"

"I knew what he was doing. I watched the bond between you both strengthen. It was amusing, his patience with an eleven-year-old girl, teaching such difficult lessons, but then, you were an excellent student. You wanted to impress him, and you were eager to learn. He had always been such an enigma to you. You were delighted at the attention and rose to the challenge. He met his match in you, I felt."

Fallon traced the embroidered pattern on the tablecloth. "Can I defeat Kian?"

Colette rose and began gathering the dishes. "You can," her voice was almost hesitant, "and Kian knows it. So, I am not sure how he will approach it. But as in the past, everyone you love is in danger. He will try to cripple you with loss. It has long been his single tactic with you."

Anger coursed through Fallon. "Then Jacob had better begin teaching me quickly."

* * * * * * *

Jacob returned two days later in the middle of the night. Fallon awoke to the sound of the shower running; it took her a minute to process what the sound was and what it meant. Realizing he was back, she jumped out of bed and ran towards the bathroom. "Jacob!"

The only answer was a faint groan of pain, and she went quickly around the privacy wall of the shower. There she found Jacob standing naked under the full blast of hot water. Fallon stopped abruptly with a small, startled cry. Her gaze started at his feet and worked its way slowly up his strong body, taking in the range of injuries—the blood and the bruises, the cuts and abrasions. She finally made it to his handsome face, where she found three cruel lacerations on his left cheek. His long, wet hair was clinging to his neck, and his blue eyes were watching her.

"My love," he greeted her gently, his weary voice nonetheless filled with happiness to see her again. He winced as the water hit a particularly raw wound on his leg, and Fallon watched as blood continued to swirl around the drain. Jacob shook his head. "I don't want you to see me like this."

But as her eyes filled with tears, they stayed locked on his eyes, and she began removing her clothes. "And I do not want you to feel pain, Jacob." Naked, she came over to him and wrapped her arms around him, pressing her body against his as the hot water ran over her skin. She turned her head to look up at him. "Is it all surface injury? Nothing deeper?" Seeing the terrible marks on his cheek caused her blood to burn. She reached up and touched them lightly with a shaking hand.

"More or less," he confirmed. "A lot of things hurt; I'll say that. Nothing is broken. Fallon, please don't cry," he pleaded, kissing her cheek. "This is simply what I must do sometimes. It happens, now and then. Many of the things I am required to do, they are not easy. There is danger, death, and violence—it cannot be avoided. But I have survived thus far, haven't I?" He smiled at her fondly. "I will be alright in a few days."

She pressed her tear-stained cheek against his chest and tightened her hold on him, closing her eyes.

A moment later Jacob felt the power wash over him—he caught his breath at the sensation as his entire body began to slowly heal. He tried to speak, to stop her, but the force of her will was overwhelming. In the end, he could only cling to her.

After what Jacob estimated to be around ten minutes, Fallon's hold on him loosened, and she slid towards the floor. He reacted, crouching down and catching her before she hit. Sitting down under the direct spray of the water, with his back against the wall, he pulled her onto his lap and cradled her against his chest.

She had healed him. Entirely. Every scrape, every burn, bruise, and cut, even every aching muscle—all were restored. He tentatively touched his cheek, but the lacerations were gone as well.

He was astonished. He'd been well aware that her skill for healing had improved dramatically since she'd healed the long cut on his arm when she was only twelve. But he marveled at the change in her ability even since she'd healed Jack Lane's arm several months before. It could not be merely her increased confidence causing this. He wondered if by removing the premonition ability, all of her other skills had been strengthened and sharpened? It gave him hope, in regard to her odds of defeating her father.

"Fallon." He touched her cheek and looked closely at her, kissing her lips. "Fallon."

Her eyes fluttered open and then she smiled.

He kissed her forehead. "That was unnecessary," he murmured. "But appreciated, all the same. Thank you."

Her fingers tenderly traced the old scars on his chest. "I didn't want you to feel more pain. You've had enough."

The surge of her love washed over his body like a powerful wave, and he felt himself blinking away tears. *I will never have enough of you*, he thought.

The next morning, Fallon slept long and hard. Jacob lingered in bed with her, physically exhausted from the night before and emotional regarding what she had done for him. It was noon when he finally rose and headed into the kitchen to prepare a nourishing meal—sausage, eggs, rolls, yogurt, and fruit—which Fallon happily devoured when she joined him.

Eventually they were outside in the sunshine together. Fallon held his hands and closed her eyes, turning her face upward and feeling the warmth on her skin. When she looked back at him, he was watching her with affection.

"Where were you?" she demanded. "Who hurt you? What were you doing? Were you fighting someone? Tortured?"

Her distress hurt his heart. He pulled her hair back from her face. "Oh, my love." He sighed. "Fallon, I will never tell you what I do. There is enough darkness in the world. I have no doubt that the darkness will touch you now and then, but I will not immerse you in it by sharing the details of my brutal tasks, my sweet girl."

She wrapped her arms around his neck, and he held her close, running his hand soothingly over her back.

"You need to train me," she told him. "So that I can put this awful thing with Kian behind me and place all my focus on you."

Jacob held her back a little. "I do love when your focus is on me," he murmured, and she smiled slyly. But what he told her next surprised her.

"The secret about your powers and your training is, there's no great secret." He took her wrists in his hands and rubbed his thumbs over the tattoos. "These tattoos are the gateway to all the power you possess. And remember, I've told you that you are extremely powerful. Press those two tattoos together and everything inside you unlocks. Every last bit of your power. That is why when Kian takes you, they bind you with a cord to ensure your wrists can come nowhere near each other."

She held her wrists up, frowning. "I touch them together and what, though?"

"You have to focus. And there has to be a fire," he touched her chest, "here. Your heart must burn with fury, with a desire to destroy or at least to unleash everything that is within you." The skin near his eyes crinkled with a smile. "I cannot teach you what will happen next. It is something that you will simply know. Your mind and body will work together to manifest whatever needs to be done."

She narrowed her eyes. "That's my lesson?"

"How else could I get you here for weeks, uninterrupted?"

Fallon smiled. "For that, you only had to ask."

"There is a reason." He tucked her hair behind her ears. "You must meditate. Focus. Strengthen your mind and your heart, your will. You must be rock solid. Unshakeable. Your father is incredibly vicious and strong. Ruthless. Heartless. You are stronger, but you are not ruthless. You must be steady and single-minded, ready for anything. Your reflexes must be sharp." He felt her tremble with doubt beneath his touch. "Fallon."

Her gaze met his.

"You have a warrior heart. It has always been that way. You are a survivor. You will be ready." Taking her hand, he led her a short distance down a path. There he sat in the grass, in full view of the sheep, pulling her down with him.

"You have strategically placed me in view of the flock to calm me," she accused.

"Perhaps." He sat cross-legged, facing her, his knees against hers. Taking her hands in his, he turned them over to expose her wrists and the two tattoos. "Kian and his people had, for a long time, contemplated the harnessing of powers using tattoos. Of course, it's been done before, but every madman thinks his ideas are new and unique. Kian is no different. Years ago, your brother was taken at age twenty solely so that your father could enact his experiment. Since your brother had moderate power, it was considered that he would be a safe test subject.

"It takes powerful magic to capture power, to create portals out of tattoos in order to funnel that power. Your father's artist is not a genius is this area. He has little talent, but he is a long-time crony of Kian's, and therefore no one dares challenge his place, nor do they alert Kian that his man may be weak. When you are in such a position as Kian is—hated, feared, and respected—people are going to react, not for your good, but to keep themselves safe."

"Did it work? With Luca? With the tattoos?"

He shook his head, rubbing his thumbs over her tattoos in a way that made electricity coil up pleasantly inside of her.

"Do these tattoos react to you differently than anyone else because you're the one who made them?" she demanded.

He gave her a charmingly wicked smile. "Possibly." He leaned forward and kissed her, but finally she pulled back, breathless.

"I want more of the story."

"Luca's tattoos were poor, as I've always said. Laughable, when you understand what the intent had been. They did nothing, really, at all. By this time, your father was well-aware of how powerful you are, and he knew that trying the same tattoos on you would be riskier, both for you and possibly for everyone in the direct vicinity. Kian is fully knowledgeable that my skills with tattooing magic are unmatched, but it was only when his artist went temporarily missing that he relented to allow me to be the one."

CHAPTER TWENTY-FIVE

Her tone was low and soft. "And with me, it worked. Didn't it?"

He nodded, pressing his thumbs into her tattooed skin, causing her to catch her breath. "It worked." He let go of her and leaned back. "Obviously, you are powerful without the tattoos— they don't give you power. You are filled with the talents for countless abilities, many of which you don't even know about. So, imagine it this way—within you this all manifests as a swirling, glowing mass of power. The power is what fuels your abilities when you use them. It is always there in you, resting just under the surface. The idea is that, when the tattoos touch and you engage fiery focus, the power unleashes from you, and you can direct it in whatever manner you choose."

She looked puzzled.

He touched her chin. "This is why I say it cannot be fully explained. The power is yours, not mine. I have never known anyone with your level of potential, of inner strength. I can't say what will happen when you lock those tattoos together and seek to do whatever you might do. I'm sorry that it is vague."

"I burned Jack with this tattoo." She held up her right wrist. "Without intending to."

"You unconsciously summoned the magic to accomplish what you desired—to get him off of you. There is no telling what you will eventually be able to do."

Fallon sank into her thoughts, appearing troubled. "It had never happened before."

"Which?" He was smirking. "A man trying to take advantage of you or burning someone with your tattoo?"

"Both. I've been able to avoid treacherous situations with men because I can usually read their thoughts and intentions. I always knew who to steer clear of. Jack is different because his intentions are all over the place, and honestly, he didn't intend to become so rough with me."

"Maybe that is why the tattoo did not kill him, only injured him."

Fallon's eyes widened briefly. "That would have been traumatizing," she remarked lightly. "Luca had a black bird on his wrist, was it supposed to be a raven?"

Jacob snorted. "Possibly. There is a lack of imagination in that camp. I can tell you that the artist was instructed to choose two images and place them on Luca's wrists. For whatever reason, he chose a bird and an eye. To stay consistent, when it was time for yours, I kept those two elements. It worked nicely with my desire to tattoo a raven that was linked with mine. Your eye tattoo enhances your ability to see and includes the protection from being fooled by disguises, by shapeshifters and the like. But there was no grand plan in the choice of the eye and the bird. I simply made them adhere to my purpose when it was my turn to tattoo you."

Fallon crawled onto his lap, straddling him and laying her arms loosely on his shoulders. "This can't be it. There has to be more to preparing me."

Tracing her jaw, he gazed at her. "There will be tests. I will do what I can. But in reality, slamming those tattoos together and funneling every bit of power that you have at your enemy is your foremost lesson." He covered her mouth with his, devouring her as she pressed forward against him.

CHAPTER TWENTY-SIX

"Colette said you have other places that you stay."

Jacob nodded. They were sitting side by side on the blanket on the precipice, enjoying the view. "Yes, that's true, I do have several places available to me."

"Did they...come with the job, so to speak, or...?"

"Hmm." He leaned back on his elbows. "Let's just say, about all the others, that I acquired them here and there along my journey. A collection, if you will. This place, though, I sought out. I always felt my soul brought me here. Once I got the land and the cottage, I spent decades making it into a secure sanctuary."

"This place is special," she agreed. "It speaks to me. It heals me."

He smiled at her. "Sometimes I think that I created it all for you."

She rested her head against his shoulder a moment. Then she sat up. "There's been something else I wanted to bring up. I noticed something strange, after I started seeing Bret last year."

He looked at her expectantly.

"My raven tattoo. Out of the blue, it would start tingling uncomfortably. Most often when I was interacting with Bret in some way."

A nearby blade of grass suddenly seemed to hold all of his interest.

"Jacob."

He gazed into her eyes with a sigh.

"Was it you?" she asked quietly.

"Yes. It was me." He sat up straighter. "Usually, but not always, unintentional. I was jealous. Though I had seen you with men before, this was different. You had an emotional connection with him. It brought out not the best emotions in me. After this life I have led, I am unfamiliar with jealousy. But seeing you with him, it unlocked that particular emotion in the harshest way. And was so strong that it found its way to your wrist."

"In December, it was much worse," she remarked, laying her hand on his chest. "In December, it hurt."

He ran his hand along her cheek. "Because I had just seen you, held you in my arms, only a month before. After being away from you for so many years, it was all I could do in Nashville not to kiss you. It made seeing you with him later all the more painful. I am sorry."

She slid her arms around his neck and pulled him close. "No apologies. If you had kissed me in Nashville, I would have come completely undone and never gone back out to them."

He grinned, pressing his face against hers. "I know. I wanted to take you home with me that night, believe me. I desperately wanted to bring you back here. Immediately saying goodbye to you was like a knife in my heart. But I knew, for one, that your conscience would not let you run out on those two without explanation, causing them worry and distress. And also, I knew that I was about to be gone for a month, and that when I got home, I would likely be in much the same shape you found me in the other night. I didn't want you to be faced with that so soon. That is why I did not return to you till London."

She pulled back and held his face in her hands, looking into his eyes. "And were you, after that month? Injured and bleeding, like you were the other night?"

He grasped her wrists, sliding his thumbs over the tattoos, sending pleasant shocks through her body. "Yes."

Tears filled her eyes. "You were alone."

"Fallon." He cradled her head in his hands. "I have always been alone." Her eyes closed as his lips went to her throat. "You are the most wondrous thing to ever come into my life." His lips found hers again, then he sat back. "My beautiful girl, you have become everything to me. The love you show me is an elixir to my dark, lonely existence, to the trials that I face, the sorrows I have endured. You will never fully know how you have saved me."

Tears crisscrossed her cheeks as she wrapped her arms around him. Laying down together, they fell asleep on the blanket, entangled with each other, faces touching.

When they woke up later, he rolled over onto his back, smoothly pulling her on top of him in what was now a practiced move. He stroked her hair as she stared at the landscape.

"You have more questions," he guessed.

"Are you reading my mind now?"

He gave a low chuckle. "I wish. No, there's a little clicking sound you make with your tongue when you are preparing to ask me a question."

She rose up to look at him. "Seriously?"

He cocked at eyebrow. "Seriously."

Lowering herself back down, she grinned. "I do have a question." She felt the silent rumbling of laughter in his chest. "Why did Simon die?"

Jacob took his time, scanning the sky, following a dark bird that was flying overhead. "Kian always detested Simon. He didn't like his involvement in yours and Luca's lives—again, Selah's survival surprised me—but I advised him early on to let things alone with Simon. Especially when I saw the relationship between Simon and your brother taking shape. And so, he did."

She raised up to watch him as he spoke.

"But later, when Kian had your brother killed and you completely fell apart, and then immediately embarked on an unfortunate and twisted physical relationship with Simon as a way to further destroy yourself," Fallon bit her lip, avoiding his gaze, "Kian's revulsion to Simon deepened."

She cut her eyes at him. "I doubt you were a big fan, either."

He shifted uncomfortably under her. "I knew what you were doing, I understood why. You were in so much pain. It was difficult for me to see you hating life. I was devastated that I couldn't go to you and sweep you away, to comfort you, to heal your grief. But things were still too tense between Kian and I regarding you, and as he had just had Luca murdered, I knew he would swiftly kill you as well if I pushed him too much. I was helpless to do anything but watch you self-destruct." He brought her hand to his lips.

"Selah brought me back to life."

He nodded. "As I knew, or at least hoped, she would."

"So, what happened? It was many years later that Simon was killed. He had been away from me and out of my life for a long time."

"You and he had been back in touch," he reminded her. "It sparked something in Simon, maybe due to the immense grief he still harbored regarding Luca's death, and so he began digging too deeply into sources he should have avoided in order to attempt to untangle the mysteries in your life. He was becoming obsessed, unbeknownst to you. He had not been on Kian's radar for years, but as soon as he learned what Simon was doing, he reacted immediately and ordered him killed, eager to finally be rid of him."

She stared at him, feeling a strange tension in her bones. "Was it you?" she asked, voice barely a whisper.

He shook his head. "Fallon, no. I would never agree to harm anyone in your circle. No matter how I felt about them. After I was ordered away from you when you were younger, it created a deep rift and Kian never asked anything of me again. His trust for me was broken. Which was a relief, to me."

She lay her head back down against his chest.

CHAPTER TWENTY-SEVEN

"**S**omehow I never knew sheep could be so soothing."
Jacob laughed at Fallon's observation. She was sitting
on one of the stone pillars that supported the wooden
fence around the cottage, and he was standing nearby. Together
they watched as Colette walked amongst her flock, talking to the
sheep. Though she was at a distance, they could see her smiling,
peaceful face. Fallon looked at Jacob and noticed how he was
watching Colette, the satisfied smile on his lips.

"You didn't create this place solely for you and me."

He looked at her.

She gestured at Colette and the sheep. "You did it for her,
too. None of this can have been easy for her. She hasn't faced
the same violence and darkness you have, but all the same, she
lost the life she had before and is chained to you for all time.
You've said before that she is in her element here. I know you
must have also had her in mind."

Jacob came closer. "I have always felt an obligation to
bring her comfort, knowing that being tethered to me was not
her choice."

Looking around, Fallon bit her lip. "Do we know for sure that Kian will try to kill me?" Everything surrounding them was beautiful, so much a piece of heaven. Birds were singing nearby. She sometimes had a difficult time imagining that Kian was truly a threat.

Jacob took both her hands in his, his expression somber. "It is a certainty, Fallon, I am sorry. Kian is a bully, a sadistic egomaniac. But he is a coward. He has been afraid of you for a long time. His greed is what has kept you alive till now. He believed one day he might possibly use you, that he might add you to his arsenal. Control you. From things I picked up on over the years, I feel he thought he might eventually sway me to his way of thinking. I know that, at one time, in order to regain my allegiance, he fully intended to offer you to me as a creature to be possessed, so that I might do what I liked to you." He winked at her as she blushed, laughing. Softly he brushed her lips with his.

"He never knew how I loved you all along; no one would have ever expected that from me. As we said, it was the great plot twist—the cold and heartless Ravener would never in a thousand lifetimes have fallen deeply and completely in love with the sweet, elusive Fallon Quinn. It was not in my character to do so." He gave a slight smirk. "I have long been what people expect I am. It is easier to be ignored that way. It brings less conflict into my realm. But now, knowing that you and I are in love, as completely entwined as we could possibly be, Kian will be panicking. Yes, I said he would take his time. He will. But you can be assured that he is frightened. That he is regretting all the times he could have destroyed you but did not.

"I have heard all the underground rumblings, Fallon, as well as the news that is shared with me by people in his circle who maintain a degree of loyalty to me. Kian wants you dead. By his own hand. He will not rest. You saw what nearly happened in Amsterdam. He hasn't changed his mind; he knows that with every passing day, you grow stronger, more aware.

"That is why you and I are about to take further steps in preparing and protecting you. If he attacks you, I will burn myself to the ground defending you, but he knows this, and he will try to separate us. I need you to be strong enough to face him alone, just in case."

She was trembling under his touch, her eyes full of fear. Unable to imagine the scenarios he was painting for her.

He wrapped his arms around her, pulling her close. "Fallon, I believe in my heart that you can do this terrible thing. That you can face him and come out the victor." He pressed his lips to her forehead. "I know it is not anything you asked for, nothing you could have expected. This has all been playing out behind the scenes for your entire life. I hadn't been looking forward to the day when I had to lay it all out for you, to tell you the truth about Luca and about Kian. But that day has come, and you now possess this knowledge; I know the weight of it wants to break you. But I also know how emotionally strong you are. How mentally strong you have become. I would bet on no one more so than on you, my love.

"One thing Kian cannot easily do is kill you in this world. In your world. He is weaker here. He will try to pull you to his realm, where he has the upper hand. The longer we can hold him off from doing so, the more frustrated he will become, and there will then be the chance that he will attempt something here.

"I have seen the lines in your mind. They are similar to Violet's, with a few key differences here and there. The raven, when you were attempting your mind tricks last August, saw your lines clearly, and because of that I now have the image in my head, like a map. There is a copper-colored line—it is nearly hidden behind the gold and red lines. Into this copper line you must place two bends. That will strengthen you against being stolen by outside forces. It is not fool-proof, especially against someone as powerful as Kian, but it will add extra protection." He looked thoughtful. "There is also a tattoo I could try. I've used it once before."

"On Violet?"

He shook his head. "On another."

She didn't ask.

That evening, Fallon sat on the ottoman in front of the fire. Azul was asleep on the rug in his usual spot. Jacob reclined on the couch behind Fallon, watching her.

Resting her hands on her knees, she closed her eyes and concentrated on breathing deeply for a minute or two. When she was relaxed and centered, she fell back deep into her mind. There she could see a group of shimmering lines, each a different color.

The first thing she noticed was the blue-green premonition line; it had always glowed the brightest, dominating the other lines with its presence. It was into this line that she had put a gentle bend the year before, in order to enhance her premonition ability. But she saw that now the line was no longer whole. It was snapped in two, the ends curled up and blackened as if burned. Even though she had known the premonition line had been cut by the two silver tattoos, it was still shocking to see.

Fallon had somehow always known about the lines in her mind, even before Jacob began teaching her. Each line represented a different ability, though besides the premonition line, she was never sure which color matched with which skill. Jacob had been able to teach her a little about them, but even he didn't know them all. There were far more lines in her mind than the number of abilities he had awakened in her.

Luca had surprised her once by admitting he knew about the lines, though he had only seen them; he had never thought to manipulate them. He had three other lines besides the premonition line, which he assumed must be the abilities of mental telepathy, reading people, and seeing in the dark. All were things both siblings could effortlessly do back during their youth. When her brother had asked her what color her other three lines were, and she looked in her mind and saw an endless canvas of lines burning with a rainbow of colors, Fallon was scared and lied to him. Luca went to his grave never knowing how full her head was of the unknown.

Now she looked around amongst the lines until she finally spotted the red and gold ones. Behind them she could see the copper-colored line Jacob had spoken of. With care, she focused on it, being sure not to touch the red and gold. The copper line hummed happily under her attention, glowing warmly. Slowly she began to bend it.

From the couch, Jacob saw Fallon's breath quicken with the effort it was taking to bend the line. His heart shattered with the love he felt for her. He wished she knew how brave she was, how strong and capable. Her kindness broke his heart. Her goodness overwhelmed him. The shadows in her eyes, which he'd seen when she was younger, were all but gone now.

The universe had cruelly cursed him so long ago, stealing his family, his life, his future—all that he knew and loved. He'd walked in darkness for so many years. But now Fallon loved him, and it was all he could see. Every time she smiled at him, it washed away more and more of the scars in his old, battered heart, making him feel new. She awakened things in him which he'd long ago forgotten. He wondered where this path they were on would lead them, for he'd learned ages ago that nothing was forever. But Fallon, he thought, was forever. No matter what hell brought to him, he would never let her go, even unto death.

Adding the second bend to the copper line took everything Fallon had left, her mind already exhausted from the first bend. She slipped once, but narrowly avoided the gold line. She had no idea what the gold line represented or what might happen if she hit it, but when it came to the lines, caution was best.

Finally, after an hour had passed, the copper-colored line held two bends. Fallon looked over her shoulder. Jacob had fallen asleep on the leather couch. She crawled off the ottoman and lay down beside him, sliding her arm around him and burying her face against his chest. She felt him kiss the top of her head as he wrapped an arm around her, and they both fell asleep.

CHAPTER TWENTY-EIGHT

The next morning when she woke up, Jacob was gone. In the middle of the night, his body achy from their entanglement on the couch, he had gotten up and carried her to the bedroom. Laying her down on the bed and then carefully lowering himself onto her, he'd kissed her and told her he would have to leave in an hour.

"I'll hopefully be back by evening. I want to get started on your tattoo then."

She kissed him back hard, snaking her fingers into his hair. "Let's make this next hour memorable, then," she challenged, and he grinned.

But now she was alone in the bed, the mid-morning sun shining in. Pushing aside her deep worry about what Jacob was doing and if he would be injured like last time, she forced her brain to contemplate other things. She thought about Tayce, wondering how the rest of the tour was going for him, missing his camaraderie. She felt sadness regarding Kat and Paul, their new way of life. And she worried about Bergen, who was now not only separated from her father, but only able to communicate with Fallon by letter.

Apparently, the raven was able to deliver mail. This discovery had delighted Bergen, though Fallon tried not to think too hard about it. When she gave Jacob a quizzical look, he pressed his lips together and shook his head, disavowing knowledge of this particular magical facet.

One day in her bedroom, lonely Bergen had written a letter to Fallon, pretending that she could mail it, though she knew she could not, since Fallon was with Jacob. It had brought her comfort, putting pen to paper—Fallon had long encouraged her to keep a handwritten journal, and maybe, she reasoned, this was why.

As she slipped the letter into an envelope and lay it on her desk, a clattering and flapping at her window startled her. A large black bird with gleaming eyes was trying to gain entrance. Thinking immediately of Fallon and Jacob's tattoos, Bergen had opened the window without a thought. The raven had flown in, snatched the letter off her desk, and then departed as suddenly as he'd appeared, leaving one glossy black feather in his wake.

That evening, he had reappeared to her bearing a letter from Fallon. And thus, their secret mail service was established.

"He likes her, I suppose," Jacob allowed, when Fallon pressed him again about why the raven would be acting in this way, despite receiving no order or direction to do so and remaining unseen for the past hundred years. "Possibly she reminds him of you when you were a child. He is devoted to you, believe it or not. You have been his focus for so long. Remember he sometimes left you a feather as a token when you were younger." He chuckled. "It caused very reasonable and logical Selah much consternation."

Now Fallon rubbed a hand over her face as she sat cross-legged in bed. Trying to set her mind on other things had not worked. Subconsciously, she was still worried about Jacob, and now she missed Tayce and Bergen as well. Getting out of bed, she splashed water on her face and got dressed.

No one was cooking breakfast for her this morning, which was fine because she wasn't in the mood for conversation. Making herself some hot tea, she sat at the window and stared out at the perfect blue sky. She nibbled on a slice of toast. At one point, two sheep ran by, Azul chasing gleefully after them, and Fallon smiled.

After putting away her breakfast things, she returned to the bedroom and began folding laundry. As she had learned, Colette usually handled most of the household chores, but lately Fallon had been taking over more of these tasks, as she and Jacob preferred that no one interrupt them in the cottage. Fallon had never minded folding laundry. It was the one mindless chore that calmed her.

She began putting things away in drawers, wondering where Jacob purchased his clothes. Such an odd thing to think about, she mused. Some fancier items came from Paris and London; she supposed that being around for as long as he had, he would by now know where to get the best things. He had definitely developed his own style. Money seemed to be no object, and she speculated if that had come with the Ravener position.

As she tucked a shirt away into a drawer, her hand hit cold metal—dark images immediately filled her head, and she flinched away. Pushing the shirt aside, she saw the silver dagger laying there before her on a piece of black velvet. The dagger Jacob had introduced her to when she was only eleven, when he'd taught her about psychometry and healing. Now prepared, she picked the dagger up, blocking its history from her mind. The images of the deaths. All at Jacob's hand.

The dagger was beautiful but cruel, and heavy in her hands. She wondered why he didn't have it with him, panicking briefly that he might need it and be without it. Then she reminded herself that he had been doing this for apparently a century. He would not leave a necessary weapon behind. Maybe he hadn't needed a weapon for whatever task lay before him today. That thought calmed her a bit.

She reflected that when his whereabouts had been entirely unknown to her, she had rarely been worried specifically about his well-being. Her concern for him had been wrapped up in all of her emotions regarding him: grief, anger, confusion, sadness, loss. But now that he was with her, the foremost presence in her life, she fretted about his safety every time he left her. Would she ever get used to it? The fear of losing him? The anguish of seeing him wounded, bleeding and in pain?

Her joy did what it could to negate all the fear. Her love for him ran wild like their river, beyond her control. Despite the chaos and the unknown, loving him steadied her.

* * * * * * *

It was cold in the cottage that evening—Fallon had accidentally let the fire die out and then had not re-lit it early enough—so she sat on a stool in the kitchen with a hot mug of spiced apple cider, a black knit hat pulled down on her head. She nibbled on a slice of homemade bread Colette had dropped off earlier, watching as the fire roared in the fireplace. Shadows danced on the walls as she felt the drink begin to warm her, and the fire slowly spread its warmth into the cottage.

Jacob suddenly appeared behind her, wrapping her up in his strong arms and holding onto her tightly. He rested his chin on her shoulder, his eyes closing as Fallon relaxed against him.

"It's a wondrous thing," he said, "coming home to you."

She reached up, placing her hand against his face, and he kissed her palm. "You've been lonely here," she observed. "Especially after I stole Azul."

He laughed. "Yes, especially after you stole my dog."

She hid a brief smile against her mug of cider. "But the raven, he is lonelier still."

Jacob loosened his hold on her and straightened up as she turned to look him over with a critical eye. He appeared to be unharmed, not even a scratch, and so she relaxed further.

"You're right, Fallon. The raven did not ask for this life any more than I did. Yes, he is always alone. Watching you."

"He doesn't need to watch me when I'm with you," she pointed out.

Pouring himself some wine, Jacob was quiet a moment as he sat on a stool beside her. "No. But that is his duty, watching you."

"What did he watch before me?"

Jacob stifled a yawn. "He more often assisted me in my various tasks and duties."

"You no longer needed him, after me?"

He touched her cheek. "I may have needed him, but it reassured me more that he was watching you." Helping himself to a piece of cheese, he took a long sip of his wine. "Lovely girl, what have you been up to today?"

She poured some wine for herself and sliced off a piece of bread for him. "Laundry. I figured out another trail to go running on. I wrote a letter to Bergen and found another book to read. I asked Azul to please stop chasing the sheep."

He laughed and tossed a bit of cheese to the dog. "His favorite pastime. He does not like to see the sheep at peace."

"Clearly he does not." She laced her fingers through his as he clasped her left hand. "I came across your dagger," she mentioned. "I hadn't seen it in a long time."

He held her hand to his cheek and stared at her affectionately. "That dagger was the single weapon I possessed when I became this. On the night I became the Ravener, I aged greatly, and that dagger was in my possession. To this day it reminds me of that event, and so it grieves me yet also makes me realize how long I have survived." He kissed her fingers.

"You didn't need it today," she observed.

He let go of her and tore off another piece of bread. "I did not. Today was not about death." He sighed, staring into his wine. "I have seen enough of death." Fallon leaned into him, sliding her arms around his waist, and Jacob kissed the top of her head. "Your tattoo must wait; it will happen tomorrow. Tonight, I am tired. I simply want to relax with you and be at peace."

Raising her head, she kissed him. "That sounds perfect."

"When you are running…" he dropped off, and she waited. There was a tic in his jaw. "You must not go beyond the boundaries of this place. The barriers are invisible and difficult to sense. I will work with you soon on how to detect them. But it is imperative that you not wander beyond them."

She cast her gaze to the side, to the shadows, then back to him. "What's out there?"

He was staring at his wine. "All manner of things."

"Not just your neighbors on the mountain?"

Shaking his head slightly, he met her eyes. "No."

A little later he disentangled himself from her and went to the refrigerator to retrieve a bowl of fruit. Returning and setting the bowl on the counter beside the bread, his stare caught on the tattoo on the back of her upper left arm. The only tattoo on her body that he had not done. *I see, but not in the light.* He rubbed his thumb over the words, and when she looked back at him, she saw lines between his eyes.

"That phrase," he murmured.

"I got that when..."

"I know when you got it," he cut her off, and she flinched. The tattoo had been born of her frustration at failing to save her brother and Simon from murder despite receiving premonitions of each event. Her feeling of being completely alone in the world.

"Where did you get it from?" he asked. "The words?"

She licked her lips, wondering why it was important. "I don't know? It was in my head one day." She wrapped her hand around Jacob's to stop the repetitive movement of his thumb, and he met her eyes.

"The terrible headaches you used to get from some of your premonitions...when was the last time you got one of those?" he asked. "Before I broke the line, obviously."

Fallon thought back. "I had one on this tour—I had to give myself a shot. But none since you returned to me in London." *Just the odd ones that seem to distress you,* she thought.

Jacob sat on a stool next to her. "That night last summer, you gave yourself a shot when you didn't have a headache." His tone was serious, and she lowered her gaze.

"No."

Touching her chin, he tilted her head up. Her eyes were full of tears. "You were trying to leave, weren't you, Fallon?"

Her face crumpled with emotion. "Everyone was leaving me. I was sure I was going to fail Bret and Bergen. You never came back to me."

Jacob leaned forward, grasping both her arms forcefully. "I am here now."

"I know, but I didn't know then!"

He wiped the tears from her cheeks. "I knew something was wrong that night. I didn't realize there was no headache involved. The raven and I cannot read your mind or your intentions. The shields you engaged years ago to keep Luca from knowing about your secret life are still in place. It wasn't until later, when Bret showed signs of figuring it out, that I realized." There was sorrow in his face. "If I'd known..." His tone was low. She saw pure pain in his eyes. "If I'd known, I would have come to you immediately."

Fallon crawled onto his lap, arms going around him tightly. "Sometimes everything gets too heavy." He ran his fingers through her hair, and she pulled back, kissing him. "I will never leave you by choice, Jacob."

* * * * * * *

The next evening, Fallon watched as Jacob wielded the needle, marking her skin. The look on his face struck her, and she felt as if this moment was no different than if he had been touching her tenderly with his fingertips, his lips brushing her skin. The love with which he was tattooing the design onto her forearm was tangible.

She thought of Sunny's strange look, of her declaration that the two wrist tattoos had been done with love. Now Fallon knew they had. But what had put the certainty into Sunny's head? Fallon watched him work for a while, then she closed her eyes.

When she opened them again much later, there was a swirl on her arm with three dots on each side. She knew that every twist and turn in the line must be important. "I'm so tired," she mumbled, yawning as she shut her eyes again, unable to keep them open.

He reached out and lay the back of his gloved hand against her cheek. "It's the magic entering you. It is powerful and difficult to achieve. But when I'm done, you should be safe so long as you stay aware and lock your mind when you begin to feel the sensation. It will feel like something inside you, trying to take over."

When he was finally done, hours later, the swirl ran the length of her inner forearm and tendrils crept out from the sides and wrapped around the front of her arm. It was beautiful.

"It looks almost familiar to me," she mentioned sleepily.

He considered her, before gently kissing her forehead. "You must sleep, my love." He swept her up in his arms and carried her to the bedroom. "As I said, it is a very powerful magic. You need to rest and let your body recover from receiving it."

As he lay her down on the bed, she grabbed his hand. "Stay."

Smiling as he removed his shirt, he lay down beside her and wrapped her up in his arms, closing his eyes. "There is nowhere else, Fallon, that I would rather be."

CHAPTER TWENTY-NINE

Fallon slept late the next morning. When she finally wandered into the kitchen, Jacob was packing a picnic in the backpack.

"I thought we could hike to the river," he suggested. "It might be just what you need after last night."

There were dark circles under her eyes, for though she had slept deeply out of exhaustion, the new magic in her system had not let her sleep well. Accepting the cup of coffee that he handed her, she leaned against him.

"I wish Luca could have come to this place," she said wistfully. "He would have loved it."

"He did frequently immerse himself in nature," Jacob agreed.

She straightened up. "Austin was a good place for us to be. Live music and lots of outdoor stuff—the two things we loved. Though if you had dumped us in the Pacific Northwest, I would not have complained."

He grinned as he zipped up the backpack and secured a water bottle to the side.

"What made you choose the Quinns, anyway?" she wondered.

Jacob shrugged. "They were safe and unassuming. Innocuous. Incurious. I knew that, based on who his parents were, Luca would grow to be an intelligent boy who would likely have at least a few magical abilities. The Quinns would be overwhelmed by this, but instead of reacting, they would ignore, look the other way. That's what I needed. Obviously, when I gave Luca to them, you had not been born yet. I had no idea that one day I'd be delivering Luca's little sister to them as well. They served their purpose. Your mother's actions against them were unfortunate, though not entirely unexpected. With a father as notorious as Kian, the two of you would always draw danger." He looked around to make sure he hadn't forgotten anything. "Ready?"

She ran to the bedroom. "Let me grab a sweatshirt."

The exertion of the walk, as well as the perfect beauty that surrounded them, was indeed what Fallon had needed to feel energized and herself again. When they got to the river, they took off their shoes and waded in the ice-cold water. Jacob laughed at her shrieks of discomfort as they were eventually chilled to the bone.

They lay entwined on the blanket as the sun warmed them back up. And they ate most of the food Jacob had brought along. He marveled at the paradise that surrounded him whenever she was at his side. But he could not forget what lay in their future.

"I have to warn you." Jacob grasped her hand. "If Kian is somehow able to take you by force despite our defenses, it will be traumatic for you physically. There will be a great amount of pain to your body and your mind. It is a terrible thing. It will weaken you for a while, but remember that it is temporary. It will not kill you. You must remember that, if it ever does occur."

"Because we have so much in place to prevent it, is that why it would be so violent?"

He nodded. "Exactly. In the past, there had been no resistance and therefore no harm done to you."

She lay on her back and stared up at the sky, listening to the river and relishing the sun on her skin. Despite being troubled by his words, Fallon didn't want to think about anything like Kian today. The whole morning had thus far been so flawless.

"Once you acquired this place, I wonder why you ever left it," she mused. "It's like a heaven."

He raised up on one elbow, resting his head against his hand and playing with her hair. "Because you were still out there, Fallon."

She looked at him. "But now I'm here with you."

He smiled. "Yes. And you're right, at times I never want to leave." He ran his thumb softly across her lips. "But everyone remains out there, beyond this place. People we wish to protect from harm."

She looked back at the sky. "Maybe one day, when they are all safe, we will stay here forever."

He closed his eyes as he leaned into her, hiding his face against her neck. "Maybe so."

* * * * * * *

The next part of Jacob's campaign to prepare her caught Fallon off guard, just as he intended. One day when they were outside, he lobbed a bit of power at her, knocking her to her knees. She stayed on the ground in shock. She had seen him flick his hand at her and then she felt a force press against her, unexpected enough to knock her off balance—it had come out of nowhere.

He came over to her and took both her hands, pulling her to her feet and kissing her forehead. "Reflexes," he murmured.

She looked at him, incredulous. "You can toss around invisible power?"

"I can do much." He gazed at her. "But Kian can do more. Let me teach you how to block it."

The next time he raised a hand at her, later that same day, she again stumbled. He raised it again and this time she raised her own hand and blocked him, as he had shown her.

"You'd have been dead with the first hit," he told her as he approached.

"I know."

"You have to sense it before it hits you."

She was glaring at the ground.

He touched her chin. "You will get there."

Holding back tears, she wondered if he was right.

* * * * * * *

One cloudy, gray afternoon Jacob came up the path to the precipice and saw Fallon standing there, barefoot in a black dress, the wind whipping her hair. One arm was extended and there was a red scarf wound around her hand and forearm. There the raven was calmly perched.

Jacob paused to watch them; he was reminded of the dream he'd had before her birth. In his mind he seamlessly went back and forth, watching her through the raven's eyes, then observing her from a slight distance as she held the raven. His mind and body were transfixed as the three main elements of his world—himself, the raven, and Fallon—came together in this single moment.

Suddenly the raven turned its head to gaze at him, the sun glinting off his prism eye. And Jacob saw himself, looking back at himself in an endless loop, as his vision and the raven's came chaotically together. Things were off balance. Glitchy. Jacob began to tremble.

Fallon broke the spell by reaching out with her other hand and running her fingers gently down the gleaming black feathers. She seemed unafraid of the black beak which could easily tear her flesh. The bird tilted his head and looked at her, and Jacob felt an enormous tension leave his body as the raven's gaze moved away from him.

Glancing back over her shoulder at Jacob, Fallon raised her arm, and the raven took flight into the sky, crying out as it flew away.

"You summoned him?" Jacob asked as he joined her, realizing she had been prepared with the red scarf. He sounded surprised.

"I did summon him," she confirmed. "He's haunted me my entire life, I figured he and I could have a face-to-face meeting."

"He's never come to anyone before, like that. He so rarely shows himself—it's odd what he's doing with you and Bergen." He touched the side of his head, still feeling strange and off-center.

"He's drawn my blood enough. He can come when I call," she said dryly, taking both his hands firmly in hers as she sensed his disquiet. Her touch immediately quelled his unease, and he was able to breathe again. He marveled at the confidence, the fierceness, which was finding a home in her. Being here with him, free from life's other distractions and blanketed by his love, was building her up, strengthening her. He could only pray to the universe that it would be enough.

* * * * * * *

Jacob raised his hand slightly, but Fallon reacted in a split second and blocked him, and he felt the force pushing back against him. He grinned as he approached her, and she continued to lob bits of power at him, taunting him. They had been practicing for weeks, refining her reflexes, her ability to sense threats and react.

When he finally reached her, he pulled her hard against himself, his lips hesitating near hers.

"Am I more powerful than you?" she whispered.

"Yes," he murmured, kissing her. "Much more."

She pulled back and threw on a feisty look. "You're not scared of me?"

He grinned. "Of losing you, yes, that does bring me fear. But *of* you? No." He kissed her again. "Even if you were my mortal enemy, I think I might gladly surrender to you."

CHAPTER THIRTY

When the European leg of the world tour was over at the end of May, everyone returned to their homes, reunited with family, friends, and pets. Bret was back in California and Bergen, out of school for the summer, immediately went to stay with him. Lisbeth and Leo were busy preparing for the move to London; while Bret had won the right to keep Bergen for the summer, he was losing his bid to keep her for the school year. The girl had already been enrolled in a private school in London along with her step-brothers. Leo's attorneys were currently succeeding in painting Bret as a mostly-absent father with an erratic rock and roll schedule that included traveling, late nights, and lots of unpredictable strangers.

Bergen hated London. She was, as ever, a California girl, spending her days at the beach in the sun and water, and couldn't fathom living full-time in a gray, misty city with no surfing, a half-world away from her father. She'd been bad-tempered since returning to him, and Bret wished again and again that Fallon could be there to provide the balance she was so good at. His pride initially stood in the way of asking.

He texted her once in mid-June, but the automatic reply from her phone showed him only a picture of a raven. He took this to be code indicating to those knowledgeable that she was in Spain with Jacob, unreachable by technology. While he was aware that she and Bergen somehow exchanged hand-written letters via the raven, he couldn't bring himself to employ that particular method of communication quite yet.

By mid-July, things with Bergen had grown more challenging. Bret was desperate. He texted Fallon again, and this time she responded.

Fallon happened to be in Gray visiting Selah for a few days when Bret's text came in. She texted back and forth with him a bit, trying to get a feel for the situation. Then she considered his request to come see them. She felt guilty that she had not been around Bergen lately, as she continued to exist in the sphere of Jacob. She knew the father and daughter were both struggling with all that was upending their lives.

Fallon called Tayce. "Hey, trouble. Want to accompany me to Casa James for a week? Bret needs help wrangling Bergen. Among other things, he apparently tried to go out on a date, and she launched a world war."

"Absolutely!" Tayce was grinning ear to ear. "I was wondering when or if I'd see you again."

"Never 'if.' Always 'when,' with you and me, okay?"

"Just say the day, and I'll be there. I'm playing a few shows coming up around L.A., but that shouldn't be a problem at all. I'm not an expert on kids, though."

"Liar. You're one hundred percent a girl dad. I'll handle her, though. I just need you there as my companion. Since I clearly can't bring Jacob."

He chuckled. "Clearly. Count me in. Being your companion is a bucket list item for sure."

"Weren't you my companion on tour?"

"Roommate," he corrected her. "This is totally different."

After agreeing on a date and time, she hung up and texted Bret: "I'll be there Wednesday. Bringing Tayce."

In California, Bret sighed in relief. "Thank you," he texted back.

CHAPTER THIRTY-ONE

J acob was not pleased with Fallon's plan to go to Bret and Bergen, mostly because it meant he would not be around her for a week. She had been by his side for so much of the past several months. He breathed easier when she was with him, not only because she filled him with joy, but because he felt he could better protect her against any threat when he had her physically with him.

"The raven is watching me," she reminded him. They were in her apartment, and she had just finished packing her bag. She was checking Tayce's progress on her phone so that she could meet him at the location they'd agreed on.

"It's not the same," Jacob mumbled in annoyance.

Fallon wrapped her arms around him, smiling to herself. She understood he was frustrated that he had to stay away solely for the comfort of Bret James. Even at night, when Jacob might have secretly shown up in her bedroom, she warned him that most likely Bergen would be sleeping beside her.

"I am sure Bret will be happy to have you back in his house. Swimming in his pool."

She covered her mouth to hide her smile. "Are you…" she narrowed her eyes, "jealous again? I packed my most modest bikinis."

He held her head in his hands, looking her over slowly all the way down to her toes. "There is nothing you could wear, Fallon, which would hide or lessen the beauty of you." His hands dropped to her waist, playing with the hem of her shirt as his fingers ran across her bare stomach.

The raven tattoo was burning on her wrist with his desire for her. Fallon pushed his shirt aside and kissed his stomach, just above the waistband of his jeans, her hands sliding over his abs. She heard him suck in his breath at her touch. *This man's body is ridiculous*, she thought with a sigh.

"My tattoo is like a mood ring for your feelings," she noted, grinning as she looked up into his eyes.

Jacob pulled her up and kissed her. "Then you already know how the next several minutes are going to go," he whispered, and she laughed.

"Yes. Yes, I do."

They were ten minutes late to meet Tayce, who was leaning against the hood of his car and staring out at the ocean when they arrived breathlessly beside him. He glanced pointedly at his watch.

"Sorry," said Fallon.

"It could not be helped." Jacob was unapologetic.

"I'm sure it couldn't," Tayce agreed, looking back and forth between them with a grin as he accepted Fallon's bag and placed it in his trunk.

After one more kiss, Jacob was gone, and Fallon turned and threw herself into Tayce's arms.

"I missed you, T! I miss being your roommate."

"Same." He chuckled. "Pale in comparison to your current roommate, though. You guys are…"

"Goals?"

He gazed at her fondly. "Yes. That."

She giggled as she got in the passenger seat, setting her messenger bag at her feet. "How much longer for Jane?"

"Next month!" He was smiling big as he got behind the wheel. "Due August twenty-ninth, give or take."

"Do they have a name picked out?"

He glanced at her briefly before pulling out into heavy traffic. "Elliot William."

Fallon touched his arm. "Tayce Elliot Williams, that's the sweetest thing I've heard this week."

"It is pretty cool." He looked enormously pleased. "You know, she's still a little suspicious as to how you were so certain he was a boy. Because you weren't just playful certain. You were certain-certain."

Fallon smiled dreamily. "I saw him for a moment. And then I knew. It's never happened before."

"You saw him, like, in her belly?" Tayce was frowning.

"No. I saw *him*, alive. Elliot. About three years old, smiling the cutest smile. Head full of wavy brown hair. Only for a second, but I knew it was him."

He touched a hand briefly to his heart, taking in the mental image she'd given him. "I can't wait. I've never looked forward to something as much as his birth, not even the births of my daughters. This is something else."

"I don't even like most kids, yet I am eagerly anticipating seeing you in your Grandpa Era."

"Fully embracing it," he confirmed.

When they arrived at Bret's house in the early evening, Bergen ran out to the driveway to greet them. Fallon thought she looked older and taller since she'd last seen her, though it had only been four months. Tayce hugged the girl tight and tousled her hair, and then Bergen went into Fallon's arms.

Fallon held her close for a long while, watching as Tayce carried their bags inside.

"I missed you," Bergen mumbled against Fallon's chest.

"I know, Bee. I've missed you, too. More than you know."

"You've been with Jacob this whole time." The girl's tone was accusatory though her expression remained neutral.

"I have, yes. Working on some things. I've been in Gray a bit as well. Hey, I have a new tattoo." She showed Bergen the inside of her right bicep, which was now graced by a beautifully-detailed black-line bee the size of a quarter.

Bergen's face lit up. "Is that me?"

"Who else?"

She hugged Fallon again. "I love you so much. Did Jacob do it for you?"

"Of course, he did. I would trust no one else at this point."

"I can see that. I want him to do all of mine as well." Bergen took Fallon's right hand and examined the other new tattoo that wrapped around her entire forearm. "Wow. What's this?"

"Something Jacob wanted to add."

A strange look passed over Bergen's face and then she looked up at her. "Are you in danger?"

Fallon felt a cold knot forming immediately in her stomach. Staring into Bergen's gray eyes, she could see the innocence that was melding with knowledge. The wariness of what the world might hold. "There are some unpleasant things going on right now, yes," Fallon confirmed.

Bergen looked off into the distance. "Does it have anything to do with... remember when we were at your apartment, me and my mom, and you just disappeared?"

"Yes. It has everything to do with that."

"And with whatever happened in Amsterdam?"

"Yes, that, too."

Lines formed between Bergen's eyes. "Can you and Jacob handle it? Whatever it is."

Fallon pulled her close. "I hope so."

Bergen breathed her in, detecting a faint citrus scent, feeling at home and safe in Fallon's embrace. "Some unpleasant things are going on around here, too," she said dryly.

"I know." Fallon rubbed her arm. "Sometimes adults can really mess things up. I'm sorry."

Stepping back a little, Bergen checked her phone and then stuffed it back into her pocket. "I'm not considered old enough to tell the courts my wishes. Every psychiatrist they make me see says I'm better off with my mom, that she's a more 'stable situation' for me—like moving me away from my dad and the beach to live in another country with my brand-new family is *stable*. And apparently," she rolled her eyes, "I'm 'moody.' I'm so sick of their attorneys lying about Dad, I don't even care anymore. I tell the psychiatrists all kinds of shit that doesn't make sense. I figure at some point they'll try to medicate me. That's what I can read off them, anyway. That none of them believe anything I'm saying and that they're super close to prescribing me drugs to make things 'easier' on everyone."

Fallon placed her hands on Bergen's shoulders, concern in her eyes. "I cannot save you from this. I can't magically fix what's going on. But your dad needs you to be nicer to him. He's fighting as hard as he can for you; you have to be able to support him like you always have. And I don't think they can medicate you without his consent. In theory."

Tears came to Bergen's eyes. "I know, Fallon. I try to be nice. But sometimes I get so angry, I can't even control what I'm doing or saying. It's like something's taking over me. Even though I'm mad at my mom, I take it out on Dad, I don't know why. I'm just furious all the time."

Pulling her into a hug again, Fallon rested her cheek on Bergen's head, filled with worry.

When Fallon and Bergen finally made their way up to the house and went inside, Bret was so relieved to see Fallon that he gave her a hug. He didn't get a chance to talk to her, though, until late that night after Bergen had gone to bed.

Taking wine outside, they sat in chairs by the pool. Bret marveled at how much everything had changed in a year.

Fallon stared at the lights reflected in the water as she sipped her wine. "She doesn't mean to be difficult for you," she told him. "I think it's a terrible coincidence that this is all happening in the midst of serious preteen angst, hormones, etc." She looked at him.

The stress of the situation was clear on his face. "I can't lose her, Fallon. But I don't have endless money to fight this, either. My team is pushing all kinds of crazy new merchandise and old back-catalogue stuff *ad nauseum* in an attempt to bring in extra cash. I'm pretty sure I'm about to be marketing my own brand of whiskey—I don't even drink whiskey. The world tour came at just the right time. I'm about to start recording a new record, but without my band this time. I did a lot of writing during the tour. Anyway." He chuckled bitterly. "Hopefully, I can get it out by the end of the year, not sure yet. Then I'll need to tour again to promote it, to make more money. Which is ironic, because that's the main thing that's hurting me—my unstable touring commitments." He looked over at Fallon. "What else can I do? I mean, this is what I do. What I've always done. I play music, and I tour. I don't have a retirement plan, and I definitely didn't plan for needing to fight legals battles till eternity in order to have my girl with me."

Fallon was deep in thought, watching the slight ripples that distorted the reflections. "Don't tour."

His eyes stayed on her. "I have to."

She turned to him. "No. You don't. Put out the album, yes. But stay home. Figure something out that you can do in California. Do some shows in-state. And figure out a music-related thing you would enjoy doing. Then plan tours for summer only when she can come with you."

"But…"

She held up her hand. "I have an account that will cover your legal fees. All of them."

He glared at the ground.

Standing up with her wine in hand, Fallon walked to the edge of the pool. Her toes curled around the coolness of the stone edge. "Don't argue this one with me, Bret. You know I love her like she's a part of me. The money is for her. It's not charity for you. I have a ridiculous amount of financial wealth. I would never use it all if I lived ten lifetimes. I actually give it away often; I can more than afford to be generous. As I told Bergen earlier, I cannot fix this situation magically. But I can help. And you can accept my help and focus on what needs to be focused on. Which is her."

When she looked back over her shoulder, Bret was sitting with his face in his hand. She knew he was going to accept.

Fallon observed Bergen closely during the next several days. At times, the girl was sweet and polite, her old self. But then she was suddenly moody, snapping at everyone including Fallon, slamming doors, and stomping on the stairs. It was obvious at times that she was trying hard to be good. At night, she slept curled up against Fallon, holding her hand. But Fallon could sense more and more of a change in her.

"I feel like in no time at all she'll be wearing all-black clothing and dark lipstick," Tayce commented.

"She's already wearing dark clothing," Bret relayed. "The lipstick is a battle she's fighting with her mother. She's already tried it a few times here. Part of me wants to let her do whatever the fuck she wants, especially if it pisses off her mom. But then part of me knows I need to be a responsible adult or whatever."

"Lots of kids go through this. She's trying to figure out who she is while also being angry." Fallon sighed. "All we can do is love her. And set some boundaries."

CHAPTER THIRTY-TWO

The next afternoon Fallon and Bergen swam in the pool for a couple of hours. It was Fallon and Tayce's fifth day at the James house, and Fallon was deeply missing Jacob. Despite what Bret might have imagined, she was not capable of curing Bergen's bad temper, and she was not going to hang out with them indefinitely just to make it easier on him. Their father-daughter dynamic needed to be able to run smoothly without her intervention.

Fallon wondered when an appropriate time might be for her and Tayce to take their leave. Tomorrow was sounding promising.

After they got out of the pool, they took their time drying off, laying in the sun on side-by-side lounge chairs and talking about Europe. Fallon was attempting to help Bergen see the positive side of living overseas with so much history to explore, but Bergen was stubbornly uninterested.

"Suddenly you want me to be happy about being away from Dad," she accused Fallon. "Do you hate him that much?"

Fallon kept her gaze on the water. "I never indicated that I hated him," she responded neutrally. "I'm trying to get you to see the potential benefit to living overseas, since it's looking like more and more of a reality."

Bergen glared into space for a while. Then she hopped up and pulled on a pair of shorts over her swimsuit. "I think we're going out to dinner tonight," she mentioned. "I'm going to go ask Dad." She disappeared into the house, and Fallon exhaled slowly.

Gazing up at the blue sky, she thought about Jacob at the cottage—it would be midnight there now, the sky ablaze with stars. Her body ached with needing his touch, his strong embrace, the firelight in his eyes. A smile curved her lips. Tonight she would tell Tayce and Bret that tomorrow they would be leaving.

Determining that her black bikini was mostly dry, Fallon pulled on a pair of black running shorts. She didn't see her shirt anywhere and thought she must have left it inside. After hanging the towel on the back of a chair to dry, she entered the house, stifling a yawn. She had not been sleeping well in this house, and Bergen was a chaotic bedmate.

As she passed through the large kitchen, Fallon could hear Bret and Bergen talking in one of the living areas, and she went in to join them.

"We're eating out tonight," Bergen informed her. "Just like I told you. Italian."

"Or Mexican," countered Bret carefully. "There's a place Tayce likes to go to."

Fallon could see the look of annoyance that passed over Bergen's face at the thought of not getting her way, and she assumed they had been arguing about this before she showed up. Father and daughter began discussing a departure time, and Bergen added in her desire to go see a movie, which Bret rejected. Bergen was incensed.

As they spoke and argued, Fallon shivered at a strange tingling that traveled all over her body from head to toe. She felt an odd pressure beginning to crawl around in her mind. Both sensations were unwelcome, but she couldn't immediately determine what they might mean. Was she in danger? Hadn't Jacob said it would feel like something trying to take over? This didn't feel quite like that. But what else could it be? Was she not interpreting it correctly?

Adrenaline flooded her system, panic rising in her chest and tightening her throat. She experimentally threw up a mental block, just in case. It took all of her concentration.

Bergen noticed that she had lost Fallon's attention. "Oh, I forgot to tell you, I had a dream last night," the girl announced. She perched on the arm of a sofa and crossed her ankles.

Bret and Fallon both looked to her in anticipation, the latter distracted.

"We were in Austin together, all three of us," Bergen continued. "You were wearing long-sleeves," she directed at Fallon, "so I don't know whether you had the scorpion tattoo or not. But one thing had changed." She smiled. "You were pregnant. Very pregnant."

Bret cocked his head. To him it sounded like Bergen was possibly lying.

Fallon's face had paled when she heard Bergen's words, too preoccupied with the strangeness in her head to truly process the validity of what had been said. She took a quick step back, trying to focus. "What? No." She sounded confused, and Bret looked over at her in concern.

"It was so real! You looked so cute pregnant. How exciting, for you to be having Jacob's baby!" Bergen's smile was overly bright. Bret narrowed his eyes at her, and her smile dimmed slightly. Definitely lying.

But in that moment, Fallon panicked. Her mental block slid a little, and she felt the tingling increasing, the pressure on her mind building. Bergen's alleged foreshadowing of the one thing Fallon had always been passionately against was too much.

Turning without another word, she fled blindly from the room, crashing hard into Tayce, who had been about to enter through the doorway. Tayce grabbed both her arms to keep her from falling, as well as to steady himself, and then there was a harsh wave of blackness, and they were gone.

CHAPTER THIRTY-THREE

Fallon was on her hands and knees in the dirt, feeling as if she was being burned alive. Screaming in pain, she shrank into a fetal position. Her face pressed hard into the dirt as she willed herself to regain control. She struggled to breathe in and out through her whimpering, her fingers clawing at the earth as she fought against her own body.

You are not dying, she told herself, crying out again in pain. *You. Are. Not. Dying.*

Then she heard the voice.

"Fallon? Why are you hurt? Where are we? I can't...I can't move."

Her eyes flew open wide in alarm, icy awareness breaking through her agony. She knew she'd been yanked forcefully into her father's world; she recognized the atmosphere, as well as the trauma to herself that Jacob had warned about. But her blood ran cold as she realized Tayce was with her. Raising up weakly on her hands, she looked around to find him sitting nearby, watching her. He looked confused.

"Did we teleport? Why are you hurt?" He was shaken and puzzled. When she looked into his brown eyes, she saw something she had never seen there before: fear. This world was different for him than it was for her. For him, it immediately began to take a toll. Panic and chaos were filling him, paralyzing him.

Still feeling as if her flesh was being cleaved from her bones, she forced herself to crawl to him, wrapping her arms around him and holding on tightly. In response, he clung to her. Burying her face against his shoulder, she tried to block out her own pain while willing him to calm down. She was in utter disbelief that he was with her—that he was now in such terrible danger.

Slowly he relaxed, his breathing evening out as her magic worked on him. She released him but took one of his hands firmly in hers, lacing her fingers through his. She didn't want to lose him if her father suddenly ripped her elsewhere.

"Where are we?" he asked again, casting sideways glances but not seeming to want to look at anything directly except for Fallon herself. He reached out and placed his hand on her cheek, concern written on his face. "You're hurt."

She closed her eyes, still trying to focus through the pain. God, it was brutal. She could barely catch her breath as she rubbed the skin on her thighs and arm with her free hand. "I'll be okay. We're not in our world, it's my father. His world. I have to get you out of here."

She touched the raven tattoo, begging Jacob to hear her, but it did not react. Surprised, she tried again, pressing her lips to it in a kiss, which was always guaranteed to seize Jacob's immediate attention. But still there was nothing. Dread crept into her aching bones. Her link to Jacob was broken.

Regardless, she was responsible for Tayce. She had to save him from this. Shoving her fear back down, she pulled Tayce to his feet. "Come on, we need to keep moving."

They looked to be on the edge of a dense, dark forest. The air was humid, a faint scent of woodsmoke curling about them. As she looked around, Fallon could see no living thing, not even a bird. With a feeling of foreboding grasping at her, she headed into the trees, wanting the cover. Tayce stumbled along beside her.

"Are we sure that going into the spooky forest is the best idea?" he asked.

"No," she confessed. "But I'm running low on ideas."

The rest of her body was finally recovering, but Fallon's entire head still ached and throbbed with the searing pain of the forced teleport, and she was exhausted. She could see why Jacob had protected her from this in the past—it was not pleasant. He had worked so hard to ensure this never happened again, and yet here she was, with Tayce in tow.

Stepping on a sharp stone, she winced, gritting her teeth. She couldn't believe that in this epic moment, she was barefoot, clad only in shorts and a bikini top. The odds had not, in the wardrobe department, been in her favor. At least Tayce was wearing jeans, a t-shirt, and actual shoes.

The reality of being cut off from Jacob was unnerving; she reminded herself that she was strong on her own, though she wasn't sure she entirely believed herself. Had her father blocked Jacob from this world? The absence of a response from her tattoo suggested that. She hadn't known that was even a possibility. Had Jacob known? Why hadn't he said anything? She clenched her teeth in frustration. Clearly, he was blocked. Otherwise, he would be standing beside her right now.

She was completely alone in her father's domain, exhausted by pain and burdened with the need to protect Tayce. He only had a few hours before his mind began to fracture, if she remembered Jacob's story of her mother correctly. Tears came briefly to her eyes as she realized how trapped she was, how in grave danger Tayce was. If this was her father's plan, it was stellar.

They paused their hurried pace, Tayce catching his breath as he glanced around. "Where are we going?" he asked.

"I have no idea. My father will try to kill me now, I assume. I can't reach Jacob for help, and I have to keep us both alive long enough to get out of here." She smiled at him sadly. "It's just you and me, trouble."

He forced a grin. "The dynamic duo. We should be fine."

* * * * * * *

Bret and Bergen were speechless, and at first neither moved. They had both watched Fallon flee from the room, seen her collide with Tayce in the doorway, and then both vanish into nothingness.

Finally, Bret launched into motion. "Did you see Jacob?" He hurried to the doorway, looking around as if he might find some remaining clue. "Was it him, Bee, did you see him at all?" There were a multitude of emotions running through him, but panic and anger were the most acute. He'd noticed Fallon's strange change in mood, obviously troubled by something, and now his two friends were gone. He was pretty sure someone would have told him if Fallon was suddenly able to teleport herself. And he knew with certainty that Jacob had not appeared with them before they disappeared.

Bergen was shaking her head, her heart pounding with terror. "I didn't see anyone. It was just them, and then they were gone. I thought," she covered her face with her hands, "I thought I heard Fallon scream. Not from the collision, but from whatever happened next." She struggled to hold back her tears, wiping her hands roughly across her face.

Bret looked at her. "I thought I heard it, too. Her scream."

"Is this the thing she and Jacob were so worried about happening?" She stared at her father with tear-filled eyes.

Bret nodded. "I think so, yes."

"This is my fault, then. Oh, my God." Bergen looked miserable, tears now spilling freely onto her cheeks.

Before Bret could respond, Jacob was suddenly standing with them. He looked like a storm. Bret could swear that the light had dimmed and the air grown cooler with his arrival.

"*Where is Fallon?*"

Jacob's voice was cold in its intensity, his eyes treacherous and dark. He had never not known where Fallon was.

Both somewhat frightened of Jacob's terrifying appearance, Bret and Bergen told him what they'd seen.

Cursing the universe as he turned away from them, Jacob screamed with a rage that shook the father and daughter. Then he sank down to a crouched position, his head bent as if in prayer.

"What is it?" Bergen demanded, approaching Jacob with caution. "What's happened?" Bret gave her a warning look, but she ignored him. "I know something was going on, Jacob, some terrible thing. What is it?"

Jacob seemed for the first time to be at a loss. He rose slowly back to standing, fury in his eyes, unable to look at either of them. "Her father has stolen her. By force. It will have hurt her tremendously. He has blocked me from that world. I cannot help her. I cannot find her." He was hoarse with emotion. "I can do nothing at all."

"Blocked you?" Bret was frowning. "Did you know that he could block you?"

Jacob's gaze was far away, turning over endless possibilities in his mind. His fingers were rubbing the raven tattoo on his forearm, as if he might elicit some answer there. "There was a chance, but I didn't think he would dare it because of the energy it would take from him to create and maintain the block. I also didn't think he would be able to pull her away from this world; I had trained her and covered her with every known protection. But she has been away from me for a week, not as focused. And the collision with Tayce would have distracted her for that perfect instance."

"Other things were distracting her as well," Bret mentioned darkly, not looking at his daughter, who shrank back from the implied accusation. "And now Tayce is in danger."

Jacob glanced at Bret. "Tayce is in the gravest danger. He could be lost forever. And she loves him—she will use everything she has to protect him, making herself vulnerable in the process." There was a tic in his jaw. "We could easily lose them both." The words tore from his throat, his voice hard with sharp edges.

The raven, wherever he was, was panicking at having lost Fallon. Clearly the bird had been blocked as well. Jacob tried to shield his mind against him, for the dark bird's distress was threatening to overwhelm him.

Bergen shivered miserably and moved closer to her father, who put his arms around her. "There's nothing we can do?" She looked at Jacob imploringly. "Nothing?"

Fists clenched and face darkened, Jacob shook his head. "If there were, I would have done it by now. We can only wait."

In a hundred years, Jacob had never felt this powerless. His heart had never felt this level of pain, of abject terror. His eyes burned, and he thought perhaps his soul was burning as well—what little soul he had left. The soul Fallon tended to with such gentleness when she filled him up with all of her love and sweet kindness.

He crouched back down, weak with fear, resting his elbows on his thighs and his face in his hands.

I have not loved another as I love you, Fallon. I will not exist in this world without you. Come back to me, my love.

* * * * * * *

Jacob's voice floated through Fallon's aching head like a distant song. His voice had never been in her mind before—her lips parted in surprise. She snatched at the beautiful words and grasped them tightly to her heart, tucking her chin to her chest and allowing herself to cry desperately for several seconds. Her whole body tensed in frustration and pain. *My love*, she answered back. *My heart.*

Beside her Tayce shuddered slightly, and she shifted her focus back to him. Fallon rubbed her hands up and down his arms. "Stay with me, T."

He looked at her and smiled. They had been there in that otherworld for a little over an hour, by her best guess, walking in the forest, meeting no one. The sky was growing dark as if with impending night, though she could see no sun at the times when the sky was visible through the treetops. She didn't want to face her father in darkness. She knew that much.

Anticipation was wearing on her nerves, and Tayce was suffering. She tried employing various tricks to keep him focused, mostly having him sing to her.

"If only you'd been clutching a guitar when all this went down."

"If only," he agreed.

Singing seemed to keep him with her, seemed to stop this strange world's slow assault on his mind. Only an hour. If she could get him out of here before two hours, maybe all would be well.

"Why do I need to sing?" he asked, not for the first time.

She squeezed his hand. "To save you."

He nodded and continued singing softly.

Fallon wanted to scream and cry at the danger his mind was in; she thought of all that could be lost. His absolute wizardry on guitar, that thing he loved above all else. His easy, charming manner. His goofiness. His close relationship with his girls. All of it was in jeopardy of ruin if she failed to get him out of this world in time.

Her lack of teleportation skills was a noose around her neck. She knew that Jacob had hesitated to teach her because of the natural skill needed, the danger involved, but she would have risked any of it now to get Tayce home safe and sound.

Suddenly the treetops above their heads exploded in sparks and flames.

"RUN, TAYCE!"

They took off through the underbrush, branches tearing at their skin as explosions rocked the earth on either side of them. Tayce was not as fast and nimble as she was, causing her to slow her pace.

After several yards they emerged from the trees and came up on a rocky precipice—Fallon dug in her heels to keep them both from plunging over the edge. Lightning zinged past her ear, she felt the brief warmth, and as she looked out, she saw a figure standing on the other side of a wide, dark chasm.

Kian.

Fallon trembled in fear, unprepared for the emotional blow of seeing in the flesh the man who wanted her to die. Even though she had never seen his face and couldn't make out his features now, she recognized his egotistical stance from the tone of voice he'd used with her before.

Grief and anger welled up in her as she thought of Luca. *You killed him,* she thought, staring across the chasm. *You killed my brother.*

Roughly, she pushed Tayce down behind a pile of boulders, hissing at him to stay still. Then she crouched beside him and tried to think. He was shooting lightning at her? Explosions? How was she supposed to battle that? She could block it, of course, as Jacob had taught her. But she did not fool herself with thinking lightning was his only trick. His attacks would grow deadlier. And he would love for her to watch Tayce die. *He will try to cripple you with loss.*

The only other element that would make this moment perfect for Kian, she supposed, was if Jacob was here to watch *her* die. But clearly Kian had known he could not go up against them both.

She held her head in her hands. She was emotionally fatigued due to her concern for Tayce, her terror for his mind and his life, and her head was still aching from the forced teleport, the pain making her nauseous. Breathing deeply, she tried to center her thoughts and calm herself, but she could not stop trembling. She was scared. Truly afraid. Why had Jacob ever believed that she was brave?

Feeling a hand on her arm, she looked up into Tayce's kind eyes.

"You are strong, Fallon. You can do this."

Love for Tayce bloomed in her heart, and she leaned forward, kissing his cheek. Then she sat back on her heels, holding an image of her brother in her head—oh, how Tayce reminded her of Luca at times—and touched her wrists together. She felt a strange but welcome spark of power as the tattoos met. Aiming her hands over the top of the boulders in the direction of her father, a sensation of electricity covered her entire body, and a stream of light shot forth from her wrists. A boulder near Kian exploded.

"Hot damn," Tayce crowed. "Look at you!"

She gave him a bewildered look as she simultaneously tried to anticipate Kian's next move and consider what she'd just accomplished. "I don't know what I'm doing," she assured him.

"As long as you look cool, though," he pointed out. Sitting back, he shrugged out of the black Queen t-shirt he'd been wearing and handed it to her. "Here, sorceress, put this on. It's getting cold, and you're grievously underdressed."

"That's an understatement," she muttered, slipping into the shirt. "Thanks."

Several minutes passed. Or was it half an hour? More? Time seemed to slip away from her as she found herself falling into the pain in her head more and more, only Tayce's hand on her arm bringing her back. Wiping dirt and cold sweat from her forehead, Fallon squinted against the continuing agony. Would it never stop? And where had Kian disappeared to? How long had things been quiet? Tayce seemed zoned out beside her, and she knew he would have no idea.

Curiosity finally got the best of her. She crawled from behind the barrier to see if she could catch a glimpse of her opponent.

An explosion sent her flying back against a row of jagged rocks. Through a fog of shock, she heard Tayce's cry of alarm. Pain surged through her shoulders and radiated across her back; at first, she couldn't see for the pain. Tayce retrieved her as swiftly as he could, half-dragging, half-carrying her back into their hiding place.

Sitting up slowly, Fallon looked in surprise at her left shoulder. She struggled to move that arm, but white-hot pain instantly rocked her whole body, swimming through her from head to toe. She leaned over and vomited, the agony overwhelming her senses.

She felt Tayce's hand petting her, one protective arm around her as he also held back her hair. She teared up as she wiped her mouth with her shirt. Sweet boy, so out of his element, his mind under direct attack from the world they were in, yet his only thought was to keep her safe and help her any way he could.

"Something's broken," she told him unnecessarily, looking at her shoulder in annoyance. He saw that her face had gone pale from the pain. "Why is there no continuous assault?" she wondered, holding her aching head in her right hand and her left arm tight against her body. "Why hasn't he killed us already?"

Tayce was taking off his belt and trying to fashion it into a sling for her arm. "He probably has to...to recharge. He's nowhere near as...as powerful as you, right?" He frowned, as if he was concentrating on the words he spoke, as if it was now taking effort to draw them from his mind. His speech was slowed down.

There was worry on Fallon's face as she watched him. More time must have passed than she thought.

"That's why we didn't...didn't hear from him for an hour after he dragged us here. It took everything out of him. It took him that long to recover. He has to...to recharge after every shot." He winked. "See, I've been paying attention in class."

She touched his face fondly, then attempted to situate her arm gingerly in the belt-sling with his assistance.

"Don't ever say I'm not...not resourceful," Tayce directed, admiring his work as the belt somewhat supported her arm.

"You're my superstar hero, T. I'll have all your clothes off before we're done."

"It's like I'm losing to you at strip poker. But not having... having a good time at all."

She grinned weakly at him.

* * * * * * * *

Chapter Thirty-Three

"Come out, come out, my Rose."

Kian's voice projected—magically, Fallon assumed—across the chasm. He had been taunting her for…for what? The past ten, twenty minutes? The past hour? She didn't know how much time had gone by. She had neither a watch nor her phone, but she was sure they'd been in Kian's world for well over two and a half hours.

Tayce was speaking less and less, and it was more difficult to get his attention when she tried to talk to him. She couldn't stop the shaking of her own body; she knew it was fear and exhaustion combined. Her father's annoying trash talk wasn't helping. There was a level of confidence in Kian's dialogue that chilled her heart every time she heard it.

"Where are you, little warrior? Why do you not show yourself to me?" Kian's voice was poison in her ears. "The Ravener is not coming—is that what you're waiting for? For him to save you like some dashing hero? I can promise you he is not coming. You are not as important to him as that. He will not endanger a century of business relationships in order to save one pretty, expendable girl. He has a hundred just like you, in various locations. Where do you think it is he goes when he leaves you? He grows bored of you and finds pleasure in other places. It has always been that way. He is restless. One woman would never satisfy him."

Fallon crouched with her eyes closed, her hands over her ears. About twenty minutes ago she had moved herself and Tayce away from the protection of the boulders not long before Kian blew them up, which would have mortally wounded them.

Now they were huddled together just inside the shadowy tree line. Hiding. Waiting.

"It's not...not true." Tayce was pulling weakly at her hand, his gaze unfocused. "What he's...saying. Lies, Fallon. He lies."

She took a deep breath and nodded. Jacob had spoken to her several times—she had not stopped to consider why or how they were suddenly communicating telepathically—and his words brought her comfort, especially in the face of Kian's lacerating verbal assault. Again and again, Jacob reminded her that she was stronger than the evil she was fighting against. That he loved her more than all the stars. She could hear the pain in his voice, the agony of his helplessness.

All she could tell Jacob was that she loved him. She wanted to say she'd come back to him, to ask him to wait for her sweet return to his arms—but every time she tried to speak those words, they felt false, and she held them back.

The distraction of Tayce being with her, of knowing that his beautiful mind was fracturing as she breathed, was damning to her focus. She was angry that they were trapped here, forced to listen to the unbearable monologue from Luca's murderer; she didn't know how much longer she could survive this back-and-forth assault.

Every time she aimed her wrists in Kian's direction, the result was spectacular, but did him no apparent harm. The distance was great, and her aim was tentative and uncertain. Fear and doubt were hampering her abilities, crippling her focus. With tears in her eyes, she knew she was failing Tayce.

You're failing Luca, too, she told herself cruelly. *You're failing everyone you love. What good are you?*

Overwhelmed with anger at herself, she crawled forward. Trying to stay low to the ground, she searched across the chasm for a hint of where her father might be. As she squinted in the dim light, however, she couldn't place him, for her ability to see in the dark was hampered by her father's world. Impatiently she raised up on her knees.

There was an instant flash of red—Kian was in view, pointing at her, and the flash was traveling through the air. She was out in the open. It seemed to take forever but she knew it was only seconds, and she knew that she was about to die.

Jacob.

Unexpectedly Tayce, who had followed her out of their hiding place, flung himself at her, shoving her aside to shield her. She screamed but it was too late. The red flash hit Tayce full in the chest, and he crumpled lifelessly to the ground.

Fallon screamed again and again; she didn't know if she would ever stop.

Kian was now lurking behind the larger stones on his side of the chasm, and she knew it would take him time to recharge. Swallowing her screams, she turned Tayce over onto his back. He was unconscious, and there was blood on his face from hitting the rocks, but otherwise he looked unharmed. For a few seconds she was filled with hope, but as she touched his wrist and chest, concentrating, she realized with horror that the life was spilling out of him—she could feel it flooding slowly away. Tayce was dying.

No. No. No. Not you. Her eyes were blurry with hot tears as she grabbed onto him desperately. *Not you, dammit.*

From across the chasm, she heard the cruelest laughter. Insidiously it flowed into her, wrapping coldly around her heart.

Fallon's deep love for Tayce turned instantly to fury—her entire body was suddenly hot with an internal fire that sparked in her heart and rapidly spread. Kian knew what he had done to Tayce. And he was reveling in it.

She leapt to her feet, eyes darkening with malice. Shrugging the belt off her shoulder, she pressed her wrists together, aimed her hands in Kian's direction and unleashed every ounce of power she could find. She poured all of herself out with blind rage, feeling the power from within her beginning to grow, threatening to overwhelm her. Sweat covered her skin as if flames burned inside of her.

Her shoulder was agony, and her wrists screamed in pain, but she held them steady, her fingers locked together. Blazing white light shot forth from her and surged brutally across the chasm. She felt heat sizzling all over her damp skin, crackling with power.

The rocks Kian had been hiding behind exploded. The ground shook and flames shot into the sky as more explosions followed. In less than thirty seconds, the entire area where he had been hiding was nothing more than a blackened scar, and part of the chasm wall had collapsed. She could see no sign of life.

Fallon collapsed back down beside Tayce. Laying her trembling hand on his chest, she willed her mind to heal him. She had no idea if Kian had somehow miraculously survived, but all her attention needed to be focused on Tayce. Tears continued to stream down her cheeks as she recognized that her mind and body had little left to give. She could slow him down, but she could not change the reality that he was dying before her eyes.

Jacob was suddenly kneeling beside her, his arms around her. A single sob escaped her lips with her relief at his appearance.

"*Fallon.*" Jacob growled her name, holding her so tightly that it hurt. He was trembling with emotion. When he'd heard her cry his name in his mind moments before, it had sounded like she was saying goodbye.

Fallon hid her face against his neck, seeking his warmth, his familiar scent, everything about him that felt like home. All of which she'd thought she'd lost forever. Clinging to him with her right arm, her tortured emotions were soaring as she felt the safety of his strong arms and chest, his hands checking her all over for major injury.

"Is my father…"

"Kian is dead. As soon as you killed him the block went away, and I was able to come to you." He released her and looked her over with concern, holding her face in his hands. "You're badly hurt."

Fallon looked fearfully over her shoulder at the charred landscape across the chasm. "Are you sure?" Tears blurred her vision. "Are you sure that he's dead?"

"Yes, Fallon." He pulled her tightly against his chest again. "He's gone." Gazing across the chasm at the blackened, eerie scene, Jacob felt a deep unease. "He must be."

She pulled away and directed his attention to the man that lay beside them. "Tayce is hurt. Can't you heal him?" she begged. She lay her hand on Tayce's bare chest and again slowed the failing of his body, feeling the enormous effort it took her to do even that. "He saved me, Jacob, he saved my life. He doesn't deserve this. Please do something."

"You know I am not a healer, Fallon." Jacob was holding his hands a couple of inches off Tayce's chest. His eyes met hers. Sadly, he touched her cheek. "A few minutes more," he told her. "That's all. The damage is great. It is not repairable, even if you had the strength or I the ability."

"*No*." She fiercely wiped the tears from her eyes with her right hand, and then saw that Tayce's eyes were now open. He was trying to watch her, but his gaze was still unfocused. She smiled bravely at him. "Hey, trouble."

With a weak smile, he spoke. "Fallon. Alive. So...so glad. You were...were brave. Badass."

She grabbed Jacob's arm. "Take us to the pond at Star Fall. It's his favorite place."

Jacob held onto both of them and in a moment, they were on the grass next to the pond, under the sycamore tree. The sun was low, and the water gleamed gold in the light. Tayce's head was propped on Fallon's lap enough that he could see, and his smile grew a little when he finally realized where they were. With her right hand she tucked aside his hair, tenderly touching his face.

"Sing me that...that song you love, Fal. The one where... I'm your friend." His voice was faint, but she heard every word. He tried hard again to look at her, but, failing, he looked away, back at the water. Fallon swallowed the painful knot in her throat.

And then she sang "Moon River," her voice shaking. Jacob sat back and stared at them, feeling his own heart breaking at her pain. Tayce watched the light dance on the water as he listened to her.

340

She only managed to sing a few lines. As she stopped, Tayce looked up at her, and when she looked back in his eyes, she saw her friend, strong and whole.

"You know what, beautiful?" His voice was husky and fading as he smiled at her, his gaze focused firmly on her. "You're my favorite magic girl."

He looked back at the water, and then his eyes were closed, and he was gone.

Jacob wrapped his arms around Fallon as she collapsed, sobbing, against him. He pulled her completely onto his lap as she screamed against his chest. He was overwhelmed by the force of her grief. He was in disbelief that she had so suddenly lost her beloved friend. And that he himself had so nearly lost her.

"What do we tell his girls?" She was shaking so badly, Jacob almost couldn't understand her. "We can't tell them the truth. The truth is ridiculous, awful, it's not even real! To everyone— what do we say?"

He stroked her hair soothingly as she shuddered against him. "I will take care of it, my love," he promised gently. "I will take care of it all. You can tell Bret and Bergen the truth. I'm going to return you to them now while I deal with Tayce. Then I will come to you and let the three of you know what the story will be."

Fallon crawled off of his lap and lay forward across Tayce's body, trembling as she held onto him. "It should have been me," she moaned. "Not you. Sweet boy. I'm so sorry." Her sobbing began anew, and Jacob shut his eyes against her pain. Placing his hands on her, he wished in the deepest crevices of his ragged heart that he could end her agony, heal her sadness. But he knew that he could not. She was his queen of loss.

CHAPTER THIRTY-FOUR

Bret and Bergen had been waiting for something to happen. After seemingly hours of misery and the unknown, of watching Jacob haunt them with his terrible helplessness and fear, he had alarmed them by suddenly screaming Fallon's name. He had shocked them further by disappearing without explanation soon after.

They had speculated for a long time. Had he gone to Fallon somehow? Had he thought of a way he could help? Was she dead? The terrible way he'd screamed her name did not give them hope—it had brought them both to tears.

And so now they were both startled as Jacob appeared in the living room, holding Fallon in his arms. With relief they saw that she was alive. Jacob lowered her gently to the ground, kissing her on the head with sweet tenderness, and then he was just as quickly gone again.

Bret and Bergen got up to go to her, but then hesitated. Sorrow was emanating from Fallon in terrible waves; they could both feel it. On her knees on the floor, she looked pale and war-weary, streaked with dirt and blood. There was no light in her eyes. She stared ahead dully, not looking at either of them. She was holding her left arm strangely against herself; every now and then she trembled as if with pain, tears running down her cheeks.

Bret searched her face as he finally knelt beside her, and there he found the answer that he didn't want. Tears stung his eyes. "Tayce…"

When he spoke that name, Fallon seemed to grow smaller, cowering in agony. "He tried to shield me." Her voice was hoarse from screaming and crying. "To save me. He was supposed to stay hidden. Out of harm's way. But he saved my life instead." She dug her fingernails into her skin. "He's gone."

Bergen covered her face with her hands as she fell to her knees.

"It should have been me." Fallon breathed in raggedly, whimpering in pain. "It should have been me." She turned her head to look at Bret, and he felt a shift in his soul at the torment in her eyes. "I'm sorry," she whispered. "It shouldn't have been him."

He gingerly placed a hand on her back, unsure as to where she was injured. "I'm sorry, Fallon. You've been through hell—we can see that. I'm so sorry."

Bret fetched some water for Fallon and helped her drink it, but other than that, no one moved or spoke again until Jacob reappeared next to Fallon half an hour later. Bret moved a few feet away to give them space.

Jacob was solemn in the face of their grief. Since everyone was sitting on the floor, he knelt down beside Fallon. She looked at him questioningly.

"I will tell you what has happened to Tayce, but the three of you can never ask how I managed this, do you understand me?" He did not wait for them to answer. "Tayce left this house twenty minutes ago to run an errand—he mentioned to you all that he did not feel well. Five miles from here, while driving, he suffered a fatal heart attack. His car then hit a tree. Paramedics are already on the scene."

Fallon whimpered, and everyone glanced at her, then back at Jacob, who took her hand in his.

Bergen got up and ran to the window. Looking out, she saw that Tayce's car was indeed gone from the driveway. "How..."

Jacob gave her a sharp look, and she pressed her lips together, waving away his stare.

"I am a friend of Fallon's," Jacob continued, "who happened to be driving by and tried to offer assistance, but realized there was nothing to be done. I also recognized Tayce as a friend of this group, so I immediately came here to give you the terrible news. Many details will be lost in the days to come, so I am unconcerned with the answers you give should anyone question you. I," his glance went to Fallon, though his words included them all, "I am deeply sorry for your loss. I know that he was a rare person. His heart was generous and kind. There was not another like him."

Fallon bent her head and continued to sob silently. Rising slowly, Jacob had his arms around her as he brought her to her feet.

"I need to speak to her alone," he addressed Bret and Bergen, "and then I must go away again to take care of some things. For now, I will leave her here in your care. Her shoulder has been shattered in places. It will heal on its own, much more slowly than usual, but I believe it will. If you could find something to fashion a sling for her, that would be helpful."

He guided Fallon out to the privacy of the back patio, and there he embraced her as she wept against his chest.

"Don't leave me," she pleaded, pain and sorrow twisting through her exhausted body.

"I'll be back for you soon, Fallon. There are some loose ends I need to make sure are tied up. The funeral will be held in a few days. You must be there for that, for his daughters and for Bret. Tayce would want that from you."

She struggled to breathe, nodding. "I know. I will."

He kissed her forehead, cradling her face in his hands. "I am so sorry, my sweet, sweet girl."

"I'm tired, Jacob."

He sat down in a chair and pulled her onto his lap, holding her close, careful of her shoulder. "My love, you did something that was nearly impossible. You destroyed an enormous power—a power even I did not have the strength to overcome—and you have been given little time to recover."

"Someone finally found my breaking point."

"Yes, I thought they might." He kissed her tenderly, and she gazed into his eyes, seeking refuge there. "You were so brave, Fallon. So very brave, even though you think that you were not. I am sorry that it turned out this way. I know how you loved him. He loved you just the same. But as soon as he ended up in Kian's world, his fate was sealed."

She lay her head on his shoulder. "He was the best person."

"He thought the same of you. The two of you truly were, as he liked to say, the dynamic duo."

The sun was low and the breeze pleasant as they sat quietly for a while. They were relieved to be reunited, though Fallon was still in a great deal of pain from her head and shoulder. All of her suffering was eased by Jacob's arms around her, the feel of his heart beating against her.

Can I speak to you now? she asked curiously with her mind. *Is that still real?*

Jacob held her closer. *Yes, love. I can still hear you. We have developed a telepathic link, you and I.*

She looked at him. *How? And why now?*

Running his hand gently over her injured shoulder, which was bruising terribly, he shook his head. *I don't know for certain. But I have never been so intent on reaching someone as I was to reach you when you were stolen away with Tayce.* He smiled slightly. *And now here we are.*

"I wonder if…" She looked thoughtful and tried to talk to Bret in her mind. But there was no answer. She tried to sense him, but could not, even though she knew he was there in the house. That link was gone. With a sigh, she leaned back against Jacob.

* * * * * * *

Leaving her with Bret and Bergen tore at Jacob's heart, he could barely stand to say goodbye, but there were things that still needed his attention. A mortal human had been killed with magic in a world not his own. While little attention was paid to this by the universe as a whole, there were those in the various realms who did take note of who Tayce Williams had truly been and the emerging fact that he had saved the life of Fallon Quinn—the Ravener's love and the lone surviving daughter of the cruel murderer, Kian. And since Tayce had saved her life,

Fallon had subsequently slaughtered her father. A fascinating series of events, for those who were interested. For these reasons and more, Jacob felt the need to ensure that every possible loose end was knotted up securely and that every story and truth shared was the appropriately correct version.

Since the moment when Fallon had cried his name, and he'd known immediately that she was about to die, darkness had been swirling around his psyche, painted with violence and grief. The idea of living his dark, lonely life without her rose up before him again and again. Again and again, he rejected it. As Fallon's life went, so went his. That was his conviction.

So many things had happened all at once. Jacob was still trying to convince himself that she lived—she lived!—and was still his. He was sure his heart had not stopped racing since the terrible instant when he realized Kian had stolen her and blocked him. Even now, knowing she was safe, his blood still burned at the memory.

I can still talk to you, Jacob, no matter where you are. Now I am truly a part of you forever.

He couldn't help the smile that lit his face as Fallon's voice entered his mind, as if she had sensed his inner turmoil. *This link is different, more powerful than any you've had before,* he told her. *It transcends worlds. There is nowhere I can go where we will not still be able to speak to each other. My heart beats for you, Fallon, and no other. I love you,* ma rose dorèe.

* * * * * * *

When Jacob appeared on Selah's front porch that night, she thought the world had ended.

"Where is she?" She grasped the doorframe, light-headed and afraid.

He sat on the edge of the porch railing. "It's alright, Selah. She is in California with Bergen. Healing while I take care of some things. I have come to tell you that she won the battle. She lives."

Selah exhaled as she came near him, watching him steadily. "You look…there is some distress in your eyes."

He nodded. "She is badly injured, in a terrible amount of pain. I am doing what I can for her. But there is a much more severe pain in her heart." He briefly explained the truth about Tayce.

Tears fell onto Selah's dark cheeks. She felt an unbearable sadness welling up inside her and knew it was because her beloved Fallon was shattered. "Tayce was a joy. I very much cherished watching the two of them interact."

Jacob sighed. "I agree. The two of them together were a joy." His gaze darted around, unable to settle. "I," he hesitated, then looked at her, "I am concerned. This has hit her especially hard, as you can imagine. Do not be offended if she does not come to you right away after the funeral. I think I know where she will choose to go."

"Of course, absolutely." Selah gave him a sad smile. "Your house, with you and Azul—there is nowhere else I would want her to be. But tell her that I love her."

* * * * * * *

After Jacob was gone from Fallon, Bret ran a warm bath for her in the large tub in the guest room. Then he left her alone, and Bergen took over. The girl undressed Fallon with care and helped her into the water. Fallon cautioned her not to lose the black t-shirt she'd been wearing, and Bergen promised to take care of it.

Bergen washed her hair and helped her bathe, rinsing away the dirt and the blood. Twice she had to empty the tub and refill it. She did everything with a determined look in her eyes and only spoke when she needed Fallon to move a certain way.

Every time Fallon looked at her, Bergen looked away.

"I know you feel guilty, Bee" said Fallon gently. "But you did not cause this thing. Kian would have found another path."

Bergen pressed her lips together tightly, trying not to cry, and nodded. Fallon knew that she did not believe her. She could feel the guilt radiating off the girl.

When she was finally clean, Fallon was too weak to get out of the bathtub, and Bergen was not strong enough to manage it. Drying her off as best she could, Bergen helped her into clean shorts and a t-shirt, and then Bret came in and lifted her out of the tub. He carried her to her room and set her carefully on the bed. Then he held up an orange bottle and a package.

"Jacob had this sent over from the pharmacy, apparently. Somehow. They delivered it just a while ago. It's pain meds for your shoulder and a proper sling."

Fallon willingly swallowed two of the pills with the water Bret had also brought. He set the sling on the table by the bed.

"Are you, do you want one of us to stay in here with you?" he asked uncertainly, as Bergen hung behind him like a shadow.

"I think I want to be alone for a while," she told him, and they reluctantly left the room, closing the door behind themselves.

When they were gone and the door shut, hot tears filled Fallon's eyes, and she lay back on the bed. She pressed her right fist hard against her face, shaking violently with silent sobs. Grief and loneliness engulfed her.

Jacob was immediately lying beside her, his arms cradling her against himself. She turned into him and buried her face against his chest as he whispered soothing things to her.

"I thought you were gone," she whispered.

He kissed her softly. "I am taking care of things, yes, but you override all of that. You needing me is the most important thing."

She looked into his eyes. "Don't leave me tonight. I can't face this without you. This first night without him."

"No, my love, no. I will not leave you." *I so nearly lost you. You know I will never let you go.*

She rested her head back against his chest. *Never let me go.*

* * * * * * *

When she woke up in the morning, Fallon's head was no longer hurting, and she knew she had slept deeply. Jacob's arms around her for the entire night had been essential. Before she fell asleep, he'd told her that when she awoke in the morning he would likely be gone, which she had accepted.

Her tears were currently at bay as a numbness settled into her chest. Something snuffled against her hip, and she smiled as her right hand found Azul's furry head. She glanced at him. He panted at her happily, licked her hand, and then returned his head comfortably between his paws.

"Such the handsome napper," she murmured fondly. "Thank you for coming." She tried to roll over but caught her breath as the pain in her shoulder reminded her that it was still very much there. Azul raised his chin in concern. Looking around, Fallon saw the sling laying on the bedside table and snagged it. She sat up in bed and examined it to see what needed to be adjusted.

An uncomfortable fluttering from the raven tattoo drew her attention. Frowning, she stared at a scratch on her wrist which she hadn't noticed before. About an inch in length, the scratch was across one of the tattooed bird's outstretched wings. She ran her tongue thoughtfully over her front teeth. Was this from when she and Tayce had been crashing through the underbrush? She couldn't recall. In the bathtub last night, she'd been careful to clean all the cuts and scrapes, but she didn't remember this one. She thought she would have definitely noticed a scratch across one of her tattoos.

Her finger touched the red line and came away with bright red blood. Faint alarm traveled through her, humming with caution. This cut was fresh.

Fallon! Are you okay?

She flinched at Jacob's sudden, panicked voice in her head. *Sure, I am, why?* Her heart was beating unnaturally.

There was silence as he considered. *Something has unsettled the raven, but I couldn't determine the cause. He is not sharing. I immediately thought you were in danger.*

As she stared at it, the cut vanished, and the tattoo subsequently calmed down. She breathed in deeply, exhaling in an attempt to calm herself. Turning her wrist this way and that, she saw no evidence of the scratch. But her body was not currently succeeding at self-healing, so where had it gone? All of the other cuts were still there, though they were clearly a day old.

Fallon? he persisted. *What's wrong?*

She met Azul's gaze. *I'm fine, Jacob, I don't know. A little panic attack, maybe, and the raven got caught up in it? I'm fine, though. Please don't worry.*

Alright. He didn't sound entirely convinced, but he also seemed somewhat distracted, as if he had been caught in the middle of some task. *I will try to return to you tonight.*

Fallon went back to working on the sling, and Azul went back to sleep. She knew that Jacob had enough to worry about today. The scratch was probably just some left over side-effect from everything that had happened the day before. She glanced at the tattoo one more time, and then she put it out of her mind.

CHAPTER THIRTY-FIVE

J ack Lane came up to Fallon after the funeral and slid an arm almost protectively around her shoulders, though careful of her left shoulder, which he knew was still tender. She was wearing a black dress that fell to just above her knees, and her left arm rested in a charcoal gray sling. There were dark smudges under her eyes, evidence of her continued exhaustion and the stress of her injuries, both physical and emotional.

The memorial service had been both difficult and joyous. There had been tears and laughter and songs. Tayce's daughters got up and spoke—everyone wept with them when they broke down and smiled at their anecdotes. It was bittersweet. Musician friends, including Bret, performed.

Fallon had sat in the third row with Bret, Bergen, and Jacob and watched it all with a face of stone. Jacob had an arm around her and held tightly to her right hand. Tears slid down her cheeks, but otherwise she did not react. The laughter made her flinch. She did not smile at the amusing stories that were recounted, the happy memories. She couldn't. He had died in her arms. He had died because of her. Her heart beat inside a nightmare.

At one point in the service, when several musicians were onstage performing, Jacob tensed up beside her. Fallon looked at him questioningly, then saw who his gaze was locked onto.

Are you looking at the older man with the guitar? White hair? she asked in the privacy of their minds.

He glanced at her and nodded.

Fallon smiled sadly. *That's Damon Rayne, he was...*

I know.

She swung her head to stare at him. *You know?*

An unreadable look passed over Jacob's face, and he relaxed. *No. Tell me who it is.*

She looked back at the man on the stage. *He's an incredibly famous guitar player, quite talented. He's been well-known since he was a teenager, and now he's nearly eighty. Anyway, he was a mentor to Tayce, they were really close. They met not long after Tayce moved to L.A. from Wisconsin when Tayce was in his twenties. Damon was instrumental in encouraging Tayce to more aggressively pursue his dreams and helping him hone his talents. Tayce always spoke highly of him and with such affection.* She squeezed Jacob's hand. *But that's not what you were going to say.*

Jacob shook his head. *No,* he was smiling, *I didn't know any of that. But it makes me happy.*

She increased the pressure on his hand.

Damon Rayne was Tayce's father.

Fallon's lips parted in shock as she looked back at the man on the stage. More tears threatened, while beside her, she sensed Jacob was feeling unusually emotional.

I am glad they found each other. He kissed the side of her head. *It was a regret I long lived with, but now I can put it to rest.* He stared fondly at her.

She couldn't believe it. *Does Damon know?*

He shook his head. *No. And now that I realize all of this, I would never tell him. He got to enjoy Tayce in his life, which is all that matters.*

She leaned against him, resting her head against his chest. As she watched Damon Rayne's fingers move like lightning on his guitar, she wondered how Jacob knew.

Bret had privately told Jack the truth about Tayce's death, as he had proven himself again and again to be secretive about everything regarding Fallon. Bret figured that anyone who had kept quiet about being burned with a tattoo and then twice healed by magic, could be trusted to keep information to himself. He also understood that the story of Tayce's death was wild enough that even if Jack did try to share it, no one would believe him.

"I'm sorry," said Jack roughly now, squeezing Fallon close.

Her gaze traveled over the room—she thought that possibly Jacob had walked out into a courtyard area with Bergen.

"He was the best damn guitarist I've ever heard and one of the very best guys I've ever known." He leaned in and lowered his voice. "But without you in his life, he'd have died three years ago in Nevada."

She looked down. Nothing he was saying mattered. She hadn't killed Kian in time to save Tayce. That was her only truth right now. She had robbed Elliot of his grandfather.

"You blame yourself," Jack went on. "You probably always will. But you know what? He wouldn't have wanted you to. I know that much."

She eyed pregnant Jane across the room. "He'd have been the coolest grandpa in the world."

"Without a doubt." Jack nodded. "But he fucking adored you, and he laid down his life for you without a second thought. He knew you'd have done the same for him."

Lines of sorrow creased her forehead. "I hate it."

Jack released her, seeing that Jacob had re-entered the room, and crossed his arms over his chest. "Tayce was a force of nature. It's heartbreaking when someone like that is lost."

She cast a glance at Jack. "You're sober and speaking eloquently."

"A funeral like this makes a man stop and think. That much talent, silenced so suddenly, it makes you reconsider things. Tayce had one of those eternal souls—you expected to see him one day at age ninety still tearing up a stage with that guitar."

She looked away. She'd always had the same thought.

Jane found Fallon later, outside in the courtyard area. Tayce's oldest daughter's eyes were red, and she looked tired, the ninth month of pregnancy weighing on her during this time of grief, but of the two sisters, she was the one who was best handling the situation, and so she was the one to seek out Fallon.

Damon Rayne is your grandfather, Fallon thought sadly. *He's about to be a great-grandfather to Elliot and will never know.*

"I'm glad you're still here, I was scared we'd missed you," said Jane. "Since she got the service out of the way, Annie can barely speak, but we both wanted you to have this." She held up the long silver chain with the crescent moon pendant.

Fallon's eyes widened, but she remained silent.

"Dad really loved you," Jane continued. "As a friend. Of course, he thought you were gorgeous, we've told you that before. But he valued your friendship. He held you in the highest possible regard. He told us you were one of the best people he'd ever had the fortune to know."

Tears streamed down Fallon's cheeks as she accepted the necklace.

"This was one of the ones he wore all the time, you probably recognize it. He left everything to us; we have all the memories we could want. But we wanted you to have something, and when we saw this, we both knew immediately that it should go to you. It's a little mystical, and he always told us you were magic." Jane laughed at the idea. Then she hugged Fallon, who hugged her back tightly with her right arm.

Fallon slipped the necklace over her head. "Thank you both, it means the world to me, to have this, you have no idea how much it means. I always…I loved this necklace."

Jane smiled tearfully and then started to head back inside to the memorial.

"Jane!" Fallon stopped her, catching up to her. "You know, your father was so close to Damon Rayne. Have you spoken to him today?"

Jane broke into a smile. "Funny you mention it. Damon came to see me and Annie yesterday, and he's invited me and Sam to come stay a few weeks at his enormous, lovely house after Elliot is born. Which would actually be a relief, since we're in that tiny apartment, but…"

"He loved Tayce like a son, I think."

Wiping away tears, Jane nodded. "You know, I wasn't sure about accepting. But you're right. He did. And Dad would want us to maintain a relationship with him. I'll go talk to him right now."

Clasping the silver moon in her hand, Fallon stared up at the sky and wept. Jacob was beside her immediately, like a dark angel bringing comfort, placing his arms around her, and holding her close.

"Get me out of here," she whispered. "Take me home."

He bent his head, and they were gone.

* * * * * * *

When they arrived at the cottage it was the middle of the night, and Fallon was weary of thinking about Tayce and death, guilt, and sadness. She knew there would be time enough for that in the coming days. Instead, she kicked off her shoes and led Jacob by the hand into the bedroom, where the fire threw around golden light and a steady warmth.

Carefully she removed her arm from the sling and tossed it aside. Turning to face him, she reached around her back with her right hand and unzipped her black dress. It slid off her shoulders and fell to the floor at her feet as Jacob slowly looked her over, flames and shadows dancing on her bare skin. She took a step towards him and touched his chest, the slightest hint of a smile on her lips.

"Jacob."

His eyes darkened with heat as she spoke his name like an incantation. "Yes, my love?"

"Take my mind off of everything."

He closed the distance between them, his hands going to her waist and his lips brushing hers. "It would be my absolute delight," he murmured.

CHAPTER THIRTY-SIX

"**I**f I hadn't run out of the room at that moment, if I hadn't overreacted, then he wouldn't have been there to die." Fallon had been speculating for nearly an hour, going back over the same points again and again.

"He saved you, Fallon," Jacob reminded her patiently. "If he hadn't gone with you, you'd have been injured more than you already were, maybe killed."

"But he'd be alive."

He held her face. "I have you here with me."

"If only I'd gotten angry fucking sooner—I could have killed Kian right away, then you could have gotten us out of there before that world hurt him. Tayce didn't have to die. I did everything wrong!" Sobs tore from her throat.

Jacob's eyes flashed. "There was no right or wrong way to handle this, Fallon. There is no playbook for how to go up against someone as cruel as he was. You kept Tayce alive for hours in an environment that was trying to destroy him from the time he got there. You did the best you could for the situation you were in."

"He'd still be playing guitar and laughing with his daughters. With his grandson. But that's all gone now. Because I couldn't find my rage in time."

Pulling her close, he stroked her hair.

"Jacob, I can't lose anyone else."

His gaze strayed down to the crescent moon that shone against her chest. "Nor can I."

She sat back. "If only I'd been stronger. If I'd been stronger, I could have healed him."

Jacob's patience with her was endless and gentle. "The damage was beyond repair. And even if you'd somehow healed his body, you know his mind was damaged." He cradled her head against his hand. "He never would have played the guitar again. His mind was wrecked, fractured—he would not have been your Tayce."

"He was my Tayce when he told me goodbye," she argued, tears welling up again. "I saw it in his eyes. I heard it in his voice. At the very end. It was him."

His tender look grabbed her heart in a fist. "He was dying, Fallon. He was crossing over. He has gone to a place where his mind is beautifully whole. He was already halfway there when he told you goodbye. You saw the smile on his face, the calm. The love for you. He was at peace. That was not simply the work of that golden pond. He was already halfway gone. That is the Tayce you saw."

She covered her face with her hand and lay her head on his lap, and he gently rubbed her back.

After about half an hour, Fallon sat back up, rubbing her eyes and gazing out at the sheep, for Jacob had again employed the strategy of positioning her in view of the flock. She watched as a furry black four-legged creature raced into the center of the sheep, sending them scattering and *baaing* in mild distress.

Turning, she found Jacob watching her intently, his expression full of love. She settled herself on his lap and placed her palm against his face, looking deeply into his eyes.

"You may go on forever," she told him. "But my life is fleeting. And I want you to know that I will spend all of it that I have left loving you beyond all reason, loving you so hard it takes your breath away. Because you are my center and my light and my heart."

His blue eyes looked momentarily glassy with tears as he kissed her. "I will not go on forever, Fallon, for I cannot go on without you. My life is yours."

* * * * * * *

Fallon stayed at the cottage for several months, slowly recovering from her confrontation with Kian. Her shoulder was still not fully healed. She spent hours in the gym with Jacob, regaining her overall strength and working on shoulder mobility. They spent even more hours in his bed, relishing the tender love and intense passion they had found in each other.

A few times during those months, Fallon recognized from snatches of thought she read off of him that he was supposed to leave to attend to his Ravener duties, but he refused, unwilling to leave her alone.

"You can say no?" she wondered, after the third such occurrence found its way into her head.

"There will be penalties later." He rested his forehead against hers. "I will deal with it when it comes. Right now, I would not leave you for the world."

Fallon wrote long letters to Bergen, not wanting the girl to feel abandoned as the custody battle continued, but finding herself unable to leave the sanctuary of Jacob and the mountains in order to visit her. Bergen wrote letters back from London, still feeling bitterly guilty for her role in it all.

Fallon mentioned to Jacob that the custody issue seemed to really be taking a toll on Bergen's attitude and behavior, which had been so poor all summer.

"You know Tayce and I were only there because Bret needed help with her. And the premonition she allegedly had, of me pregnant—I don't think she had any such premonition. I think she was just trying to get a reaction out of me. Or get attention, I don't know. Of course, she never intended for it to harm Tayce. And now she feels incredibly guilty about that." She rubbed her head. "I wish these headaches would go away."

He watched her somewhat tensely. "So do I."

She held up the crescent moon so that it sparkled in the sunlight. "This belonged to his mother. His real mother."

Jacob tilted his head a little. "What do you see about her?" he asked.

"Nothing very clear. Her name was Isla. Blond, beautiful. Not of this world. She was full of love, but also loss, fear. I could sense some sort of disobedience? But overall love. She was," she considered her words, "full of life." She smiled. "Not unlike her son. She wasn't the only one who wore it, though." She rubbed her thumb over the edge of the moon, pressing one of the points into her skin till it hurt. "Someone else. A woman. Darker spirit. Dark-haired. Also beautiful. That's all I can make out."

He reached out and caressed her cheek. "I do love you, my lovely Fallon."

She smiled at him. "Can I stay forever?"

Gazing at her, he sighed. "Forever, yes."

She kissed him. "And you. You held this necklace in your hands. Many years ago."

He was quiet for a while. Then he simply said, "Yes."

She watched him, waiting.

"One day," he promised, kissing her. "One day."

You'll tell me how you knew about his father?

Yes. I will tell you everything.

EPILOGUE

In the fall, months after Tayce's death, when cooler days occurred intermittently in Texas, Jacob brought Fallon back to Gray. They had agreed that she had no more need of the garage apartment, her home undeniably in Spain with him. He'd confessed to her his desire to take her traveling around Europe for a year or more, exploring to her heart's content, and she had happily agreed.

She'd regained a good deal of mobility in her left arm and was no longer in need of the sling, but full strength was still lacking. Her deep emotional damage and lingering physical exhaustion fueled by sleepless nights and terrible dreams were halting her complete recovery, though her body had resumed its ability to heal cuts and bruises.

She often woke up in the night screaming, fighting against some invisible force. Jacob would wrap his arms around her, stilling her, talking to her in her mind, till she collapsed in tears against him. She didn't admit to him that, at some point during those months, the nightmares had changed from visions of Kian attacking her and of Tayce dying, to mysterious confrontations with a hooded figure she couldn't identify. An anonymous man whose features were fully hidden by his cloak, who seized her roughly by the throat and whispered terrible things in her ear, choking the life out of her while he described Jacob's imminent, brutal death. She tried to fight him off, but in her dreams, she was powerless, all her magic unreachable, and so she struggled with him in vain. A few times she glimpsed a cruel scorpion tattoo covering his right hand, but otherwise she could tell nothing about him.

Every time when she awoke to Jacob holding her and speaking soothingly to her, she was so relieved to find that he was alive, and it had only been a dream, that she shoved the awful memories deep into a dark space in her mind and tried to forget them.

At the apartment in Gray, Jacob helped her pack up her clothes, books, photographs, and a few odds and ends. This they took immediately to the cottage. The rest they hauled to a thrift shop, borrowing a truck from Diego.

Fallon paid her rent through the end of the year to Ms. Landrum and told her she was moving out. The woman, who seemed frailer than the last time Fallon had spoken to her, thanked her for being such a good tenant.

"It's strange to be in the apartment without Azul," Fallon said, looking around. The dog had stayed behind at the cottage, awaiting their return.

"I believe he is looking forward to living full-time in the mountains again," commented Jacob. "He has maybe had enough of the Texas heat."

"I've had enough of the Texas heat, to be honest. Okay, I need to see Selah, and then we can go." She thought briefly about Katrine, still residing in a mental hospital in Dallas, unable to receive visitors beyond immediate family. She was sad for Paul, who had lost his long-time bandmate and his wife in the space of a few months, life as he had known it changed forever.

Fallon and Jacob rode around town in the Dart for a while, the top down. "Michael says it can stay in his garage indefinitely," she said of the car, as she shifted into third gear. "I don't know that Selah entirely likes that idea, but she does appreciate that it belonged to Luca."

"I noticed that she named her son after Luca," Jacob commented.

Fallon nodded, thinking of her godson, Indio Luca Lowe. "She loved my brother. I'm pretty sure he was her first serious crush."

She had turned the car to head north out of town towards Dutton, and she saw an unreadable look settle on his face.

"I want to go see Sunny," she explained. "To say goodbye."

"You will see Sunny again," he countered. "You are not abandoning Texas forever."

She thought he looked almost tense. "True, but it won't be as frequent. And I haven't seen her in a while. You should come in and meet her. She's the coolest girl."

"I do not doubt that she is." He leaned over and tenderly kissed the side of her head. "However, I would not want to intrude on the girl talk. I'll return to you at Selah's later." And then he was gone before she could speak, surprising her with the abruptness of his departure.

Pulling into the parking lot of Sunny Girl Bakery, Fallon parked and then sat in the car, deep in thought. She stayed in the car so long, so troubled and worlds away in her head, that she jumped when someone knocked on her windshield.

Sunny was standing beside her, smiling gently. "My fabulous Fallon friend. It is good to see you. I was concerned when you stayed in the car and much time passed—I had to investigate."

Fallon looked up at Sunny, staring into dark eyes that held an expression so familiar, yet somehow elusive. "I was bringing my friend, my love, to meet you. But he made a weak excuse and left."

Sunny nodded soberly. "Hey, I heard about Tayce Williams. I'm so very sorry; I know his loss hurt you. He seemed like the best guy." She stepped back. "Come in and have a cappuccino, on the house. I will miss you when you go away."

Did I say yet that I was going away? wondered Fallon, but she was not really surprised.

As they headed towards the bakery together, Fallon felt as if she were walking through a fog, and at one point, Sunny took her hand. There were tears in Fallon's eyes again, which had been the case daily after Tayce's death, and which she had slowly been trying to control, to keep her emotions in check. Being with Sunny, feeling her hand in hers, left her raw and vulnerable, completely exposed. Something was coming.

Inside the bakery, Sunny indicated a table for Fallon to sit at, and then she went behind the counter and began crafting two cappuccinos. Fallon watched her closely, her slender figure in tight jeans and sleeveless black shirt, her glossy black hair. The tattoos up and down both arms.

As Sunny finally approached her, Fallon's gaze was on her arms, searching.

"What are you looking for, my lovely friend?" Sunny asked, setting Fallon's drink before her. She sat across from Fallon and grasped her cup in both hands, gazing at Fallon steadily.

"I was looking for a tattoo like mine," Fallon said, glancing at the swirls on her own forearm.

"Hmm." Sunny sipped her coffee.

Fallon met her eyes. "Where were you before you opened this bakery?"

Sunny shrugged her narrow shoulders. "All over the place. I open a bakery for a while, then I close it and move on, traveling around, seeing the world. What an incredible world we live in, Fallon, and when I was a young girl, I never dreamed I'd get to see so much of it."

Fallon looked down at the table between them, tears inexplicably filling her eyes again. Then she looked back up. "How many bakeries have you had?" Her voice had the slightest quaver in it. "You barely look old enough to have had this one."

Sunny laughed, a musical little laugh that Fallon had never heard before. "Oh, I lost count long ago. They've been pleasant enough, but mostly forgettable endeavors. This one in particular has been special to me, though, I admit. I will never forget this one." She sighed. "Ah, Fallon. I am so glad that you are alright." Her dark eyes flicked to Fallon's left shoulder, then back to her face.

Fallon felt as if she were free falling slowly.

"Sunny," her voice now had a full tremor in it, "who did all of your tattoos?"

Sunny lowered her thick, dark lashes, and then looked at Fallon, her expression sly and sweet. "The man that loves you so. My brother, Jacob."

ACKNOWLEDGMENTS

Thanks as ever to Alan and Finn—for supporting me, cheering me on, and believing in me without fail. I am the luckiest girl in the world to be loved by the two of you.

Eternal thanks to the vast array of individuals who showed up *en masse* to buy "The Secret Girl" and support me at every turn. Lovely people from all over the timeline of my life surprised me again and again with their willingness to contribute to my dream. I was repeatedly humbled by the amount of support that came my way, and I cannot thank you enough.

Big, loud love to Jenn and Morgan for their willingness to read my manuscript again and again and again. And again. Your thoughtful insights and critiques and ideas helped make "The Magic Girl" what is it.

Special thanks to Janice and Saundra for being the first in-person purchasers of "The Secret Girl" and the recipients of my first ever book signings (at which I am now so much improved). Your love and support of me means the world.

Cheers to the Readin' with Rose' Book Club for your support, your willingness to indulge my questions, and your enthusiastic opinions on facial hair.

END NOTES

1. Brecht, Bertolt. *The Good Person of Szechwan (Modern Classics)*, trans. John Willett (Methuen Drama, 2015).
2. Verlaine, Paul. "Clair de Lune." *Fetes galantes.* 1869

ABOUT THE AUTHOR

Erika Fair was born and raised in Texas, where she lives with her husband and son. When she isn't writing stories or forcing her favorite music upon her family, she can usually be found hiking or planning future adventures. She has a penchant for iced coffee, and she's always watching for ravens.